Chocolate Lenin

A Novel

Graham Diamond

LION BOOKS, NEW YORK

LION BOOKS, NEW YORK

Copyright © 2012 Graham Diamond
Cover painting by Isaak Brodsky

ISBN: 0-6155-9403-4
ISBN-13: 9780615594033
LCCN: 2012934066
Lion Books, New York Hampton Bays, NY

Dedication

To my lovely wife Ann, whose help made this story come to life.

1.

The youth splashed through slush, ignoring the dirty snow piled high along the side of the street. When he reached the corner of the Polytechnic Institute of Applied Sciences he stopped as he did every day. Waiting for his brother Pasha soon became boring. He wanted time to hurry so he could get home and visit his friend next door. Shifting from one foot to the other, his thoughts drifted to full-bodied, pretty Luba, the wholesome girl with big breasts. Winter was ending, and soon school would also. "You're just a child, Nicolai," she'd chided him. Pasha was so lucky to be sixteen. Already a man. And pretty Luba didn't view his older brother as a child.

Nicolai's nose was running. He wiped it quickly, tossing dirty tissues into the muck. A glint caught his eye from something half buried in an oozing mound of evaporating ice. It was a damp piece of coated cardboard sticking up at an angle. He scraped ice away and lifted it with his grimy, gloved hand. There was writing under the sludge. He loosened it clean and stared. Letters ran along the top, rows of numbers crowded into a grid below.

"What do you have there, Nicolai?"

Pasha was strutting towards him, knapsack of books slung over his shoulder. "Give it to me."

"I just found it in the snow..."

His brother grabbed it from his hand. "It's only an old bingo card," he said with a frown. "Junk. Worthless. They lose them all the time." He made to toss it.

"Give it back!" said the younger brother.

"Take it, I don't care."

"There's writing on the back. Look." The boy shoved the card in his brother's face. "Property of the *Das Kapital Bingo Parlor*, Omsk."

Pasha laughed. "You're such a child, Nicolai. That place is an old shithole around the corner. Bingo is just a new fad from America. The place is overflowing every night with fat babushkas wagging their tongues. They have nothing else to do, so they come to play and gossip at the same time."

"Mama once won money playing bingo."

"Once, I suppose you're right. So what?" He shook his head.

"It also says, 'do not throw away under penalty of law.' And there's a phone number, too. But it's different than the parlor number on the card. It's written in pen and underlined, *call immediately if found.*"

"Show me." Pasha held out his hand. Nicolai reluctantly gave him the soggy card. The older boy looked at the numbers, and then turned the card. When he rotated it diagonally something peculiar struck him. He held the bingo card at an angle up toward the sky, shaking his head in bewilderment. "These numbers, when you read them bottom to top they display the first ten elements of the periodic table."

"What are you talking about?"

"Chemistry. This *is* weird. These are key elements of compounds and physical properties. Physics. It can't just be a coincidence…"

Nicolai puffed with delight at his find. His brother studied science. Young Pasha Ivanovich Radulov had passed a very difficult test to be accepted to the Polytechnic. This elusive trash might turn out to be worth something after all. "Use your mobile. Call the number written on the back."

The older boy nodded. He slowly punched in the provided numbers. It rang once, switched over to another line, and someone immediately answered. "Internal Affairs sub division. How may I direct your call?"

Pasha gulped. "My brother found this card. A bingo card from the *Das Kapital Bingo Parlor…*"

After a moment of silence the voice on the other end said, "Give me your exact location at once. Stay put. You are in extreme danger."

"Such is life," he muttered. Vlad Petrovsky ached. He leaned forward over his desk and rubbed at his left shoulder. Intense pain shot down his arm. Ever since he suffered his herniated disc and was told surgery might be required, he'd been in a constant challenge to avoid undergoing the procedure. Time was growing short, and the operation would have to wait. Everything needed to be ready and in place for the Twenty-Fifth Anniversary Jubilee, the eagerly anticipated constitutional celebration of the democratic New Russian Federation.

A monumental event was planned, an unrivaled gala of immense proportion, a spectacular triumph unlike anything his beloved Russia had ever attempted. Vlad closed his eyes and imagined it coming true. Continuing for three entire months, it was packed with star-studded, fun-filled festivities in virtually every city, a luminous carnival of the arts highlighting command performances from the world's best playwrights. State-of-the-art world-class hotels sparkled in 'Jewels of Russia' host cities, with special emphasis placed on Moscow and St. Petersburg, and the Volga Federal District. Luxurious, music-filled, casino riverboat paddle wheel steamers would navigate the vast Volga River and St. Petersburg's Neva River, winding leisurely from north to south and back again, rivaling the famed gambling boats of the mighty Mississippi. Russia's skies would burst with stupendous nightly firework displays from the Caucasus Mountains to the sweeping Steppes, all the way to the imposing forests of Siberia. Hot air balloon rallies and races would glide from coast to coast. Innumerable music festivals underscored Russia's tremendously rich historic traditions. Globally acclaimed composers Tchaikovsky, Prokofiev, Borodin, Rachmaninov, Shostakovich and many more would be honored during the Jubilee, all in an effort aiming to propel the nation into a world-class tourist destination.

Vlad made an effort to decisively sort through the many memos on his desk. The Jubilee would be a gargantuan, and heralded achievement for a country containing the vastest land area in the world. To accommodate so many expected international visitors the government poured enormous sums of money for infrastructure improvements; airport upgrades and new terminals, extensive production of cutting-edge light-rail metro networks, and construction of numerous road and highway interconnections, electrical grids and telecommunications capacity. Hundreds of billions had already been expended, and many billions additionally allocated by Russia's burgeoning multinational corporations, with yet more to be disbursed by various independent financiers. Peoples of all nations were cordially invited to attend and partake in the frolicking gaiety, carnivals, pageants and celebrations. And Vlad made sure no one would scrimp on or sacrifice luxuries. It was hoped the world would wait with breathless anticipation.

He smiled to himself, recalling humor his dad used to tell him.

Two Muscovites meet in the street.

"How's life?" asks the first.

"Fantastic," replies the second.

"Do you read the papers?" his friend wonders.

"Of course I read them! How else would I know?"

That was a long time ago. Russia had changed enormously since those bleak days of gallows humor—or on second thought maybe it hadn't.

At last here was the Federation's opportunity to show off, to boast, to resuscitate its weak internal market economy, extol its resources, and take its rightful place as a leader of the world's supreme nations. This was an exciting, exhilarating time, and Vlad knew how incredibly fortunate he was to have been handpicked to oversee and guide the worldwide public relations campaign for this milestone event. It was an honor bestowed personally by the prime minister.

"Vladimir Petrovsky," he was profoundly asked by none other than Prime Minister Sergei Milonov as they sat sipping expensive French wine one evening at a swank café. "Can you assure me you're prepared to take on this formidable task for your country?"

He certainly wasn't lacking ability. His media and advertising background resume was impeccable, as was his marketing expertise in television and broadcasting sponsorship. Plus he had wisely cultivated important relationships among the Kremlin's official elite. Eagerly, if not humbly, Vlad pledged that he was indeed ready and capable, and was thankful for the confidence placed in him.

That question had been posed several years before. Since then, his disciplined approach painstakingly laid the foundations. As with any such ambitious undertaking, there would be enormous burdens to overcome, delicate issues to resolve, and mind-boggling jurisdictional minutia. He was prepared, or so he thought.

No sooner had his work begun bearing fruit than his spill on winter ice near home caused his herniated disc, cervical spine rupture, C-5—C-6. How careless and stupid. Yet two MRIs, one nerve conduction test, and five medical consultations later, he was still alertly on the job, never mind requiring a regimen of physical therapy and pain medication supplemented by an occasional shot of vodka.

The world's media was set to focus on Russia like a laser beam, a mixed blessing at best. Here it was, everything Vlad sweated for and simultaneously everything he dreaded. Russia would find herself under a rapacious media microscope, and so would he. Already several of his highly touted underlings were circling like vultures, prepared to bypass protocol, and ready to pounce at the opportune moment should his lauded marketing techniques slip.

Indeed, such is life.

He wasn't about to let any slimy bastard become aware of the intensity of his pain and steal away this uniquely prized plum. He'd manage, just as he always had, overcoming adversity since his childhood in Moscow, through state-sponsored schools, and years at university. When career doors finally opened he found himself entering an ensuing endless maze of bureaucracy, cronyism and nepotism that dogged every aspect of modern Russian life. He dived right in, eager to prove himself. Now, several decades later, he stood at the threshold, the pinnacle of achievement. His title was Director of Public Relations for the rapidly looming Jubilee. This was the defining moment to demonstrate what his talent could do. Score big, validate himself by pulling it off with flying colors.

His wife, Raisa, exhaustively tried to understand the position he was currently placed in, even if his two beloved young daughters did not. 'Papa never comes home anymore,' he overheard them complain. 'Papa works very hard,' Raisa told them. The strain on everyone was painfully conspicuous, and even Raisa wasn't pleased or placated.

It would pay off handsomely he kept reassuring; the years of stringent study, his proficiency in dealing with both foreign and domestic top-ranked print media, television, and Internet. His propaganda skills were exemplary and carefully honed. Nor did his boyish good looks and easy charm do him ill as premier spokesman for the Jubilee. His job was to be innovative and creative continuously, doling out small tasty, portions and keeping worldwide media salivating and hungry for more.

Intense campaigns were already underway. The outcome might even catapult him into a permanent directorship or Cabinet post. Already his dozen assigned undersecretaries were insufficient to handle the legion of diverse preparations. Troublesome headaches would only increase as opening ceremonies steadily grew closer. The onset of the 25th Anniversary opening ceremonies was barely fourteen months away. The countdown had begun.

As he mulled these circumstances he opened the top drawer of his desk, reaching deep to locate a chocolate bar. The wrapper read '*Russian Pleasure, an exquisite blend of dark chocolate made at the Alexander Nevsky Chocolate Factory in Omsk*'. He indulged himself, eating quickly and stealthily, as a schoolboy might in an effort to hide the deed from a watchful teacher. He recalled that a century earlier the Alexander Nevsky had originated as a sausage factory. During Stalin's purges the grim joke was that your supper sausage might comprise an out-of-favor politician you'd long forgotten.

As he crumpled the wrapper he was reminded of the one nagging concern that incessantly surfaced. For weeks there had been an unusual barrage of rumors and rumblings, claiming something was distressingly amiss at the Omsk Alexander Nevsky Chocolate Factory. Ugly rumors. This most classified festival project was reputedly under a cloud of speculation and gossip of peculiar subversion, a clandestine plot to ruin Russia's glorious moment. None of it made sense. Several of his staff wondered if the Americans might have unknown motives for undermining the New Russian Federation's awaited spotlight. Others suspected the Chinese. One aide went so far as to intimate it might be some insidious, weird plot hatched by the Israelis. Of course Vlad discounted all these ridiculous rumors out of hand. What was to be gained? The very notion was preposterous. No, Russia's exposition was not fodder to induce top-secret spy intrigue. Most likely the truth would be found amid the endless bureaucratic layers of lethargy, bickering, and malfeasance that increasingly plagued his work.

The scientist appointed to direct the secret project at the Alexander Nevsky Chocolate Factory, Dr. Mikhail Sunavich, was a peculiar bird; a genius prone to incessant outbreaks of tantrums, temper and whim, storming in and out of his laboratory, disrupting meetings, and managing to irritate everyone from the lowest to the highest-positioned political apparatchik.

Sunavich got away with this fundamentally infantile behavior not merely because of his stature in the Russian scientific community, but also due to his exceptional abilities presiding over numerous teams of cross-disciplinary interaction experts. World renowned personages who'd spent entire lives delving into the complexities of molecular biology, genetics, physics, biochemistry, plant and animal sciences, and immunology, among other fields that totally perplexed Vlad. Some at the chocolate factory believed Sunavich harbored ulterior motives, feeling he'd accepted his esteemed position reluctantly, submitting finally only at the president's personal behest. Yet questions continued to linger as to whether the obnoxious man was the proper person for leading this covert, top-secret undertaking. It was as baffling as it was exasperating. He'd have made an excellent case study for Sigmund Freud.

Vlad would travel to Omsk in upcoming days; attend the usual series of meetings with jealous directors of overlapping departments. That no real illumination issued from these dreary conferences was a given. The place was a greenhouse for neuroses. But quelling ugly rumors was a primary matter of importance. World media needed assurance everything was proceeding in an orderly, if not efficient manner, and that schedules would meet all deadlines. European and American venture capitalists were watching carefully, unwilling to heavily invest without favorable incentives. He popped two aspirin, hoping the pain would subside, and wondered what fate might throw his way next.

He opened his laptop and viewed his email. Hundreds of messages waited. Most were solicitations by job seekers. These he ignored for underlings to assess. The first message he read concerned a proposed official jingle for the city of Omsk, Siberia's second largest, and its own tidy role planned for the celebration. Vlad's brown eyes quickly scanned the lyrics:

Almost heaven, Omsk city,

Ural Mountains, Irtysh River...

He groaned at the bad parody of an American folk song. His next message was more cryptic and it startled him. It read simply, "Important news. We must talk, B."

The 'B' was Boris Sokolov, Vlad knew. Boris was an older man who'd provided Vlad with excellent counsel on several government projects and had proved an astute asset in every endeavor. Assertive, wise in the ways of weaving a path through endless bureaucracy, Vlad had utmost respect for his professional judgment. Boris remained somewhat of a character, a hardheaded, irascible drinker and smoker with a special affinity for Cuban cigars. Short-tempered at times, tactful at others, few retained the connections or ear of so many disparate high-ranking officials. Vlad closed the email, took his mobile phone and punched in the unlisted, memorized number. The voice on the other end answered almost immediately.

"It's me, Boris."

"Good you called. We must talk today."

"I haven't time."

"We must."

"I have meetings scheduled all day."

"We must talk now."

Vlad heaved a lengthy sigh. "Let's meet at Red Square. We'll walk and talk." He hung up, instructed his executive secretary to delay all meetings and calls for the next several hours. Red Square was just a short distance.

The sky was an overcast lead. Afternoon flurries appeared, hopefully the last snow after Moscow's long and punishing winter. Rather than polluted the air was crispy and clean, and Vlad inhaled deeply. Moscow had evolved so immeasurably since those bleak days of his childhood during the breakup of the old Soviet Union. It had rapidly become a world-class bustling city, cranes dotting the landscape, nightmare traffic-clogged roads rivaling any European or American city. A sense of energy and controlled chaos, teeming crowds shopping countless boutiques, art galleries, bookstores, filled with elaborate diversity along major thoroughfares.

Entering the profoundly impressive Red Square he recognized the squat, muscular man with creased leonine features. Boris was standing near the main entrance of the legendary St. Basil's Cathedral. He wore a fur hat, dark woolen overcoat, and was holding a cigar. His short grey beard glinted with wet snow. Behind him the great cathedral rose in an exhilarant array of swirling colors and pinnacles. Eight onion-dome topped towers were positioned around a larger central ninth spire, forming an eight-point star, a montage of domes, cupolas, and arches bearing magnificently distinctive patterns and hues, forever a sight to behold since its original construction by Czar Ivan the Terrible in commemoration of the capture of Kazan, nearly 500 years ago.

Boris Sokolov quietly circled around a group of Japanese tourists eagerly snapping photos of this classic piece of Russia's long history. He walked with the supple gait of a far younger man.

He greeted Vlad with a firm, nearly bone-crushing handshake. "Good to see you again, my friend. You're looking worn and world-weary. Your eyes are burning with sleeplessness, not healthy for a man your age. You work too many hours. Slow down."

"Thanks so much, Boris. You needn't tell me what I already know. What's this business about today?"

"Come on, let's you and I take a little tour. We have much to catch up on." The square stretched before them and they strolled briskly over stone paving. The austere, red-granite, black-faced edifice of Lenin's Mausoleum hovered nearby, a symbolically potent resting place for the Revolution's great leader whose embalmed corpse in its crystal casket was permanently on display. Now it was stripped of the honor guard that once proudly flanked its entrance, and there was talk of removing the display permanently. Today's visitors were greeted by an odd sense of entering a place all but forgotten in today's New Federation.

Boris glanced and shrugged. "Have you time for coffee, my old friend, Vova?" He used the friendly diminutive form of Vlad's name.

"No. They're running me ragged every minute, every day. But I did read your email. You made meeting sound urgent."

"It is urgent." He looked up at the taller man. "I have a story to relay, Vlad, a story not easy to believe. So incredible and complex I'm not certain I believe it myself. Meanwhile, take a deep breath and try to enjoy life more. Good foods, fine wines, make love. Dunk it like bread soaking up gravy, what is life for?"

"Boris, *Pozhaluista*. Please. Curtail the dramatics. I have no time for this. You should understand the pressure cooker I'm working in. The Moscow City Director and his deputies have been lighting fires under my ass for weeks. Believe me, I've given him the whole buildup and hype, but I can't keep him happy. I promised discreet parties, public hosting of grand festivities and lofty gala balls spotlighting in the media, even women of his choosing, but nothing satisfies the swine. Not even a little envelope stuffed with cash."

Boris nodded with genuine appreciation of Vlad's dilemma. Amateurs and boot lickers. His own extensive experience with Moscow State Television both before and after the breakup of the Soviet Union had not been wasted. Bloated bureaucrats of every stripe delighted in preening and flattery often more than being greased with bribes. They could never amass enough, and even with all his skills and contacts he rarely managed to live up to their lofty expectations no matter how much skimming or incentives were provided. Since then this piteous state of affairs had only worsened. Russian culture was long in retreat before the brute force of money. Bribery was an art; many within the foreign diplomatic corps regarded Russia as a kaleidoscope of official corruption, peppered with criminal malfeasance. Why be ashamed of pocketing a few illicit thousands here and there while millions are shamelessly being pocketed at the highest level?

"All right, my friend. I sympathize with your agitation. Your position isn't easy. But hear me out. Listen and please don't interrupt." The sky was retreating into a white haze, snow falling more intensely. "I've received communications from someone I trust. Someone safeguarded in Omsk, burrowed deeply as my informant at the Alexander Nevsky Chocolate Factory. I assume you realize I requested our meeting because of what's ensued regarding Dr. Mikhail Sunavich."

Vlad nodded impatiently. "I've heard different accounts, but as usual no one's bothered to explain anything. I'd appreciate being filled in. I admit it has me concerned."

"*Horosho*. Good. Then permit me to come directly to the heart of the matter. He whistled softly as they walked. "We have reason to believe Dr. Sunavich has not only betrayed the State, but also the closest colleagues most associated with him. These endless delays he's increasingly caused have been outrageous and provocative, as doubtless you already appreciate. However, a further more perfidious element has inserted itself; it seems Dr. Sunavich has disappeared."

Vlad's eyes widened. "What? Left his post without authority? Has the project been halted yet again?"

"*Da*. Yes. Unfortunately, it's true. Worse, he's absconded seizing indispensible reports, destroying or compromising all hard drives and memories from his personal computers as well as those of confidential associates. Our security people have rifled through his private offices and laboratory, painstakingly searching. They're pulling their hair out. It's all gone. This whole matter isn't for the faint-hearted, Vlad. As far as I'm personally concerned the little degenerate could secede from the human race." He lifted his face upward to feel the snow and boyishly licked at it with his tongue. "I love the taste of wet snow. Clean, fresh. Taste, taste it yourself." Vlad declined. Boris continued, "Listen, what I'm about to divulge is challenging for anyone to accept, so please trust I'm confiding it openly as an old friend and colleague."

"Off the record? Not as a cloak-and-dagger agent for the prime minister's office?" It was said veteran spies regarded Boris an old warhorse symbol of the defunct KGB and all it represented.

Boris chortled softly. "Why do people always suspect me of double dealing? I don't know. Paranoia lurks everywhere. But back to business, this Sunavich, the sneaky whore's son, you understand he's always proclaimed himself an unabashed revolutionary and counterrevolutionary?" He gestured with sharp motions of his powerful hands. "And you're also aware he's switched political allegiances like curling salami, more than the total number of parties we have sitting in the State Duma. However, we've always known his true colors. Sunavich remains an adamant disciple of the old school, a defiant Bolshevik, a Trotskyite, a Maoist."

"I'm well aware of his reactionary background, Boris. If I recall, you yourself emerged back then from the same radical school."

"*Pozhaluista*. Please, my friend, I asked you not to speak yet. This whole affair is onerous enough as it is. You see our clandestine experiment is all but finished." His voice lowered, teeth flashed. "We've succeeded, Vova. Our 'project' is accomplished and we've prevailed beyond anyone's wildest dreams. As hoped, our scientists have regenerated the sum total of every cell, every fiber supplicated distinctly as the man breathed in life. Cloned, utilizing an exclusive newly designed blueprint containing formulated light chocolate molecules throughout his bloodstream. Incredible, eh? Neither of us are scientists, but to the extent I grasp it, I'll explain. Entire body organs have been coupled, incorporating every strand of coded DNA. Vlad, my prize television prodigy, this is more than a replication. It's him as he lived—down to his corneas, toenails, moles, even pubic hairs. The heat of his body, flesh and bone marrow, fashioned with sheer perfection. You'd never believe it, but a blended plasma and red blood compound incorporating subatomic chocolate particles inside and out, courses through his most vital organs to his epidermis. But I digress. Mark my thought; this is a scientific earthquake, an undisputed, unparalleled achievement."

Boris momentarily swelled with pride, then thrust it off as they approached *Lobnoye Mesto*, known as the 'Place of Skulls', a circular platform in the shadows of the cathedral's teardrop domes where for centuries czarist edicts were proclaimed.

But then a look of increasing concern crept over his face and he seemed rocked with despair. "Our project's official unveiling could have been announced well in advance if not for that opportunist's purposeful procrastination. Because of him we find ourselves derailed, scrambling to get out of the nightmare we've been placed in."

The air grew chillier. "Dear friend, allow me to enlighten you with the most convoluted and formidable details. No sooner had Sunavich successfully cracked the essential codes than he stole every set of genetic DNA compounds his laboratory concocted. Somehow or other he imported critical malware to sabotage the primary lab's computers, wiping them clean, erasing backups, hard drives and servers. He infected everything with an unknown vicious virus specifically written to attack and destroy information. It worms across networks and ruins everything in its path, botching our investigation. Meanwhile, other computers providing essential services have been compromised—including sophisticated military systems from Moscow's Central Command. Our people found massive infection overriding error detection. It caused near-total hardware failure. Government servers are no longer fault tolerant. It's havoc, I tell you."

"That's impossible. Military computers are administered under strictest classified control, codes written by the best programmers and engineers."

"Not impossible! That man's caused howling bedlam. Always remember, in the garden many types of potatoes grow. Rootkit software is causing unstable power supplies, and the military is in a frenzied uproar. They're ready to shut down the Alexander Nevsky completely—and could you blame them? The malware cyber worm damaged critical command codes. Sunavich went completely off the rails, berserk if he believes he'll get away with it." His words tumbled out in a torrent. "This episode has escalated straight to the top, I'll tell you. The president is fully aware and is, of course, profoundly concerned. State security's been impeded. It's going to take time and incalculable treasure to repair—if only that were the end of it, because there's more." The old spy's gaze was earnest and bleak.

Vlad cocked his head, riveted by the far-fetched story. "What else did Sunavich do?"

Their shoulders were covered in a fitful sea of snowflakes. Boris buttoned his coat, flicking wet flakes off his sleeve. "I have scant details, but regarding the formula I'm advised all numeric genetic compounds for the counterpart were purposely scattered and lost while this vindictive, contemptible snake fled into the night."

"Where can you 'scatter' genetic compounds?"

"I'll tell you. After an all night frantic search they were tracked down and partially identified. Who in their right mind could devise such a thing? They've been glibly hidden among tens of thousands of newly issued bingo cards at the *Das Kapital Bingo Parlor* in Omsk. Don't laugh, please."

Vlad laughed anyway. "And how did you discover it?"

"We didn't. Two schoolboys found a stray card in the snow, probably planted the same way others were. Schoolboys! We think Sunavich itched for us to find out. We quickly shut down the *Das Kapital*. A scientific team did a preliminary exam of these bingo cards. It appears each and every one contains some quantified singular element, a simple letter or number combination of molecular DNA, base pairs in every cell containing a nucleus. I'll read you a coded fax I received." He took a paper out of his pocket.

"Unauthorized RNA editing by Dr. S. is exceptionally widespread. Specimen DNA transcribed to RNA, and triplet bases translated into specific amino acids for protein building. Genome exam complete, further findings to follow..."

The explanation posed more questions than answers. Boris had unspoken specific justification for sharing this classified information, reasons Vlad knew he might not like. "What does this mean?" he asked with concern.

Boris lifted his eyebrows in a shrug-like gesture. "I don't understand this science, either. Sunavich, the dybbuk, probably brewed his scheme while new bingo cards were printed. The number of possible combinations within those cards is staggering, effectively countless. Imagine them stretched like peasant carts heading to a market fair along the banks of the Volga. The world's greatest geneticists might take months to unravel them into proper sequence. If what I suspect proves true, it's impossible to recreate his code or repair damage in a timely manner because the permutations he inserted approach infinity."

Boris retained his steely smile and composure. "Even my famous sense of humor has its limits, Vladimir Petrovsky. There's more. He administered blood transfusions into the prototype, maturating it utilizing a secret ingredient to mask the chocolate by blending it with rum. The two are intertwined and cannot be separated."

"This whole narrative is a joke, right? My life isn't complicated enough?"

"No joke."

"Blood and rum transfusions mixed with chocolate coursing through his veins? What are you talking about?"

"Precisely that. Engineered within Sunavich's rum formula the *thing* was inoculated, infused with a 'life force'. Understand now? This is his ultimate achievement, the ultimate achievement of all science. Until that point the duplication was perfected but not functioning as intended. Single-handedly Sunavich consummated into existence a living, breathing replica of the illustrious man himself. Because of this accomplishment the world as we know it is forever transformed."

"Are you telling me Sunavich successfully created a viable, living entity without permission...?" As they strolled towards the banks of the wide Moscow River, Vlad's face drained of color. The mind-warping story rattled and mystified him.

Boris touched his arm. "Are you not feeling well, Vova? Has this unsettled you?"

Vlad's mind careened with the enormous scope of these fantastical events. Foreign governments would eagerly pay fortunes to unearth such secrets of an organism's genomes, enabling them to also furnish such a 'life force'. The world's foremost scientific experts doubted such a feat could ever be produced. They were wrong. But it necessitated a creative madman like Mikhail Sunavich to prove their long-held axioms fallacious. With this substantiated evidence the little doctor with bad eyesight had made fools of the entire establishment. Not to mention that this revelation could potentially spoil, if not ruin, the upcoming Jubilee. Already Vlad could hear the incoherent barrage of endless quarrels, recriminations, and denunciations. Stepping back and looking at the broader picture, total cancellation of the festivities would be a foregone conclusion.

The aging master of chicanery and deceit drew his lips close to Vlad's ear and lowered his voice to barely above a whisper. "Now you know our country's danger, and the domino effects it can have. A bitter pill to swallow, isn't it?" He waited, then added "I've been requested by the highest authorities to form a small working group to assist in this matter. And I have an unorthodox request for you, Vova. I'm asking for your help to assure everything's kept under wraps, safe from leaks until we can solve this disaster."

"Me? *My* help?"

Boris regarded him with utmost seriousness. "There are so few people a man can really trust." He put his hands on Vlad's shoulders. "I believe I can trust you. Admittedly, we found ourselves asleep at the switch, and we mustn't be caught sleeping again. It's a jungle out there. That little man, Dr. Sunavich, is a devil, my friend." He gazed downward. "Or maybe he is the devil himself."

The cell phone rang. Vlad had forgotten to put it on vibrate before going to sleep. He put the receiver to his ear. "Petrovsky."

Beside him Raisa drowsily stirred. She was a pretty woman, just the wrong side of forty, with bright, engaging brown eyes resting above a petite nose and a winning smile. "It's after one A.M., Vova," she reminded, using the affectionate diminutive in a husky voice filled with annoyance.

"Please forgive this late intrusion, sir. I'm ordered to inform you your presence is urgently required at the prime minister's private quarters."

"Do you know what time it is?"

"Yes, sir. A car will arrive at your front door in ten minutes. Please be ready."

"*Spasibo.* Thank you. I'll be waiting." He turned to his wife and kissed her lightly, squeezing her hand. "Go back to sleep, Raisa, everything's good. I'll be back home soon. It's an emergency meeting."

"This is becoming too much," she muttered irritably. "One more unavoidable meeting—again."

"This is one I can't refuse. The prime minister wants me there."

"They always want you there, Vova." She turned over, burying her face in a pillow.

Vlad sat on the side of the bed wiping sleep from bleary, bloodshot eyes. He needed strong coffee right now. He'd been in a deep slumber and was barely thinking straight. There hadn't been much time for sleep all week, and now this sudden flurry of craziness was taking precedence over everything else in his life, with no idea of what any of it meant. He hurriedly dressed. The pain in his aching shoulder waxed and waned.

The car turned near Manege Square onto wide, Tverskaya Street, an avenue lined with Western shops and impressive imperial grandeur, complimented by people coming and going from late-night lounges and restaurants, underscoring the new modern Moscow. It was a veritable playground, home to upper class Muscovites. The limousine driver honked, zigzagging amid traffic, passing the pink-façades of grand old buildings embellished with gold gilding and elegant cornices. A thin dusting of snow covered the streets. Minutes later the car cornered the street into the low-key and low to the ground buildings of *Kitai-gorod* and adjoining *Tretyakovksy Proyezd*, another upper crust neighborhood designated for Russia's patrician elite.

The car pulled in front of an imposing stone building. As he climbed the steps he was greeted by a pair of carved, leering, gargoyles on either side. A uniformed security guard checked his identification. Jacket slung over his shoulders, Vlad entered the P.M.'s private quarters. The prime minister was waiting in the boardroom. "Ah, Petrovsky, do please join us. Good that you live close by. I trust we haven't inconvenienced you too much. I think you're acquainted with almost everyone here."

He thanked the prime minister and shook the hands offered. They were a dour group, largely political flunkies, carefully handpicked. Relentlessly and remorselessly, the P.M. always made a point of surrounding himself with advisors smarter than himself. It remained fascinating to Vlad that a crass functionary like Sergei Milonov could acquire such a prominent office, but then again under the unfettered rules of the New Russian Federation anything was possible. It was a departure from a harsher era, when such a notoriously mercurial man would not by any means obtain a position higher than third-rate apparatchik. These days, influence, money, and effortless lechery went far.

"Take a seat, have some coffee." The prime minister gestured to a silver samovar. His frequent facial tics and lateral eye shifts were more marked than usual. Milonov was a middling man in age and size, square-faced with a pointed chin. Bushy eyebrows beneath a creased forehead and soft features disguised a quick, raw temper. Ordering and countermanding were his habit, a constant seesaw of changes in direction, unpredictable, purposely confusing and draining subordinates, leaving no doubt who was in charge.

Vlad greedily poured the strong brew. "May I enquire why I'm summoned tonight? I have a string of meetings lined up beginning in five hours. The first is with the Associate Director of Channel One—"

"Oh, that nuisance? Don't fret, he's not as important as you think, Petrovsky." Milonov had a penchant for conflict and drama, and chuckled with concealed knowledge only he was privy to. A gold front tooth glinted in the soft light. "No one promised climbing the ladder would be easy, eh?" Several associates grinned with ass-kissing appreciation. Those who curried favor enjoyed special privileges sparingly doled out.

"All right, back to business." The prime minister altered course and speedily passed around a number of folders. His laptop computer sat closed in sleep mode. Vlad looked over the rim of his glasses and skimmed the material. It was composed of recent dispatches, letters, requests, and the like. Nothing appeared to be particularly noteworthy.

"Excuse me, sir, but I understand we have a situation," Vlad said in a quiet tone. "A national security concern of far-reaching consequences..."

The prime minister stroked his chin with his right hand. "You're badly misinformed. Matters are far beyond a mere 'situation.'"

One of his lackeys spoke up, a slender man with a pockmarked face, a long neck, and bobbing Adam's apple. Vlad vaguely recognized him; he was a scientist with extensive experience, a club-footed, austere man hampered by a severe limp and little humor. His name was confusing, Rimsky or Kimsky, or some jumbled combination. "My fax is humming non-stop, Mr. Prime Minister, my laboratory assistants working without stopping."

"To your credit. But truthfully, have you resolved anything at all?" Milonov tapped his fingers impatiently.

Rimsky-Kimsky glowered with the nuanced rebuke. "I'd like to be more forthcoming, but I can't. We've marshaled multiple resources using different methodologies. To put our current situation in perspective, we're dealing with open-ended blame throwing resulting in unresolved allegations, denunciations, and accusations. Our A-team scientists at Omsk are panic-stricken finding their work trashed."

Sergei Milonov, often short with insubordinates, listened with irritated indulgence matched by a cold impatient glare. "I'm not insensitive to your frustration, but their behavior is understandable when one's entire output is flushed down a toilet. I need answers, not excuses." He was met with stony silence from his bureaucratic hive. "Comments, anyone else?"

Reluctantly, Vlad lifted a hand. "Sir, I'm at a loss. Everyone in attendance is aware of events I'm not informed of. Today Boris Sokolov from Internal Security contacted me. We met near the Kremlin and he intimated a number of ambiguous, inconceivable matters. Dare I refer to it as a 'phenomenon'? Am I here because of the classified Omsk project?"

"Correct, Petrovsky."

"I can fill in the details," offered Rimsky-Kimsky.

Sergei Milonov clicked a ballpoint pen he clutched. "I'll do it," he overruled. "It isn't inconceivable anymore, Petrovsky. To be point blank, our esteemed Dr. Sunavich has disappeared, vanished without a trace. You are aware of that much?" He tamed his authoritarian fervor.

Vlad nodded. "I was told all his findings and formulae have been removed. Notes, computer drivers wiped clean. And somehow he's compromised an entire network of servers via carefully calculated malware attacks."

Milonov annoyingly kept clicking the ballpoint. "Correct again. Sunavich initiated an infection, a noxious, deadly worm that endlessly reproduces, targeting what I'm told are known as 'programmable logic controllers.' These all-embracing buggers have seriously compromised state security networks in power and scope, a feat as ambitious as linking the Volga with the Don." He referred to the canal connecting the two great rivers, unfinished from the time of Peter the Great until actualized by convict labor during the mid-twentieth century.

A pestering cat in the corner meowed as it rubbed itself against a catnip-filled toy mouse. The prime minister quieted it with a snap of his fingers. "Hush, Tinkerbelle!" His stern gaze returned to the conferees. "Because of this herculean breech our project is placed in dire jeopardy. Had we learned of Sunavich's perfidy as little as three days ago we might have prevented impending disaster; shut down all labs at the Alexander Nevsky, instituted a lockdown, and placed the complex under immediate military jurisdiction. Sadly, that horse has fled the barn. You see, Petrovsky, one son of a bitch has managed to compromise our entire effort and scientific breakthroughs. I don't pretend having knowledge in these areas. I have less understanding regarding genetics, DNA, genomes, than anyone here. Nevertheless, I do understand one thing; the combination of ingredients Sunavich secretly compounded surpasses all our combined expertise. Our original intent was simple; announce to the world an unmatched scientific achievement, a lifeless replication of our historical revolutionary leader, Vladimir Ilyich Lenin. In the cynical spirit of our age, what Sunavich instead unleashed is a twenty-first century variation of Dr. Frankenstein's monster."

Vlad was repulsed at the blood-curdling metaphor. "My dealings with this project are limited, basic information meant for public consumption. This is far beyond my paltry expertise."

Milonov nodded, opened his laptop, and fiddled with the keyboard, saying in a businesslike voice, "We all failed to foresee the cataclysm that was underfoot, but we can quickly clear up a little of your bewilderment. Tell me, how much do you know about Vladimir Ilyich Lenin?"

"I'm acquainted with what everyone's taught at school. Lenin was the primary leader for Soviet socialism and shepherd of the Great October Socialist Revolution. He was a lightning rod, and a champion of the proletariat. His radical Bolsheviks seized political power and inaugurated the Communist regime. To solidify authority, Russia was thrown into a civil war lasting five long, horrible years before we finally experienced peace and stability. Once in command Lenin turned his strategic vision into reality. Even today our national identity remains profoundly shaped by his hand." Vlad quickly added as an afterthought, "I know my own grandmother venerated his memory, and because of her I share his name."

"Concise and well said, Petrovsky. You recognize the circumstances that brought about the 1917 October Revolution, the overthrow of Russia's provisional government, and the demise of the monarchy. You understand Lenin was the Soviet Union's preeminent authority, a superior orator, a man beloved, blessed and worshipped by the masses. He stood as an icon, exalted and praised by worker, soldier, and peasant-elected councils alike. With fiery passion he organized and reshaped Russia's proletariat, and as leader of the Bolsheviks became the very embodiment of revolutionary Russia."

Vlad recalled other things he'd been taught. Women threw themselves at Lenin and men willingly gave their lives. At no time in history had Lenin's prominence been questioned. He dwarfed all rivals, but died at the pinnacle of power. Surviving several assassination attempts he was never the less seriously damaged and eventually suffered a series of strokes, passing away in January 1924. This left a huge power vacuum. He was only fifty-three years of age. For many the shock of his loss had never healed. The undiluted truth remained that if Lenin had survived Russia's entire twentieth century history might have evolved quite differently. True, there were those who hated him and plotted his downfall. Yet countless others canonized him still. Adoration for Lenin never quite vanished.

"Therein rests our predicament," asserted Milonov. "We are facing a dead man brought back to life."

Alina Vera Galina was tall and graceful; appealing in a studious sort of way, creating an impression of being anything but the honored scientist she was. With dark wavy hair that fell to her shoulders, a patrician face often sheltered by large dark glasses, she seemed more suited for the role of an espionage agent in a film. Born in St. Petersburg, she relocated to Moscow and completed her studies at the prestigious Landau Institute for Theoretical Physics. Her achievements granted her not one, but two prized fellowships. First she received an appointment as the research assistant for the brilliant Asher Isaac Titlebaum, PhD, one of the most critically demanding minds of his generation. After her tenure alongside him she next became a valuable subordinate to perhaps the most lauded man of scientific accomplishments, Dr. Mikhail Sunavich.

She paced the parlor of her spacious flat in Omsk in a foul and angry mood. Omsk was a city well known for dramatic swings in weather, and today's weather, like her disposition, was dramatic. Adorned in European vogue she was wearing a checkered top, a dark cotton skirt, and low-heeled pumps. Her parlor's windows overlooked Omsk's famed Dom Prirody Museum of Natural History, a gem amid otherwise oppressive and drab architecture. She stared as she drew a deep drag on an American cigarette, hastily snubbing it out in an overflowing ashtray.

"So between them, which of the two do you believe is the smarter, Alina Vera?"

"How am I supposed to answer a question like that?"

"In your personal opinion, I mean."

She swung around and glared directly at the man slouching comfortably relaxed on her dark velvet sofa, below a copy of the famed Chinese painting, *Lotus and Mandarin Ducks*, by Zhang Daqian. "Smarter? How do you distinguish which genius is more of a genius than the other? You explain that to me, Boris, and I'll answer you. It's absurd."

Boris Sokolov chewed his Cuban cigar, glancing at the aesthetically tasteful Majorcan linens and block-printed Turkish textiles adorning furniture that attested to her wide and varied artistic appreciation. "Ah Alina Vera, I wish you'd give up fighting the world and find yourself a man twenty years younger than me. Someone my age appreciates finding myself sitting in the most prestigious apartment block in Omsk, chatting with one of the loveliest women I've ever known."

"Save your flattery," Alina Vera hissed, her back stiffening. "What you easily can do is leave my flat the same way you came in. The front door is directly behind you. The lift to the lobby is waiting down the hallway."

He stretched his arms wide in a Christ-like posture. "Here I've travelled all night on the Trans-Siberian train from Moscow just to visit you, and I find myself unwelcome. It's true; life can be so unfair."

"You didn't travel here to visit, Boris. You came to interrogate me. Don't deny it. You exude trust and friendliness, but in fact you're duplicitous as hell. Which clown in the Kremlin is pulling your strings today?" She placed slender hands on her hips and glared. "Sucking up to some hack who reports to the president? No? That money-grubbing pig whose stolen millions got him elected mayor of Moscow? What about our sticky-fingered prime minister? Or some unheralded ambitious military man savvy enough to purchase your loyalty?"

Boris laughed hard and clapped his hands in approval. "I do really love you, Alina Vera. Even at ten years old, when your mother put sharp pepper under your fingernails at night to keep you from biting them, you were a hot-tempered gypsy. Your mouth burned so badly, but you refused to cry. Alas, I made a promise to your father that I'd always keep an eye out for you, and my loyalty to him is unshakable. He requested I make certain you didn't find yourself in trouble, serious trouble. You know what I mean, the kind you encountered during your university years. Dr. Galina, you do recall requesting my help when your bad behavior was confronted with expulsion? What was that ugly student fascist group you stupidly signed your name to?"

"They weren't fascists!" She stamped her foot on the richly tiled floor. Without doubt the vibration made the downstairs neighbors jump. "They were honest students refusing to have their allegiance purchased by embezzling thugs and legalized criminals stealing our country with money stolen by faceless tycoons running the government behind the scenes."

"What criminals? They were legally elected legislators. Very well, my dear Alina Vera. Being a patriot doesn't suit you anyway, loathing authority the way you do. Call them what you may, but you must admit I conveniently managed to prevent your name from appearing on several undesirable lists. You professional career could have ended before it began." He shrugged with his eyebrows. "And now, unfortunately, the shoe rests on the other foot. It is I who come in need of your help."

She sighed with exaggerated exasperation. "Having pangs of conscience, Boris? You don't need anyone's help, you old double-crosser. How dare you misuse the word 'patriot' to me? I know all about you and your games of intrigue too, remember? You chose to evade, mislead and lie about the good old KGB days you swept under the rug. What about those frightened friends of my parents who quietly disappeared? And I know all about that Turkish belly dancer hidden from sight at your country dacha. You think I don't know details of your life?" Even with this flash of anger her movements remained gentle and feminine, he saw. "So, exactly what is it you're fishing for today, Boris Sokolov? Tell your kleptocratic masters I can't possibly be of service to you or them. Your presence is as welcome as a bout of malaria."

He leaned forward stroking his beard, an ardent expression in his indecipherable eyes. "This is strictly a professional call. I've come here concerning a very tricky, serious matter, Alina Vera. And I'm confessing to you that the very security of the State could be at risk."

"Oh, please. *Pozhaluista.* You change politics like weather. Get off your soapbox and spare me the jingoistic lecture, yes? You've declared nothing. Explain in simple Russian what this is about. I haven't seen Dr. Sunavich for a week or more. He's gone to Timbuktu for all I know—or care. And as for Asher Titlebaum, it's been several years since his departure from the Academy. At least Asher had the courage and foresight to walk out of that politically poisoned place. Your sneaky disciples couldn't ensnare him. He walked out standing tall and proud."

"I see you're still quite fond of that Jew."

She flinched internally. "I certainly am. What of it? Asher is a great man. An insightful thinker and visionary, too good for you and your slimy breed." Nostrils flaring, she pretended to spit on the floor. "He's one of the finest intellects I've ever encountered. Without his efforts the whole Institute might have buckled under political pressure forced on it. It might have shut down permanently, without any regard to the outstanding work we were doing. By the way, did you finally arrest any of those scientists you continually harangued? Root out those who the police claimed were subversive? Or were your cronies content merely ruining a few careers as an object lesson? It was a travesty."

"There were no arrests. It wasn't necessary. And I was not the one responsible for what you accuse me of, despite what you believe. As for the tax police, they'd have been happier accepting a fat envelope than making arrests."

Concerning Asher Titlebaum, Boris well recognized the professor as a most valuable asset to the Institution and to Russia. A man who'd cultivated a well-deserved reputation for nurturing his students, of whom Alina Vera Galina was a prime example. Professor Titlebaum was routinely nominated worldwide for so many distinguished prizes he could never recount them all. Still it was a shame, Boris thought. How sad that a man of his acumen, at the pinnacle of career and reputation, had arbitrarily chosen to throw it all away. Retreating instead, to some forsaken village, sequestered amidst endless shelves of dusty books and mystical missives containing subtle texts defining the infinite of the cosmos, seeking explanation to inconceivable questions without answers. Boris admittedly held a grudging admiration for the esteemed aging scientist, yet simultaneously felt a twinge of contempt for someone who so easily relegated a magnificent career into the dustbin.

"All right, when am I supposed to receive this phone call?" Alina Vera said sonorously. There was no point in continuing to argue, she knew. Boris Sokolov secured enough political clout to make any refusal all but impossible. She never trusted him, but then she rarely trusted anyone.

"As soon as our friend Vladimir Petrovsky arrives at Omsk airport they'll advise us immediately."

"You told me his plane would arrive before ten."

"Alina Vera, do I look like an air traffic controller? I know your father was a police magistrate, but that doesn't give you the right to interrogate me."

"You're a sarcastic bastard, Boris Sokolov! In any case, I don't understand the point of having some muckraking public relations man getting involved. What's he supposed to do, put out a *press release*? He has no business being dragged into this mess."

She turned away and walked into her kitchen.

Boris smiled. "Obviously you don't understand the formidable clout of the media. They're astonishingly convincing. They brainwash the public over and over. Vlad Petrovsky happens to be one of the best communications experts in Moscow. He has the personal skills of an accomplished politician, and is an expert spin-doctor, if I may use a term I hate. He deals routinely with major foreign television networks, news agencies, tabloids, and journalists from all over the world. He's adept at fending them off with lightning verbal dexterity."

"You mean he's good at bullshit?"

"Yes, as a matter of fact, he is."

"I see, another glib, smooth-talking mover and shaker itching to make a splash. His type is anathema to me." She pretended to vomit.

"Unfair for you to speak like that. In the battle for public opinion the media can defend or delegitimize us. Today choosing to be our ally and tomorrow become a lethal political foe. Have you heard of TV's *Primetime Russia*, or *Russia Today*? Both are top-notch, world-class quality programming. He was chosen for promotion from nearly one hundred candidates, and placed in charge of the agency's foreign media division. Petrovsky gets the credit, spending years at one and then the other, fine-tuning. Never underestimate the power of the press. Cornering good public relations is more valuable than an entire army in the field. Ask the Americans."

"Enough already, whatever you say," she called out. "Do you want another beer?"

"*Da*. An American one, please."

Alina Vera handed him the beer and plopped down on her chaise lounge. Outside, a robust wind began to howl. From the height of her fifteenth-story apartment she could see the sprawling lights of Omsk twinkling between heavy, swirling snowflakes. She'd come to loathe this isolated, dreadful place. Why in heaven's name had she accepted the diabolical assignment here leaving behind the grandeur of Moscow, traveling nearly three thousand kilometers to a far-flung hinterland in Eastern Siberia only to toil at a miserable edge-of-purgatory chocolate factory close to the borders of Kazakhstan? She lit another cigarette, inhaled. Boris Sokolov was correct, she admitted as she calmed. It was all about ego, jumping at the opportunity to work closely again with venerable Dr. Suna-vich, although she certainly wasn't about to admit it.

Boris popped the lid and liberally drank it American-style, directly from the can. It was cold and tasty, reminding him of the brews he so enjoyed at the bars of New York, during the years he served as a member of the Russian delega-tion to the United Nations, and covertly as a spy for the security police. "What do you feel made Professor Titlebaum abandon his career that way? Honestly, I really value your opinion. You knew him as well as anybody while you were both at the Institute."

She stared toward the window, pressed a fist to her lips. Her voice soft-ened with her mood. "I think he craved more than science could provide. I think he sought something essential to embrace and nourish. As with everyone at the Institute back then, I suppose I didn't realize the depth of his hungry need for spirituality, or the urgency to connect to what he considered necessary to sus-tain him. Life in a laboratory can be hollow. An excessively pessimistic empty existence I can't put into words. I heard him speaking of 'spiritual healing.' He was always something of a mystic, questing and lost in unearthing nature's role amid metaphysical boundaries, and seeking to fuse the two. He gave himself an impossible task. A few colleagues said he was slipping, but I knew better. The day he chose to make his official announcement everyone was flabbergasted. I'd like to believe I understood, but I didn't really, still don't."

"When he handed in his resignation you never saw it coming?"

She shook her head. "No. Asher's temperamental, too. He values his pri-vacy and shares very little with anyone except for his wife, Esther. He'd threat-ened to resign before but never actually went through with it. For a long time we assumed he wasn't serious. He can be a very witty man, you know. Not doc-trinaire in the fashion Sunavich is. Asher relishes occasional vodka with friends, a good joke, and a fine meal. He's able to recognize joy and the pleasures in life, and partakes of it when offered. That's one of the first things people see and like about him. He's also quite a gentleman, very unlike Dr. Sunavich who's so base and crude. I always found Asher polite, well mannered, and thoughtful. I don't mind admitting that I cried when he left. It was never the same. It still isn't."

Boris tugged at his earlobe, still unable to grasp the famed scientist's motivation. "So what made him finally chuck it all away?"

"Asher's the only one who can answer that question. As I said, we were all surprised—no, we were shocked. No one could have predicted it. He announced he was leaving Moscow for some misbegotten muddy village. He said he was determined to delve into new studies at some acclaimed historic yeshiva, famous for centuries. He became a Kabbalist, you know. A spiritual mystic."

"You think he's happy in this new incarnation?"

"Don't be acerbic. I know he's happy. And don't underestimate him or ever believe you can understand him. He didn't do it because he was weary of the establishment. He wasn't going to fall into the fissure like the rest of us. He did it because of sincere ideology, and Asher will prove as good a rabbi as a scientist. Albert Einstein said, 'Science without religion is lame. Religion without science is blind'."

Boris closed his eyes and massaged at his temples. What kind of manic people was he dealing with? Here was a beautiful woman more attracted to microscopes than men. Sunavich was a feral, vainglorious, genius willing to destroy the whole nation if necessary in the name of extreme political beliefs, in short, a lunatic psychopath. And then there was Asher Titlebaum, another man of such brilliance that he might have rivaled Einstein, but instead threw everything away to grow a long beard, garb himself in a black coat and hat and become a Hasidic rabbi. The older Boris grew, the more he came to believe the human condition really was absurd.

The telephone rang. Alina Vera grabbed it. "Dr. Galina. All right. Thank you. I'll give him the message." She hung up the telephone. "All right Boris, your friend from Moscow has finally touched down in Omsk."

Boris smiled. Everything was falling into place. "*Horosho*. Good. Get your coat and let's go."

2.

The walls were commanding slabs of thick stone capped by steel, with discreet security towers at each end monitored by armed sentries. The scene was anything but pastoral. From the twisting road it appeared more a ghastly gulag rather than a highly sophisticated labyrinth of science laboratories. The preeminent Alexander Nevsky Chocolate Factory, located at the far outskirts of Omsk, had served multifarious purposes since its original construction nearly a century before. Originally built for sausage making during the effort to industrialize, then converted for weaponry during the Second World War, today it remained an austere, warehouse-like edifice with no sign, no numbers shown on its black metal entry doors, a building likely resembling the dingy, harrowing prisons Stalin filled without remorse. Heavy grim gates swung open, the limousine passed through. Guards on either side dutifully stood at attention. One by one the late-night visitors exited the limousine, and in an opaque mist followed the high-ranking officer who greeted them with an attentive salute. An array of medals glinted. He and Boris were well acquainted, and exchanged whispered words.

This man was Colonel Dimsky, renowned military commander and counterterrorist intelligence expert. Dimsky was a broad shouldered, craggy-faced man with projecting cheekbones and a meticulously trimmed brush mustache. A handpicked advisor reporting directly to Internal Security and the Kremlin, he was reputedly a man to be taken seriously, an overseer with a gilded future ensured beyond the army. Known for careful attention to detail and an irreverent bent, his sole relaxation was in playing his cherished balalaika, a three-stringed, long-necked fretted lute with a triangular body and guitar neck. He never failed to keep the instrument of Turkic origin close at hand.

Vlad glanced about timorously. Alina Vera grew impatient to learn the purpose for their visit, while Boris remained contained and controlled, taking it all in stride. Two others behind them walked inquisitively. The man with the marked limp and bobbing head Vlad recognized as the prime minister's trusted eyes and ears, the club-footed scientist with the confusing name dubbed Rimsky-Kimsky.

A long draughty corridor winded downward. Dull lighting cast elongated shadows against concrete masonry. The air was dank, and an eroded trace of industrial bleach solution assaulted Vlad's nostrils. The prodigious chocolate factory necessitated constant, copious scrubbing, needing to be cleansed in the same fashion a physician's surgery required daily antiseptic disinfection. Tall steel doors were tightly shut and locked. There were no sounds except for their echoing footsteps. Vlad had visited the Alexander Nevsky several times in the recent past, but under very different circumstances. Then he was here to meet with civilian managers and executives, and this underground labyrinth of abstruse laboratories was foreign to him, a sullen, different world than the aboveground confectionary facility where premium chocolate was actually manufactured.

Invariably in this confidential location there was a steady hustle and bustle of lab technicians in white frocks, studious assistants scurrying to and fro, up and down the Byzantine maze. Today all was deserted, miscellaneous impressions of a sterile barren shell of itself. "This way, please," the punctilious military man said, gesturing to another passage. "Dr. Sunavich's personal office is the last door on the right. His exclusive lab is annexed. I've taken the liberty of unlocking both doors."

"Thank you, Colonel," Rimsky-Kimsky muttered. In the dim his face was just a pair of eyeglasses reflecting faded light.

The private office suggested the same drab, cheerless atmosphere as the hallway; a large metal desk at the center, a fluorescent lamp, and a calendar taped to the drab grey wall behind, and no recessed lights overhead. Shadows played patterns. A dark, long window overlooked a desolate semi-subterranean stone courtyard. "The son of a bitch ruined everything," grumbled Rimsky-Kimsky, his jaw set. He limped from one useless computer to another, climbing over obstacles to find switches and sockets. All hard drives and memories were burned beyond reconstruction. The powerful computer programs designed to model protein structure and function were erased and shredded. "We'll be unable to restore anything. Troves of extensive trials, files, all obliterated."

Alina Vera surveyed the replication of a war zone in total dismay. Barely a week earlier she'd worked long hours at his very site. "I can't believe he'd do this. Why?"

"Sunavich is a hard-wired maniac," scorned the colonel under his breath at the bone-jarring sight.

Overwhelmed with outrage at the insult, Boris gritted his teeth and struggled for self-control. "We've seen enough. Take us to what we came for."

Dimsky obligingly consented without hesitation. "Of course. Follow me, please." Another narrow corridor led to a steep flight of stairs. Strong air conditioners hummed as cold air flowed from unseen ducts. Alina Vera folded her arms, rubbing at goose bumps. Vlad also felt the chill, along with a rising sense of dread of things beyond his scope. Rimsky-Kimsky and his colleague appeared ill at ease as well. Only Boris outwardly maintained his unflappable bearing, to all appearances unbothered by the monstrosity.

They walked inside a wide, well-lighted chamber. The lab was crowded with numerous rows of long tables and metal desks topped with highly powered electron microscopes, an army of dynamic three-dimensional state-of-the-art computers, plus a diversity of elaborate specialized monitors.

"Note the wanton destruction," the colonel casually remarked. Video conferencing screens were pulled off walls, loose, color-coded wiring dangling high and low. The mainframe's multiple routers and interconnecting computer networks were hijacked and customized with useless network interfaces. Even old landline telephone connection cables were ripped out. As a final touch, the recently installed impressive alarm system was cleverly deprogrammed and loudly replayed a loop of depressing Latin medieval laments.

"Periodically it also plays carnival organ grinder music," the colonel commented.

"Well, just shut it off!" ordered Boris.

Colonel Dimsky found the switch. The medieval hymns ceased.

"He screwed us royally," bristled Alina Vera, sniffing at a rancid odor. "Why didn't he use a sledgehammer and save all the trouble?"

"His little joke. Dr. Sunavich's worm disabled alarms and fed bogus computerized log reports, assuring our engineers everything was operating properly. All labs were blindsided, allowing him access and freedom."

Shadowed cameras with broken lenses pointed down from the ceilings at the lab's carcass. Near the far exit end stood a row of knee-operated surgical scrub sinks and tubs. The air was potent with the smell of aseptic disinfectant. The lab's activity and bustle had barely been vacated. The military had culminated the task of evacuating the entire quadrant scant hours before.

"Before being allowed entry to the adjoining chamber everyone needs to surgically scrub," Dimsky told them. They quietly walked to the sinks. Learning from watching others, Vlad pressed the knee panel to activate the water flow. The bactericidal soap panel pumped, soap dispensed through a stainless steel spout. When he finished washing he fitted his surgical gloves and hat. White lab coats hung nearby on hooks. The colonel handed him one.

Boris impatiently drummed stubby fingers, peeking with antipathy in every direction, appalled at the deplorable waste and havoc. He walked deliberately, surveying with utmost attention uttering "Miasma, miasma."

"Before proceeding inside the confidential area does anyone wish to view anything other than our finalized prototype?" Dimsky asked. They all shook their heads.

"Please show us the specimen," said Boris.

The long-faced military man astutely complied. "What you're about to view cannot be described, only revealed," he said. With that cryptic remark he opened another door. It led into a tiny room. At the near wall the colonel punched in a series of codes and placed his right hand against a black glass screen embedded into the wall. A computer purred with instant handprint recognition. Beyond was the final, most important and least conspicuous of the inconspicuous doors. It required a code only a handful had access to. Dimsky was one. He reached and released open an undisclosed narrow alloy drawer concealed within the wall. It squeaked on a metal track, rolling into full view. Suddenly the chamber sprang to life with greenish fluorescent light. Vlad momentarily shaded his eyes. The scene made him feel they were unwelcome visitors to a lonely morgue.

"Is this the accumulation of what's left to study?" asked Boris.

"Our technicians assure this is the sum total remaining. Prior prototypes have been destroyed or compromised. All evidence of random experiments were either removed or invalidated. Traces of completed work and accomplishments are missing. We have nothing else to show from the intense efforts of two whole years. This single composition alone remains intact. Whether left untouched in plain sight purposely or not we're unsure. Please view for yourselves."

Slowly the group formed a semi-circle and peered inside. Laying flat upon a refrigerated marble slab, reposed within a long plain box resembling a coffin, rested the diminutive form of a human being less than a meter in length from head to toe.

"Amazing," muttered Rimsky-Kimsky. "Unparalleled."

Vlad peered over the rim of his eyeglasses. What he saw was beyond imagination. Before him rested a perfectly proportioned figure bathed in light cream-colored chocolate, incredibly complex in every detail, so perfect it appeared almost alive. Its open eyes were disturbingly lifelike, eerily staring, unblinking, and unimaginable, as if conscious and cognizant, functioning and knowing. A faint odor of chocolate lingered with a hint of ammonia. And for the very first time Vlad Petrovsky stared in mesmerized horror and wonderment at the flawless miniature of Vladimir Ilyich Lenin.

The macabre scene simultaneously repulsed and fascinated him. He shivered with cold, burying his nervousness with a series of calming, yoga-inspired breaths.

"Mother Volga," Colonel Dimsky rasped in an undertone, his eyes widening. "This is also my first viewing. It's been explained to me that this specimen is composed stringently as instructed by Dr. Sunavich. He developed this formulation according to his own specific design." The colonel spoke in a flat staccato voice, devoid of emotion. "You've been brought to see for yourselves and draw conclusions." He looked at Boris. "Your task is gathering information, and assisting in what course of action the government decides. In this effort I've been personally assigned to cooperate in every way."

"Thank you," said Boris. "Your help will be needed."

"Are we discussing a finalized prototype?" asked Alina Vera.

"We refer to it as a 'scrupulously accurate example'," corrected the military man. "It's not within my expertise to decide if its composition was finalized. You are the panel of experts. Incidentally, this pocketsize structure system is code-named 'Little Man'. It's how we're all instructed to address it."

Rimsky-Kimsky's colleague pushed himself forward and contemplated. He leaned over, intently studying the figurine, using a scratched, worn handheld magnifying glass. "Astonishing," he gasped, overcome with professional admiration. "Brilliant."

Every microscopic infinitesimal iota of the tiny man's skull, face, eyelashes, wrinkles, were impeccably recreated. Sinewy muscles from head to toe, shoulders, chest, abdomen, penis and testicles were perfectly formed. "Has this 'Little Man' prototype been subjected to the rum and chocolate serum injection?"

"Only a partial dosage, I was told. A single syringe's worth as far as we can ascertain." Everyone stared in awe. Rimsky-Kimsky and Alina Vera investigated its frame, struck by its perfection.

"Have you made an initial evaluation?" the colonel asked after a while.

Rimsky-Kimsky shook his head. "Not by a long shot. It requires prodigious inspection of its physiologic functions. This is no standard textbook representation. As an immunologist I must analyze for viral or bacterial infection, streptococcus pneumonia strains and the like, to be confident its immune system hasn't been compromised. Currently we have no efficacy data whatsoever. Has its brain been chemically modified with forms of carbon? Was amino acid leucine applied within the spinal fluid? Its testicles appear well descended. There's so much to do, so much." He sighed, limping away, hastily making notes in his workbook computer.

"I fully concur," said Alina Vera, whose field was molecular biology. "I can order tests immediately. But I'm particularly concerned with liver function. Is the hepatic artery properly carrying oxygen-rich blood from the aorta? Do we know? Is it producing adequate bile? And the flesh color, will it have the same chocolate tone?"

"First we must undertake a complete analysis. The information it yields will be significant, and nothing less will suffice. But the *finalized* prototype pigmentation, that I suspect will closely resemble our own skin tone; indistinguishable physical makeup."

"Exactly as the man in life?"

"Exactly."

Vlad was greatly impressed by the professionalism revealed under this monstrous circumstance. He also discovered that Rimsky-Kimsky wasn't at all the miscreant he'd initially judged. None of them were.

"I suggest placing this factory quadrant under strict quarantine," Boris said with an unhesitating air of unquestionable authority.

"Better be careful not to alter the ambient temperature in the slightest," Alina Vera cautioned. "It needs to remain constant twenty-four hours a day. Any minor variation could do irreparable damage, leaving us with nothing at all left to work with."

"I believe we can address your concerns," the colonel assured.

Rimsky-Kimsky interjected, "I think it best we begin with a thorough examination of vital organs. Focus on the spleen, liver, and kidneys. We need to probe for reduced immune response or infection. Until that's done I'm most hesitant to proceed with routine immunization, most hesitant. If you agree, I suggest undertaking a limbic study as well. I need to learn as much as possible about 'Little Man's' potential for conventional emotions, behavior, or atypical irregularities. We'll require an MRI cross-sectional scan of its brain to ascertain ability for typic, reasonable memory abilities. Monitor blood flow to be certain it's maintained throughout the integral system of veins and capillaries. I'm afraid there's a lot of ground to cover. Dr. Sunavich has placed us at quite a disadvantage."

"Quite a disadvantage, indeed," agreed Alina Vera. Her laboratory, one flight directly above, had yet to be viewed for damage. Although its importance to the project was relatively minor she shuddered at what might have happened to her work. "I can begin by running a partial DNA profile, if you want," she offered.

Rimsky-Kimsky demurred. "With a partial profile not all targeted loci will show in the sample, and in taking a sample there's risk of contamination. We need to do better."

"Because of potential sequencing errors?"

"Perhaps, if the RNA does not match the DNA. The only way of being certain is to re-sequence large numbers of edited genes. Either way, it should prove most fascinating."

Vlad couldn't hide his bewilderment. The scientists were discussing the DNA of a specialty compounded chocolate figurine as though it were a living organism, an engineered mutation. The immense extent of the secret project at the Alexander Nevsky Chocolate Factory was far beyond anything he had previously conceptualized. He uncomfortably caught a glimpse of the gravity in this current situation. Lenin's clone was never intended as merely a sideshow highlight of Jubilee festivities. He sensed something else, something as insidious as it was unbelievable. Here was what Boris had warned, and the consequences were unfathomable; he suddenly felt queasy, and his heart pounded against his ribcage.

"By dawn tomorrow we expect the new Moscow team arriving in Omsk," pronounced Boris, taking command of the situation. His undeniable dominion was yet another jolt to Vlad. How high up in Kremlin hierarchy did his old friend actually go?

"This new group may initially appear unconventional," Boris continued, "but they'll follow your directives to the letter. You have my word each and every concern will be addressed."

Alina Vera looked askance. "What's this 'unconventional' team you're referring to?" she asked resentfully. "We already have an outstanding working group, and I like to feel I'm part of it."

He sought to clarify her misgivings. "These people are handpicked, personally approved by the president. We can't risk the possibility of any team member having been contaminated by Sunavich. You of course are an exception, Dr. Galina. Incidentally, you'll be most interested to learn this new group includes someone very close to your heart."

"Titlebaum? You're telling me you got Titlebaum to pull you out of this mess? Please. You don't have enough money to buy him off."

Boris shrugged with indifference, saying bluntly, "if you're thinking he was tormented and dragged into it, you're mistaken. He's the most qualified man, isn't he? Weren't you telling me what a genius he is? Rabbi Titlebaum was first to be selected. In fact, when he was informed of our dire straits he actually volunteered to lead the science team. He declined all monetary offers."

"I don't believe that. Asher vowed to never come back. He's not some ass-kissing apparatchik."

"Oh dear Alina Vera, your Asher Titlebaum may be a rabbi, but fortunately he remains a true patriot. I expect he'll not only lead the team, but I'm reasonably certain he'll ask you to play a part."

"Will I have any choice?"

"Of course you'll have a choice."

"And should I decide to decline?" She looked at him defiantly, unwilling to leave the impression she could be bought or bullied.

Boris smiled indulgently. "You won't refuse an opportunity to work with Titlebaum again. Not when you come to your senses and realize the severity of what we're dealing with." His tone was foreboding. "Remind yourself that you remain first and foremost a scientist. When the diagnosis and prognosis of Dr. Sunavich's work is fully explained, you'll not turn his invitation down. I'll wager you'll salivate for the chance to rejoin the rabbi, if for no other reason than because you'll be making history."

He turned, focusing on Rimsky-Kimsky. "Do you have further requirements today, Doctor? No?" He looked at Vlad. "I surmise all this comes as a quite a shock?"

He was greeted with silence.

"All right then," he told the colonel. "We've seen enough. Time to return to Omsk. I'll request the president and prime minister convene an emergency cabinet meeting. Luckily our 'Little Man' prototype is intact. It's all we have to work with. I pity whoever has the task of informing the president that not only has Dr. Sunavich disappeared, but our Lenin creation was stolen by him."

Colonel Dimsky cleared his throat. "That job falls to me. It won't be easy to report we're tempting the laws of Providence."

Vlad received new instructions from Moscow early the next morning. He'd slept badly, unable to put everything witnessed at the Alexander Nevsky out of his mind. His latest directives were straightforward. Not to return to Moscow, his normal everyday responsibilities summarily canceled until further notice. He was considered on special governmental assignment, the Kremlin informed. His title as Director of Public Relations remained intact and waiting, but until his latest duties were fulfilled he would not be returning to his former position. A deputy was temporarily assigned to handle routine matters until he could resume his functions. For the time being he was to follow Boris Sokolov's instructions to the letter. He was now a member of a newly formed, special security team.

The hot shower was refreshing, the blended Turkish coffee tasted good and he felt if not exhilarated, at least in a proper frame of mind to carry out his unfamiliar commission. Everyone gathered this morning seemed to share a similar disposition. Only Alina Vera appeared out of sorts, vaguely troubled. She was an idiosyncratic type, given to moods and whims, yet something about her spirited personality beguiled Vlad. Her name seemed vaguely familiar although he was sure they'd never met. She was seasoned enough to be duly treated with deference as a noted scientist, but not so veteran to be viewed as matronly. Quite the contrary. From the corner of her eye she noticed him looking her way. He averted her glance, feeling intrusive and embarrassed.

"I'm sorry I'm late," said Boris, hastily entering. "Let me start with a little background. The fellow we're going to interview is an ordinary wage earner with little education. He's labored in factories all his life. His name is Ivan

35

Pushkin, the same spelling as the famous writer." Boris's demeanor remained serious although his blue eyes twinkled with hints of humor. "How's that for coincidence, being named after one of Russia's most eminent authors?" Vlad also found himself fighting a smile. "In any case," Boris continued, "Our Ivan, the factory man, has an excellent work record; he doesn't drink—too much—he's never been sacked, his health is good. He's married, has several grown children and is a grandfather. When he was initially questioned no one took him seriously. Luckily for us, the floor manager at the brassiere factory contacted the prefecture at Omsk. All bureaucratic officials had already received notice that anything pertaining to the work being done at the Alexander Nevsky Chocolate Factory should be immediately brought to the attention of the authorities. It was then I received a telephone call from the local police constabulary. I instructed them to forget this fellow and drop his file, but to personally deliver Ivan Pushkin. He's waiting outside now, eager to tell his enigmatic story. He's already related it to me. I don't label it truth or a hallucination, and I don't call him a liar. You'll have to decide for yourselves. However, I do say that Ivan Pushkin believes every word of his story. That much I'm sure of. And yes, we've had psychologists evaluate him, with no coercion whatsoever. The shrinks found him quite sane, normal, with above average intelligence for a man of his stature and abilities." With that, Boris opened a side door and said, "Ivan, do come and join us."

A shabby, bespectacled man shyly entered the room carrying a proletarian cap. He was bulky, clean-shaven and well toned for his age, his heritage Cossack serf, and his degree of discomfort obvious. His leathery features were pockmarked, with a widened red nose bulging below a patch of straight, untidy hair. His shoes were chafed and worn. His dark shirt was slightly stained at an open collar. Curly chest hair thickly rose to his neck. Ivan kept his head bowed, avoiding their eyes, feeling humble and nervous amid ranking members of Russian officialdom.

"Please take a seat," Boris told him. "You needn't be afraid. No one is going to shame or make fun of you." The worker looked up, nodding with intimidated eyes. "Would you like tea, water, a soft drink, Ivan?"

"Thank you, sir. Cold water would be nice."

Boris gestured and an aide quickly handed him a bottle of mineral water. Walking with a pronounced stoop, Ivan took his chair, wrapping his large hands around the bottle, nervous and sweaty, silently waiting.

"We don't have many questions, Ivan. If you would, please begin by telling my colleagues your story exactly as you told it to your workmates and supervisor."

Ivan nodded, clearing his throat several times. "My given name is Ivan Pushkin, I'm fifty-nine years old. I was born in Babrujsk, Belarus, not far from the border, but travelled here to Omsk many years ago to find work and marry my wife. My wife is born and raised in Omsk, the fine daughter of a butcher." He coughed again, spitting into an old handkerchief. He twisted the cap off his mineral water and took a sip.

"Go on," said Boris without a trace of impatience. "Just refresh for us the events of that morning two days ago."

"Three days ago, sir. Excuse me for correcting you, sir."

"Please, go on."

"Well, sir, I work in a large factory. In my factory we make brassieres, women's undergarments of all sizes for women of all ages. It's a good place to work. We make fine quality brassieres. Cotton, nylon, sometimes silk if there's a special order. Usually such an order is for a small quantity and only specialized workers are allowed to fill it." With pride he added, "I am one of those."

Alina Vera shifted with a mixture of discomfort and curiosity as the hapless worker went on. "It was like this you see, the morning shift had started, but weather was bad and my bus arrived late and I hadn't had time to use the toilet at home. My boss must have noticed my discomfort because he gave me permission to go. I'm no idler, sir. My job is fitting padded forms. Not many people realize how much need there is for a padded brassiere. It's important work. That morning we had a large special order for uplifting brassieres of European vogue. We copy the French style. The cups have to be carefully tended to, you see. Few realize how much discomfort a bad cup size can cause—"

"How do you determine the size?" Colonel Dimsky asked with absent curiosity. Boris shot him a displeased glance. "Just get on with what happened, please."

"Yes, sir. I was sitting in one of the stalls. All the toilets were cleaned the night before because usually they're dirty and by day's end the place smells terrible. While going about my business I heard one of the urinals flush and someone turning on the cold water in the sink. We have no hot water we only have cold water. It was running and someone was washing his hands. We're instructed to always wash our hands, you see. A worker can be sacked if he

37

doesn't wash his hands properly after using the toilet. Worker or supervisor, it doesn't matter. It's a strict company rule because hygiene is very important in my factory. I flushed several times, pulled up my pants and tied my belt. I left my stall and there before me, a few meters away, I saw him. I swear by our Holy Mother Church, he was standing naked as a baby; only he was a full-grown man. I looked at him. He looked back at me. I didn't know what to say, but I recognized him. Standing there, halfway between the urinals and the sink was the leader of the Revolution, beloved Lenin himself." Ivan Pushkin bit his lip, looking one by one at those staring at him. He hoped they didn't think him deranged. Would they have him hospitalized? Shipped off to Kazakhstan? Worse, would he find himself in so much trouble he'd be sacked, losing his hard-earned lifetime job? He had but meager savings and his wife Lenya would be very angry. She would shout and wail, maybe throw him out for good this time. He sat paralyzed with uncertainty, a single drop of sweat hanging from the tip of his nose.

Realizing his fears, Boris comforted the witness reassuringly. "Think of us as your comrades, Ivan. As mates, or a part of your dear family visiting from Moscow."

"But I have no family in Moscow, sir."

"Right. Your family from Pinsk, then."

"I'm from Minsk, sir."

"Of course, Minsk. Now be a good fellow, Ivan, and tell us the rest."

"He was a normal man, no taller than me, rather short. I was surprised, I expected him bigger. He had no hair on the top; he was mostly bald. But he had his famous small graying beard just like in photographs. My grandmother told me he was so handsome and now I see why. His skin color was pale, the color of cream and sand, and I thought he suffered from a lack of fresh air. But when he looked at me he looked straight into my eyes and saw into my heart, into my soul. It made me frightened. He said, 'Do you know who I am, *Tovarich*, comrade?' I didn't know what to answer. I said, 'Sir, you look very much like Comrade Lenin. I've seen many pictures. Are you Lenin? Where are your clothes?'"

"Mother Volga!" murmured Dimsky.

"He asked my pardon. He said he was travelling with his friend and they argued and then his friend threw him out of the car without clothes. He was so strange. He told me that in fact he was seeking new clothes now, and could I spare some. Decent garments, not fancy. He was hoping to borrow things from the men's locker room. He swore he'd never steal from honest working folk. I was so confounded I had no words. Then he asked what are my duties. So I told him. I explained that for some women it's easy to find bras that fit in styles they like. But many others aren't so lucky, spending so much time and money. We specialize in bra design and construction. Clasps and hooks, cups, elastic and straps. Our motto is: 'Your Comfort Is Our Pride'. He listened and said people like me were important, valuable assets to a State that abuses us. He said I made Mother Russia great, not the politicians or apparatchiks. Not rich exploiters who control globalization. People like me were Russia's backbone. I saw tears in his eyes. He said he bore great love for all brother workers, including me. That's the truth."

"He bore love for you?" mimicked Dimsky. Rimsky-Kimsky snickered.

"Yes, sir. He loves all workers, all common folk. His heart was open to us. He asked if I was unhappy. He used words I didn't understand like, 'trampled', and 'violated'. I said I wasn't unhappy. I said I have a good job and I like my work. My wages aren't big, but we do all right. My wife and me have food on the table every night. The government rents a little flat we live in. We have a shower with hot water most of the time. He listened and then said we should prepare because a new day was dawning. I said, 'Sir, dawn came hours ago. Have you just woken?' He smiled. He said he'd returned to help, come back because the Motherland needed him, and he couldn't rest until things were put right. Then he talked about our leaders ruining the land, bringing capitalist disaster upon our heads. I didn't understand the big words, but I knew what he meant."

Ivan Pushkin shook his head slowly, unaware of the confounded shock etched into his listener's faces. "I'm only a simple man from Babrujsk, I said to him. He clapped his hands. He had many friends in Babrujsk, he told me. And he was so happy to meet me."

"What else?"

Ivan Pushkin hesitated. He took a long draught of water. "These things are confusing, sir. I don't know what he wanted, but he did say a new revolution is coming. And my wife, my children, grandchildren, and me were what this revolution was fought for. I told him, please, sir, don't start a revolution on my account! Russia has enough troubles. But he repeated himself and spoke using more and more big words. His passion was like dragon's fire." Ivan Pushkin looked straight on. "That's the way it was. Then the funny stranger with no clothes said goodbye. He didn't use the door. He climbed out the window and was gone." The story ended and Ivan sat expressionlessly with a heavy weight, as if the world was about to fall on him.

Vlad and Dimsky exchanged flummoxed shrugs. Vlad asked, "Tell me, Ivan, did this visitor say in his own words that he was Lenin? Or did you surmise it?"

"Forgive me, but I don't know what that word means."

"It means, did you figure it out yourself?"

"Oh no! He told me his name proudly. 'I swear an oath,' he said, 'I, Vladimir Ilyich Lenin, do promise you, Ivan Pushkin, brassiere maker, to fight on your behalf, for your fellows and countrymen.' He made to leave but lost his balance climbing onto the ledge. I lent a hand. It wasn't easy for him to get back up without stumbling. I thought maybe he was a little drunk."

The enigma deepened and a heavy silence blanketed the room. Boris raised one eyebrow. "Is that everything, Ivan Pushkin?"

"Only one small other thing; before he fled the lavatory he told me to be strong and have faith. I didn't see him again. I stood waiting there, not knowing what to do."

"So what did you do?" Alina Vera asked with startled interest.

"I zippered up my pants, and went back to my workbench. My boss was angry I took so long and told me so. He asked if I was constipated. I told him, 'no sir, not at all.' My co-workers laughed, laughed and made fun of me."

"What happened after they stopped?" said Boris.

"Then I told them all the truth. They laughed harder. They said I was lying. They said I was crazy; I'd lost my mind. They told me go home and sleep it off. But I don't drink sir, only a little, and I wasn't drunk. And I don't think I've lost my mind. Have I?"

"No, Ivan," Boris said emphatically. "You most definitely have not lost your mind. We believe what you told us. You're a good man and we're pleased you agreed to explain today."

"And my job, sir, will I lose it?"

"No. We'll see to that. You won't lose your job."

Ivan was relieved.

Boris regarded his colleagues. Rimsky-Kimsky's mouth hung agape. Alina Vera scrutinized Ivan Pushkin from head to toe, assessing him, making mental notes of his disposition and demeanor. Colonel Dimsky rubbed inattentively at his brush moustache as he jotted a few scribbles into his tablet computer. His cased balalaika sat outside the entry and he regretted leaving it. A happy tune might have gone well with the brassiere maker's story. Vlad sat mute, marveling at what he'd heard, and a hundred questions he found himself unable to articulate. Rimsky-Kimsky laboriously lifted himself and limped slowly out of the room, shaking his head with puzzlement.

Ivan Pushkin cleared phlegm again. "What does all this mean, sir? Why did Lenin appear to me? Why me? Has he really come back from the grave?"

"Boris answered cautiously, "I don't know, Ivan. I don't know. Maybe he has."

The taxi advanced slowly along the congested street. Alina Vera was dropping Vlad off at his hotel before returning to her flat. A turbaned man chattering on his mobile phone infuriatingly drove the car in front. The taxi driver honked and honked to no avail.

Alina Vera lit a cigarette and looked at Vlad. "Why were you sent here, anyway? I don't understand it. You're not a scientist, you're not military, not some bloated Kremlin bureaucrat. What reason does a public relations man have for getting involved with this business?"

Vlad brushed his hands over tired eyes. He was weary, and the pestering ache in his shoulder resumed. The climate in Omsk wasn't to his liking. He'd telephoned and texted Raisa three times today, all in vain. No reply. "Didn't Boris explain why I'm here? I've been placed in charge of developing governmental press response regarding this intricate situation. Mainly fabricating a good story the press will swallow. I guess Kremlin bureaucrats are expecting me to find a way out for them. Somehow keeping the lid on this whole sordid affair before it explodes in everyone's face. Dealing with the media is my specialty. I've been in this business for twenty years. Aren't you aware of the intense pressure applied on Russia because of the Jubilee? We're playing a high stakes game. Hundreds of billions are at stake."

She frowned petulantly. "So it's all about wasted money? Please. Most of that spent money is squirreled away in numbered Swiss bank accounts. Larceny's been legalized," she scoffed. "Whom are you really working for, and why? Boris has secret dirt on you? Skeletons in a closet he threatened to use if you refuse to help?"

"No such thing. I'm my own man. I report directly to the Minister of Culture, one of the highest ranking members of the Presidential Council."

Alina Vera gnashed her teeth. "You're joking, right? The Minister of Culture is a clown. Come on, who do you *really* work for? National Police? Internal Security?"

"You're quite a suspicious one, aren't you? I could very well ask the same questions. Who are you really working for, Dr. Galina?"

"Me? I'm a scientist; I work for the State. I have a PhD in microbiology, and my credentials are exemplary. And until a week ago I was working alongside what I thought to be one of the finest minds in the world, Dr. Mikhail Sunavich. As of this moment, I don't have an inkling of whom I'm actually working for. I only know that, like you, I've been assigned to Boris Sokolov's new security strike team." She inhaled, rolled down the window, and blew a long plume of smoke outside.

"As a scientist you should know better than to smoke," Vlad said caustically. He turned and stared out the opposite window.

It was almost dark. People were hurrying home on overflowing trams and busses. How much she missed Moscow, the culture, the sophistication, nightlife, theatre, and friendships. Only sheer vanity possessed her to accept this position in the first place, she knew. Never could she dream Sunavich with his inscrutable smile would wind up making a fool of her, making a fool of them all. Life could have been so much simpler. There had been several positive relationships in her life, the last one culminating not so long ago. Perhaps she'd have been happier had she accepted an offer of marriage, desired and sought after. Instead she'd spurned the idea, insisting on forging her career, establishing a first-class reputation among scientific academics and colleagues, and in so doing left several good men dejected and saddened. She hadn't meant to be harsh or hurtful, but back then her budding profession appeared everything worthwhile in life. And now, these years later, how much her worldview had changed; in reality, what did she have to show for her modest achievements? No husband, no children, no one to come home to. Not even a dog. All traded for several minor awards, a handful of articles published in respected journals. She had succeeded in achieving a degree of success; several papers had indeed been considered important and received with universal acclaim. Her professional reputation was known among a smattering of scientific communities beyond Russia's borders. But achieving this small triumph was hollow. She felt like an empty vessel, a footnote, an asterisk. She envisioned herself becoming a moody, lonely woman, and wondered what life might have been had she welcomed those proposals.

Her reminiscences vanished as Vlad's strong voice pulled her from her thoughts. "Since you worked closely with Dr. Sunavich perhaps you could answer a question for me? I'm puzzled. Can you clarify exactly what's going on at the *Das Kapital Bingo Parlor*?"

"You know about that?" She looked at him askance. "You'd like me to explain it in scintillating detail? Listen Mr. Petrovsky, you seem a nice sort, even if a bit naïve." This Moscow veteran media man certainly didn't fit the typical role of fawning, self-assured go-getters that usually came her way, she knew. "It's all about the numbers, Mr. Public Relations Director. Numerical calculations. Somehow our Dr. Sunavich encoded his breakthrough work amid thousands upon thousands of bingo cards, taunting his colleagues to find the needle he placed in a haystack; one sequence here, one sequence there, making it almost impossible to piece the strings together. Personally, I think it's all an adroit ruse to confound us. Our scientific teams are already overloaded and exhausted, leaving him entrenched to plot and scheme whatever madness he envisions next."

"What *is* his game? Is there any rationale?"

"Rationale?" A hint of irony crossed her features. "When dealing with Mikhail Sunavich you don't expect reasonable explanations. Analytical motivation is not something he's concerned with. You're looking for some logic to decipher what he's done and why he's done it. There isn't any. He's totally irrational, totally illogical. The universe Dr. Sunavich inhabits isn't the same universe you and I live in. He's a double-faced villain and I wouldn't put anything past him. He may have been sabotaging the entire project from its inception. It wouldn't be the first attempt. I think there were others."

Vlad remained perplexed. "Do you always believe in conspiracy theories?"

"I'm a scientist. I believe what I can conclusively prove. I don't like speculation, but Mikhail Sunavich has never been considered trustworthy. If it weren't for his exceptional brilliance I'd guess he'd have disappeared some time ago, a prisoner consigned to oblivion in a forsaken Dante's Inferno. Or just taken out and shot."

"So how did a deviant character like this garner such an important commission? Why was he chosen to lead the Lenin Project?"

"A genius of his caliber can never be ignored. It's exploited. Human beings are complex social creatures. You have to separate the man from the work. Over the years his accomplishments have been staggering. No one can deny it.

He attains results others never would. At the same time, you can bet there were those paid to keep a watchful eye. Obviously they didn't do a very good job, or maybe he persuaded them to come over to his side, making it worth their while. Or possibly some high-up government official so infuriated him he reacted like a child having a tantrum. He's like that, unexpected fits and outbursts. His politics are radical enough to make him turn. Maybe he was offered a great deal of money. Don't look for integrity or loyalty."

"Then why go to all the trouble of completing the Lenin Project if only to subvert it?"

She had an imperceptible smile. "At first Sunavich probably did believe in the project, but it's impossible to get inside his mind. His insane views change according to what's convenient at the moment. You really are naïve, aren't you? I thought marketing and advertising was considered a shrewd, devious game. After all, isn't that what public relations really are, promoting something or someone? Sunavich was probably available to the highest bidder, so a better question might be who wouldn't wish to subvert the project? Any rouge state, possibly the Americans, the Chinese, or anyone harboring grudges. I'm sure you can find numerous reasons Russia's enemies nourish hope for our failure."

Traffic stopped again. Vlad faced her. "You're right. PR *is* a shrewd, rough game. It's learning to psychologically manipulate, play on people's greed and vanity. Convincing a target audience to buy products and services they neither need nor want. Profiting from making them spend hard-earned money and feeling happy about doing it. Smiling as they empty their wallets. It's devious exploitation, taking advantage of the human psyche, and I'm good at it. Very good. So I may not be quite as naïve as you believed." Clearly piqued, he leaned forward, earnestly regarding her. "I appreciate you filling me in, Dr. Galina. Thanks for the ride. I need some air. I'll walk to my hotel the rest of the way."

"As you prefer." She spoke to the driver. "Please stop the car. My guest is getting out. Good night Mr. Petrovsky, I'm sure we'll see each other tomorrow."

"Count on it, Dr. Galina. I also take my work seriously."

She quickly extended an apology before he got out. "Please excuse me. I didn't mean to sound belittling. That wasn't my intention. I do feel you're sincere, and I hope you don't get involved in over your head. This business is a menacing ordeal, more complicated than I think you understand."

He hesitated. "How do you mean, 'over my head'?"

"Just look after yourself, Mr. Public Relations Man."

3.

When Rabbi Asher Isaac Titlebaum entered a room everyone knew it. He cut a robust, imposing figure; broad shouldered, quite tall, striking in his black coat, black hat, with a long, black and silver-streaked beard. He had dangling arms, oversized hands and an oversized smile. He carried himself with notable dignity, whether in his former life as a distinguished, world-class genetic physicist, or in his current role as a Hasidic rabbi and Kabbalist; a religious scholar who'd penned three books in the past several years, missives translated into a dozen languages. Rabbi Titlebaum travelled the world freely, lecturing in venues such as Paris, New York and Tokyo, as well as across Russia. Few understood why he'd chosen to settle in such an isolated location more than two thousand kilometers from Moscow on the road to Odessa. The rabbi never provided explanations, he simply spoke his piece and let it go at that. He continued to be well received among members of Russia's nouveau riche aristocracy. Several internationally famous pop stars and renowned models had pronounced him their mentor, a mixed blessing at best. His numerous lectures were popular on the Internet and freely translated. Former colleagues at the Landau Institute for Theoretical Physics still held him in the highest regard as one of their own. That he had decided to turn to a religious vocation at such a late stage in life did not perturb them. They were not as fascinated by idle gossip as were the chattering classes of Moscow and St. Petersburg.

"Well look at you!" said Prime Minister Sergei Milonov, clasping the bigger man with both hands, kissing him on each cheek. "How long has it been, Doctor, or should I say, Rabbi? Three years, four? So you remained untamed by the perks of academia after all. I never dreamed I'd see you wearing a frock coat and a black hat; you cut quite a colorful figure. No wonder your Jews love you."

Asher Isaac Titlebaum laughed heartily. He was a man of great vigor and great appetite. His quest for knowledge was boundless, as was his ability to remain on friendly terms among the most coarse and vulgar. "Prime Minister now, eh Milonov?" He put his hands on his hips and roared. "How many people did you bribe to achieve this golden nugget?"

"Probably as many as the number of equations you've had to solve," Sergei answered deftly. "Have you eaten supper? I can have something hot brought. Meat patties with potatoes, smothered in butter, garlic, onions…" He described a hearty peasant Russian meal. Milonov snapped his fingers. "Ah, but I forget. You're strictly kosher now, you can't eat my food."

The rabbi kept his broad smile. "*Spasibo*, thank you. No food, but I can still drink your vodka. Where do you keep it?" He took out a small zippered plastic bag filled with green grapes, cashew nuts, and raisins.

"How is your back pain?"

Asher gritted his teeth. "Still aching, still worse during winter. I'm becoming an old man. But why talk of vertebrae, ligaments, muscles and nerves? I manage. Hot baths help, Esther's massages are a blessing."

"You must take good care."

"I try." They sat. The rabbi found a comfortable spot and savored a handful of grapes. "Have some, Sergei. They're sweet and seedless. They make a healthy, wonderful snack."

Milonov declined, pouring vodka into a disposable plastic cup. "Still the same Asher, I see." As a scientist and a rabbi he'd always managed to have the same snack at hand.

Although their careers diverged on very different paths the two men had known each other since youth. Few Jews were permitted to reside in the comely quarter of Moscow where Sergei was raised. The Titlebaum family was one of a small number of exceptions. Asher's father was a noted scientist in his own right who'd carved out a renowned career in medical research. The family had prospered. They always remained good card-carrying Party members during the heyday of the old Soviet Union, allegiance to the State unquestioned, even during the darkest times when many other Jews were under suspicion of divided loyalties. Gorbachev himself admired Asher's father, it was said. And as for their patriotism they were amply rewarded; a large flat on a most-desirable street, a respectable lifetime stipend, plus the opportunity for their children to enter any Russian university they chose. It was Asher, the plum of his father's eye, who excelled most. Asher said he'd known since the age of five that he would also become a scientist. His early postgraduate work invigorated the field of endocrinology, making possible major advances in research and diagnosing hormonal maladies. Later, his outstanding discoveries often challenged the accepted understanding of the body's immune system. Sadly, Moshe Titlebaum never lived to witness the accomplishments of his eldest son.

"So you've gotten yourself into a bit of trouble, Sergei, is that it?" Asher reclined, eyeing his host closely. "This time I trust it isn't due to women or drink." He said that with a wink and an engaging smile.

"You still retain too many ears in too many places, Rabbi."

They downed another shot. As Sergei raised the bottle again, Asher shook his head. "Enough for now; I don't want my mind clouded. Let's talk seriously, Sergei. Why am I sent for?" His gaze drifted towards the sleepy cat under the desk, playing with a mouse toy. Catnip kept the feline purring softly.

It took time to fully unravel details of the highly secretive Lenin Project. Under normal circumstances he'd never have breathed a word of it to Asher Titlebaum. But circumstances had drastically altered.

The rabbi listened intently. He gently placed his black hat on his lap and affixed his black yarmulke firmly on the crown of his skull. The Lenin project was not unknown to him. Discussions of it had begun long before his resignation, and he was well aware that his old rival, Mikhail Sunavich, headed the Omsk scientific team. "So what is it you expect from me?"

"Your help." His voice was flat and honest. "The president has hastily formed a new scientific team. I'm sure you'll recognize almost all the names." Sergei handed the rabbi a piece of paper. Asher squinted without his reading glasses, scanning it quickly.

"An laudable list; I'm familiar with most. By and large I'd say they're well chosen. I can vouch for any if that's what you'd like. I'm certain they will be worthy of whatever your requirements are."

Sergei heaved a long, hard sigh; there was no precedent for what he needed. "It isn't that simple. You see your old chum Dr. Sunavich has played quite a game with us. He's knocked us totally off balance. In fact, it's a debacle."

Asher took notice that the prime minister's nervous right eye twitch had worsened. "A bad situation, and you expect you'll convince me to get involved? Is that why you brought me to Moscow?"

"I—we need you here. That's the truth. You realized it from the moment you received my phone call."

"I assumed something serious was amiss. The urgency of your tone gave you away. Lucky you found me at home. Generally I spend entire days at my yeshiva. And if it were Shabbat, the day of rest, no one in my household would have answered the telephone. Esther gets annoyed every time it rings, and I don't approve of telephones very much, either. Always interrupting, bothering me, disrupting my studies." He zipped his bag of grapes and cashews.

"But Asher, think of how much money the State raises in taxes from the telephone company every month. You have no idea." He grinned.

The rabbi's eyes beamed. His long-time acquaintance and sometimes opponent remained forever the bureaucrat. Ledgers and numbers were his bottom line, after the correct skimming of a small percentage off the top. Business as usual in Moscow. Some things indeed never changed.

A jolly group of four men came shuffling from the alley laughing and singing. They strutted along narrow winding streets, dressed in sackcloth shirts, woolen jerseys, open jackets, and proletarian caps. The city was asleep and the streets were silent. One friend mumbled a joke and they giggled like disobedient schoolboys. The air was frosty but the strong alcohol pulsing through their bloodstreams provided artificial warmth. There hadn't been much opportunity to gather after work lately; tonight provided a cheerful exception. Three of the friends were married and now the fourth was betrothed. To celebrate they'd shared several bottles of good vodka, enthusiastic camaraderie, and now were ambling toward home. Few vehicles traveled the main boulevard at this late hour evincing good fortune because in such inebriated states they might not notice oncoming traffic. "And when you finally throw your mother-in-law out of your house the first time," advised the lean chum smoking a pipe, "be sure to toss the old baggage out with the old bag." The joker threw his head back and roared with mirth.

"Only fools laugh at their own jokes," observed one of his companions.

"You're one to talk, Dmitri," replied another, clumsily trying to light a cigarette. They stood in a semi-circle shielding the matches from the wind.

"Comrades, can you please spare a moment?" The voice coming from the alley caught them off guard.

"Are you speaking to us?" the friend sporting a walrus moustache warily inquired.

"Yes, Comrade. I'm addressing you."

The eldest of the group furrowed his thick brows. "Why do you refer to us as 'comrades'? No one speaks like that anymore."

The figure stepped slowly out of the dark. In the amber glow of street-light his features remained partially hidden in shadow. He appeared little more than a gaunt silhouette dressed in a suit and tie. Tenuously, the stranger said, "*Spasibo*. Please, may I have a word with you gentlemen? I could use a bit of assistance tonight."

"Oh? You're lost? Trying to find your way home, Papa? If you are, you're plumb out of luck. We're pretty damn lost ourselves!" They heartily slapped one another's backs.

"Gentlemen, could you please help me find my way out of your city?"

The pipe smoker considered the question a fair one. "Well, the central bus station's not far. And there's also the train station." He indicated the direction. "This street here is Prospekt Marksa, a main avenue. Where are you going?"

"My business takes me far away. And I must be gone tonight, you see. Can you assist? I would be so grateful."

"Then try Lyubinsky Prospekt. It takes you everywhere. Even the old quarter, out by the little house where Dostoyevsky once lived."

"Is it far from here? Maybe I could stop to refresh myself there."

"*Refresh* yourself, Papa?" The groom-to-be said with a slurry intonation. "What kind of speech is that? You a tourist, snooping around town, living it up? Here for our famous architecture, or maybe looking for girls? We have plenty of both. Omsk is a real attraction for foreigners with lots of cash—and we do our part to make sure they dispose of it fast." Everyone enjoyed the wisecrack.

"*Da*. Yes. You could call me a visitor, passing through on my journey."

A car whizzed by. "There goes a taxi, Papa," another said. "For a price they chauffeur foreigners anywhere, even find women for you."

"You have taxis?" The visitor spoke with genuine surprise. "Motor cars are for the rich. What about ordinary wooden wagons? Transportation for peasants, that's good enough for me. We all must sacrifice. Please, do you know where I can find one?"

"You want to ride in some old wagon?" parroted the woozy fellow in the fur hat. "Papa, what do you want to do that for? We have no horses to pull them anymore. You need a car. A fast car, with a woman's warmth for company, eh? Or is that ride too rich for your blood?"

"Maybe he'd rather joyride with a boy."

They guffawed, slapping high fives.

The stranger cast his gaze downward in disappointment.

"Listen, Papa, don't be offended. We're just having fun. No one rides in rickety wagons anymore. Not in our New Russian Federation. Don't you know anything? We're all Europeans now, ain't we?" The cheery mates snickered.

The oldest of the group scratched his face, saying, "Look Papa, down there you can get a bus to the train station. I don't think it runs until dawn— which I guess is pretty soon, anyway." More joviality followed. "Of course you could try and catch the late train to Moscow. It only takes about forty hours."

Another added, "How about it, old timer? Care for a spin on the Trans-Siberian? That's the train, eh? Bring you from one end of Russia to the other"

"I think the bus would suffice, gentlemen. How much does it cost to ride to the train station?"

"A pittance, Papa; a handful of kopecks. City bigwigs keep the fare low so working folk have a way to get around while they pilfer the city's coffers."

The stranger couldn't understand what they found amusing about public theft and abuse. "Thank you, for your explanations, comrades. Where do I find this public bus? A ticket is a few kopecks?" He held out his hands, palms forward. "Please don't be offended, gentlemen, but I don't seem to have any money. Not a single kopeck in these pockets. You see, I borrowed this suit, and unfortunately...If you would be kind enough to lend a stranger enough for the bus...?"

The groom-to-be eyed the curious stranger suspiciously. "A well- dressed man like you? You talk like an aristocrat, and act like a rich man, Papa. Are you lacking in cash? Did some bargirl pickpocket your fat wallet?"

"No, please, you don't understand, I found these clothes in a nearby Laundromat."

"Stole them, did you? You can try swimming across the Irtysh River. Swimming's free—if the ice melted." More laughter erupted.

"And then Papa can hitchhike a fishing boat all the way to Mother Volga," another hooted sluggishly.

The imposing figure moved from his concealment. His stance was proud and erect. The eldest of the friends squinted. "Don't I recognize you from somewhere, Papa? I swear by the Holy Church we've met before. I know your face but I can't place it..." He tightened his gaze. Things weren't too clear in his semi-stupor. He leaned against the wall to vomit. The others recoiled with feigned aversion.

"Gentlemen, a small loan of a few rubles will not be squandered, I promise. I labor for a worthy cause. To lift the lowest, put an end to their squalor and misery. To rid the land of exploiters who suck lifeblood from the breasts of the masses. I stand steadfast beside honest workingmen." He spoke as if speaking before a great crowd.

One giggled childishly. "Sure, Papa, shoot the damn bloodsuckers!"

"We're all good Cossack workingmen!" proclaimed the pipe smoker.

"Of course you are! I can see by the stoic tolerance etched into your humble faces. Steady and reliable, a bulwark against tyranny. I am a true friend to those who toil and earn their bread honorably. Our Motherland's self-respecting folk must likewise remain steadfast. Those whose backs have been bowed by the ever-oppressive capitalist yoke soon will stand tallest."

"Oppressive capitalist yoke? What kind of foolish talk is that, Papa? Are you looking to get us in trouble? Are you another damned politician? Listen, Papa, my gentle mother owns her fruit stall in the Central Market. It took years of saving to buy, and then pay black-market fees for her license. The damn inspectors pluck a big slice off the top every week. Understand? She sells good farm produce and the finest vegetables at fair prices. No decent, more honest Cossack woman ever lived. She's a saint, I tell you." A flood of tears flowed from deeply set blue eyes. A friend consoled him.

"She nourished me and my sisters even while my old man lay snoring drunk. She loved him and cared for the bugger, even after the bastard stole the last coins from her purse to spend in the tavern. What do you think of that, Papa? Where is it you said you came from?"

"Forgive me, good fellow. I would never disparage your honest, hardworking mother. Surely she is indeed a saintly, kindly woman. A woman to be praised and admired."

"Hold on a minute!" called the happy-go-lucky groom-to-be, his eyes brightening. He poked an index finger at the wayfarer. "I know who my friend says you look like. Sure, I see the resemblance now. You're exactly like that crazy old fanatic, Trotsky! That's it! That devil socialist, Leon Trotsky! That damned Bolshevik of the October Revolution, Trotsky, the Jew." They gasped.

"Is it true, Papa?"

"No! No! You're mistaken, brothers," the man from the shadows strenuously objected. "I assure you, I most certainly am not Trotsky."

The groom's dearest friend forcefully slapped him across the back of the head. "You drunken lout! Can't you hold your booze? Crazy old Trotsky's been dead a long, long time. Isn't that right, Papa?"

The stranger stiffened, visibly shaken. "You say Trotsky is dead?" he asked tremulously.

"Yep. Kaput. Food for worms. Dead as a Czar." A sneer crossed the pipe smoker's face. "Murdered. Bang, bang, assassinated. Everyone knows the story. The Party did him in, they say. *His* Party. Agents of that detested cutthroat, Stalin." He spat. "They found old Trotsky hiding out somewhere in Mexico and finished him off good."

The visitor panted at the utter depravity. "I never trusted that awful man, Stalin," he sputtered at length, his voice subdued. "A power hungry maniac. A criminal devoid of scruples or morals. I warned them about him. I warned everyone. But no one listened." Saturated with sudden melancholia, his shoulders hunched dejectedly, and he forlornly turned around, slowly heading toward the protective anonymity of the shadows.

"Wait a second, Papa! Where are you rushing? Here, take this." One of the friends reached into his pocket, pulling out a handful of crumpled bills. "It's only a few rubles. Go on take it, Papa. Get to the bus station, or train, or the airport, or wherever you want."

The quaint man reluctantly but gratefully took the offered money. "Thank you for this kindness. I'm deeply indebted. Please know that in my heart I shall never forget your good deed." He haltingly went on his way, glancing back at the quartet. "You were right, good friends, you certainly have seen me before. And have no fear. I vow that you will soon see me again."

Asher Titlebaum stood quietly staring from the window at the sterile panorama before him. Omsk looked gaunt and lonely. He knew when he accepted this assignment it would be arduous; difficult to be absent for a lengthy period from his beloved wife Esther, as well as his adored synagogue. Alina Vera Galina sat with her legs crossed in a plush chair examining her fingernails. Boris Sokolov brooded astride the plain wooden desk, unhurriedly nourishing his drink and chomping on an unlit cigar. Across the room sitting on a couch, Vlad Petrovsky futilely rubbed at his aching shoulder.

The rabbi had been hastily flown to Omsk hours before. A dossier of each elite group member was neatly tucked into his photographic memory. The prime minister believed a sense of patriotism persuaded him to take charge of the scientific team. The truth lay elsewhere.

For decades Mikhail Sunavich had been Asher's associate and colleague, if not friend. Always the wily radical had somehow managed to exceed Asher, from university days through academia; winning a higher honor, granted a larger endowment, bestowed with a tad more authority. Throughout the years they'd been competitors, never quite mates, often rivals, adversaries, sometimes cordial, sometimes not. Always mistrustful of each other, they remained brilliant minds contending for science's highest accolades and distinctions.

With this new turn of events they were now archenemies. Whatever Sunavich's political motives, Asher grasped that the aberrant little man would relish the thought of his longtime nemesis being called upon as his foremost opponent. He'd regard it a chess match, an aging boxer's final bout to determine final supremacy against a perennial opponent. Whatever tricks and maneuvers his antagonists might attempt, Mikhail Sunavich would instinctively realize that Asher Titlebaum, the Hasid, the Kabbalist, would approach this deadly game with equal enthusiasm, endure any anguish to be worthy of this unique struggle. Asher relished the challenge. Thus the gauntlet was thrown.

An undersecretary quietly entered the room. "The Kremlin is ready for your video conference," he announced, setting up a wide-angle computer camera. Within moments the somber-faced president appeared on the screen. Her sharp eyes followed each movement as the group took seats around the table.

Everything about her radiated strength. Her mouth and jaw were set with determination, any suggestion of age set off by sun-tanned flawless skin and high patrician cheekbones. Her eyes were bright and narrow. She wore small gold earrings, a scarlet scarf around her neck. She held herself proudly, as if boastful to be a descendant of the flamboyant, renowned Count Pasha Aleksandrovich Stroganoff of the Court of Catherine II.

"Good day, Madam President," said Boris. "I hope we find you well."

"Very well, thank you. And good day to all of you. Has everyone on your team arrived?"

"Colonel Dimsky begs your pardon. I requested him to return to the Alexander Nevsky and make certain everything pertaining to Codename Chocolate Lenin is progressing per instruction."

"Dimsky, yes. Have you assigned him to take charge of 'Little Man's' research?"

"I have, Madam President, he's overseeing it. With the prompt arrival of Rabbi Asher Titlebaum our team is completed and functioning well."

After an opaque glimpse of each one present she appeared satisfied. "So Boris, we've really mucked it up this time, haven't we?" She began. "Our Chairman of the Russian Council of Ministers, the prime minister, has filled me in on all the fine details. Rumors are seeping out, snatches of gossip spread far and wide. On a pain scale of 1 through 10 it sounds as though we're nearing 10, teetering on the edge of calamity. Do you concur with my conclusion, Boris Sokolov?"

"In my view this dilemma might yet be managed," replied Boris with as much reassurance as he could muster. He clasped his callused hands atop the desk. "Our prime minister also informed you of the so-called 'Lenin sightings'?"

"Lord yes. He certainly has, in strong, frenetic terms."

"It's no longer only the worker at the Omsk factory, Madam President," said Vlad. "We have a confirmed sighting by a group of street celebrants, as was reported by the prefecture in Omsk."

The president browsed a thin stack of papers spread out on her desk. "If you're referring to the antics of drunkards marking an upcoming wedding, I do have several security reports. Frankly, they convey more questions than answers. If I understand properly, all four workers of these revelers claim to have personally seen and spoken with him?"

"That's what they say. We're having them individually questioned by Internal Security, but their story seems solid. None have criminal records, arrests for public drunkenness, or disturbing the peace. They come up clean. And like Ivan Pushkin, there's no known record of mental disorder or imbalance. They do admit drinking that evening, but all four versions match and we believe they're telling the truth. There's no justifiable reason to detain them."

"I see. But nevertheless they said they had a nice chatty conversation with our confection fugitive?" Her tone of dry ridicule was transparent. She sighed, placing a slender hand to her forehead. "Accepting these facts at face value, where might our elusive, rabble-rousing outcast have sought to go?"

"Anyone's guess. We don't yet know if he's travelling alone, and at this point we have no indication if anyone else, apart from Dr. Sunavich, might be involved. We staked out the Omsk train station and searched with sniffer dogs, and also had the nightly Trans-Siberian train departing for Moscow held up.

We've begun examining passports and internal ID cards of all departing passengers, but unfortunately a number of intra-city buses had already departed before checking. We considered shutting Omsk's airport but decided arousing undue suspicion was unwise and could alert the media, heaven forbid. Currently, we've posted Internal Security units at all public transportation venues. They've been given descriptions and are on the lookout. Nevertheless, I assure you he'll soon be tracked, arrested, tried and convicted."

"Meanwhile, that still leaves a great deal of ground to cover," said the president. She leaned back in her chair, lightly rocking. "Can any of you tell me, if you were in his shoes, where might he seek refuge? Does history provide us with clues?"

Vlad lifted a cautious hand. "Madam President, I've been carefully studying Lenin's past. Based on historical events, I'd assume before dare risking showing himself in St. Petersburg or Moscow he'll likely retreat to the countryside. Places where those professing sympathy with the Bolsheviks could provide asylum now. From such a sanctuary his likely recourse could be to slowly gather steam the same way as during the October Revolution. If it worked successfully before, it may prove successful again."

"An interesting speculation, Vladimir...Petrovsky, is it? Oh yes." She briefly glanced downward at a photograph. "You're our appointed Director of Public Relations for the Jubilee, aren't you?"

"Yes, Madam President. You probably don't recall, but I've had the honor of personally meeting you on several formal occasions. The prime minister personally appointed me, and—"

"You're wrong, Petrovsky," she cut him off. "I recall you well, in fact. You don't have to enumerate credentials. If Boris Sokolov chose you for this assignment that itself speaks volumes. Don't keep us in the dark. What are your thoughts on where this 'creation' may find his safe haven?"

"Only conjecture, Madam President. Historically, during the initial onset of the October Revolution Lenin retained a tremendous following in regions like Odessa. Military draftees adored him, particularly naval recruits. He frequently spoke of the Battleship Potemkin, its famed 1905 mutiny at Odessa's naval base being the first true step on the revolutionary road. He stoked it like bellows to a fire. People there proudly remember."

"Most commendable, Vladimir Petrovsky. Yes, the Czarist Imperial naval base on the Black Sea. The environs of the city could provide an ideal location for camouflage. Unfortunately, Odessa is no longer under our jurisdiction. It's part of Ukraine, and our relationship with our neighbor these days is strained at best. I doubt very much Ukraine authorities will give us carte blanche to send our people swarming over one of their largest cities. But your reasoning is plausible, and I commend you for your opinion." She paused, contented. "Meanwhile, Boris Sokolov, your report regarding difficulties at the *Das Kapital Bingo Parlor*?"

"Alas nothing, Madam President. The bingo parlor has been placed under stringent armed guard. All stamped bingo cards have been duly confiscated and boxed for scientific inspection. We've procured computers, telephones, and assorted paraphernalia, and have large numbers of crates ready to be hauled. We've undertaken the severe step of holding a number of uniformed employees in detention under the National Emergency Terrorist Act. Draconian measures, surely unconstitutional, as these people are members of the Salvation Army. But under these extenuating circumstances we had no choice but to confiscate their national ID registry cards. Meanwhile, our engineers are developing new software to break encrypted codes while normal means of communication with the bingo parlor have been shut indefinitely. Nothing comes in and nothing goes out without express permission. Personally I doubt Sunavich operated in collusion with Salvation Army 'spies'. I think the paranoid bastard acted alone, but better safe than sorry."

"Recruiting from the Salvation Army sounds half-witted to me, but it's your call and your head. However, I can't hold the State Duma at bay forever." President Natasha Stroganoff's quick eyes darted, and she spoke in measured tones. "But listen to me, all of you. I don't care what Prime Minister Sergei Milonov may have told you. Sergei is prisoner to his own ambitions, but this is neither the time nor place for that discussion. I want you to know that after I awoke this morning I received word that the Americans are sending a special envoy directly from Washington. It's imperative that under no circumstance any word of our situation gets out. I have reason to believe the Americans may already have some inkling of what's transpired at the chocolate factory. I can't say how, but I have strong misgivings. We could have a leak."

"Madame President?"

"I mean a mole, Boris; a foreign agent surreptitiously in collusion with Dr. Sunavich."

Alina Vera shifted uncomfortably. "Someone who worked closely with him?"

The rabbi placed his palms on the desk and leaned toward the computer's camera. "I will personally interrogate every member of the Omsk scientific team myself, Madam President. Despite any differences we might have had in the past, rest assured you can count on me and my entirely new, screened scientific team."

"Thank you, Dr. Titlebaum. Excuse me, I should have referred to you as Rabbi."

Asher bowed his head respectfully. "Thank you, Madam President."

"Who is this American we're expecting?" asked Boris "And what does this person have to do with all of this?"

"I'm discussing him because I don't want this man snooping around anywhere near the Kremlin, nor in Moscow for that matter. Not at such a delicate moment. That's why I've decided to place him in your hands. The American Ambassador has personally requested that we welcome and assist this man with his assignments, and I acquiesced for the time being. Information they've presumably discovered is clearly making them uncomfortable, so they want firm assurances from me."

"I understand, but I don't see what we're supposed to do with him."

Her attitude remained distant and indifferent. "Personally, I don't care what you do with him. I'm told he works for the State Department, but likely he doubles covertly for the CIA. We have no background information, no records whatsoever. The Americans obviously plan to poke their unwelcome noses into our business, gathering data, hoping to learn a little here, pick up some information there. You know the routine. I expect you'll find this fellow an apt illustration of a smooth and shrewd operator, so don't be misled. I suggest you select a member or two from your team to occupy, profile him, and throw him off track; provide liquor, women—or even men if that's his preference. Sweep his rooms, and of course you'll photograph everything uncouth or unfitting, should we need to blackmail him later. My only requirement is that you keep him totally out of my hair, and leave my reputation unsullied. And keep his contact with the rabbi to a minimum while he's managing our project. Be quite sure this American is unable to gather anything of value, at any cost. I'm counting on you. Am I clearly understood?"

"Your instructions are clear, Madam President. Will that be all?"

"*Da.* That's all. Oh, I almost forgot. This American, his name is Floyd Dingus. An odd name, isn't it? I'll be having him shuttled to Omsk no later than tomorrow. That should appease the American Ambassador for the moment while we try to get a handle on all this. I'll remain in touch. Please accept my sincerest gratitude to all of you for your dedication. Your country is proud." The screen went dark.

Vlad turned to Boris. "So what do we do?"

Boris had no ready answer; the president's unexpected request caught him as much by surprise as any of them. This tawdry saga was growing more outrageous, more absurd by the day, and this unfortunate circus sideshow wasn't helping. "We'll need to find something meaningful to keep him occupied. Or, Vova, shall I say *you'll* have to find something worthwhile, seeing he's part of the public relations aspect." He cast a sidelong glance. "A woman's touch always works well, don't you think, Alina Vera? I'd like you to work alongside Vlad."

4.

It was a short taxi ride to Tsentralny Airport, some five kilometers southwest of the city. Alina Vera picked Vlad up in front of his hotel. He was clearly over-wrought, she saw. Vlad had been eager to speak with his wife, Raisa, she knew, and it wasn't taxing for Alina Vera to perceive how disconsolate he seemed. It was natural for Raisa to be distressed and angry at her own situation, Alina Vera understood. What woman could be expected to be content living with a part-time husband, and then suddenly have to accept him as a nonexistent partner?

She well realized from her own experiences how the system sought to control your life. The State was eager to grab the best and the brightest young people straight from university, dangle prized careers, and endlessly exploit them until little remained but an emptied husk. Vladimir Petrovsky epitomized the precedent for the role. Clever, intellectual, and ambitious, he was eager to perform whatever responsibility was set before him. She understood that like so many others sooner or later he'd be transformed into a burned-out shell of his former self. She'd witnessed it again and again, and not simply within the con-fines of the scientific community. It was grievous, even heartbreaking to watch, but Alina Vera was used to seeing admirable people meanly manipulated. She vowed it would never happen to her.

"I know this isn't any of my business," she said as they drove, "but is ev-erything going well…at home?"

He regarded her with vacant, despondent eyes, unsure what to say. His face was sunken, his eyes red. He was sure she could tell he'd been weeping.

"You can talk to me. Strictly between us, I promise." Her calm voice was assuring.

"Can I be honest with you?" he asked. "I know you don't trust me; I sup-pose it's only natural. But there's no one for me to turn to here. I feel so—lost. These past days I've been tense, so wrapped up with work my closest friends don't bother telephoning anymore. And who'd blame them? At this stage I pre-sume they've given up."

Realizing his anguish was genuine she found herself feeling a twinge of compassion. Vladimir Petrovsky was near to her in age, but had chosen a very different career path and maintained a very different lifestyle. Nevertheless, it wasn't hard to identify with him. She recognized that in many ways their lives could be considered virtually interchangeable. "You're wrong about me," she said at length. "I have no reason not to trust you. Maybe it seems that way because I'm peevish about my own sorry world. I've seen too much, Vlad, too often found myself at the wrong end." She sighed. "But what's happened with you? I'd like it very much if you did tell me."

Clasping his hands, he nervously mirrored her attentive gaze. "My wife, Raisa, informed me she's decided to leave. I didn't realize it, but she'd been contemplating divorce for some time. And I didn't see it coming. I've been so absorbed trying to fix all the broken pieces for the Jubilee. My job's kept me so distracted, swallowed up; I don't know what to think anymore. Raisa said she feels we've never had a real marriage, a normal marriage. Now it's gone beyond bad, constant phone calls in the middle of the night, an endless barrage of meetings, and functions I'm expected to attend. She's sick of lonely meals without me, drained with nothing to say when I finally do come home. An empty life with a boatload of empty promises I've never kept. She says I might as well be a prisoner of the State."

He was dejected and contrite, Alina Vera saw. "These things happen far too often among people like us," she empathized. "We're so devoted to our work we can't see what's happening right in front of our faces. Do you have children?"

"Two young daughters, Katya and Aleksandra. Raisa says she's taking them with her to St. Petersburg today to spend time with her family. Her parents miss her and the children, so she's calling it an extended holiday to mull things over. She's a freelance photographer and she mentioned something about an assignment offered there. A German magazine is doing a special section on St. Petersburg. She wants to earn some extra money for my younger girl's ballet school tuition, and for piano lessons for our older daughter. Personally, I think Raisa's already got her mind made up. She isn't filing for divorce—at least yet, but she says she's reached her breaking point, and there's no turning back. She advised me that I needed to hire a lawyer." He bit at his lower lip, holding back fresh tears. "Our problems aren't new or unusual, I just never expected this...I honestly don't know what to do or which way to turn."

She put a hand lightly on his slumped shoulder. He was exhausted mentally and emotionally. "I'm so sorry for your grief, but listen to me, Vlad. This is important. I can tell how crushed you are, but you need to try and remain focused. Right now you can't afford to reveal any sort of weakness, no matter how painful, or whatever the cost. The wolves are at the door, ready to pounce." She lowered her eyes, fumbling to find the right words. "I'm aware of incidents you're not. All of us involved in this sordid mess—we're in it above our heads, more than you can know. As painful as it is, you have to hold yourself together, and for a short while set your family situation aside. That's vital. Don't give anyone reason to doubt you—and don't be so trustful. Never betray your flaws. Never give an opportunity to take advantage of you, because they surely will."

"Why are you telling me this?"

Alina Vera toyed with the small gold necklace around her slender neck, thinking carefully. "I suppose because sometimes people need to trust each other." He nodded, appearing to her like a forlorn child. "And now may I confide something to you?" she asked. "I've had some trouble of my own lately and I don't know what to make of it. I haven't told anyone because *I* don't know who can be trusted."

"I'm a good listener, Alina Vera. I promise, anything you confide is confidential. It goes no further than here."

"All right, listen to this. For a while now I've felt like I'm in some sort of danger. I think I've been followed in recent days, although I can't prove it. I also think my telephones are tapped. Sometimes I'm even afraid to use my computer because maybe I'm being shadowed by eavesdropping software, scrutinized by Internal Security, or worse."

He was perplexed. "I don't understand. Why would Internal Security have reason for that? You have top government clearance, the same classification as me."

"Don't forget I'm a scientist. For quite some time I've worked closely with Mikhail Sunavich. It's true I've never been a part of his inner circle, but some may be convinced I'm withholding knowledge regarding his secret work."

"Who'd think that?"

She pursed her lips, eyes cast away, shaking her head. "I'm not sure. There are possibilities; secret police probing my own work, maybe an incriminating dossier from my past has surfaced, or an unrevealed collaborator of Sunavich is trying to incriminate me. To you and the rest of the world Dr. Sunavich appears an old radical, an aging curmudgeon, a coarse loudmouth, but nevertheless harmless. I assure you he's anything but. Those who took him lightly in the past paid a heavy price. Believe me, he's vicious. I've seen him turn savagely on the closest collaborators who invoked his wrath. That's partly the reason Asher Titlebaum is so important for us. He's a bulwark beyond anyone's reach." She stopped. "I can't offer more details now. Please understand."

"What's in it for Sunavich to put you in danger? Everyone says he's a loner, paranoid, mistrustful of everyone and everything. Why go out of his way to harm you?"

"Just speculation, I don't know anything for certain. Possibly it isn't him. For all I know some Internal Security officer may be having everyone followed. Perhaps the prime minister is having it done. He's devious also, and capable of anything. You've worked with Boris Sokolov in the past, I was told. You're aware that over the years Boris engaged in many roles, sometimes playing both ends against the middle with our abusive elite. Even though he was a close friend of my father I can't be positive someone hasn't gotten to him. We're all vulnerable. In this country anyone might be for sale. And I lack the comforts a Swiss bank account affords." She laughed with self-depreciation. "So you see, Mr. Petrovsky, there's good reason for why I no longer trust. My sister in Moscow is an aide working for a high-ranking deputy in the Foreign Ministry. Right now I'm not sure I'd even confide in her."

"You also said you believe you're in danger."

She hesitated. Could she really disclose anything to this team member who remained a virtual stranger? Was this talented public relations director really what he appeared to be, above suspicion as the impression he conveyed? She weighed her options and decided to take the risk. "I'll tell you this: Last week a car tried to run me over in the street. I'd been working late. It was already almost dark and I was exhausted. I carried my laptop with me. There wasn't much traffic when I stepped from the bus. As I walked toward the pavement an oncoming headlight nearly blinded me. The car was moving fast, too fast. I threw myself forward and rolled onto the sidewalk in time."

"How can you be sure it wasn't some drunk driver?"

"It wasn't. Not twenty meters away I saw the car come to a screeching halt. I could see his side view mirror and the driver was looking back at me, watching. I was shaken and scared. I tried to get at least part of the license plate number but the car drove away, no longer speeding."

"Are you suggesting he wanted to kill you?"

She shook her head. "I'm not suggesting anything. I don't even know what I'm really trying to say, except I'm frightened. This assignment is more dangerous than you realize. I doubt Boris warned you."

He listened in silence while she lit a cigarette and calmed herself. Vlad glanced at his watch; their taxi was approaching the air terminal, and the Aeroflot plane from Moscow would land soon.

"I mean you no harm, Alina Vera," he told her as the taxi pulled up at the arrival gate. "I'd like you to believe that."

"I think I do believe you—but you're the one not aware. You could also find yourself in danger."

"Why? I have no connection with Dr. Sunavich. The infrastructure of ports, roads, and telecommunication is my concern. We're way behind, more than I care to say. The only times I even visited the Alexander Nevsky was for meetings with marketing experts. I'm not a scientist."

"You must at least know this much: The entire project carries significant, and far-reaching implications. It's inherent in the nature of what we're doing here. Our efforts are considerably more valuable to the State than you realize. This 'Code Name Chocolate Lenin' isn't meant merely to impress the world with smart scientific achievements, as you've probably been led to believe."

He sat questioningly, looking at her obliquely. "You must consider me a very inane man. I've been aware for a long time this classified project carries deceptive overtones. That national security is involved, although I admit I don't know how."

"Sometimes it's better not to know. Russia is a proud country, ruled by vindictive, ambitious men with enemies at every turn. Power-hungry personalities determined to play a major role on the world's stage. We can't expose its corruption and incompetence, but nations would stop at nothing, pay any price, to decipher the success accomplished at the Alexander Nevsky Chocolate Factory."

He listened with unease, fully aware that Dr. Alina Vera Galina was perceived as a cold, suspicious, discreet woman. Now he was beginning to understand there was validity behind her continual aloof and reticent façade, not irrational paranoia. "Whoever these enemies are," he said, "I'm not one of them. I'd really like to have a friend here, if you'll let me be one."

She smiled slightly. "I think I'd like that, Vlad. Thank you. But I wouldn't want to be the cause of placing you at undue peril. You don't deserve that. You're an outsider."

"You keep talking about some unknown menace lurking nearby. But I still don't know who or what this danger is." The taxi came to a sharp stop. They'd arrived at the Aeroflot terminal. Traffic was heavier than normal with an influx of European businessmen planning trade shows for the Jubilee.

"I'm glad we had this talk," Alina Vera said as Vlad paid the driver. "We'll talk more. We'd better hurry to meet our guest."

They rushed to the arrival gate, dodging a crowd incoming passengers. "Has the flight from Moscow arrived?" Alina Vera asked the uniformed Aeroflot gate agent.

"Yes, it's landed. Passengers are disembarking, but you'll have to wait for them here. I can't allow you to pass beyond this point."

Vlad presented his government identification card, Alina Vera held up her security card. The gate agent's eyes visibly widened. "I'm sorry," he stuttered. "We weren't instructed in advance that government officials were receiving this flight. Follow me this way, please." They were hurriedly led to a small VIP lounge.

"So how do you intend dealing with this American?" Alina Vera asked, seating herself comfortably in an oversized leather chair.

"I don't have a clue." Vlad paced awkwardly. He smoothed his hair, cleaned his glasses, and stared toward the pale lights of the runway. "I'll do exactly as Boris suggested; offer him drinks, women, and whatever else you can think of."

"Then we'd better think quickly," she advised. She glanced diagonally and pointed.

A stout, suntanned man about Vlad's age and rolling a small black suitcase was walking their way. His sandy hair was closely cropped, and pushed back. On his head he wore a Chicago Cubs baseball cap. He had a wide nose, fair skin, and numerous freckles over beefy cheeks. His eyes were round and adolescent. To Vlad's surprise, rather than wearing a hand-tailored custom American suit, he wore a colorful Hawaiian shirt splashed with palm trees, pineapples, and sensual hula girls. His shirt wasn't tucked into his pants, and the pants, too tight around his waist, were made of polyester. He wore white athletic socks, and had large feet covered by scuffed sandals. The sole of the right shoe flapped slightly. He cut an unorthodox figure, and was a sartorial nightmare.

Perfect white teeth smiled broadly, "Excuse me, but are you *Gospodin* Petrovsky?" The American used the common Russian equivalent of 'Mister'.

Vlad was taken aback. "I am Petrovsky, yes. May I also introduce my distinguished colleague, Dr. Alina Vera Galina. Welcome to Omsk."

"Thank you." He held out a strong hand, kept a direct gaze. "A pleasure *Gospodin* Petrovsky, Dr. Galina. I believe I'm the one you're expecting. My name is Floyd Dingus."

After settling their guest at his hotel the attractive scientist took Vlad and Floyd Dingus to her favorite restaurant; the renowned, cosmopolitan Old Omsk located near the center of the city. The cozy lounge with whitewashed walls and dark beams suggesting a 19th- century cottage had a busy dinner hour for a weekday night. Most tables were already occupied. The American inquired what was tasty and she recommended *lobio*, a thick red bean soup; piles of meat-filled dumplings, known as *khinkali* and spicy meatballs called *abkhazura*, along with a bottle of imported select Romanian wine. The smart, uniformed young waiter filled their glasses and they drank a toast.

"This sure is a nice place you picked out, Dr. Galina. Old European mixed with Asian charm. Very eclectic. Real linen napkins, linen tablecloths, crystal goblets and fancy cutlery. The whole works." He looked admiringly at the prodigious, refined décor of colorful wall tapestries; Asian inspired art, and tailored gold damask draperies, displayed for the restaurant's clientele.

Alina Vera and Vlad regarded each other with heightened mystification.

The wine arrived and was poured. The American sniffed at it and took a sip. "Good choice. It has a nice subtle earthiness. Usually I make do with New Jersey wine. In fact, mostly I eat my meals at a booth in my favorite diner. Cheeseburgers, fries, a cup of java. Coffee. Do you have diners in Russia?"

"No, I don't believe we do."

"Too bad. It's a way of life back home. Once I was eating at the counter between these two guys. One was an off-duty cop, and the other just some local character. The cop keeps looking over and finally said, 'Didn't I arrest you last year?' The guy on the other side of me says, 'Yeah, you did. Please pass the sugar'." He laughed.

Again the media expert and the scientist seemed puzzled. "Have you ever been to Omsk before, Mr. Dingus?" Vlad asked, switching the subject.

"Please, no honorifics, just call me Floyd," he said convivially. He raised his glass high in salutation. "This is my first trip here, and I'm very pleased and excited. I hope we'll quickly become friends."

"Let's hope we do," chimed Alina Vera. Glasses clinked. "Although," she deftly added, "we're not sure why an American representing the American State Department is being delegated to join us at the edge of Siberia."

Floyd Dingus smiled his toothy smile. "The State Department? Heck, no. I don't work for them. Who told you that, Sport?"

Vlad glanced quizzically at the scientist. "Oh, perhaps we've been misinformed," Alina Vera quickly said. "Which American agency do you represent?"

"Actually, I've been assigned here by the Department of Agriculture," Floyd responded proudly. "Generally my job takes me all over the States, mostly inspecting cattle, checking for diseases, making sure birds, poultry and other livestock are given a clean bill of health. I look for things like wheat pasture bloat, or obesity deaths due to high gluten content fed by greedy cattlemen. Sometimes it really gets serious. You all remember Mad Cow Disease, don't you? That was a real bummer. Bad stuff. Congress isn't happy when Americans start getting sick and dying, whether from botulism, salmonella, or anything else."

"You're a contamination, toxic bacterial and viral expert?" Alina Vera noted. "How curious."

"Mostly, yes. My original background is veterinary. I graduated with honors. I guess I'm an animal lover, too. In fact, you can call me a sucker for all critters."

"We Russians love animals, too."

"But now let me compliment you; your command of English is excellent, both of you. I'm very impressed. So few Americans bother learning other languages. It's a darn shame. I sure wish I could speak some Russian."

"Remain with us for a while and you will," Vlad responded pleasantly. "Studying English is mandatory in our schools. Personally I was lucky enough to have attended a British university for several years. But what was it you began telling regarding your own line of work?"

A busboy gracefully refilled their water glasses and deftly stepped back. "Oh, my work's pretty dull, but it does beat refilling hand-soap dispensers for a living." He cut a slice of thick black bread, smeared it with jam, and took a large bite. "This is scrumptious," he said, talking and chewing. "Absolutely delicious.

66

Who'd have known? Food here is as good as anything you'll find in Washington, D.C."

"Yes, this is undoubtedly my favorite restaurant in Omsk," Alina Vera told him. "This city has grown quickly in recent years. It has the title as being Eastern Siberia's capital."

"Over a million people," added Vlad. "They have several very famous fine museums and galleries. Omsk is trying to become sophisticated, no longer just an Eastern Siberian hub. Hopefully you'll have opportunities for touring while with us. Outside of the city there are numerous operating farms dating back centuries. Perhaps you'd like to familiarize yourself with local livestock, make comparisons with breeds you're familiar with. If you like what you see, we might find a way to work out a new trade agreement, something mutually beneficial for both our countries. What do you think, Floyd?"

"We American's are always looking for a deal. Isn't that what a market economy's all about? I'll take you up on those visits, even though my feet are sore and aching from this running around airports. Thanks for your generous offer."

"Wonderful. I'll arrange excursions for you. How long do you expect to be remaining here?"

The American shrugged, taking another big bite. A small blob of jam adhered to the side of his lip. Vlad was tempted to take his napkin and clean his face. "I'm not quite sure how long I'm staying, Vlad. May I call you Vlad? Good. You see, my instructions were hasty and not well defined; I hardly had time to pack, things got so rushed. When I got the call I was watching a curling match on TV. Canada vs. Russia." He glanced admiringly around at the restaurant. It was a good choice. "I see these customers are pretty dressed up. I hope you don't mind this shirt I'm wearing. I'd been on vacation in Hawaii until last week, and bought myself a half dozen of these beauties, figuring I'd give a few as gifts. I have a young nephew back home in Iowa; he'd enjoy one, I bet. Say, I hope I'm not being presumptuous, but maybe you'd like to have one, Vlad. Would you accept it from me as a small gift for a new friend?"

"I'd love to have my own Hawaiian shirt, but no, I couldn't accept. We're strictly forbidden from accepting presents. It could be construed as a bribe by my government. But thank you for offering."

Floyd laughed affably. "Well, I sure wouldn't want to get you in trouble over a shirt."

The waiter brought the main course, nimbly placing each porcelain plate on the table. The trio sat quietly and ate. Alina Vera had chosen well from the menu. The food was excellent, the ambiance an interesting mixture of the old Russia and the new. Outside, a soft rain was falling. Vlad watched a tram as it sluggishly rumbled along the street.

"So how else can we be of help, Floyd?" Vlad said after a while.

Floyd downed the last of his wine. "Well, the Secretary of Agriculture personally instructed me to take several unguided tours of your world famous chocolate factory."

"Oh? You're referring to the Alexander Nevsky?"

Floyd nodded, dipping another slice of black bread over gravy and sopping it up. "Yeah, that's the one. Nevsky, a grand Russian hero, I've heard."

"That's true. Alexander Nevsky, Prince of Novgorod, a revered figure in our history. He led the Russian people in battle, defeating the Swedes in 1240, and routing the Teutonic Knights in 1242, a great victory during the Middle Ages. He became supreme ruler and defender of Russia. A Russian proverb says, 'the sovereign is the father, the earth is the mother'. Thus, he was the father of our nation, as the land is our mother. So beloved that the Russian Orthodox Church proclaimed him a saint, canonized in 1547."

"Sainthood. That says a mouthful. He must have been quite a guy. And now he's famous for chocolate, too. I never knew Russia was renown for exceptional chocolate. We should be importing it. I'll make a note and pass it on."

"Thank you for the compliment," said Alina Vera. "It's been my privilege to be employed at the Alexander Nevsky for several years."

"Really? I didn't realize chocolate making had become an arm of science. You're a scientist Alina Vera, if I may call you by your given name?"

"Of course you may." She smiled almost flirtatiously. "You'd be amazed how much scientific knowledge is required these days for making chocolate. Competition is fierce in our global economy. But my own role isn't really important only a small matter of toying with elemental molecules for increasing flavors. Our primary aim is to make your mouth water."

"Sounds fascinating. I'd love to hear more."

"Well, I can't divulge any chocolate secrets," she said with a smile and a wink. "However, I don't suppose anyone would mind me discussing my personal specialties. Tell me, Floyd, have you ever eaten a creamy, dark chocolate with wild blueberries in the center?"

68

"Can't say I have. Sure sounds good, though."

"Another of my concoctions is taking tangy orange peels and drenching them extravagantly into a smooth, silky milk chocolate. My own favorite uses Arabica beans; full-bodied beans usually found in gourmet coffee. Dark roasted in small batches by a specialty roaster. Espresso beans, and not just any kind. Then each bean is dripped with chocolate from secret recipes. Sometimes we add crisp honeycomb molasses centers, together with a heavy coating of milk chocolate. How does that sound?"

"It sounds like you sure know your stuff."

They all laughed. "At least your work's a lot more fun than mine, Alina Vera. Better being around chocolate all day than smelly cattle." He chuckled as he wiped his mouth with his napkin. "You know, I don't mean to sound ignorant, but I haven't the faintest idea how chocolate is made."

Vlad swallowed hard. Why was this veterinarian, Floyd Dingus, so interested in the Alexander Nevsky? Could it be the American knew more than he let on? Had Floyd Dingus learned of classified secrets surrounding 'Code Name Chocolate Lenin'?

Vlad had little idea himself how chocolate was manufactured. He hoped Alina Vera had enough background to explain and make it sound plausible. Any mistakes might cause this suspicious American to realize she wasn't what she claimed to be.

"I'm glad you asked me," she said. "I do so adore describing compounds. But first, you must realize chocolate is the product of a long and sophisticated refining process. In Russian we pronounce it, *shokolad*. Can you say it, Floyd?"

He mimicked, "Shok-o-lad."

"Very good. *Shokolad*. Now, have you ever heard of a Theobroma cacao tree?"

"Nope." Floyd shook his head emphatically.

"Well, Theobroma cacao literally means 'food of the gods'. Ancient Mayan and Aztec cultures held the cacao bean in holy reverence; they believed cacao came to earth from heaven, and regarded it as divine. In tropical countries Theobroma trees produce bean pods all year long. Our biggest shippers are African, although we also buy from South America, as you do in the United States. There are three types of cacao trees, but I needn't bore you with details. Suffice to say, we harvest cacao pods year round, first splitting them, making certain fruity pulp surrounds the beans. This pulp we use for drinks and desserts. Then, beans and leftover pulp are scraped from the pods and left to ferment. This is crucial, Floyd, because the fermentation process mellows flavor and enhances taste. Without proper care beans would become astringent and bitter, and not good to market. Once we're finished with fermentation, the beans are spread out in direct sunlight and left to dry. Only after this process are they packaged and shipped to us and other chocolate makers all over the world.

"When they arrive at our facility that's when the fun begins. We roast them. Temperature and timing of the roasting depends on the type of bean. If we roast it right, out comes the most intense flavors and colors in the chocolate. Next, the beans are transferred to a winnower, a special device for removing the shells and leaving only what we call nibs. These nibs are the very essence of a cacao bean; filled with cacao solids and cacao butter. Are you following me, Floyd?"

He nodded, dazzled as she explained.

"These nibs," she continued, "are then ground into a thick, rich, paste. This we call chocolate liquor, but liquor is a misleading term because there isn't any alcohol in it, but it *is* the foundation for chocolate products. At this stage the nibs begin to resemble and smell like conventional chocolate you'd recognize. After that, the liquor is pressed to remove cacao butter. We use that for cacao powder, but if the chocolate is going to be of high quality then we add the cacao butter to the chocolate liquor. Vanilla, milk and sugar are added next. Then our chocolate travels through a series of rollers, which smooth out the texture on their way to our final step, the conching machine. This determines its ultimate texture and flavor. It's called a conching machine because the original invention resembled seashell conches. These machines massage and knead the chocolate mixture, ranging from just a few hours up to several days. Temperature, speed, and length of the process determine the outcome. When conching is done, our confection is tempered in machines to cool the chocolate to precise temperatures. And finally we pour the chocolate into molds of whatever clever designs we've formulated. What do you think happens next?"

"Haven't a clue."

"We wrap it and ship it, delivering it to fellow chocolate lovers all over the globe."

"Wow." Floyd sat spellbound.

Vlad heaved a long sigh of relief; his gaze briefly met Alina Vera's. Her eyes mischievously twinkled and danced. "Do you think you've learned enough about our process?"

"I'm amazed, and gratified. Thanks for the lesson. You sure can strut your stuff. With terrific people like you in charge I bet the Swiss and French are gonna be in for one hell of a shock from their newest competitors."

"I'm grateful for your confidence, Floyd," she told him. "But as I was discussing earlier, I play only a small role in the whole process. My only ambition in life is making chocolate taste so good that people like you will keep on buying. Turning you into chocolate addicts." She smiled with her eyes.

Floyd blushed. He couldn't be sure if she was flirting. He changed the subject. "So are the two of you locals to these parts of Russia?"

"Not at all," said Vlad. "I'm a born and raised Muscovite. Alina Vera originally came from St. Petersburg and resides also in Moscow, although I know her work takes her numerous places in various cities." She nodded in agreement.

"And you Vlad, I've been told you're the Director of Public Relations for the New Russian Federation's 25th Anniversary Jubilee, is that right? They're calling this the biggest bash the world's ever known, far larger than any international exposition or World's Fair."

Vlad agreed, sipping his wine. "Our plans are enormous. Wait until you see it. It'll be the most extensive, preeminent celebration imaginable. As for being named Director, that's the title they conferred, but as you say, I'm nothing more than just another bureaucrat among an army of bureaucrats."

"I hear you loud and clear." Floyd stifled a yawn. "Pardon me, but it's sure been a long, tough day. But Vlad, how did you ever snatch a sweet job like that? You must have lots of big wheel friends up in high places."

"Not really. My university major was in Marketing and Western Advertising. I studied in Moscow then spent several years in London. After returning home I went to work for Russian State Television. They offered a stint as Program Director for 'Russia Today,' one of our most highly rated shows. It wasn't as exciting as it sounds; we were always hunting for new sponsors, especially in the European market, and pushing our own products. We worked hard and managed exporting lots of Russian wheat overseas." He smiled with satisfaction. "Now Russia is considered a premier exporter of wheat. These days we find ourselves locked in direct competition with the United States. Friendly competition, that is."

Floyd's eyes flickered with merriment. "And tough competition you guys are, costing us plenty in lost exports! Now, if only we could find some way to have you to lower the price you extort for oil…"

Vlad laughed in response, holding up a hand. "Please don't get me started on that topic. I have absolutely nothing to do with oil or the price of oil. It's a very touchy matter in this country as well as your own, as I know you realize."

"I sure do." He poured the final contents of the wine bottle into each of their glasses. "This was such a wonderful experience tonight. I'm so grateful. Nothing personal, but the food they serve on Aeroflot airlines leaves much to be desired. I was practically starving by the time we landed." He cleaned his hands with his napkin. "So when can you arrange for my first tour of the factory? I'm really looking forward to observing."

Alina Vera put an index finger to her lips. "That might not be as easy as you would think."

"Oh, is there a problem?"

"Not a problem," she said, "but the Alexander Nevsky is temporarily shut down. Mostly for mandated sterilization and sanitation. Before new production goes on line all facilities need to be decontaminated and disinfected from any previous routine bacteria. Producing mass quantity chocolate is more intricate than most people dream. We're legally required to pass a rigorous inspection before starting up. But we'll certainly invite you to be an exclusive guest at the earliest opportunity."

"Thank you, Alina Vera. I do appreciate that. My business over here isn't all that simple either. I'm under strict orders from my people to personally tour and inspect your Alexander Nevsky factory."

"We have a number of other high-quality chocolate factories in Russia," Vlad quickly interjected. "Very likely we'd be able to get an exclusive tour of one within the next few days."

"No can do, Vlad. I hope this doesn't hurt our friendship but you know America has satellites buzzing above the earth, as you do." He indicated with his index finger something going round and round. "And you'd better believe they never discuss anything vital with me when it comes to classified info. But I do know my government believes something really odd is going on here in Omsk at that particular chocolate factory."

Vlad and Alina Vera exchanged glances and shrugged. "I have no idea what you're talking about," said Vlad.

"Nor do I," she agreed.

Floyd placed his glass down on the table and folded his hands in his lap. "Your president herself said I'd receive total cooperation from your people out here, Sport. You've been made aware about that, haven't you?"

"Of course we have, Floyd. Our government has asked us to treat you with top priority. Russia values her friendships. That's exactly why we're here extending ourselves for you." Vlad snapped his fingers. "But I'll tell you what. Which hotel are you staying at, Omsk City Center? After we drop you off, I'll personally ring our contact man, Colonel Dimsky. He's in charge of quality control and management at the Alexander Nevsky these days. Everything concerning our 25th Anniversary Jubilee currently has some military jurisdiction or other. Dimsky is a decent fellow. I'm certain he'll be happy to do whatever he can to get you inside. However, you must understand he has superiors to report to also, like the rest of us."

"Heck, I expected that much."

"Then you do realize our dilemma? America and Russia are good friends, and we've maintained excellent relations for some time. I assure you that whatever your government suspects, nothing unusual is going on at the Alexander Nevsky, nor anywhere else America needs to be concerned about."

"I realize you're probably right, but just before coming to Omsk, someone with contacts at the Kremlin informed me about this spy affair. Do either of you know what I'm talking about?" They shook their heads. "Somebody, either in Moscow or Omsk was arrested, I was told. They claimed it's an agent for a foreign government; a spy caught hacking into one of your super computers. I could be wrong, but I think they've accused him of espionage for the Israelis. I guess nobody's above suspicion these days."

Neither Vlad nor Alina Vera could tell whether Floyd Dingus had purposely inserted this ominous note. "Neither of us have knowledge of this," said Vlad. Alina Vera confirmed as a nicely dressed couple at a nearby table got up and left. The jovial mood subdued and they needed to rekindle it.

The waiter returned with strong coffee. "Would you care for a famous Russian dessert?" he asked the American guest. "I suggest *kissel*, fruits mixed with honey, and decorated with cream. Or perhaps a Russian cheese tart pastry?"

Graham Diamond

Alina Vera asked, "What about chocolate vodka for dessert? Grated chocolate sprinkled in warm vodka and poured over ice cream? Does that sound good? I highly recommend it." Her eyes were smiling at him again.

The American winked. "You've sure tempted me. Chocolate vodka over ice cream sounds delectable."

"Chocolate vodka over ice cream for all," Vlad said in near-perfect English, grinning at the American. "If you have free time tomorrow, I'll bring you to visit another closely-guarded secret location; the shop to buy Omsk's best American-style milkshakes."

5.

At the farthest end of the Primorsky Boulevard pedestrian walkway, near the Mother-in-Law's bridge, stands Vorontsov's Palace. In 1917 it served as headquarters for Soviet Red Guards and also for the first Soviet of Workers and Sailors. The palace was a lovely, pink and white-columned stately edifice, a shiny crown in the city pleasingly known as Odessa, the Jewel of the Black Sea. Only a portion of the grand palace remained, but it timelessly continued to be a delightful attraction with its grand Gothic and Moorish architecture. Wide steps spilled from the arched entrance, and at the bottom of these steps a podium was placed. This location remained a proud landmark of the epicenter of the October uprising. And this night it would serve as a new platform for stirring the enmity still simmering across generations.

At dusk people began to congregate, a patchwork of workers, shopkeepers, the unemployed, and the haggard homeless. Some young, others aged, a mixture of the prosperous and poor, the pious and blasphemous, the sacred and profane. Some came attired in European finery, others in blue jeans, yet others clad in traditional threadbare frocks. Some attended out of boredom, some out of curiosity. But the news that something important was occurring spread across the city by word of mouth, rumor and fact. Tonight, at the literal place where pious citizens had hailed their leaders during the October Revolution, Bolshevik Red banners aflutter, events were stirring anew. Now the resolute people of this lovely port city would again listen and be inspired.

"Who's coming to speak?" a grumpy old woman asked.

A raw-boned worker removed his proletarian cap and wiped a sweaty brow with his forearm. It was a warm early-spring evening, and if not for the urgings of his brother he'd have gone straight home, eaten supper and turned on his television. "They say it's someone famous. My brother thinks it's a politician, but I'm hoping it's a celebrity. Maybe a famous film star." He envisioned a voluptuous Italian actress.

The crowd formed bit by bit, a handful here, a little grouping there, inquisitive students, strollers, passersby, joggers from the nearby park, assorted merchants and a few businessmen, until it became a hodgepodge of Odessa's diversified population. The moon was bright at dusk. The brown landscape of winter was beginning to be replaced by green. Vendors soon appeared at the edge of the crowd, one cart selling sausage and cabbage, another ice cream. A third was doing a bustling business selling imitation American soft drinks. Several city policemen appeared on the scene, puzzled as to what was going on. Proper permits had not been issued, but they weren't bothered. In a boring job an hour or so of unanticipated entertainment was always refreshing. Stars glimmered, wispy clouds rolled along. In the distance the steady clacking of the train was muffled.

As dusk faded into night, an enigmatic figure appeared unaccompanied from atop the palace steps. He rigidly walked down to a hastily placed make-shift podium. But for his paunch he was slender, bald, a spade beard peppered with grey sprouting from his chin. His facial features were distinguished, his comportment well bred and mannered, convincing in a grandfatherly fashion.

He stumbled slightly upon reaching the podium, and patiently waited until the crowd grew quiet. Then he glanced at a few papers held between thumb and forefinger. The assembly was small, but it was a beginning. It would serve its purpose. He knew these fine people of Odessa to be a sturdy, honest breed, gentle, but hot-blooded and strong-willed. No folk more resilient were to be found anywhere.

He carefully adjusted his eyeglasses over the bridge of his nose and behind his ears. "Comrades," he said at length, "Hear me, Comrades!" Many started at the word 'comrade'. It was a relic of the past, long since abandoned.

The speaker shuffled a few papers before him. "I know the hour is late and many of you are hungry and haven't eaten your supper. I know you've suffered a long day's work or study, but I beg for a few minutes of your time. I bring good tidings for a new beginning for the glorious proletariat, and spit on the contemptible intelligentsia."

"Heaven save us!" someone shouted. "I think he's another bible sermonizer!"

"Find him a priest's robe!" Muffled laughter rose.

"I do not preach religion." His voice was agitated.

"So are you looking for votes?" someone else called. "What government job are you standing for?"

"Politicians are worthless scum, anyway," yelled a heckler.

There was more laughter amid the crowd. Several young mothers stood suckling infants. A small child cried. These listeners were a brusque, demanding lot. He focused on his scribbled notes, proclaiming loudly, "No comrade, I am not looking for your votes." His tone betrayed his own dislike for politicians of any stripe.

"Are you an entertainer then?"

"Can you sing or play guitar?" A festive mood of gleeful relish germinated in the air. "Maybe the Moscow circus is coming…"

Another replied derisively, "Brother, *that* circus has been here for decades!"

"Maybe he can he tap dance?"

A rowdy youth with a ring in his lip bellowed, "He must be a clown! Look, he's bent over like a pretzel!"

Hoots of general bemusement reverberated. Ignoring it, the speaker patiently said, "I come tonight on serious business, to restore hope among our weak and downtrodden. To assure swift demise and retribution for the devastating greed and corruption that has befallen our land. True enough, a worker must earn his bread, but it is bread he earns with the sweat of his own brow." His ardor brought little enthusiasm.

"Oh, this one's a reformer! He'll point out our errors for us." Joviality rollicked the dubious onlookers who nudged each other, and stamped their feet. The crowd craved diversion, a free show, and small amusement at the end of a long day was most welcome.

The ice cream vendor eagerly did brisk a business as children grew restless.

"Hear me, Odessa!" This time the voice thundered above the clamor. "I'm speaking of a new order, Comrades. People of our Motherland united again in solidarity, restoring workers to rightful supremacy. Raising high our flag, the banner we hold dear, the proletarian flag, the Red flag."

At mention of the communist banner, the assembly quieted and began paying attention. Officially, the Red flag was forbidden to display. But strong memories from their parents and grandparents remained fresh among many, and silent supporters of the discredited Soviet way were startled. For some, the speaker appealed to forfeited convictions secretly held, his words as clear as pure spring water, delivering forgotten hopes that things need not be as they are.

"Who sent you?" a blatant voice called from the back, an ageing disenfranchised Party member.

"A fair question, brother. Are you old enough to recall the blood and sweat during the protracted, formidable battle we fought, you and I? When the People's Collective overthrew the tyrants who dared make themselves custodians of the land? This is the same ilk that now has seized power and brought national shame. I am here to revoke that ascendancy, and restore justice."

It was true; Russia's Duma and Council of the Federation were largely composed of deputies handpicked by the Kremlin, and one needn't strain to imagine how these wealthy, well-connected worms acquired office. There were no indebted governors or bankrupt ministers to be found. Well-greased palms assured a structure tolerating and highly susceptible to exploitation. A corrupt bureaucracy ran rabid; schools, hospitals, medicines, licensing, the courts, even the police. Laws against malfeasance were window dressing, ignored while ordinary folk watched helplessly, seething silently with resentment. This man made vivid their distress. How much more humiliation, injustice, inequality, and immunity for misconduct could they take?

The speaker was peppered with questions. Lobbing fiery invectives, he had made intimate connections among those hating the government's brutish contempt for people wishing to be free and equal in the Motherland.

"We've heard such promises before!" some decried.

"Show us proof!" they demanded.

"Comrades, shall I recount those who sought to murder me in my sleep to prevent our noble struggle? Do you wish to view the scars where an assassin's bullets pierced my flesh?" He trembled with intense emotion, made airy hand gestures that demonstrated burning anger. "Honest, stoic people of Odessa, you cannot disregard the drumbeat of your ancestors. Our Collective yet lives, our cause honorable. My presence proves that all things are possible." He outstretched his arms. "Have the fruits of our battle been erased? Have you forgotten the brutal fight we waged, the terrible destruction, and uncounted lives wasted? Tonight I vow Odessa's freedom-seekers will pave freedom's way.

"I look into your eyes, Comrades. I see despair, but I also see hope. Those who believe the battle lost, leave now! The rest stay. Our fight is not relinquished; we shall vanquish this new set of privileged, these heirs of decayed demagogues, buffered by thugs stealing bread from children's mouths." He uplifted a veined hand, and pointed a rigid index finger skyward. "Even now these unbearable moguls congregate and fester within the walls of the Kremlin, gorging upon the fat of the land. *Your* land, plowed with *your* sweat. Comrade citizens, why are you docile, so fearful that you lose your will?"

There was momentary silence, then a question. "You ask us to fight the might of the government?"

"I challenge the established order of this elitist world. I say we can expunge these oppressors. Men posing as benefactors while selling cheap vodka to addle your brain, ready to stomp jackboots upon your necks if you complain. Good folk of Odessa, I will bring down these debased governors, restore dignity, return you to your rightful places."

A thickset, middle-aged woman with a white doughy face shrilled. She pointed directly at the articulate speaker, her hand shaking with nervous excitement. "Look! Can't you recognize him? Don't you know history? It's Lenin! By heaven, it's *Lenin*!"

"Lenin!" The cry was picked up. "Lenin!"

Spontaneous, emotional outbursts followed, the crowd simultaneously aroused yet pensive. Could it be? Was it possible? Lenin was dead, his corpse on display in Red Square. Confusion grew.

"How can you prove you're not an imposter?" someone yelled.

With eyes inflamed, veins straining, the speaker roared, "I am no charlatan. Look, see for yourselves my scars!" He ripped open the collar of his shirt, exposing blemished flesh, displaying a maimed neck where an assassin's bullet had pierced and almost taken his life. It was indisputable; his wounds were identical to Lenin's

Those nearest the podium gawked and gasped. "It's true! I've seen photographs!" An old pensioner cried.

The volatile crowd looked about, doubtful, boiling up inside, heartbeats thumping at this extraordinary rhetoric. "I've been hearing for days rumors of his return," one worker said.

"So have I, brother. It's everywhere, whispered in the streets."

"Listen to this," another breathlessly agreed. "My brother-in-law told me of a worker in Omsk who saw and spoke to Lenin at his workplace lavatory. Not an apparition, but the flesh and blooded martyred man."

"People swear he's alive. Maybe he never really died. What if he was in hiding, alive and waiting—?"

"Or a second coming!"

"If this man can end our misery, what matter does it make?" cried a squat babushka. "He's not one of them—he's one of *us*!" Like others of the downtrodden she was frustrated that promised economic opportunities for her children and grandchildren rotted with stagnation.

"It *is* Lenin, without question!" It was a little man in thick eyeglasses speaking furiously, agitating the sense of drama, arousing the crowd, prodding and whipping them into a storm of frenzied belief. He knew how badly these blunt, candid folk wanted to believe, how much they needed to believe. Who but the larger-than-life hallowed leader of the true Revolution could lift them from desolation and anguish, and restore their faith? The people were stirring, aroused and angered. Tonight was but a beginning; one triumphant campaign would soon follow another.

A one-legged veteran, his fleshy face awash in tears, stepped forward with the aid of a crutch. "Tell me the truth, Comrade. My body took bullets and shrapnel in the duty of our Motherland. We trusted those leading us to wars, and brave comrades died in filth and agony lying upon foreign dirt. No lies, please, brother. Do not dupe my friends and neighbors. Our humble folk cannot bear more blows. Are you truly our father, Vladimir Ilyich Lenin?" He moved closer, scrutinizing this self-proclaimed, would-be defender of the people.

Hushed and transfixed, the assembly held a communal breath. Somberly the speaker nodded, a tear of his own forming, then falling. "Yes, beloved Comrade. I understand your suffering, your dishonor. I feel your pain. But be assured, I have not returned to tell lies." This was no hollow hyperbole. "Corruption and counter-revolutionary enterprise will again be punishable by death!"

All became silent, as if listening to a profound, soundless wind. Under the old regime that was the law. Then suddenly a cry, "It's a miracle!"

The chant was picked up and recited. "A miracle!"

"Dear children, I am here to serve. Through my long, bitter darkness I heard your cries, your pleas. I listened until I could bear it no longer. I fight to emancipate you, to bring liberation! Children, trust my love is boundless, and through that affection I have been given renewed life."

Tears welled in many eyes. "Lenin loves us!"

An earsplitting rousing round of cheers and whistles ensued from the traditionalists, buoyed by a euphoric expectancy that decades of abuse might at last come to an end. Some wept openly, others stood meek and mute, shock and awe engraved across each peasant face. If ever a great leader were needed the time was now. They were fed up with the lies ruling autocrats fed, preserving a system enabling incompetents to control the nation. Official misbehavior was the norm, and this speaker well understood the curse of such unrestrained exploitation. Perhaps, somehow, this haunting image of Lenin had indeed returned to be champion and liberator. Here he stood in the flesh, the icon of their yearnings. Truly the greatest miracle of all.

"Lead us!" they acclaimed. "Lead us, Comrade Lenin!"

"And so I shall!" the speaker exhorted, his vocal chords raw and powerful. "Liberation from servitude, oppressive bondage, and evils of capitalism. An end to persecution. I vow never to repeat blunders of the past. Enlist in my campaign, stand at my side, and become recruits in raising our glorious banner. Shoulder-to-shoulder in solidarity, workers of the world, united and invincible!"

A ripple effect emerged; energized, enthusiastic voices crying, "Bless you, Comrade Lenin!"

"Comrades, united we shall restore our sense of national purpose, and conquer the world! The People's Soviet remains alive within. Nothing can withstand this surging tidal wave! We'll crush the fascists sapping your strength and breaking your backs!"

He closed fists and lifted his arms higher, speaking with his famed emblematic fervent zeal. "These merciless stooges who obediently grovel at their masters' feet will be pounded into dust, cast from majestic thrones built upon suffering. Now is your turn to repay in kind. I will not desert the faithful at this moment of great crisis.

"Hear me, Comrades! I promise a long, arduous journey. Swear your oaths and loyalty, and in return I pledge absolute devotion. Redeem our sacred soil, reclaim beloved Mother Russia!"

Mighty cheers swelled, hot defiance restoring Motherland patriotism. There were only those eager to sign up for the cause. "Lead us! Lead us to victory!"

The clamor became so great he pleaded for quiet. "When the time is at hand we shall march together. What is begun tonight cannot be reversed, a thirst that cannot be quelled. We shall take up every weapon, marching onward to Kiev, Lvov, and Omsk, joined by our sisters and brothers, following the long, winding road. We'll retake Petersburg, and finally reach the beating heart of beloved Mother Russia, Moscow. Forging the Kremlin walls, emancipating the throngs waiting to join our righteous cause. Tonight we declare the Second Revolution!"

A chilly wind whipped low to the cold, hard ground. Stars glimmered from behind black clouds. What he said was true; there was no going back. The crowd stood silent with adulation for a time, then thundered with violent electricity, feeling it in every fiber like a flame.

6.

Rabbi Titlebaum leaned over the desk, intently studying a book on Gematria resting before him. His usual small mixture of grapes, raisins, and nuts nestled in his pocket. He adjusted his yarmulke, skullcap, at the crown of his head. Gematria is a mystical system of assigning numerical value to letters, words and phrases. For long years Asher had studied this weighty, philosophical connection, frequently in seclusion before deciding to resign his positions both at the Landau Institute for Theoretical Studies and the Steklov Institute of Mathematics.

Seeking to comprehend the nature of the universe and creation had overwhelmed Asher. His acutely insightful mind assured him the answers he sought were beyond science's meager interpretations. We know and understand so little of the nature of things, he realized, and it pleased him that science might serve as one channel for ideas owing more to mysticism than worldly dispassionate study.

To his satisfaction the sacred text of Kabbalah conclusively demonstrated that God created the world partly by utilizing the twenty-two letters of the Hebrew alphabet. The building blocks of the universe itself were created using forms of sacred numbers together with the twenty-two letters of the Hebrew alphabet. Merged in variant combinations, these interacted in ways he only dared pray he'd begun to grasp.

Asher turned from his texts and looked at the woman standing at his side. "I know how confusing this seems, but can you understand that the 'essential force' of a thing's name, such as a lion, for example, will also be found somewhere in its numerical value?"

Alina Vera sighed with impatience. "I comprehend you've become an impenetrable mystic, Asher, while I've remained a scientist. I don't see how any of this is helpful. Are we supposed to review medieval perceptions of alchemists?"

He answered with avuncular compassion. "Keep your cool, Alina Vera. I myself was like you—until I discovered the very foundations of the universe can be understood beyond microscopes and quantum physics. These texts reshape our view of life sciences, as well reevaluating all our advanced technologies science has made possible. I study both, and combining sources, I searched for simple words in the text and translated them into numbers. After that I compared and contrasted them together with other words."

She tapped her foot edgily. "What does this explain?"

His voice was as calm and unruffled as it always had been during their work years. "I believe this is how Sunavich managed to extrapolate genetic codes and incorporate them among endless letter and number possibilities of the bingo cards we found at the *Das Kapital Bingo Parlor.* He definitely left these clues to confound us. Wickedly clever on his part."

"I never underestimated him, Asher."

"I'm pretty lost," reluctantly Vlad admitted. "These heady concepts aren't easy to follow."

The rabbi offered the same dispassionate indulgence to his new colleague. "I'll put it this way, the doctor stole mystical concepts from the Kabbalah, adapting them as necessary for his own purpose. He employed numbers in place of letters, then letters in place of numbers. In effect, the Zohar, the book of Jewish mysticism, became his guidebook of sorts. He used his genius to acquire procedures, screening his covert codes so only the most adept minds might comprehend. He lodged these disclosures as a riddle for us to decipher, laughing, no doubt, at our clumsy attempts. If you consider the matter, it's conceptually brilliant. Holding the whole of Russia's scientific community at bay. The toil of a madman ingeniously inspired." Asher spoke of the rogue doctor with grudging admiration.

"But Sunavich isn't even a Jew," Alina Vera protested. "What would prompt his interest in manipulating Kabbalistic theories?"

"Therein lies his brilliance! He recognized how badly it would hamper our efforts to decode. His devious plan causes maximum confusion and havoc, having us bicker, fight among ourselves, and pulling our hair out trying to reconstruct his formula. Countless delay after delay." Asher sighed with appreciation of the complications it must have caused even Sunavich. He rubbed his beard and regarded the charming younger scientist as a grandfather explaining a homework enigma to his favorite grandchild. He realized mystical realities were difficult to illustrate to any novice. "Barely a handful of learned men in the world can glimpse an iota of the vast truths found in the Zohar's complex wealth of thought. What it shows regarding the design of the universe is astounding and beautiful, a masterpiece drawn by divine hand. In believing he's accomplished such a feat, I venture to think Sunavich delights in the idea of likening himself to the Almighty. From skimpy notes, we managed to piece a few clues together. Here, look with me."

He pointed a long forefinger, carefully demonstrating a single line of text. "When you take the first and last letter of each of these Hebrew words, translate them into Russian, you will discover the confusing acronym DKBP. Four ordinary letters from the alphabet, seemingly random, without meaning, and easily overlooked. Yet they are hardly harmless. You'd rack your brain searching for connotation, but in reality it's deceptively simple. You see, the anagram DKBP stand for the initials of the *Das Kapital Bingo Parlor*."

Everyone suspended breath, stood tongue-tied, astonished at the rabbi's capacity to arrive at such a stupefying conclusion. Alina Vera clutched Vlad's sleeve. "And the numerical value of each letter," Asher went on, "again when added, correspond to the precise address of the bingo hall. This is how I concluded I was on the right track." He leaned back with satisfaction, chewing with gusto another handful of grapes.

"Who else in this world could have worked out that deception but you, Rabbi?" Vlad said haltingly, in awe, marveling with deference. It became abundantly clear to them all that the rabbi's intellect and vision surely rivaled that of his adversary.

"Thank you for the flattery, but the fitting indebtedness dates back to the origins of the Zohar, the very foundation of mystical beliefs called Kabbalah. That's where I discovered keys for unlocking the numbers. Nevertheless, we can never underestimate the talents or abilities of an obsessed, misguided fanatic perverted by a god-complex."

A frosty glare overtook Alina Vera. "Sunavich thinks himself a deity? Mikhail Sunavich isn't a misguided fanatic, he's a bloody lunatic. You know it, I know it, and now the whole world is going to know it. Listen Rabbi, I've been assigned to this project virtually since inception. Don't forget I studied under both Sunavich and yourself in theoretical and practical science, and still I don't fully comprehend what he's achieved. I wasn't given classification or authorization as part of the project's inner circle. All I do know is suddenly all hell has broken loose. I'm supposed to be assisting you. Dozens of the finest scientific minds available are also assisting you. Each of us at your beck and call—yet no one has a clue to what the fuck is going on."

"Maybe Sunavich went off his meds," Dimsky matter-of-factly offered.

The rabbi lifted his brows at the remark, turned and regarded Alina Vera warmheartedly. "Dr. Galina, I know it's not my business, but I believe you're still young enough to bear children. I wish for you many, many blessings, an admirable match to share your life, along with healthy offspring and numerous grandchildren." He chewed another handful of grapes.

"What's that got to do with anything?" She turned away exasperated, pacing, clenching and unclenching her fists. There were no cigarettes handy, but if ever she needed a smoke this was that time.

"All right," Asher reluctantly agreed. "I'd best fill you in. What I'm about to disclose was classified for my eyes only; however, under the circumstances it's abundantly clear I need to share these theoretical explanations with my team. First, you must realize that 'Codename Chocolate Lenin' was never intended to advance this far. Even before I resigned from the Academy we'd realized our work was moving toward this possibility. Already we'd achieved the probability of imbuing an elementary artificial life force analogous to what the Chinese call *chi*. A living being, totally created in the laboratory. Some believed we'd conceptually proven it, *theoretically*." He stressed the last word. "A biologist asks, 'what is the origin of symmetry in the genetic code? What triggers its breakdown?' It was discovered that base modifications, mutation of RNA editing, *could* change genetic code. Our lab's intention was to eventually create a toad or a mouse in gradual steps. I admit this gave me great concern at the time. As a scientist it was an arousing concept; but moral chaos aside, I feared its ramifications and possibility of widespread abuse. It took a great deal of soul-searching and prayer for me to come to terms with it." He looked up. "Now I have.

He continued. "Sunavich is a sly opportunist. He understood what he was doing every step of the way. In my opinion, the real secret isn't to be found within the normal range of human genomes, nor any elemental structuring of DNA. I'd wager we find the code's final resolution directly within the synthesis of the rum."

She stared. "The synthesis of *what*?"

Generally unflappable, Colonel Dimsky sat still and attentive. He carefully put aside his balalaika. "Please decipher what you mean."

"Colonel, as a professional soldier you've studied combat strategies as applied on the battlefield. Correct me if I'm wrong, but historically no military leader from Julius Caesar, to Napoleon, to Dwight Eisenhower, ever placed his troops into harm's way without first considering every conceivable consequential outcome."

"That's a correct military assessment." Dimsky agreed.

Asher continued, chewing another grape. "Although this project remains top secret, at this juncture I can't be faulted for providing background. I doubt even our president realizes the full extent of Mikhail Sunavich's treachery. He didn't dream up early-stage 'Little Man' as a prerequisite for instilling life, as we understand it. Over the years, biologists accumulate large amount of genetic code variants. Based on these data, they study how changes occur. After going through a primordial phase of evolution, genetic code was frozen into its current form. However he overtly utilized his highly camouflaged amalgam of rum and chocolate-blended serum, slyly administering an alcoholic substance into its final plasmic composition. Initially this was strictly intended to induce flavor and aroma, not hiding his formulation. That changed when he committed this reckless, prohibitive act, which he neglected to share with colleagues or superiors." Asher's voice dropped an octave lower. "Now he's unmasked. If he had treasonous accomplices, I can't say. But our present paramount directive is to reverse and eliminate his accomplishment by any means."

Aghast, Dimsky stood to his feet. "You're insinuating Dr. Sunavich invented a procedure to reconstitute Vladimir Ilyich Lenin back to life? Restoring a heinous *thing* from the grave even while Lenin's corpse lies in the State Mausoleum?"

"I'm not insinuating; I'm informing. This highly developed being now set free bears no resemblance to the precursor you safeguarded, aptly called 'Little Man'. This actualized prototype is a living being."

Vlad rubbed at throbbing temples. Had he heard right? "Rabbi, these Omsk sightings, the throng in Odessa—this so-called Lenin is alive because of elements Sunavich injected into cloned veins? Compounds of chocolate and rum?"

"That's specifically what Rabbi Titlebaum is saying," Alina Vera said. "I'm not sure I fully comprehend, but if I do, it means this life-size composite of duplicated molecular DNA is an oxygen breathing entity as alive as you or I."

"Living, breathing?" parroted Vlad. "Is it natural, is it *human?*"

Asher rested back in his chair, rolling grapes in his palm. "'Natural' and 'unnatural' are not scientific categories. And chemicals in a test tube won't spring to life. Before the entity received injected serum it hadn't yet breathed its first breath. Therefore clinically, it wasn't 'alive'. Now we can draw the conclusion it's painstakingly and perfectly infused, a hallmark of attaining what I call actualized 'life force'. Not artificial. No different that you or I. Electrical impulses to specific regions assure its brain waves function normally. Its heart beats no differently than yours or mine. It feels the range of human emotion; anger, laughter, hate, maybe even love. I'm loath to describe it this way, but yes, the replicate is technically alive." His lower lip quivered; it was plain the rabbi was struggling to maintain his composure. Dr. Sunavich had succumbed to the basest human impulses, violating universal sacred laws of nature.

"Has everyone gone mental?" protested Dimsky. "Are we chasing a walking, talking, *chocolate bar?*"

"In a perverted way that's correct," Asher dourly responded. "Sunavich turned that lump, that fleshy amalgam of rum-infused chocolate DNA fiber into something the world's never seen. He succeeded beyond anyone's wildest imagination. When you first viewed 'Little Man' you learned of the project, but not the complications that weren't divulged. This effort didn't start with ideas conceived at the Alexander Nevsky. They've been long dreamed, devised, and evaluated at the Academy as well as other institutions throughout the world. It was just a matter of time until we closed the gap separating inanimate and animate. The difference is that Sunavich knowingly debased science for his venomous political agenda." Asher allowed time for this reality to sink in. Then he continued.

"He remains a staunch Marxist-Leninist, believing capitalism can be overthrown only by ruthless class struggle. This process provided a way to jumpstart such strife, and he expertly adapted and revamped his serum's formula right beneath the State's nose. Under the guise of injecting aromatic rum, his serum stealthily transformed and inserted an original molecule from a test tube that evolved and replicated itself, delivering the decisive spark, the supreme ingredient required for initiating life. It's disturbing to conjecture how he achieved it. My personal theory is that his remarkable chocolate-based molecule manipulated the cell's mitochondria."

"Explain, please." said Vlad. "It's over my head."

"I'll try. You see, within every human body there are approximately 100 trillion cells. The mitochondria I mentioned are organelles located outside the nucleus of a cell's cytoplasm. Organelles are cellular powerhouses responsible for energy transfer. When DNA was initially studied we recognized it as the master molecule of life, controlling development of every living thing. DNA consists of long strings called polymers, strands of simple repeating units. Utilizing influences of his serum, Sunavich doubtlessly obtained total molecular control over polymerization, in effect overriding natural cellular replication. There are degrees of conscious awareness, and by stages this allowed him to artificially manipulate a phenomenon referred to as paradoxical excitation. At some point when complete cognitive response was diligently achieved…Voila!

"His rum-laced formula was then diluted when injected, thus disguising the dilution and all other influences. How many random tests were required until a pattern of neuronal firing was perfected we'll never know, but perfect it he did."

The notion of the mad doctor's achievement was breathtaking, a recreated embodiment all but impossible to believe. "So this manufactured rum-and-chocolate-base masks the serum's secret formula?"

"It does. And by so doing makes our work all the more difficult."

Vlad asked, "Does alcohol in his bloodstream impair his faculties? Does he behave as though he'd been drinking?"

The rabbi remained thoughtful; it was a complex concept. "Your question is what? Is he perpetually drunk? I understand how one might surmise the notion. I'd say it's reasonable to deduce Lenin does hover approximating an inebriated state."

"Then he *is* drunk?" asked Alina Vera. "How drunk? Wobbling in a stupor?"

"The ratio of measured alcohol is probably low enough to keep him below legal limits of inebriation. Of course it would vary according to weight, anatomy, structure, and so forth. Alcohol will certainly have reached his brain, with the rum retaining a limited dilution. Overall, I'd diagnose him as being slightly lightheaded or tipsy."

Dimsky could not come to grips with any of these matters. "You're telling us this *thing*, this preposterous chocolate abomination, is a drunken 'life force' freely roaming around Russia?"

"Well, yes and no," demurred Asher. "If my assessment is right, he's unceasingly had 'one too many.' At times he'll appear lethargic, other times talkative, even combative. Naturally we can't be sure without obtaining a fresh sample of urine to compute fixed alcoholic content." He shrugged absently. "At times the level may variously exceed legal limits, at other times not. As with any living creature, his blood courses continuously throughout his body, round and round like a carousel. However, his thought processes will undergo little alteration from any other normal human who's had a drink or two. Although," he mused, "I wonder how efficient his liver and kidney functions are?"

"This is a pathetic comedy," uttered Dimsky.

"It's no comedy, Colonel." Alina Vera turned and regarded Asher fretfully. "Despite limitations, am I correct that this 'Lenin' will be nobody's fool or puppet?"

Asher nodded. "Quite so, Dr. Galina; his thoughts and decisions will be his own, like anyone else."

"Would Dr. Sunavich likely be able to control him?"

Again the rabbi gave the question concentrated reflection. "To some extent—but not entirely. As our prototype experiences real life conditions and situations he'll start feeling and believing in his own vigor. Eventually he'll gain independence, much like an infant first leaving its mother, only speeded up. A baby crawls and learns to stand. Stumbling a bit, assuredly, but sooner or later he'll not only stand but soon walk on his own."

"Oh fine," rasped Alina Vera. "So all we have to do is catch him."

"In a nutshell, that's it," conceded Asher. "Vlad, your conclusion on Lenin travelling to a location such as Odessa was astute. Any inclination where he'd next seek refuge?"

"Difficult to say; I'd guess he'll keep close to the countryside, agitating locals. Small crowds of workers are his best audiences. Probably he'd play a similar role as during the Revolution, spouting platitudes praising socialism, and the necessity for decimating the oligarchy. Only now his rehashed writings and speeches will get plastered all over cyberspace in the name of clean, honest government. Expect coalitions of alienated youths to start nightly protests in restive cities. I'm not sure how seriously the world's media will pay attention right now, but the military won't hesitate to prevent civil disorder. If this nascent revolt causes violence there'll be a sharp response to crush seething tensions. Then we'll face real blowback. Widespread backlash will fuel a logistical nightmare to refute. Foreign correspondents will besiege Moscow like a plague, decrying the military's tactics, demanding answers and explanations, seeking ever-bigger stories. Bigger means more notoriety, and media thrives on a good feeding to improve sagging ratings. They can alternately cast Lenin as a villain or designate him a folk hero. Media frenzy will cannibalize our PR efforts within days. We'll see an onslaught of hyped, wrenching, ideological and provocative stories mocking our denials. It doesn't matter who wins or loses. To them, only the story counts."

"This travesty must cease!" snapped Dimsky, rising to his feet, visibly agitated. "I don't care if this glob of primordial ooze was constructed from garbanzo beans! We'll never knuckle under to street protesters!" The military man glowered at the crackerjack PR expert. "Petrovsky, your prime duty is managing every public aspect of this horrid affair. Get to work! Deny everything regarding this primate's sightings. Nip it in the bud. We'll show backbone, call a national press conference, and denounce this phony redeemer."

"That's the wrong tactic," Vlad firmly disagreed. "This is my job, that's why I'm here, so allow me to handle it my way. We need to appear calm and unruffled, displaying confidence. The official view is that there's some unbalanced psycho running around the countryside proclaiming to be Lenin. All right. We'll stress that the authentic revolutionary leader died in 1924. That's undeniable. There's nothing peculiar about unsound people making outlandish claims. We've seen such impersonators before. They're more to be pitied than laughed at.

"Moreover, countless people swear they've personally witnessed the Virgin Mother appear to them, while others maintain they've spoken to holy saints and been given commands to follow. UFO sightings are perennially popular. As far as we're concerned this matter fits into the same category, and not in any way hampers national security. My job as government spokesmen is to assure everything's under control, the nation functioning normally. Besides, negative press will certainly make our friend Floyd Dingus more suspicious than he already is. And the damn Americans can nurture a lot of PR damage if they decide."

"But what if Lenin's following keeps growing?" asked Alina Vera. "What if stupid hotheads take up arms and do launch a popular insurrection?"

He faced her squarely, speaking with honesty. "I won't lie. It could happen. It's a pretty desolate picture, having today's lost generation heedlessly searching for any would-be savior. Resourceful, impassioned rabble-rousers could easily take advantage and provoke trouble. If it gets out of hand the P.M. will mobilize his hated secret police with a snap of his finger. We can expect massive roundups, security forces patrolling the streets night and day. Standard procedure. It's up to us to prevent the situation from deteriorating to that level. If we can't come up with a workable plan, Boris will have our heads on a platter."

"They'll likely have our heads anyway," bemoaned Dimsky, sinking into a funk. "I'm obligated to report directly to the Kremlin. In my view, this intoxicated perversion poses a severe threat to national stability, arousing and beguiling society's most vulnerable, making promises he can't deliver."

"Historically wasn't that his sole aspiration, fermenting unrest? His entire life was devoted to preaching insurrection. Yes, peaceful protests can quickly turn violent, and we have to avert that. Yet as the rabbi explained, this new incarnation of Lenin is a different creation evolving into his own man, and there's no telling in which direction he'll guide his crusade."

Alina Vera took a series of deep breaths, fighting to alleviate her rising concerns. "You mean a campaign for some renewed dictatorship of the proletariat? Hello, people! This is another century. Lenin fashioned a rural revolution for a long disappeared agrarian society. Aren't we supposed to be living in a new 'golden age of worldwide market capitalism'?"

"Sounds to me like a nice way of saying 'worldwide market greed'," scoffed Vlad. "Impassioned youths desiring to risk their lives for this bombastic populist with zero credibility is shameful."

"Tell it to *them*." Alina Vera pictured masses of today's deprived young people forming coalitions, mindlessly following friends into waiting mayhem. It was a hair-raising scenario, frighteningly plausible in a time of globalized information technology.

"Vlad's right in one respect," she admitted. "People are angry. It won't take many sparks to hijack nonviolent protests. Remember the exuberant Arab Spring with all its promise? Crackdowns, mass arrests, torture, indiscriminate killings. Residue from those conflicts is still simmering." She shuddered; her own family had endured enormous suffering during the furious upheavals following the October Revolution a century before. Russia's Civil War had been long and brutal. If Vlad was correct the nation faced being ripped apart again.

Vlad sought to calm her anxiety. "All this is just hearsay, encouraged by a tiny fraction of fanatics. A meager crowd gathered in Odessa doesn't signal insurrection, nor is it a newsflash. I don't believe Russians desire some invigorated 'dictatorship of the proletariat'. Not anymore. And so far not a single television network or news website has picked up the story."

"The blogosphere is on a roll," Dimsky pointedly said. "They're paying attention. A volatile mix of scummy freebooters is orchestrating incitement at highly promoted English language sites. Not long ago the notion of mass gatherings organized in real time over wireless devices was sheer fantasy. Not now. The Internet's open environment has speeded up the world. Individuals can take on any challenge faster and faster, from disseminating new ideas to taking down vulnerable governments. So far mostly cranks and bellyachers are gloating over these crazed ramblings, and we're hacking to pinpoint ringleader mischief-makers. Unfortunately there are thousands to verify. My men are busy crosschecking search engines, reviewing whenever the name 'Lenin' receives hits. We take down as many sites as possible, but encounter more popping up by the hour. We're also scanning and tallying hits on word searches for 'revolution', and 'insurrection', monitoring, and disrupting them. But web pages revamp content within minutes. It's an endless ordeal. And these notorious social sites are even bigger irritations, instantaneously spreading disorder with pet peeves, disseminating grievance after grievance. If a time comes when revolutionaries do vigorously organize into an army, our backs will really be to the wall."

"There's no way of preventing online chats or instant messaging," Alina Vera pointed out. "It's freedom of speech."

Dimsky looked at her with knitted brows, his voice cantankerous and opinionated. "Maybe, but the power of social media frightens me, especially this insidious FacetoFace site, prowled by harassing provocateurs and geek ringleaders. It's a barometer for the whole Internet. A motley conglomerate wooing and wowing supporters around the globe, articulating their visions, and shouting for widespread riots while hiding behind computer screens. We've empowered these spineless jellyfish, yet we don't dare deny public access unless the government's prepared to totally blackout cyberspace."

"Which itself will cause massive riots," said Vlad glumly.

"I cooked up a new handle to check out some of these opportunists. I called myself, 'Hambone', and joined every protest group I came across. Mother Volga! My mailbox is stuffed! Hundreds purport to be Revolutionary agents, common swindlers implying that by forking over a little cash they'll be happy to set Russia's streets afire. Meanwhile, other cyberpunks claim they're reincarnations of John Wayne and Father Christmas. One says he's Shakespeare's dog looking for a home. Sick!"

"I didn't know he had a dog," quipped Alina Vera.

"That isn't the point," Dimsky caustically replied. "They have the latest tools at their command. Perverts and defects ask my age, my sex, and attach animated obscene videos. I routinely receive requests to send them photographs before going out on a date. Long-lost 'friends' invite me to share in multi-million dollar bank accounts they need my help to access, if only I'll forward a little money now. Triple-X sites offer free trials. Masseuses propose visiting me at home at no extra charge. I've never been so popular."

"Nor has Lenin," said Alina Vera. "We're at a crossroad. Maybe these malcontents you've ferreted out can be discredited, but since you say publicity counts so much, look what's going on at Lenin's Tomb, and how do we deal with that? The lines to view his corpse grow longer by the day. People want to know if that stiff under glass is real or not. If it is, who's this uncanny imitation? Everyone's suspicious and jaded, even normal, decent people are confused. What a farce. Everyone knows Lenin is *dead*."

"Knowing and believing aren't always the same," said Vlad with unexpected severity. "That's the nature of this crisis; the longer it continues, the more confusing it gets. Half the country thinks the body on display is bogus, that there never was any authentic corpse in the crypt, just a wax replica. Perception is reality. We'll be globally stigmatized if they find we're propping up a phony dummy. They'll accuse us of irresponsible, megalomaniacal efforts to dupe the world. That spells big trouble; our credibility's already sagging. In the court of public opinion we'll be creamed."

"Quite right," Asher soundly agreed. "The acceleration in stature of this loathsome *resurrection* is explosive. Ambiguity in official pronouncements doesn't help. We have to be outspoken and clear, otherwise it will turn toxic like poisonous radiation. We ignore these warning signs at our peril."

"The rabbi truly believes in the rationality of the people, but I don't," Dimsky said with a casual air. "The populace has the memory span of a gnat. Lose control and society will crumble. The mobs in the streets will happily raise this pygmy onto their shoulders like a cult icon. You'll need bulletproof vests and goggles to go out and buy groceries."

"What is he, a fucking *rock star?*" said Alina Vera. "You make it sound like the end of the world. The prime minister would have reason to have us certified as lunatics—and who'd blame him? Do you realize how insane this conversation sounds if anyone were listening?"

"Maybe they *are* listening," Vlad speculated. "Evade, deny...profess ignorance...we're all just pawns in a drama of political exploitation, aren't we? Spy rings everywhere. What if the State is already monitoring everything we say and do?"

Dimsky threw up his hands. "Damn it, Petrovsky, don't you know who you're working for? We *are* the State! You're falling for your own media mumbo jumbo."

"Oh? You're saying computers and smartphones aren't being hacked? That every time someone connects online their personal data, ID, and email aren't at risk?"

"Not legally," groused Dimsky.

"Not *legally*? You yourself break into confidential data every day!"

"Only when necessary."

"Settle down," soothed the rabbi, desiring to calm tensions and keep the lid on a steaming kettle. "Gentlemen, let's not get carried away. Reassure us, Colonel. We'd all like to know. Our conversations aren't bugged, are they?"

Vlad stared at Dimsky intently. "Well?"

The colonel stiffened. "Absolutely not! It's ridiculous, delusional, and paranoid." He scowled, hesitated. "At least I don't think they are."

With a streaming sigh, Alina Vera pursed her lips and looked away. A feverish, demoralizing mood was overtaking them, she saw, and its implications were catastrophic if they didn't get back on track. "Let's stop this pointless bickering and get back to work. These are the hard facts we can agree on: A man-made monstrosity has been set loose. He's escaped, running wild and free, creating anarchy in his wake. We have no idea where he's hiding, and no leads where or when he'll appear next."

"Exactly. We're stymied," said Vlad. "We've hit a brick wall."

"So it seems," Dimsky agreed as an afterthought, repentant for his near run-in with young Petrovsky, whom he genuinely had come to respect. "After more than three decades of counterintelligence work even I admit feeling rattled and discouraged by chasing down this enshrined *anthropoid*. It's true what they say; it's a jungle out there."

Vlad heard the doleful tune of a flute sounding a mournful note in the distance amid rain pounding against windowpanes. A great elm rose near his window, beside an aged wooden wall. Spring grasses were growing and that made him smile. He thought of other times and memories; Raisa's winning smile, their wedding in St. Petersburg and intoxicating honeymoon in Paris. The memorable day they'd taken possession of the handsome flat they purchased in Moscow, and the flustered pounding of his heart at first news of becoming a father. All these things and more ran randomly though his dozing mind.

The shrieking of the whistle woke him abruptly.

The clacking of the train's wheels was lulling. Most passengers were fast asleep. The Trans-Siberian midnight train to Moscow wouldn't arrive at its destination for eleven more hours. Direct orders from Sergei Milonov himself removed Vlad and the strike team from Omsk relocating them at the capital. It was an ambivalent command Vlad recognized to be a precursor of increasing apprehension seeping within the Kremlin, and a disturbing symptom of the prime minister's intensifying uneasiness. Faceless bureaucrats had taken control of the chocolate factory, among them Russian, plus a smattering of trusted Chinese, German, and Swedish scientists. The *Das Kapital Bingo Parlor* was directly under military control. All scientific abstracts were allocated for scrutiny under the circumspect direction of Director Rimsky-Kimsky, who in turn reported solely to Asher Titlebaum.

Across the aisle, Rabbi Titlebaum rested as far back as his seat allowed, sanguine in a light sleep. Colonel Dimsky, ever the true soldier, sat rigidly upright, his eyes shut, balalaika in its case at his side. Only Alina Vera Galina remained fully awake, attentively studying her view of the dark countryside passing outside. Vlad observed her. She was a striking woman, he recognized, and he mused at what might lay behind her customary façade of calculated aloofness. In another day or time he might have found the smart scientist not only attractive but also captivating. Yet this wasn't that time, not with the pain of Raisa's decision of separation and considered divorce. How very much he missed being near his daughters. Travelling to visit them in St. Petersburg was out of the question, and he had no idea how long it would be before he could see them. His coveted directorship had already cost far more than he'd ever expected, and he dared not speculate on what might happen next.

One thing was certain, 'Codename Chocolate Lenin' was out of control. Trying to hide it from Russia's press or the far more sophisticated Western media would become impossible if the situation wasn't competently and quickly handled. The slightest misstep would bring Stroganoff's wrath directly upon his shoulders. He was the fair-haired boy, the media expert toast-of-Moscow who could do no wrong—so far. Now he questioned if the accolades and honors were merely a guise, their way, should plans go awry, of heaping blame and making his head the first to roll. He couldn't afford any miscalculations. Was he becoming overly suspicious like Alina Vera Galina, he wondered, discovering threats lurking at every turn? He gave her a sidelong glance, which she noticed from the corner of her eye. He looked away with embarrassment.

The train began to noticeably slow, wheels churning, squeaking as brakes were forcefully applied. As it slowed a distressed conductor hastened through the carriage. He spoke in hushed tones into his two-way radio, crossing into the next car. "Is something wrong?" asked Alina Vera.

Vlad stood and tilted off balance, tightly grasping the back of his seat. "We're stopping but not at a station."

Dimsky's keen eyes opened wide. He set his jaw firmly. "We're stopping in the middle of nowhere," he groused. He looked at his smartphone's GPS. "A thousand kilometers from Moscow."

Rabbi Titlebaum stirred, his lower back feeling the sudden jolt. "Can you get a coded line to the Kremlin?"

Dimsky sat keyboarding. "*Nyet*. The signal's weak and distorted. Any of you have a signal?" Vlad and Alina Vera checked their phones. They were dead.

Another conductor rushed through the car. Dimsky adroitly stood up and stepped in his way. "Tell me what's happening here."

"I'm not authorized to discuss it," the conductor responded. "Now let me pass!"

Dimsky rose to his full height. "Mother Volga, you *will* discuss it with me!" he bellowed, flashing his official identification card and holding it close to the conductor's nose. "Do you recognize this seal? Does this authorization mean anything to you?" The identification clearly disclosed Colonel Dimsky as a high-ranking, military Internal Security official.

The conductor paled and stuttered, "Please, sir, I don't want trouble. I've been ordered to say nothing, but of course I do recognize your jurisdiction."

"Good. Now tell me what's going on."

"There's been some sort of commotion ahead, a little hindrance. I don't have many details, but I think drunken rowdies set something ablaze on the tracks. We're ordered to stop and wait for further instruction."

"What else?"

"Rabble causing a nuisance is all I know. Please let me pass. My supervisors are waiting." Satisfied, Colonel Dimsky nodded and stood aside.

"All we can do is bide our time," said Asher with a sigh, resuming his seat. He folded his arms, yawned, and made himself as comfortable as possible, grateful his back pain eased.

"You're pretty sedate," said Alina Vera. Asher shrugged and made no effort to answer. The train ground to a complete halt. Mingling passengers began to grow restless.

"Look, they're giving out sandwiches and coffee," said Vlad, motioning to the back of the car to where two conductors rolled a large cart.

"They must expect us to be stuck for some time," said Dimsky. He played again with his smartphone, scanning for a boosted signal. "Nothing," he told his colleagues. "I'll look for a better location."

"Sit down, try to relax, Colonel," said the rabbi. "There's no use in becoming agitated. Stress will only raise your blood pressure. You too, Vlad, Alina Vera, take seats and try to make the best of it."

Dimsky raised a hand, snapped his fingers at a conductor. "We'll take coffee over here." A young man came hurrying with a tray laden with Styrofoam cups. The coffee was steaming. They all took one except the rabbi.

"We'll never get home on time if we're bogged down in this forsaken rat hole," Alina Vera brooded.

"I trust you've already taken your blood pressure medication?" the rabbi joked to the comely scientist. She ignored his attempt at humor, recalling sometimes Asher liked displaying a childlike quality.

A tinny, loud voice came over the intercom. "Ladies and gentlemen, we regret this unfortunate delay. There's been an incident ahead, but nothing to be concerned about. Please remain in your seats. We expect the train shall be moving again shortly." The message was delivered in Russian, repeated in thickly accented English, and given for a third time in French. Many of the passengers were foreign tourists who needed extra calming.

The tinny voice continued, "As a gratuity we will be serving Western-style cold sandwiches. We have prepared a good selection. We have ham, ham and cheese, and we also have tuna and sour pickles. We will be serving complimentary peanuts, chips, and a selection of Russian chocolate bars. Please give your choices to your conductor, and enjoy. Thank you."

Vlad lifted his eyebrows at the irony of the chocolate.

"Maybe they'll pass out chunks of Little Man," Alina Vera said with dripping sarcasm. With a straight face Dimsky slipped her a small, decoratively wrapped piece of Alexander Nevsky chocolate. "I've been saving this." She flushed with his offer. "Sure, why not? Thanks."

"A piece of exquisite chocolate for you, Rabbi?" The colonel tried to refrain from smiling at his own little joke. Rabbi Titlebaum shared the humor.

"Not me. Thoughts of chocolate turn me off these days. I brought along a kilo of fresh seedless grapes and a tin of cashews, sent by Esther. However, if you find a soft drink in a bottle, that would be nice." Dimsky nodded and sauntered off, whistling.

After a while, Alina Vera said to Asher, "How do you keep yourself so calm?"

"Calm who's calm? I'm trying to meditate. Center myself, and listen to my breathing and heartbeat. Inhale deeply, then exhale. Repeat. We Jews meditate too, you know, not just Buddhists."

Dimsky unexpectedly came rushing back in haste. Beads of perspiration dotted his forehead. He paused to catch breath. "The train's been halted to bring aboard a special passenger," he announced.

Before questions could be asked the doors leading to the next car creaked, and opened wide. A snap of frigid air accompanied a young woman hurriedly ushered inside. A uniformed policeman flanked her on one side, a train conductor at the other. Her shoulders were shivering, and a thin blanket was wrapped around them. Her straw-blond hair was unkempt, long wet strands pressed against the sides of her face, her thin lips blue and trembling. A few of the passengers waiting in line for sandwiches were gruffly jostled and bulldozed aside to create an open path.

"Please keep moving and clear the aisle," implored the policeman. Again Dimsky interfered. He stood stiffly, a menacing presence blocking the way; again he flashed official identification.

The policeman quickly snapped to attention, saluting. "Sir, this woman has been rescued from extreme harm, and escorted to the train for her safety," he informed.

"What happened to her?"

"It appears an attempted kidnapping was underway, Colonel. Luckily, local police were stationed nearby and saved her before she could be bundled off."

The girl had large expressive blue eyes, wetly bloodshot. Her fresh pretty face was daubed with grime, tears and mascara. Her toned body shook with an anxious reaction she couldn't suppress. She greedily accepted the cup of hot coffee Colonel Dimsky ordered a conductor to give her.

"She'll be safer remaining with us," he instructed the policeman. "We're aboard tonight on official Kremlin business, and we'll take over from here. On my authority, this woman is to be considered under official government custody, understand? I commend you both for admirable duty. Sit her gently down over there and provide more dry blankets." He gestured toward a nearby double seat. The policeman and conductor respectfully settled her, saluted smartly and departed.

The girl shut her eyes and sipped. She pushed blond, disheveled hair aside with a quick gesture, ingesting the drink, and feeling its warmth. Something was inexplicably familiar about her, Vlad thought, as he observed. Do I know her from somewhere? Have we crossed paths?

"You're most kind," she said as they made her comfortable with a fresh blanket.

"Are you hungry, dear? Would you like something to eat?" the rabbi asked.

"No, thank you. I don't feel very well—" her eyelids fluttered, then she fainted. In an instant both the rabbi and Vlad kneeled by her side. Asher felt her pulse. Ever prepared for an emergency, he quickly pulled smelling salts from his knapsack and waved them under her nose. The ammonia and eucalyptus oil worked. She stirred and regained her senses, looking around with doe-like wide eyes.

"You're going to be all right. You're in safe hands, I assure you. You're aboard the *Rossiya*, travelling from Omsk to Moscow. You can rest as long as you wish. When you're feeling better perhaps you'll share what happened."

She slowly sat up and cleared a parched throat, coming out of her fog. "Forgive me. You're so kind, all of you. You have no idea how thankful I am. We—we were in my car, the two of us, lost, driving along some wicked, black, winding road, looking carefully for directions to the main highway. I don't know how we became so lost. We had to drive slowly because the road was narrow and bad. Suddenly our car was surrounded. These ghastly individuals were standing together, huddled over the road. They yelled at us. One of them stepped in front of my car and I hit the brakes. He fell. I was afraid I'd hurt him. Several of these crazy men started shouting at us. I don't know what. A few were carrying torches. They were plain country folk, dressed in sheepskin hats and fur vests. I have no idea what they wanted. I think I started screaming when they banged fists on the hood. Then they hit the car with sticks and pipes. I tried to step on the gas. They broke the windows, and the next thing I knew I was being pulled from the car together with my manager, Ilya. They yanked me one-way, Ilya another. She shouted but I couldn't hear, and don't know what happened. These barbarians shoved me to the ground. A few taunted, calling me names; a capitalist, a greedy swine, a whoring slut…" Her voice cracked and she wept with shudders. Those listening looked down with dismay.

After sipping more, she quietly continued. "I begged them, please, please, let me go. They refused. They laughed. I'm on my way to the Moscow Spring Invitational, I said. I implored them to show mercy. I offered them the money in my purse. They weren't interested. I tried to make them listen but they didn't hear a word I said. Then came threats. One said he'd beat me to teach me a lesson. They laughed. Another said, no, I'd be more valuable if they took me to some hiding place, kept me with a ransom on my head. The brutes listened to that man. He seemed to be a leader. I cried and pleaded. I swore I'd pay a lot of cash if they set me free. I said they could have all my tournament money just to let me and my friend go. 'Shut up!' someone said, and pushed my face into the mud and told me to eat it. Dirt was forced into my mouth. I spit it out. A moment later I was pulled away and dragged. I fought as hard as I could, but I was exhausted and almost passed out. The next thing I heard was a loud siren. The police, it was the police. Some of the thugs ran. There was screaming and shouting, and loud noises like gunshots. It was so dark I couldn't tell what was going on. The next thing I remember the police were lifting me up, and I was free. They drove me to this train. I still don't know what those horrible men did with my manager."

"We'll deal harshly with that cannon fodder," Dimsky vowed.

Vlad's mouth hung open. "Wait…I *have* seen you before!" he blurted. "I *do* know who you are. You're Anya Andropova, the tennis professional." Everyone stared. It was a well-known name in the world of professional sport.

She took notice and lifted her face. "Yes, I'm Anya. My manager and I were on our way to the Spring Invitational in Moscow. My preliminary match is scheduled for the day after tomorrow. We were planning on driving all night. I was going to spend tomorrow at practice…" She started crying again, head lowered, her shoulders quaking.

Rabbi Titlebaum kneeled before her on one knee and looked straight into her dispirited eyes. "Anushka," he said, using a diminutive, "listen to me carefully. This is very important. These brutes, this gang of lowlifes, try to recall the things they shouted. We need to know their motives. It's imperative to learn all we can."

Nodding, Anya said, "I understand." She thought long and hard, her child-like face streaked with drying tears. "Most of them were sober, I think. They yelled slogans about citizens' rights, injustices to the proletariat. The leader called for a revolt, things like that. It's all a blur, the shouting and the fire, the shadows. One of the men held a flag of some kind, waving it and shouting orders. I saw it clearly. It was a red flag with the hammer and sickle—you know what I mean, the old Soviet flag."

"The USSR Communist flag, Anushka? Is that what they were waving and claiming to fight for?"

She nodded emphatically. "That's right, it was the old USSR flag. I recognized it. The Communists. We learned about the old regime in school, the way things used to be before I was born. And this beastly man who egged them on, giving orders, demanding they take some old wagon and burn it, setting it on fire across the railroad tracks. I saw him standing and staring while the flames grew higher. He was entranced like a crazy man." She shuddered.

Vlad and the rabbi exchanged probing glances. "Thank you, Anushka, you've told us what we need to know. Rest now, little one. You're safe. My friends and I are government officials. You're aboard the midnight train to Moscow, and we'll be arriving at our destination by morning."

"We'll need to question her further," said Colonel Dimsky. "Have her placed in quarantine."

The rabbi regarded him with a sharp, abraded glance. Alina Vera put a finger to her lips. The girl was frightened enough, couldn't Dimsky see that?

"Don't be scared, Anya," she said. "We'll take good care of you, you have my word. If you wish, you can remain with me at my home in Moscow until you're feeling better. Take a nice hot bath, sleep in a comfortable bed with down pillows." She introduced herself. One by one the others did as well.

Dimsky's smartphone rang. He'd regained a strong signal. "Yes?" He stood motionless, listening to the voice at the other end. "*Da,*" he repeated, then quickly put the phone away. "Anya Andropova's version of events is confirmed," he said. "There's an outlying village not far from here. It's named, Gorki. A mob was assembled under the auspices of an unknown firebrand. The leader exhorted them to anger, and they lost control and burned several vehicles. They dragged an old hay-wagon over the railroad crossing, also setting it on fire. Police were called and order restored after a brief scuffle. Most of the criminals were captured, but it's reported that the man inciting them managed to flee. Roadblocks have been set up along all routes. The suspects being held in local custody will be arraigned before a magistrate in the morning. Meanwhile, they're under lock and key in isolation."

Vlad regarded his associates one by one; they grasped the alarming meaning as if of a single mind.

Scant days ago, what was impossible became implausible. Next, the implausible turned possible. The possible had become likely. Now what became likely turned to fact. The carefully planted seeds of insurrection were sprouting.

7.

"**W**elcome home, Sport," said Floyd Dingus, grinning from ear to ear. A Chicago Cubs baseball cap dangled from his hand, he wore another prized Hawaiian shirt. Beside him stood a stern paramilitary policeman with a holstered handgun at his side, a uniformed member of the feared Internal Affairs Service.

The Kazansky Train Station was noisy and busy. Loudspeakers blared arrivals and departures. Eagle-eyed, plain-clothed security police mingled amid scurrying passengers.

"What on earth are you doing here?" a mystified Vlad said, lugging his suitcase. "I thought you were in Omsk."

The American beamed sheepishly. "Well, you know how it goes. My embassy got word of some funny business up here, so they requisitioned a private plane to bring me back. Then I heard your train trip was delayed by some kind of trouble."

Vlad hid his astonishment at discovering Floyd Dingus reached Moscow long before they did. "How did you know we'd be on this train?"

Floyd dodged a direct answer. "You rode on the famous Trans-Siberian, huh? Sure wish I'd get a chance. Who'd want to pass up an opportunity like that? Yarns are still written about this extraordinary train. Anyway, it only took a little straightforward arithmetic to figure out when you'd arrive. Say, Vlad, I heard something about the hoi polloi getting pretty unruly and out of control out in the countryside. What was that bonfire on the tracks all about?"

"Our trip was extremely tiring. I'm exhausted." Now it was Vlad handily ignoring Floyd's question. This was neither the time nor the place. "Forgive me, but I'm going straight home to sleep."

"You do look pretty bad, Sport. Look, I have a car waiting outside. Come with me, I'll bring you right to your door." He glanced around. "Where are your friends?"

Boris, along with several plainclothes security agents, remained unseen amid the crowd. He greeted Rabbi Titlebaum and the others, quietly whisking them out of sight. Vlad knew it was now up to him to keep Floyd Dingus occupied. Debriefing wouldn't be until tomorrow. It was decided Anya Andropova would stay at Alina Vera's flat for the time being. Vlad handled a press release for public consumption saying that due to a bad sinus infection she was forced to bow out of the Moscow Invitational. She'd be questioned separately.

After the ride from the station Vlad invited Floyd to come in.

"Sweet!" Floyd said, glimpsing the spacious parlor. It was a large flat, overlooking a tree-lined street, well furnished with antiques and collectables, Scandinavian rugs, a variety of pastoral watercolors complementing lightly painted walls. "Your home is swell."

"We were very lucky to find this residence for sale. Our neighborhood is highly sought after and not many flats come on the market."

"Well, I sure like it." Floyd peered from the window at a car moving slowly amid the gardened, manicured route. "Bet this place set you back plenty."

"It cost enough. My wife fell in love with the area. It's really an ideal neighborhood, close to parks and shopping, but quiet and serene. A good place to raise children." A small ragdoll was lying on a chair; Vlad felt a flush of emotion, not knowing how he'd handle this separation. He walked to his small bar, his back to the American. "What will you drink? Scotch, brandy, American whiskey?"

"A small glass of vodka would do fine, thank you." Floyd lightly sat himself down on a plush velvet settee, feeling the quality fabric. "You have wonderful taste in furniture, Vlad. I'm envious. If you ever came to D.C. and looked at my messy place you'd collapse. But I do have a good autograph collection of curling champions. It's my favorite sport."

Vlad smiled without commenting and poured two glasses, handing one to the American. "If I do ever get to Washington I'll certainly look you up. Here, this one's for you." He lifted his glass. "To friendship."

"A long friendship, I hope." They downed their drinks. Floyd exhaled. "Whew, Vlad, this damn stuff's on fire. Where's it from?"

"As a matter of fact, it's vodka made in America."

Floyd Dingus laughed heartily. He slapped a hand on his knee. "Well, that's something! Here I am finally seeing Russia, mingling with honcho locals, and what do I find? American vodka. The world sure can be funny."

"That's for certain." Vlad relaxed in a recliner opposite. "I'm sorry you never received official permission for that tour of the Alexander Nevsky. It couldn't be helped. We did try. I hope your superiors aren't disappointed."

"They'll just have to deal with it." Floyd toyed with his glass. "By the way, maybe you'd know where I could get my hands on a good English-language translation of Marx's *Communist Manifesto*?" His smile was expansive.

The question was unexpected and Vlad pretended not to be taken by surprise. "You can use my laptop to look online. I'm sure it's readily obtainable in Moscow. Heaven knows, I don't keep or want a copy of it in Russian, English, or any other language."

"You were never a communist, Vlad? I guess not, you're probably too young. Maybe you're parents were."

"Back then it was prudent to endure the Collective, especially if you hoped for a good career, needed a decent place to live, and food to feed your family."

"I've read that Russia's had some pretty rough guys for leaders over the years. Stalin, Brezhnev, Lenin…."

"You had to be a tough guy to remain in power. Our Revolution wasn't like the American Revolution. We still don't know how many people perished. And matters substantially worsened after Stalin took control. Labor camps sprouted, overwhelmed with political prisoners, gulags across Siberia. Millions vanished and died during those atrocious years. But the Party assured jobs for everyone, pensions, and free medical care—at least for those who didn't cause trouble. There are many Russians who remain nostalgic for the old, discredited Soviet regime, despite its horrors."

"For sure Stalin was the worst, a savage, murderous paranoid. But from what I've heard Lenin also was a badass."

"He was. He formed the first Bolshevik government, and made endless promises to the people. But enemies lurked everywhere, and some faction or other was always trying to kill him. They almost succeeded when he was shot and nearly assassinated. He didn't live much longer, anyway. Shall I pour another drink, Floyd?" He lifted himself, reached for the bottle.

"I guess a small one won't hurt." Floyd winked. "You know, I'd still like to give you one of my Hawaiian shirts as a gift. I wish you'd reconsider."

Vlad pictured himself attired in one of the outrageously gaudy shirts. "I appreciate the offer, but again, no thank you. I'm legally forbidden to accept, remember? Anyway, why do you want to read *The Communist Manifesto*?"

Floyd leisurely nursed his drink. He leaned back, crossed his legs and stifled a yawn seeming to settle more deeply into the chair. "Well, the big kahunas at Ag asked me to do some brushing up. They don't think my knowledge of Russia is sufficient, and they're probably right. Heck, I didn't ask for this assignment, Vlad. Sure, it's nice meeting you and other good folks like your friend the pretty scientist, but I'm no expert in Russian affairs. Who's kidding whom? I never even ate caviar. So what do I know about this nasty revolution business, or Lenin and those boys?" He reflected. "Although I did once go see this humongous 16-foot monster Lenin statue they shipped to Seattle. It's on display in the street and a lot of people there sure aren't happy about it."

Why was Floyd repeatedly mentioning Lenin's name, Vlad wondered. What was this seemingly guileless, untainted American really up to? Surely, he couldn't be the jejune bumbler he outwardly portrayed. "*The Manifesto* is boring reading, Floyd. However, if you like, I can have a copy sent to your hotel. One of my aides will dig one up, if it's important."

"That's not necessary. I'll just call the Embassy and tell them to find one, pronto. The Ag people in Washington have given me lots of latitude here. I can pretty much write my own ticket, stay as long as I need, do whatever I need to do. This assignment must be more important than I realized. Between you and me, I was speechless when they arranged a chartered plane for me at Omsk. I was just getting a hang for the place, too. Until this jaunt I'd never even heard of Omsk." He stared into his shot glass and shook his head. "Yeah, life sure can be funny. But as the wise man said, wherever you go, there you are." He downed the last of his drink, stood up and stretched. "I've kept you awake and I apologize. I didn't mean to be rude. You've got sagging bags under your eyes, and I see you're exhausted. So I'm just going to slip back downstairs. Don't worry about me. I'll get an embassy car to pick me up." In the hall entry he noticed several portrait photographs on the wall. "Are those your daughters? Pretty girls."

"They are, thank you. Katya and Aleksandra are the lights of my life." He felt a tightening knot in his gut as he escorted Floyd to the door. He wished his girls were with him now. Petersburg suddenly seemed so far away.

"By the way, my close friends call me, Vova. It's a nickname. Please feel free to use it."

"Thank you, Sport. I will." They shook hands firmly. "I'm sure we'll have the pleasure of seeing each other again soon, Floyd."

Floyd Dingus smiled his toothy smile. "You bet."

Boris Sokolov stood at the window, hands clasped behind his back. The tree-lined cobblestone streets of the old city of Moscow majestically splayed out before him. He treasured the old city and its ancient ways. The grand palaces and churches of the Kremlin were being encroached by taller and taller skyscrapers stippling the horizon. Surviving artifacts of ancient Moscow were becoming rarer, replaced now by a hodgepodge of ultramodern office towers, multinational corporation headquarters, and outrageously expensive highrise condominiums. The Moscow of his youth had all but vanished, reshaped into a neoteric mega-metropolis blend of London, Paris and New York, to which he felt deep antipathy.

"I suppose you don't need me to inform you that our prime minister isn't happy," he said gruffly. An antique clock on the wall ticked softly, a classic heirloom he cherished.

"We did everything specifically as you instructed," Alina Vera replied, unwilling to accept undue blame.

"The P.M.'s not placing responsibility personally on me or you. He's increasingly upset with this misbegotten farce—especially this latest round. He just wants the mess to go away, and it won't." He turned on his heels and looked at the group. "So this tennis star, Anya Andropova, tell me her story."

Vlad had done a careful background check. "She's well known and well-liked as a professional. She's barely nineteen, began playing when she was five, taught by her stepfather. She quickly gained attention as becoming a promising athlete. Anya's a highly energetic girl, competitive, and has good stamina. She's known for taking her game seriously. She's extremely determined, and practices endlessly in preparation for Grand Slam tournaments. The word is she has excellent concentration, and stands to win lots of trophies and make lots of money. Some pros believe she's got real potential, and maybe could elevate Russia's current lackluster position in the competitive world of professional tennis."

"Do you think I care a tinker's damn if she can play tennis?" Boris grumbled through cigar smoke. "I don't hang around locker rooms, and couldn't care less how many matches she's won, singles or doubles, or how many sponsors she signs with. My concerns are simple. I want to know what the hell is going on? Exactly who is this other woman traveling with Anya, this Ilya Evgeny, and how the hell does she fit into this?"

"She's been Anya Andropova's manager for the past few years," said Dimsky, skimming notes. "Reputedly she's a very strong-willed, ambitious woman, also known for high aspirations within Moscow society circles. My operatives believe the drunken riff-raff snatched her kicking and screaming. Likely she's been hauled to a safe house, held hostage, as far as we're aware. I expect Anya will soon receive ransom demands. But from what I'm told her captors will have hell to pay preventing Ilya Evgeny from escaping."

Fingertips to his temples, Boris rolled his eyes. "Colonel, how dated is your information? Ilya Evgeny *escaping*? Has your brain frozen? Subsequent intelligence from Gorki claims Ilya Evgeny has become an operative *for* Lenin—and maybe has been one all along. Possibly even a plant placed by Sunavich. Evgeny is a shady character with a questionable past, a provocateur, and maybe a willing conspirator. Now let me really blow your socks off: She's more than likely become Lenin's constant companion, his consort."

"Lenin wants a woman?" Dimsky put a hand to his mouth.

"Do I have to spell it out, Colonel? If he's really a living man, he's acquired a man's natural desires. If it's true that they're lovers, it puts events in a very different light. We may indeed have a wide conspiracy on our hands. But I digress." Face reddened, nostrils flaring, Boris struggled to keep a semblance of aplomb amid this litany of woes. "My updated report indicates not only isn't this gang isn't holding Evgeny against her will, she may well be an enthusiastic participant. She's reputedly merciless in a self-serving quest for fame and fortune. An ambitious woman indeed! She likely recognizes her prize as a potential power-broker, Russia's warrior and savior, not some skuzzy, ragamuffin hothead. She envisions great opportunities coming her way. A clever girl can go far as the woman standing beside a great revolutionary."

The rabbi, quietly listening, suddenly grew more attentive. "Slow down, and watch your blood pressure. This is significant. Important news. A huge turn of events, possibly containing considerable implications for us."

"Oh?"

Asher leaned forward, speaking calmly in a lowered voice. "Listen to me, if this woman is bedding Lenin, their sexual encounters can prove extremely valuable."

"How?" said Dimsky. "Selling online X-rated photos?"

"Pipe down, Colonel," rasped Boris. "Let the rabbi finish."

"I'll explain the simplest way I can," Asher said. "If Evgeny and Lenin are copulating, there'll be substantial amounts of his DNA we can systematically catalog, so-called 'control switches', promoters, enhancers and repressors, as well as suites of genes designed to act in a tractable and predictable manner..."

"Meaning?"

"Meaning, if we can obtain a single sample for analysis, his sperm could resolve our difficulty in identifying Sunavich's categorical life force formulae. Obviously this is an inspired leap for us in understanding it." He punched a fist into his open palm. "You see, within Lenin's semen lies the empirical evidence we're lacking. I urgently require a set of samples for study, cardinal features I can deconstruct for reduction of complexity, and then reconstruct on a subcellular level. In short, I want as much sperm as we can locate. Which also means it's in our interest for him to ejaculate as frequently as possible."

"He's capable of ejaculating?" said Vlad.

Asher spoke with enthused dynamism. "Of course! He's a fully living, if not quite thoroughly human entity, created far beyond any current modest genetic engineering. Remember when the Americans experimented with salmon? They produced exquisitely engineered duplicates, true masterpieces of nature. This prototype is likewise such an exquisitely engineered duplicate, complete with gonadotropic hormones produced by the anterior pituitary. I believe it likely his healthy gonads are capable of manufacturing quality seminal fluid. Prime spermatozoa. Needless to add, Ilya Evgeny possesses a female's potential to regularly drain his testicles, and while so doing perhaps exhaust his life force."

"His own sperm will betray him," Alina Vera came to understand.

The rabbi stood in thought, scratching his beard. "Most interesting, isn't it? Of secondary noteworthiness is the question whether Lenin is capable of impregnating a woman. Spawning his own duplication would be another scientific triumph, wouldn't it? Certainly it presents disrespect for nature's law; nevertheless it's fascinating speculation for debate. Without drawing moral conclusions, we can't learn anything definitive before acquiring a superior specimen and running a complete sequence of tests."

Asher turned to Dimsky, a tiny muscle pulsing at the side of his face. "Colonel, I request you to alert all principals of our scientific team. Instruct them to prepare for analysis as quickly as we can obtain specimens." Next he looked at the pleasing but moody scientist. "Dr. Galina, do you concur with my hypothesis? What's your professional opinion?"

"Let's hope Boris is right and she's fucking him."

Vlad winced.

"Well and good," said Dimsky. "But we're blindsided. Where's this protozoan life form holding up? It's tough finding something when you don't know what you're looking for."

"My good Colonel, learning definite whereabouts isn't necessary. They could have made love on a steaming dunghill. We only need establish where they were. Outside the body ejaculated semen survives mere minutes up to a few hours. If Internal Security can calibrate his hideaway, successfully obtain a sample and hurry it to a controlled atmosphere, we can provide it with far longer life—maybe several days' worth under proper conditions. A few well-timed sheet swabs can contribute everything we need. Every minute counts, Colonel."

This tidbit buoyed Boris' spirits. "I like it! It has a strange poetic justice—utilizing his body fluids against him. You may be as mad as Sunavich, but your strategy is masterful. Sheer ingenuity. Let's get cracking, Colonel. Who's our primary man at Omsk, Rimsky-Kimsky? Get in touch immediately, with instructions regarding exactly what the rabbi requires." Again he looked to Alina Vera. "Meanwhile, your directive is to befriend our innocent star tennis player, and learn as much as possible regarding Ilya Evgeny. Find out her habits, likes and dislikes, what kind of men she's attracted to, what foods she enjoys, what clothes she shops for, the perfume she prefers, music she listens to, anything and everything."

"And me?" asked Vlad.

"Let me put it delicately, Petrovsky. Let's say you'll show an earnest interest in this girl. Flirt and be amorous if you find it necessary. But find out whatever you can."

Colonel Dimsky adeptly keyed numbers into his smartphone. The rabbi scribbled a memo. Vlad and Alina Vera exchanged brief glances, and Boris made an attentive note that the shared look between his colleagues lingered a bit longer than it normally should.

"Is Anya Andropova still at your flat?" Boris asked.

"She was asleep when I left. By now she's probably up, online, blasting alternative rock music. She realizes she can't go anywhere. Plainclothes police are standing vigil outside. They'll block any exit the moment she tries leaving."

"Good. Well then, Vova, I suggest you accompany Alina Vera and get to work."

Vlad felt ill at ease with Boris's instruction; he didn't approve of being placed in such an awkward position, nor did Alina Vera appreciate her own role. For now, though, they'd have to go along; there wasn't any choice. Anya Andropova and Ilya Evgeny were tightly bound together, and what affected one would surely affect the other.

8.

"Is that you, Petrovsky?" Vlad stirred from his slumber. He recognized the voice from Moscow. It was a well-known television producer from Channel One's nightly news program. He scratched his head trying to shake himself awake.

"Nadia, is that you?"

"Of course it's me. Are you sleeping? What are you doing sleeping? They told us you were incommunicado, so busy with top classified security business you didn't have a moment to spare for old friends. But never mind that official rot, Petrovsky. I want you to listen and take a few notes."

"Nadia, I'm officially removed from Jubilee business, remember? It would be better to contact one of my deputies—"

"Bullshit. I need *you*, Vova. Look, I have no idea what they have you involved in. Rumors say you're embroiled in an effort to catch this lunatic traipsing around Russia calling himself Lenin. Plus some babble about a real rebellion..."

"I can't discuss any of these things, Nadia. You know that." He sat up, tried to stretch, but the pain in his shoulder hurt like hell.

"Alright, boss man. I won't pump you for info. Hear me out though, okay? There's this woman I've met. She calls herself a psychic. A seer. She's been pestering the network day and night for more than a week demanding access to me. I have no idea how she found out who I am, but she buttonholed me the other night as I was leaving the studio. She claims to have valuable information she can only share with you, and perhaps your colleagues. I told her to tell it to me, and that I'd pass it along. She blurted some muddled nonsense regarding chocolate, scientists, and all sorts of bizarre doings. She clung to my sleeve. I told her to get away from me, that whatever her problem was she should take it up with the police, and if she didn't get satisfaction there she could try contacting some local press organizations."

Vlad held the phone closer to his ear. "I have no time for this. Sorry, but I have to go."

"Don't hang up! Please, Vova. There's more. I'm well attuned to this type of trivial nonsense, but I've come to believe this woman may know things. She was waiting outside for me again late last night, pleading, 'Tell your friend he's in danger.' I told her to go away or I'd have her arrested. She looked at me with plaintive eyes. 'All right, I won't bother you anymore. But please warn Vladimir.' I stopped in my tracks. I asked her whom she was referring to, and told her I didn't know which 'Vladimir' she meant. She shook her head. 'You won't listen either, will you?' she said. 'But maybe *he* will. The one called Vladimir is surrounded by danger. Imminent danger coming from the chocolate factory. Some mustn't be trusted. I saw him in my vision, surrounded by scientists and spies and something else I can't explain.'" Nadia bit her lip. "This is going to sound even crazier, Vova. She said next, 'in my vision I saw a dead man sucking at the bosom of a woman whose breast fed him poison. But the poison didn't kill this man; it was bringing him back to life, coursing through his veins.' I realize she sounds like a crackpot, Vova, but I believe she's sincere. Her message rings powerful and heartfelt. She absolutely believes every word, I'm sure. And there's something hypnotic about her eyes…"

He listened. Nadia Ivanova was a valued friend and colleague for many years, and he was unaccustomed to hear her sounding at her wits' end. He sat stunned. Nadia wasn't the type to parlay a story or make frivolous middle-of-night phone calls. She was a highly esteemed, respected television producer with credentials and awards dating back many years. These events obviously troubled her greatly. The tale this seer imparted to Nadia contained scraps information no one outside of his team could possibly know. *Chocolate factory, scientists…*Evaluating it he felt goose bumps, and in his mind's eye he drew the portrait of a dead man sucking at the poisonous bosom of an unknown woman. "All right, Nadia. Tell me who she is."

"She calls herself, Madam Zaza. She looks like a hot-blooded gypsy, but she's not. I admit she has me spooked. I did a little background checking. It's so strange. Maybe she's a nutcase, but she isn't dangerous, I'm certain. Jot this address; you won't have trouble finding her. She says she'll be waiting—expecting—you. This whole business scares me, Vova. I think she might know some things you need to hear. Nobody knows what to believe anymore, not with all this paranoid disturbance…we don't want to lose you. Be careful, Vova, please."

That was the end of the conversation. Vlad sat in place, rubbing at his shoulder. A psychic, a seer? *A dead man sucking poison at the bosom of a strange woman*...Boris would laugh him out of the room and off the team. So would Alina Vera. They all would. But he couldn't just ignore Nadia Ivanova's frenetic, pre dawn call.

He went into the bathroom and washed his face with cold water. How would this person have the slightest knowledge of anything regarding the Alexander Nevsky, he asked himself. Was it some sort of prank? Or could it be a setup? Chicanery from someone out to glean secret information? It made no sense.

Madam Zaza's address was in an older part of the city, an area highly desirable at one time, now faded and fallen on hard times. It wasn't too far away. He quickly decided that Nadia fully believed what she'd heard, and would never have phoned if she was not legitimately frightened. He decided to wait and not discuss this with anyone, at least yet.

"Send for gypsies," the old man cried jovially. The campfire was warm, the night air clammy cold.

A garrulous, senescent, skin-and-bones woman cackled as she spread emaciated hands over the flames. She embodied the rustiness and infirmity of advancing years. "Yes, where are they?" she mimicked. Her smile was like a small black hole, excluding a handful of decaying yellowed teeth. "You men keep sharp eyes on your purses. Gypsies are slippery thieves." Mirth and frolic encompassed the camp.

A neglected youth of about ten nervously approached the old man, a proletarian cap askew on his head, his head framed by straw-colored hair. He held an unfurled red flag in his hands. Holes in the soles of his shoes were covered with old newspaper. "What shall I do with this flag the strangers left?" he asked.

The old man regarded him with lifted bushy, glistening eyebrows. "Maybe it'll make a warm fleece for cold nights—unless you find me a warm woman, all the better." He stretched his blistered lips into a crooked smile. "But you'll learn these things soon enough, boy! We all lose our heads over pretty girls. Don't be bashful; every man's had his face slapped. A man's soul wants to carouse, don't it?" The baffled youth stood mum, dropping his eyes under the old man's squint. Haughty laughter ensued.

This ramshackle encampment of tents and blankets on the outskirts of town had remained entrenched for weeks beside the road. Surrounded by pale-hued skies and a dark forest of abounding trees, their tiny habitation was barely noticeable save for flickers emanating from the fire. This homeless coterie had not caused trouble, so for now local police hadn't found need or reason to relocate them. There were many such disorganized homeless encampments across the Motherland these days. This particular campsite was comprised of a group of about twenty, vagrants, veterans, jobless workers, men and women plus a handful of ragged children. There was little room for their sort in the New Russian Federation. Shoved aside, they were mostly harmless folk. Townspeople had designated them as drifters and derelicts, not to be paid attention to. But those of the camp felt themselves as liberated, free to greet life on its own terms. They'd throw dirt in the devil's eye, spit upon insufferable bourgeois morals and civility, defecate upon those middle classes who despised them and whom they despised. If God desired men to live in houses they'd be born provided with walls and a roof above. These semi-nomads regaled in freedom, lived by impulse, pursued carnal desires and quenched their appetites, dousing fears of death with indolence, indulgence and debauchery. When necessary they were compelled to beg while at other times they stole, occasionally lifting a tempting bourgeois purse or wallet. Yet other days they were forced to go without.

Along the nearby rock and pebble-strewn road a dilapidated wagon rolled sluggishly. Its aged driver sat hunched forward clutching the reins tightly, big hands thickly layered with calluses. The worn, dispirited mare plodded sullenly along, ears flat, neck outstretched. "Hey driver, where are you going?" the old man beside the fire shouted. He held up a dented tin can filled with a diluted swill made from the cheapest vodka. "Share a drink. C'mon, it's free."

"Thank you friends, but I can't linger," the driver declared. Bundled in a shabby greatcoat, its collar pulled high and tight to defend against wind, his steely eyes were delineated by thick eyebrows, roughened face leathery and spotted, a condition caused by endless and merciless frigid winters.

"Why the rush?" inquired another camp inhabitant, a wiry little man with curling gray nose hairs and a bulbous boil on his forehead.

"Important business takes me to town, friend," he said considering the matter. "If you're still awake when my work is done, and haven't devoured every last drop, I'll be happy to return and share the rest with you."

"Oh, what polished manners," the hoary woman babbled. "Maybe we'll hang him and maybe we should! He smells like hot vodka at your grandmother's funeral." With a movement of his hand the old man curtly cut her off. "What business could be so important on a cold night?" he inquired.

118

"Customers, friend. Some upper class gent with his lady. They'll pay up front, they said. I'm off to collect them by the old mill up the road. City folk, always in a hurry to some place or other before going somewhere else."

Sparks leaped from the fire's flames. "That poor stiff jointed trotter of yours is on her last legs," observed the old man, who as a youth worked as a groomer. "Give the poor beast a rest and new shoes. She looks worse for wear than you. Let the nag end life peacefully. Buy a taxi."

"Me buy a car? Can anyone see me driving a car? Ha! I don't have a license and my eyes aren't good. Besides, this old filly has shared many years with me. I couldn't part with her, friend. But blessings to you." He drove on with a good-natured wave, wagon wheels creaking and groaning, sinking along ruts on the road, horse's tail thrashing.

"And give the priest our regards," the old woman blathered, pointing an arthritic, nimble finger. "Tell him to stop yammering like a banshee! Remind him my curses always work, so he'd better watch it." She prattled with hilarity, sitting near the burning logs, surrounded by a collection of potions and charms.

As the wagon slipped into night's shadows, the drinking and levity among the little group continued unabated. The old man hunched closer to the fire, wrapping his broad chunky hands around the dented tin can. "Who'd travel on a night like this, eh? Better to stay among friends, and enjoy this life while you can, that's what I say."

Another gaunt hand reached out to him. "Give us a swallow, eh? Don't be a miser; share and share alike."

In the hilly distance, thunder rumbled over a clouded sky, followed moments later by a blinding flash of lightning.

"It sounds like canon fire," the old man muttered with a small shudder, recalling conscription days of long ago. He chuckled to himself. Days before he'd been told of the seething revolt. None of his companions believed it true, but he knew better. It was repeated in hushed tones in the village. They said the Bolsheviks had returned, come to toss out the bankrupting scum who raped both the land and people year after year. Here was the chance to settle old scores at last. Maybe regain his lost pension, reclaim the cozy room at his cramped boarding house. Maybe his wife would return, wherever that closed-fisted washerwoman had fled with her tattooed Tartar.

Widespread words of discontent had swelled quickly, propelled by basic human longings for dignity, justice, and the right to control one's own life. Others may have given up hope, but not him. The moneyed rich would pay the price and dance to a different tune. He took a swig and passed round his tin cup. Fire arose in his belly, and he said, "Drink to Comrade Lenin! Round up the wealthy bastards and shoot them." His thirsty friends nodded and drank greedily. The toothless old woman chortled.

Down the road behind the derelict mill, the wagoner adjusted his shabby sheepskin hat over untidy hair, patiently humming while waiting for his passengers. "The train station's a long way off, sir." He urged them to make haste.

"That doesn't matter," replied the well-dressed man. "Permit us a minute more." He slipped off amid nearby bushes.

The woman took crumpled paper money from her purse and with a surly gesture handed it to the wagon driver. He took the notes. "Don't touch me with your filthy hands," she reprimanded. Her complexion was fair, with striking cheekbones and narrow catlike eyes. Her skin was supple, hips wide, body muscular and limber. She was tall, taller than her companion, with generous breasts and long legs. Her temper was short. "Go on, take your pay."

The driver counted the cash nimbly and eagerly, trying to avoid staring at her ample bosom. The payment was a bit more than the arranged price, he saw. "Thank you, Madam. Holy blessings for you and to your husband. Please climb aboard and we'll leave. Pardon if my wagon is dirty. Since dawn I've been lugging milk cans and carting lumber."

"All right, just make the trip fast!" The woman disapproved, but turned her attention toward the darkness. She called out, "What's taking so long? We're finally ready to leave this cesspool."

A muffled reply responded from the bushes, "Wait a moment, will you? I'm not finished urinating."

"I can tell! I hear it. I think you pee too much, dearest. You really should consult a doctor when we reach our destination." She looked away. "Hurry as best you can. You're the one who said we mustn't be late."

"All right, don't badger me, woman."

She rolled her eyes and tapped an impatient foot.

At length the well-dressed man with a nearly bald palate trudged toward the waiting wagon. He finished zipping his pants hastily, saying, "You labor very hard, driver. You're a good man and believe me your toil hasn't gone unnoticed." He stumbled as he assisted his female companion up. The driver noticed she was more capable of climbing aboard than he was.

There was a foul, fetid odor in the rickety wagon, and she wrinkled her nose with disgust, and spat. "What's that hideous stink?"

"Forgive me, Madam. A bit of this morning's milk must have spilled and soured. I had no time to clean up before loading my lumber. But I keep a pile of rags in the corner, if you'd like to wipe the spill yourself. I deliver milk cans every day. I've been doing it for so many years I can't remember when I started. I bring it for my family, neighbors, and friends every morning, even on Sundays before church. My wife complains I work many hours for little pay, but I say work is what a man is born for. What good is a man without work? I may be poor but I'm honest, and nobody dare call me out as a liar." He proudly displayed sinewy, brawny arms.

"Enough jabberring," castigated the woman. "Button your lip, you churlish oaf."

"Oh no!" protested her friend. "Don't harangue him, dear. Permit the fellow his opportunity to speak his mind. His folk, the millions he represent are the essential soul of our sweet Motherland. Working from dawn to dusk, baking in the heat, and drowning in the rain. I'll update my old stump speech 'Concessions to Peasants', and that will make it clear for you. We sorely need these fine folk on our side. It's we who must bend to them. Worthy men like this driver make our revolution possible. They are the backbone of the land. Driver, please do continue your tale."

The nag tossed back her muzzle. "In truth, there isn't much more to tell, sir. Since I was a lad, I've worked to exhaustion with these strong arms of mine. I labored as a tree cutter, a gravedigger, then and a builder of roads. I've held many jobs, raised strong children. While my friends spent wages drunk at public houses, I kept my pay sewn in my shirt, the way my mother taught. It took a long time but I saved enough to purchase this very wagon and horse. Life is good when you're your own boss and no man dare stomp your face into the mud. This old mare and wagon, they've been good to me. Without them I wouldn't be able to earn my living."

"Now do you see, Ilya? Listen to his story. Appreciate his strenuous labor. This is exactly what I've been trying to say! Solid, strong, unyielding, yet containing so much warmth and decency despite life's merciless struggles. What

121

marvelous endurance!" A tear rolled down his cheek. "They are the secret ingredients of our army. If I am not to be their champion, who shall be?"

She gnashed her teeth, doing a slow burn, staring straight ahead, not uttering a word. The wagon continued painstakingly onward. "Just get us to the train station quickly, you old bandit," she finally lashed. "You don't fool me."

Her companion on the slat bench lifted his small suitcase and several books and placed them in his lap. He took a lengthy deep breath. "Oh, how fond I am of this bucolic countryside. How I adore simple country folk, how much pleasure we glean from their company. And how sick I am of bogus intellectuals, predatory politicians, and thieving landlords. I long for the day we resume the Collective. Drive on, good fellow, and don't be faint of heart. A new dawn is arising." He cleaned his spectacles, smiling fully, pleased with his proclamation.

The driver blew his nose into a worn handkerchief, cracking his whip. The shabby, drooping mare clapped forward into the night as quickly as the overworked animal could manage.

The radio alarm rang loudly. Alina Vera stirred in her bed, struggling to open her eyes and glance at the clock. "Oh, shit."

Sluggishly she composed herself, touched the walls as she made her way to the shower. She ran the water as hot as she could bear. Before grinding coffee she peeked inside the guest bedroom. Anya Andropova lay in a sound sleep. The tennis star was sprawled across the bed lightly snoring; one arm this way, one arm that, one leg this way, one leg that. Alina Vera closed the door. She shuffled into the sunlit kitchen.

Her spacious flat originally had belonged to her grandmother, Yulia, and the plaster walls were adorned with Yulia's framed black and white photographs, taken many decades before. Yulia when she was a child, riding her bicycle, posing with her parents and siblings. Alina Vera fondly remembered her grandmother. She had adored the spry perfumed lady. The flat remained in the family's possession after Yulia's death, and Alina Vera was grateful to learn it was available for use during her first years of study in Moscow. After bitter, acrimonious disagreement, she eventually managed to buy out her siblings' shares, and now finally owned the fashionable apartment outright. She wished nothing more than to remain in Moscow, away from the hellish tour of duty she'd agreed to in Omsk. The phone rang just as she was opening a vitamin bottle. "Doctor Galina," she said groggily into the receiver.

"Good, you're awake. I trust I didn't arouse you from your beauty sleep?"

"Good morning, *Tovarich*, Comrade Boris." She chided.

"And how is our little tennis player this morning? Is she well? Does she need anything?"

"You're more interested in Anya's well-being than mine?"

Boris crowed approvingly. "Of course. Anya Andropova is far more valuable for us than you. But then I digress..."

"Why are you calling? Our meeting is already scheduled for ten."

"Meetings take place when I decide," he corrected. "As a matter of fact, I'd like you to rouse our little pumpkin right away and have her accompany you."

"Oh? Is Anya now a part of the team?" Her sarcasm was ignored. Alina Vera drummed fingernails on the counter while the coffee brewed. The aroma was rich and strong.

"A car will be arriving as usual. Please be ready with our little tennis star in half an hour. I appreciate punctuality."

"Whatever you say, Comrade." She hung up the phone.

Laptop held close, Vlad hurried into the conference room. A pale sun was shining. He seated himself quietly. From the windows he could see the rising skyscrapers complimenting Moscow's skyline; but within these thick walls many highly placed government leaders huddled pensively, aware this revolution in miniature was a ticking time bomb. Vlad noticed Anya Andropova's early presence at the meeting and was surprised.

"It's Friday, the Jewish Sabbath starts tonight," Rabbi Titlebaum informed. "So please allow from sundown tonight until after sundown tomorrow I won't be available. I'll be at synagogue."

Boris nodded, keeping his promise. He'd spent the entire night poring over latest reports. Cyber activists across the blogosphere were appealing for huge protests to take to the streets. "There's a great deal of ground to cover this morning," He announced, thumbing through a folder. "And, Anya, I wish to personally thank you for joining us this morning."

"I'll be glad to help if there's anything for me to help with." Anya remained puzzled as to why she'd been summoned.

A low-level clerk entered, carrying a large tray with coffee, tea, and a plate piled high with sweet butter rolls and jam. Dimsky greedily helped himself with a heap of hot buns and butter.

Boris regarded him askance. "I trust you'll leave a little for everyone else, Colonel? Thank you. Now let's get on with business." He clasped his hands, interlacing his fingers. "There's more news from the vicinity of Gorki, where Anya was nearly abducted. Local intelligence reports indicate the mob leader may have crossed the porous frontier from Ukraine into Belarus." Everyone listened intently.

"A bureau policewoman from that area reported that a man and a woman fitting the exact descriptions of Ilya Evgeny and our prime suspect were seen at a municipal train station. He'd apparently just delivered a short lecture on 'Labor Discipline' to a bunch of villagers. According to the report, the would-be despot appeared to be inebriated. The policewoman justly demanded he produce his identity papers. At that point she was accosted, and prevented from doing her job by the suspect's companion who quickly stood between them. She reputedly whacked the policewoman with a heavy handbag, knocking her off her feet, loosening a tooth. Amid the frenzy and ensuing melee the suspects fled. This leads me to believe our secondary suspect, Ilya Evgeny, is deeply implicated, perhaps playing a central role."

Anya Andropova emblazoned dogged defiance at the idea of it. Offended, she shifted uncomfortably, and said, "What has Ilya got to do with any of this crazy stuff? Why would she evade the police? We were pulled from my car *together*. I watched her get *dragged* away."

"Anushka," the rabbi gently said, "don't be upset. The truth of the matter is somehow Ilya has fallen in with these reprehensible people."

"No way! That's not possible! Ilya would never do anything like that. She doesn't come from that sort of low class ruffian home. She's a quality woman from a respectable family. Good, church-going people. Her sister is well liked among the most respected circles. In fact, her uncle is even a monk, recently delegated on a special mission to join a sacred monastery in Novosibirsk."

"*Hello!*" repudiated Alina Vera. "The church hurried the ascetic slob to Siberia to keep him far from public scrutiny. For your information, Ilya's uncle was caught up in a flagrant scandal that included underage girls, sex, and drugs. It received major headlines in the press for weeks. It's all out there on the Internet, Anya. Wisely, to save themselves from too many questions, the church shuffled him off to the most remote place to minimize damage to their reputation."

"That isn't true! Those stories claiming he hid two young girls in his rooms and impregnated them are horrible lies. Fabrications meant to ruin his lifework. He was framed, and said he's going to sue the papers for every ruble they've got. He told me so himself before leaving Moscow." The girl's nostrils flared. "And he assured both Ilya and me he's gone on this retreat solely for prolonged prayer and guidance, and to beg forgiveness for his rotten tormentors."

"Did you think he was entertaining socialites and philanthropists in his room? Dear Anya, when someone is shipped off to a dismal place like Novosibirsk it's not an assignment you requested. It's an exile, plain and simple. Banishment. Tantamount to an admission of guilt." Alina Vera darted her eyes, quickly adding, "The colonel has obtained all pertinent files regarding the incidents of this case, if you're interested in reading them."

"I can show you an explicit video shot in Super High Def.," offered Dimsky. "Mother Volga! He convinced himself he possessed mysterious Rasputin-like abilities. When the police broke into his secret chamber I'm sure he was disappointed to discover he didn't. The underage girls tattled on him immediately. And the file photo of him in handcuffs isn't flattering."

Anya looked mortified.

"I was stationed at Novosibirsk for a time," Dimsky added, shivering at the memory. "I don't suppose you've ever been invited to play tennis there? You'd leave the court with icicles hanging from your nose."

Tears outlined the corners of the tennis star's eyes. She pushed curls from her face. "Why is everyone constantly so down on Ilya? Anyway, what has her uncle's problem got to do with her? Ilya's my manager, not my sister. I don't live with her. Alina Vera, you're always prodding me to discuss my private life. Why? And yesterday when Vlad came over he also kept asking questions. Personal questions. I appreciate you all helping rescue me, and I do want to be a help to you, too. But what else can I say that I've not already said?"

Boris tried to be tactful. "It may appear unfair, Anya, I understand. I believe we all understand. But sometimes it can't be helped. For example, while you're playing an opponent on the court, even though off court that person may be a good friend, during the match they become a savage rival, no? You go after them mercilessly to win, don't you?" He waited to let Anya take it all in. "No one's suggesting Ilya Evgeny is a person of ill repute. It's even possible she's been brainwashed by her captors. Perhaps she didn't choose of her own will to do the things she's doing. In that case, we must do everything in our power to help her."

"That's what I don't understand," insisted Anya. "Will everybody please stop speaking in circles? I'm not a kid; so don't treat me like one. If you think Ilya's been taking advantage of me, you're very wrong. She doesn't receive any more money than other managers. In fact, she's been like a second mother to me. Some of you already know I don't get along with my own mother. She's such a pain. We rarely talk, and when we do we either argue or have nothing to say. It's a constant hassle. It just turns into fights all the time. My mother's practically disowned me. She says that what I'm doing is a disgrace and shameful. Well, it isn't. I'm proud of playing professionally. Tennis is my life."

"And all of Russia is proud of you, too," Vlad replied honestly. "That's the truth. I've watched you play in tournaments several times. You're an outstanding athlete. Your backstroke is amazing, the finest I've ever seen. I know how hard you train to keep in top shape. In the future I firmly believe you'll be acknowledged as one of Russia's all-time outstanding tennis stars."

Her eyes grew wide and wet with the unexpected compliment. Asher handed her a box of tissues. She sniffed and blew her nose. "Mr. Petrovsky is absolutely correct," agreed Boris. "Any of Ilya's dealings have absolutely nothing to do with you. You're under no suspicion whatsoever. Your reputation is intact. But as I started to say, there are several questions we still need to ask. Our nation's national security could be at stake. Can you understand our position, Anya?"

She nodded. "Yes, I do. I'll tell you everything to the best of my ability, although I still don't believe Ilya's fallen in with hoodlums."

Rabbi Titlebaum rubbed a hand along his bearded chin. "I wouldn't put it quite that way, Anushka."

"Not at all," agreed Boris. "Maybe she's also a victim. It's my guess she may have fallen in love with the leader of these hoods and believes what he's told her."

Anya recoiled in horror. "Ilya fall for some lowlife? A street pimp? No way! Anyway, for months she's been in love with that super footballer from Novgorod, Alexei—what's his name? She dotes and slobbers over him like he's a prince or something."

"Didn't you say last year she fell in love with a Polish film star, and even considered running away to Warsaw to make movies?"

Anya fumed.

Alina Vera smiled warmly. "Boris is blunt, but he's just trying to help. It's straight talk. You yourself admitted Ilya's been smitten over the years by quite a few men."

Anya sipped from her teacup. "I wouldn't say she was in love with them all. Ilya just likes having nice things and enjoys meeting fashionable men of the world, especially handsome, rich ones. I guess what you're really asking is, has she had many boyfriends?"

"Exactly, Anushka," the rabbi confirmed.

Boris picked up his thread of thought. "The police have good reason to believe Ilya Evgeny has indeed fallen in love with this underworld criminal we're seeking."

"Underworld? You mean like the Russian mafia?"

"Not exactly, but nevertheless a renown gangster of another ilk. And this criminal is causing a great many predicaments for us. More trouble than I can deny. We have a solemn duty to find and stop him any way possible before he hurts anyone else."

She placed her hands in her lap and thought for a moment. Her mouth remained slightly open. "Oh. You mean like in the movies?"

"Yes," said Boris with a wan smile. "Like in the movies."

"But he isn't an amiable criminal like Pepe Le Moko," opined Dimsky.

Boris was baffled to find a beautiful, international celebrity like Anya so naïve. As a young woman nearly twenty, she sometimes acted and sounded more like a fourteen year old.

"Okay. Now I get it. What do you expect me to do?"

Gratified at her abrupt turnaround, Boris said, "We believe your manager will soon try to get in touch. In fact, we're hoping she does. So you see, Anya, it is we who need your help. We want you to gather as much information as possible when she makes contact. Try to learn her location, places she's been hiding, and especially where she's spent recent nights. That alone would be an enormous help. If we can arrest this monster you'll have done the Motherland a very great service. You might even be called a hero, right Dimsky?" Boris looked to the colonel.

"Without doubt she'd receive her country's sincerest gratitude," agreed Dimsky. "And I myself would personally request Anya be bestowed with the National Medal of Valor."

The girl listened in awe. The idea was overwhelming.

"When did you last communicate with Ilya?" asked Vlad.

Anya sat thoughtfully. "Not since that awful night. How long ago was it? I've lost track. I want to block it out."

"Not long," assured the rabbi. "You still have possession of your mobile phone?"

"Yes. I hid it in my bra. They stole my purse, took my money and credit cards. But I fooled them with my mobile."

"Smart girl. Your telephone is very important. We'll take care of the rest," said Boris. "There's just one more thing we need you to do. It's not very difficult and will only take a few minutes. Down the hall from here there's an official conference room. Vlad is going to escort you there."

Vlad nodded. "I'll be at your side every moment. There's going to be a national press conference, and we're set to start in just a few minutes. All we need from you is to make a short statement. A plea for Ilya's release. We'd like you to inform the press of the fact that Ilya Evgeny, your manager and dear friend, was abducted by unknown persons, possibly terrorists, and that it's vital for Ilya to somehow get in touch with you. Reporters won't be permitted to ask any questions regarding tennis, upcoming matches or cancellations. Assure the media it's your fervent hope someone out there will recognize Ilya and alert their local prefecture or National Police. They'll know what to do. No names need be given. All information will be accepted anonymously, and a substantial reward will be paid to the informant who provides information leading to Ilya Evgeny's release. Payment will also be made anonymously to a national bank with a special code number we'll provide." He handed the girl the written statement.

Asher spoke in his grandfatherly fashion. "Anushka, child, you'll be doing a great service. Let it be known your intentions are purely in the interest of Ilya's safety, and your wish is to help her in any way possible. Be polite, and thank everyone profusely for his or her cooperation. Let them photograph you as much as they wish. Vlad is an expert at this sort of thing. He'll handle and forestall any difficult questions, and make sure no one causes you the slightest distress. Will you do this, dear child?"

Vlad added, "In a few days, we'll be planting our own story in the newspapers and across the 'Net. Credentialed journalists will spread it for us. I'll read you a draft.

'Anya Andropova is sorely disappointed at the lack of results in the case regarding the abduction of her closest friend and manager, Ilya Evgeny. She's deeply concerned for Ilya's safety. Ilya's life is considered to be in danger. Therefore, Anya herself is offering to pay a generous reward, money saved from her tennis winnings. She desperately hopes a Good Samaritan will appear to help. Anya is fervently praying she'll hear word soon.'

"That's it. We believe the lure of money will trigger new information. And again don't fret, I'll be there to keep them off your back."

Anya sniffed and wiped her eyes. "I know what to do. I've held press conferences before. You can count on me."

"I think I've always been in love with *Patriarshiye* Ponds," said Vlad as they rambled near the sloping embankments of the peaceful lake setting, Alina Vera tossing breadcrumbs to the pigeons and occasional crows. Nicknamed *Patriki*, the Patriarch, it served an affluent residential area in the much sought after downtown *Presnensky* District of Moscow.

He fondly related stories of his formative years, a time when he frequently visited and enjoyed the famed greenway, its odor of moist earth, the great pond itself, and the nearby boulevards adorned with architecturally perfect residences representing so many periods of history. He spoke of settling beneath old leafy trees, eagerly reading adventure books until time to go home for supper, dreaming of faraway, exotic places he'd one day visit. "My boyhood hunger was to circumnavigate the globe on a ship", he told her, a twinkle in his eye. "Becoming a modern Magellan soaking up experiences, in time maybe writing tales of my own worldly exploits like a Russian version of Joseph Conrad or Melville. I did travel a bit after graduating, learned to speak a few languages…but where are the novels I planned to write? The good things I hoped to accomplish with my life? I don't know. I never imagined one day I'd be living in such a posh neighborhood. I don't belong here. I traded all my cherished aspirations for what resembled a glamorous career."

Alina Vera listened attentively, picturing a young innocent Vlad dreaming his childhood dreams, stalking untraveled territory to excavate eternal meanings and truths beyond shallow yearnings for mandatory good grades that would assure a valued place at university. There was so much of her own struggle in what he was saying, she saw. A kinship, sharing the same insights, gradually coming of age only to exchange what made you feel fully alive for the lure of ambition and success.

"Look across the street," she said, pointing. "My elderly great uncle lived his final years at that residence, 'The House of Lions'." It was an imposing pink building adorned with Corinthian columns, and great lion sculptures at either side of its wide steps. Prized housing built by Stalin for Red Army marshals and other important military personnel.

"Party members lived in the lap of luxury back then," she went on. "I remember as a little girl my father holding my hand as we left the *Pushkinskaya* metro station to visit my uncle. He remained a big, strong man to the very end, and I felt so small beside him that he always scared me. He'd be dressed in an immaculately pressed uniform with so many shiny medals on his chest, proud of each. The old codger remained a cavalier relic of the past until his very last day." She glanced sentimentally at the great house while reminiscing. "If I behaved properly, my parents would take me to *Tverskaya* Street, let me stare in the windows of the fancy shops. I promised myself I'd have all the fine luxuries one day. I begged my father to stroll the entire street with me so I could gape all the way to Pushkin Square." Slight dimples appeared with her smile.

"Sounds like your family has an influential old regime Party background."

She tilted her head, pitching a handful of crumbs to nearby birds. "Party membership was required for people holding good positions. Of course, one never knew when you were being spied on, or when to expect a rude midnight visit from the KGB. Membership was a double-edged sword; it kept you on your toes."

They casually meandered, zigzagging amid blooming, gnarly rooted trees. A frog croaked along the lake's bank, a squirrel dashed across their path. "My nickname was Verochka," she told him, looking at the arrangement of leaves on the twig of a tree.

Vlad laughed as a flock of birds flew over their heads. Winter had relinquished its struggle, the pond's use as a winter skating rink concluded. Since returning from Omsk he could feel the change of season in the air. "Didn't the rabbi own a flat nearby?"

"He did, on a lovely street usually forbidden to Jews. The Party always remained suspicious. Many still do. I've always been curious why Asher decided to remain in Moscow. He could have emigrated, and lived practically anywhere he desired. Universities from Paris to Chicago offered lucrative positions. Once he spoke of an offer he received from Princeton." She became amused. "He said they expected him to be their new Einstein. He turned the offer down, saying Russia was home no matter what, and he wasn't going to leave her. The day he announced his resignation everyone at the Academy was stunned. It created a huge disruption. But he'd set his mind to becoming a rabbi, residing in some far away backwater village and studying Kabbalah for the rest of his life. Asher's so gifted, such a wonderful mentor to so many of us. I didn't understand how anyone could give up that much influence and respect. The scientific world lay at his feet, and he renounced it."

Vlad listened with interest. "I've really come to like him, and I wouldn't judge so harshly. He's decided to pursue a profound spiritual intimate relationship, discovering where he belongs. I envy him. What more can anyone ask? I wish I could say the same." A shadow of sadness crossed his features. She touched his elbow with her fingertips.

"It's been terribly hard for you, I know. I can't even imagine how you feel."

His shoulders sank. "Not being able to share life with my girls hurts more than I can describe. I know I made mistakes. Maybe I didn't appreciate what I had." He paused, shifting his focus, admiring the encroaching trees and shrubbery the park was famous for. "Raisa and I were different from the start. She's pragmatic, knows what she wants and finds ways to get it. For her life is strictly black and white. It's not like that for me. Maybe I've been far too absorbed with work, it's true, but I doubt I've ever could be the husband she'd hoped for." He cut his introspection short. His tone didn't reveal all his thoughts, but Alina Vera had no trouble reading the burdening questions and doubts she could see in his brooding eyes. They walked for a time without saying anything.

"When I was a boy I loved taking long walks all over the city," Vlad said after his silence. "But I especially liked *Patriki* because it's so filled with history. Centuries of it right beneath our feet."

"Oh? Tell me something."

He was proud of his knowledge, and he wondered if he was telling this to show off like a teenager. "Well, did you know the trees from this park were chopped down for fuel by Napoleon's freezing soldiers during the 1812 invasion of Moscow?"

"Interesting. No, I didn't know that. You'd make an excellent tourist guide, if you someday decide to throw away your career." She smiled mischievously, picking up twigs and snapping them, dropping a trail of crumbs while they walked. She paused, looking into his face, regarding him with sympathy.

"I appreciate you being so candid about your family. And I'm sincerely saddened your marriage may be ending this way. Please know that. I can tell from the pain in your voice how much your daughters mean to you. This might be difficult to believe from someone perceived as cynical as me, but I sacrificed several chances for a family because of my work. Happiness only meant a fulfilling career to me then. That's what I convinced myself I wanted, the only thing I wanted. But it turned hollow, empty, and lonely. Sometimes I feel I eschewed so much for a microscope. It makes me sound awfully shallow, doesn't it?" Her inflection was wistful. It became his turn to glimpse the deep currents stirring within Alina Vera. Not the unreachable scientist, the extolled woman of the world, or the glib talker ever ready with a quip. But an unseen side, a simpler side; images of a vulnerable young girl who'd once constructed bird feeders so she and her friends could watch and photograph from their bedroom windows. Now she'd learned life's sober lessons, resigned and surrendering to her fate, discovering safety inside her cocoon of dense armor.

When their eyes briefly met she realized he was fathoming her thoughts to their depths. Off guard and embarrassed, she looked away. He reached for her arm. She didn't pull away. "Are you sorry things worked out the way they have?" he asked.

Her hair blew gently amid a light gust of wind. She clenched her hands inside her jacket pockets. "I admit to wondering what my life would be like had I chosen another direction. By now I'd have a couple of kids who'd probably be abominable teenagers. They'd dream of running far away, the same as I did. I have a brother and a sister, and both do have children I used to visit often. Not so much anymore. Don't misunderstand, I love them all dearly, but it's painful sometimes. And it does hurt, realizing what I've missed. But eventually, you resign yourself to the kind of life I've had. Locked away in laboratories, research, and experiments. You convince yourself it still retains importance, meaning, something worthwhile..."

"Worthwhile for the State?"

"No, Mr. Public Relations Man, never for the State. I'm too much of an idealist for that." She spoke in a familiar way, as though he were a long time friend she could spill her heart to. "I'd like to think my work is for the good of humanity, but it's so grueling to pretend...pretending you've kept your idealism intact. I've still clung onto some dreams, though. Pursuing cures for disease, new and better ways to heal and to comfort. I could get in real trouble for openly saying this, but frankly I don't care a damn about the State. I loathe politics, all politics. I suppose my ego's too big for my own good. Maybe I'm obsessed with delusions of grandeur. I should have been a dermatologist, better yet, a plastic surgeon. I'd earn tons of money, minus the stress." She laughed again. "I apologize for unburdening myself on you."

Across the path, a young couple was lost embraced in a passionate kiss.

"Life at their age was sweet," said Vlad. "I had so many half-baked plans, too; the world was a photo album of endless mysteries I planned to fathom. I also set out to make a name for myself, daydreaming I'd single-handedly become the man responsible for elevating Russia's image and status, and hoisting myself with it. Becoming the darling of Europe, envy of the world. Being appointed to this Anniversary Jubilee business almost made me feel I succeeded. But that illusion's gone. I've started to grasp the world we inhabit for what it really is. My dreams are stale and ancient, fanciful delusions hatched a million years ago by a boy's rash imagination."

"It *was* a million years ago, Vlad. You were as idealistic as me. Who had the bigger dreams?"

"I bet both were bigger than Russia's sky, Verochka." He used the diminutive of her name, and looked at her questioningly. "Is it all right to call you that?"

"Sure. Just not in front of the team, please. I don't enjoy being teased." The wind began blowing colder.

"Do you enjoy keeping people at a distance?"

"I suppose you've discovered my last retreat. My loftiest degrees come from the school of hard knocks. But I suspect we've both had our ideals tarnished and cling on by our fingernails." She returned an unlit cigarette into its pack. "Come on, it's getting late, and we're both cold and hungry."

They crossed the wide boulevard, away from a departing tram and toward a narrower side street. The traffic light switched to yellow, then red. They stepped from the sidewalk. Vlad shouted, "Watch out!" He yanked her by the arm, roughly forcing her to tumble backward. Clutching tightly onto his jacket sleeve they stumbled together to the pavement. A dark sedan bolted past, headed away.

"My God, are you all right?" Vlad said, gasping to catch breath. She slowly found her bearings and nodded, swaying dizzily. One knee was scraped, her hands scratched. Several passersby hurried to assist.

"I saw that car flying down the boulevard, I saw what it did," said an elderly man clutching his walking stick. "The fool didn't try to stop...but he must have seen you step into the street."

"You were very lucky," a student in the crowd said. "I left the park right after you. It sounded to me like the driver was gunning his engine. When I looked up I saw the car shoot like a bullet. Where are the damned police? He needs to be arrested."

"Another drunk on the road," someone else said. "As if we don't have enough already. Sooner or later he'll kill someone for certain unless he's stopped."

Vlad looked around. "Did anyone see the license plate number? Anybody see anything?" The small crowd made no reply.

"Do you want a doctor?" the student asked. "Or go to an emergency room? I'll flag a taxi."

They declined. Vlad helped Alina Vera to stand firmly. "No. We're shaken up, that's all." As he reached for his phone, Alina Vera drew close, whispering. "Don't call anyone, don't tell anyone yet. It's safer." Against his better judgment he reluctantly agreed. They carefully made their way across the street amid a larger group.

"Maybe now you'll believe what I've told you?" she said breathlessly. She held a bruised elbow beginning to hurt.

"I believed everything before, but this time I'm not sure which of us they were after."

"Either—or both. Don't trust anyone, Vladimir Petrovsky. Don't trust anyone."

9.

"I want you to pay close attention," Vlad said. Remote control in hand, he replayed the nightly international news.

"Meanwhile, in Russia," the attractive young news anchor behind a large desk began reading, "it appears a mystery is unfolding. We have a growing number of accounts—unconfirmed at this point—of peculiar sightings across the country of the iconic Russian leader of the 1918 Revolution, Vladimir Ilyich Lenin." The reporter barely hid a droll smile. "In one of the strangest stories we've ever aired, international news agencies are recounting crowds gathering in various venues to listen to a man proclaiming himself to be the very same Lenin. According to reports, many individuals say they've witnessed, heard and spoken with this Lenin, or at least someone sharing an uncanny likeness." A flattering photograph appeared on the screen, an old black and white picture of Lenin passionately speaking at a podium.

"These reports," the presenter continued," have been steadily streaming in from a number of both Russian and Ukraine cities and towns. Among them, the Western Siberian city of Omsk, thousands of kilometers southeast of Moscow, also at the Black Sea port city of Odessa, where he reputedly delivered a rousing speech. Some accounts additionally tell of this so-called Lenin convening an audience at the peaceful city of Lvov, in Belarus, and then at the doorstep of Russia's former capital, St. Petersburg. Voice recognition equipment is said to verify that this man's voice seems have almost identical qualities as Lenin's. Facial recognition analysis studies in a closed test stage report similar findings; initial computerized indications detect interchangeable patterns in expression, as well as eye and mouth movements. These examinations, however, are not considered foolproof or conclusive.

"The Russian government declines to formally make any official response to WNN's request for its view on these bizarre sightings. Unexpectedly stopped while leaving an unofficial dinner, Prime Minister Sergei Milonov, when asked, shooed away reporters with an angry, inappropriate gesture. However, one highly-ranking government advisor did indicate off the record that these sorts of accounts amounted merely to some prank or hoax, whose sole purpose is to cause discord and disharmony among Russia's many varied ethnic peoples. In an effort to seek further clarification, our correspondent in London chatted several hours ago regarding this baffling episode with noted author and renowned psychologist, Dr. Ralph Guttmann."

A heavyset, truculent man wearing a blue, buttoned cardigan sweater appeared on the screen. The shock of salt and pepper hair spilling across his crown and forehead did not quite match the hair on the sides of his head.

"Doctor, as an experienced expert, what do you personally make of these peculiar ongoing sightings?" the off-screen correspondent asked.

"Ahem." He cleared his throat. "These signs appear to be symptoms of mass hysteria," he answered, calmly and solemnly, embarking on a long, rambling discourse. He was experienced in front of television cameras. He spoke in a deep, authoritative voice laced with a thick upper class London accent, his nostrils flaring. "May I point out this is certainly not an uncommon phenomenon in contemporary Western societies. We witness it occurring across the world at various times, especially during prolonged periods of increased stress. With economic barricades remaining severe not just across Russia but Europe and America as well. When citizens feel their governments and institutions violate the principles of fiduciary and moral responsibility in pursuit of personal gain, I am not surprised to encounter people pursuing comfort in an effort to find something greater than themselves."

"Are you implying, Dr. Guttmann, those individuals claiming to have personally sighted or spoken with this so- called incarnation are behaving in a delusional manner due to angry perceptions of their political system?"

"No, I'm not saying that at all. I'm expressing my conviction that certain individuals, especially when faced with mounting apprehension, have always claimed to come in contact with famous figures from the past, often of a religious nature, and sometimes not. For example, I'm sure you're aware of numerous revelations of the Virgin Mary appearing these past several years. I dare to say we have counted hundreds. In a similar vein, UFO sightings are routinely observed on an almost daily basis on every continent. Additionally, we also have the matter of crop circles. Theories abound on all such sightings, of course, yet we amassed no evidence whatsoever of other-worldly visitations."

"Excuse me, Dr. Guttmann, but are you likening these reports from Russia to sightings of Unidentified Flying Objects?"

"Ahem. In a manner of speaking, I am, although, surely not in a literal sense." He sniffed and curled his lip, appearing in turn vague, surly, assured and concise. "Psychologically, we human beings have a primal need to believe in something beyond our own limited capacities, if you're able to follow my train of thought. When someone claims to have witnessed a UFO on a particular night there will quickly follow a putative flurry of additional sightings both near and far."

"You mean copycat sightings?" asked the reporter.

"Something akin to that nature, I would presume. Ahem. My own studies of such psychological phenomenon have certainly taught me to never discount the creative dexterity of the human mind. I believe that probably each and every one of those who say they've seen or spoken to 'Lenin' are quite sane, and quite capable of explaining meticulously when, where, and how it occurred. In other words, you see, they trust what they perceived, and in that interpretation they are absolutely telling the truth. As an example, I was told of a factory worker who claims to have personally met and spoken with this reincarnation while using the men's room. He purportedly professed that Lenin appeared to him stark naked, but nevertheless ostensibly prepared to ignite a nationwide revolt. A nude representation of one of history's most distinct figures seems to be a rather fantastical claim, yet went unquestioned at every level by the tale's narrator. The worker was arduously examined by medical authorities for aberrant psychological symptoms, and found to be quite sane."

"Not a loony?"

"Not a loony at all."

"So again, Dr. Guttmann, you attribute these reports from varied areas of the New Russian Federation as evidence of some sort of mass hysteria? A derangement due to current severe economic conditions, work-related stress, and that hardship brought on by unemployment contributes to the passions and mania behind many of these so-called sightings? Is that your diagnosis?"

The esteemed doctor sat deep in thought, squeezing blackheads on his nose before smugly answering. "My opinion, yes. Let's not quibble over semantics. It so happens I quite recently lectured upon a similar theme at The International Psychological Symposium, hosted in Montreal. Permit me to elucidate, if I may. When a toiler loses his employment and helplessly watches his income decline, perhaps suffers divorce, or the loss of a loved one, during such a period of excessive mental duress, the body's emotional and physical immune system is increasingly depleted, becoming an impotence susceptible to all manner of external stimuli."

The lauded psychologist went on, "I've been evaluating varied anomalies for some forty years now. And I've written numerous papers on such examples of extreme upsets where patients have sworn to have been in touch with, spoken to, and witnessed first-hand, everything from departed loved ones to encounters with creatures from outer space. Indeed, I've even interviewed several gentlemen swearing they were forced into having sexual relations with female intergalactic travelers, usually of royal bearing. Compelled into it by their captors, they recount their stories with great detail and greater fervor, explaining that said alien females covet Earthmen to impregnate them. Once their tryst is completed they are cast aside by the princess or queen female and returned safely home to Earth." His face remained severe, betraying no hint of bemusement. "Therefore, I would find it highly irregular if these touted Lenin sightings were not only to continue, but even increase under current circumstances. However, I will gladly offer fresh evaluation if and when supplementary indications of this phenomenon acquire broader scope compelling further investigation."

"Forced sex with royal intergalactic travelers," Dimsky derided. "I hope his shrink can straighten him out."

"In conclusion, Doctor, do you mean you'd accept these reported findings as being factual?" said the news anchor.

"Well, I'm not quite ready to say that. My expertise in explaining these marvels has proven my hypothesis to be conclusive time and time again. My numerous books on this subject speak for themselves." He held one up briefly for the camera, pointing out that it could be easily ordered online at a steep discount. "Therefore, I can state with categorical confidence there is no more likelihood of this so-called 'Lenin' coming back to life than there would be of, say, Abraham Lincoln's resurrection in the United States."

The screen returned to WNN's appealing news anchor sitting behind her desk.

"Thank you so much, Dr. Ralph Guttmann in London, for your most insightful opinions. Of course, WNN will continue to track this puzzling story as new developments arrive. Turning to other news, in a headline fresh from the wire services, the Saudi Arabian women's activist group says—"

Vlad clicked off the television with the remote control.

"Dr. Guttmann's hairpiece was lopsided," said Dimsky.

"So, major news networks have finally begun picking up the story." Boris heaved a deep, frustrated sigh. "Yesterday they reported on a lecture Lenin supposedly gave to a bunch of workers, called, '*The Democratic Tasks of the Revolutionary Proletariat*'. A geriatric rehashed piece of mumbo-jumbo from the 1920's. After being spoon-fed by that boring, grandiose imposter I have to conclude the wolves are banging at the door."

Dimsky grimaced. "We still have several voice samples to analyze. But so far our experts say his speech patterns continue to show definite similarities with recorded speeches Lenin gave during and after the Revolution. They can't rule out his authenticity. Hence, his mystique."

"At least Guttmann's negating Lenin sightings so far," Vlad said optimistically. "That's a good sign. A story like this gets airplay only on slow news nights. And it wasn't very important or convincing. But if the press keeps plugging away, we'll have to dream up some snappy answers, give our own spin, and face questions. The worst thing is allowing this to gain substantive international traction."

Dimsky made no effort to hide his considerable chagrin. He grabbed his balalaika, staying calm by plucking strings one at a time. "Damn the Internet and cyberspace," he sulked. "Damn hyper-connectivity. Ads and ad blocking, freezes, pop-ups, cookies, viruses and virus protection. Phishing, ID theft, intellectual property theft. Cloud computing, cyber espionage, hacking. Updates ad nauseum. Streaming video hucksters pitching everything from intimate ladies' underwear to anachronistic busts of Mozart. Online marketers gone viral. Millions and millions of people sitting at computers day after day, bored out of their minds, waiting for something, anything, to brighten up their lonely, miserable lives.

"And smartphones aren't better, choking us with endlessly clogging apps, upgrades, and add-ons. Carcinogenic cellular phones, dropped calls, non-stop text messaging. Isn't there anything better in life? Damn this electronic media world we inhabit. Instantaneous communication is the bane and scourge of the world. Worse, abominable social networking sites like FacetoFace only compound matters. Social networking provokes protests anywhere, any time. Just how many simultaneous cyber friends can a normal human being collect? Don't any of these people have jobs? The Web is the new fuel for inciting insurgency. Hundreds of millions of hits are counted every single day. Do you know how much drivel I myself tally online? There's a newly formed international anarchist group calling itself 'Lenin Lives!' Within its first hour of inauguration tens of thousands of hippie utopians signed up as members."

"Are you done yet?" asked Alina Vera.

"Be that as it may, Colonel," jibed an impatient Boris, "on this point Vlad is absolutely correct. Immoral or not, one way or another we have to come to terms with it. Online networking has a vast reach and immediacy we can't contain. We need a way to cushion the bilge spewed by TV and the blogosphere, a manufactured, superb counter story that will stand up to public scrutiny. Be as creative as you can, Vova. We're counting on you. Unless we frame a believable line of reasoning we're sunk."

No one said anything after that.

Alina Vera swirled remaining hot water in the teacup and poured residue into its saucer. Then she turned the teacup upside down, held it for a few moments in her right hand and placed it back right side up. The dark, stubby tea leaves were dried and scattered in various places around the bottom and circumference of the porcelain cup, turning it into something resembling a kaleidoscopic design.

"What are you doing?" Anya looked on with curiosity, her elbows resting on the table, chin in her hands.

The scientist ran a finger along her lower lip. "I'm going to read your fortune. My grandmother taught me when I was a child. Let me show you. Allow the tea leaves to dry after you finish your tea. The leaves dry very quickly. Next, turn the cup upside down, and then back. The way the leaves settle will show you images. The Chinese began this during ancient times thousands of years ago, reading the dregs of their cups for symbols and omens. Grinds found at the top and rim of the cup indicate what might be happening soon in the future. Look here." She offered the teacup around the table for viewing. Vlad noticed a single clump and nearby grouping, and thought it resembled a house with a chimney. Colonel Dimsky, ever the skeptic, toyed with it in his left hand, his narrowed eyes alerted to spot some intriguing pattern. "Old wives tales," he muttered.

"Well, my grandmother was an old wife, I suppose."

Anya giggled girlishly. "Tell me what you discover, Alina Vera! That's my teacup you're examining."

"Go ahead, tell her," said Vlad, with interest. "We're just hanging around waiting, anyway."

Alina Vera fastidiously examined in an exaggerated, theatrical manner. She put her left eye close to the cup and stared. "It's imperative we concentrate to be accurate. Remember, Anya, your stirring the tea with your own spoon gave the leaves their shapes and position, and so this is a personal reading exclusively for you. Look," she indicated with her pinky, "these speckles trickling downward along the side, I think it represents rain. That could portend something. Below, stands a house, a country house or dacha, I think. Vlad was correct in seeing that. Now over here I can see an old stone chimney badly in need of repair…"

"My Aunt Grusha's house!" Anya exclaimed. "It must be! She lives in the countryside in an old place like that. And her roof is in really bad shape. She made me promise to fix it when I win my next tournament." She smiled with self-approval.

"I also see a loosely curled sprig—very curvy—like a woman's shape… yes, I do see a woman…"

"Ilya! It's Ilya, isn't it? Maybe it's showing the place where they've abducted her."

"Perhaps," the reader agreed. Before Alina Vera could continue a deep voice interrupted.

"Good evening," Rabbi Titlebaum said, taking off his coat. "Forgive me for taking so long. I decided to do a reexamination of my formulae, hoping our new Omsk team would be farther ahead by now. Unfortunately, things are progressing painfully slowly. I've requested duplicates of Little Man's complete genetic blueprint. Perhaps working on a parallel track, tweaking programs, I can identify code specifics to move the process along." He sat down wearily.

"Glad you're here, Rabbi," said Vlad with a good-natured glance at Alina Vera. "Our in-house scientist is busy explaining the theories of tea leaf reading."

Rabbi Titlebaum laughed. "Ah, tea leaves? We Jews invented reading tea leaves, you know."

"I always thought the Chinese got the credit," said Dimsky, quietly strumming his balalaika. Everyone had developed a taste for his lively folksongs, music learned from his grandfather during his Siberian childhood.

Without hesitation Asher replied, "It's an established fact that Jewish caravans travelled the ancient Silk Road trade routes from Samarkand and Cathay.

We were great merchants and barterers, you know. I'm sure it was a Jew who gave the idea to the Chinese." His fun loving approach disarmed Alina Vera, who sat listening with fascination.

The row of silent computers sprang to life. Everyone froze with baited breath for the telephone to ring. "Any moment," anticipated Boris.

"Please," muttered the rabbi. "Let it be, let it be."

Dimsky snapped his fingers and pressed a button. A bank of systems programmers in the high-tech security room stiffened. Satellite and broadband frequencies instantly tuned in. The wired, landline black telephone sat solitary on a shelf. Vlad held his breath, the rabbi closed his eyes, and Boris clenched his fists. The telephone rang.

"Calm, stay calm," Boris gently instructed the nervous tennis player.

"Don't freak," added Dimsky.

Boris continued, "Remember, try not to sound too excited. Listen more than you talk, but be sure to ask the questions we've told you. Keep her talking as long as possible. The more time we have, the easier to denote precise coordinates. Good luck."

Anya nodded, swallowed hard, and reached for the telephone. "Hello."

"Anya, are you there?" Computers began tracking, copying, transmitting to the subterranean central command at the Kremlin.

"Yes, Ilya, it's me! Is that really you?"

"Yes, Anya, it's me, too." The voice sounded distant and unclear. Dancing red bands on computer screens indicated how precariously weak the signal was. "They must be hiding in a cave," drawled Dimsky. He sat upright at his keyboard, locked in on the indicator, struggling to enhance the fragile signal's capacity. There was an additional flurry of activity outside the room as security men tweaked the delicate straying bands.

"Thank heaven. Ilya, I've been *so* worried, you have no idea. I've prayed you'd find a way to contact me. Where are you?"

"I can't answer that, Anya. I'm sorry. I know you've worried. I've read the newspapers, and I've been waiting for an opportunity to get in touch. We..." she hesitated. "...Your phone is tapped."

"Tapped, who'd be tapping us, Ilya?"

"Internal Security, secret police, any or all. What does it matter? Your line must be under surveillance. Listen, I watched that fake press conference the police forced you to give. It wasn't very convincing."

"The police have been no help whatsoever, Ilya. I can't believe how inept they are. I've refused to work with them any more. And, no Ilya, they didn't force me to hold that press conference. It was my idea. Couldn't you tell how on edge and frightened I am? I've been sick to death waiting to hear news about you."

"The police aren't listening in now?"

"No, Ilya they're not. I hope you believe me."

"All right, Anya. It doesn't matter. I can only talk for a moment."

"Just tell me if you're safe. Are you really all right? Have these kidnappers harmed you?"

"I'm quite safe." She spoke more rapidly in a hushed voice. "So much has happened, but I can't explain it now. Hopefully you'll soon know and understand everything. Something important is going on; something wonderful, with the potential to change our lives forever."

The girl was frustrated by Ilya's lack of clarity. Boris looked to Anya and mouthed the words 'remain calm' twice. Anya's heart was pounding wildly, tiny beads of sweat dotting her forehead. "Don't you realize how concerned I am, how concerned the whole country is about you? This bunch of horrible terrorists—"

"They're not terrorists, Anya. Don't let anyone brainwash you. Listen to me carefully. I read in the newspapers that you're putting up your own money to help me get released. Did you mean it? I hope so. It's essential I get everything deposited from your last tournament. Every last ruble, in cash, converted into dollars. I'll need it, Anya. I'm sorry to ask, but please try and raise as much as you can."

Anya gasped. "They *have* kidnapped you!"

"No, Anya, they—" Static interference interrupted the conversation. Ilya's voice was broken, barely discernable. Dimsky continued working frantically. The voice crackled, Ilya said, "It's essential for the cause…to raise money…." Unintelligible words followed, then, "…New orders, soon…"

"You're breaking up badly, Ilya. Yes, I'll get the money. Don't worry. And every ruble of my savings, too. Nothing matters except your safety. But how will I deliver it? Are you still near that horrible village?"

"No, far away. I have to go, Anya. Collect the money. In cash, understand?"

"Yes, I understand. When will I see you? When will I give it to you?"

"Soon. You'll be contacted."

"On my mobile?"

"I don't know yet. Take care of yourself, Anya. No one can be trusted in these dangerous times. Please don't believe the lies the police have told you about me. Don't believe them, Anya..."

The line went dead. A young computer expert ran into the room, panting, "We've got it, sir! We've homed in on the signal, already designating perfect coordinates."

Dimsky barked commands into his smartphone. "Get me three fully equipped Special Force combat platoons deployed immediately! Armed helicopters waiting on the pads at every base within a thousand kilometers. The moment exact coordinates are established the mission is a go. I repeat the mission is a go."

The atmosphere bristled with tension. Vlad sucked in a lungful of air. Dimsky wiped sweat from his forehead. Asher ground his teeth. "It looks like her money well has run dry," said Vlad. "With luck, maybe we can track them down tonight."

Various scenarios sped through Boris' mind. "Not so fast," he admonished. "Something isn't right here. We knew Evgeny would contact Anya, but this was...too easy. She fully knows her call was traced despite Anya's protests. Yet she knowingly endangered herself and maybe Lenin, disregarding our manhunt."

"You're thinking they don't care if we traced their location?" said Dimsky.

"My conclusion is *she* doesn't care. She knows she's hunted, and she put Lenin at risk anyway. It doesn't add up."

Vlad sensed an undercurrent of duplicity. "She has her own agenda for making the call. We've underestimated this Ilya Evgeny, haven't we?"

"I think she's toying with us," affirmed Alina Vera. "Anya means nothing to her, and maybe Lenin doesn't, either. Possibly she feels she can twist him for her own purposes. Has she emerged as his pawn—or the reverse? She'd like us to believe anarchy is so widespread that tracking her doesn't matter. She's untouchable. Obviously her sole motivation is money for helping herself. Do you think she cares a fig about fomenting revolution?"

Boris stood fervidly attentive, reviewing the possibility, arranging potential puzzle pieces into place. The scientist's hunch made sense; Alina Vera was proving to be her father's daughter. "You'd have been a keen cop. You're imply-ing this tennis coach was Sunavich's accomplice all along?"

"How else can you explain it? If we catch her, she'll protest innocence, saying she was forced. And if she gets away with it she gets the money and pos-sibly power too, if the revolution succeeds." Alina Vera stood her ground.

Boris grunted with a dismissive wave of his hand. "Evgeny wasn't abduct-ed, was she? It was a set-up from the start." The nucleus of the insurgency was uncoiling, exposing a cold-blooded growing menace. "I wouldn't be surprised if she planned the whole damned episode herself."

Asher interrupted. "There's time to figure it out later. Right now, it's car-dinal for me to determine if Ilya's copulating with him. Whatever Evgeny's true objective, it mustn't obfuscate my need for obtaining vital sperm samples. His semen's DNA encodes important genetic information. Colonel, can your infor-mants locate safe houses where they've spent nights together? Without quantum level detection and understanding of their molecule patterns, I can't progress."

Dimsky shot the tennis player a look of strict business mixed with a plea. "Can you help us, Anya?"

The tennis star felt momentarily torn, wishing to give Ilya any benefit of the doubt. But she realized she couldn't ignore facts. "It's true, Ilya does have a sensual way with men," she affirmed, reluctantly conceding what she didn't want to believe. "She uses men. I've watched her at parties and sponsored events. Places where elite big shots with money and power get together. She knows how to use her charms to manipulate, and she especially enjoys mingling among important businessmen. For a long time she'd dated this guy, one of Russia's most notorious black marketeers, some kingpin. But she said it wasn't true, that he was only a high-flying gambler...Oh my God! Maybe he really *was* a mobster! I thought she was just bragging, you know, trying to impress me, get me to hire her for a high salary..."

"Try and recall everything," Asher urged.

"Everyone said she was crazy about this gambler, smitten real hard. Some months later this boyfriend died mysteriously. An unofficial police report claimed it was suicide; that he jumped off the twentieth floor of his luxury flat likely due to gambling debts. It was tragic. Ilya didn't buy it; she was shaken and frightened, certain someone pushed him out the window, execution-style. Her boyfriend had many enemies, she said, notorious men with government ties. It tore at her, ate her up. She believed people in power wanted him dead because he knew too many things, and could cause too much trouble...

"Soon after his death several of his close associates disappeared. Officially they're still missing persons, but Ilya believes they were murdered. A thorough police investigation was promised but never completed. A while later the case was closed for lack of evidence, they said. To Ilya, evening the score became an obsession. I told her to let it go, but she doesn't listen to me. Ever since, she's been wrestling with vengeful impulses for revenge."

These new links the tennis star provided were important and insidious. Boris's mind worked furiously. Ilya had grown melancholy, harboring deep hatred to the point of paranoia, prime for becoming a conduit between Sunavich and Lenin in her quest for retribution. If so, who might have introduced and involved her in the conspiracy? He asked the question they all were thinking, was Ilya's antipathy drastic enough to spur her into becoming an active part of a dangerous insurrection?

"She never got over her lover's death?"

Anya seemed uncertain. "It's kept her bitter, that's all I can tell you. All this happened shortly before I hired her. The Ilya I know loves life; she has good taste, and likes buying expensive things, especially jewelry. I suppose it's also true she'll do practically anything for money. I see that now."

"And in her desire for revenge she's blinded by hate. She'd risk anything," said Vlad.

"That hatred will be her downfall," said Boris. "Rabbi, I'm trusting in your theory. With a coquettish, skillful woman like Ilya seducing him, Lenin will greedily bed her. She'll stir him on, all right, like a couple of rabbits. Let's clench our teeth onto this and hold on tight. We need to ferret out locations they've spent nights together. Then, Rabbi, we'll be able to provide all the swab samples you'd ever want."

"No shortage there," scorned Dimsky.

Alina Vera soberly added, "Let's also hope Lenin doesn't bother using condoms."

10.

"Have a look at this," said Vlad. "This is the woman Nadia Ivanova from Channel One mentioned when she phoned me in the middle of the night." The newscast showed an agitated woman in a black dress being dragged away from outside a police station. Two uniformed officers were uncivilly pulling and shoving her down the street. One shoe fell off and they wouldn't allow her to pick it up.

"Do you see what they're doing?" the abused female croaked loudly to no one in particular. The TV cameras were running. "Do you see them hurting me?"

"Go on, get out of it," shouted one of the policemen, "and don't come 'round here again—ever. Or else!" His warning was explicit.

The woman made to spit at those accosting her, but thought better of it aware they'd drag her to a holding cell, and lose her amid the maze of police files never resolved.

The fallen shoe was thrown at her.

"You should never spit at the police," said Dimsky. Meanwhile several television reporters, microphones in hand, scurried to the agitated, trembling woman.

"Did you film what they did?" she railed, hobbling on one foot while putting the shoe on the other. She was a dark skinned, gypsy-looking woman with curly black hair covered by a colorful scarf. Heavy makeup was applied in a failed effort to make her appear youthful.

"Why were you tossed out of the police station?" one reporter inquired.

"Because they're nothing but ignorant philistines! I've been coming here every day for weeks, asking, pleading to speak to someone in authority. Someone has to hear me, the police, State Security, anyone with clout. I have important information, but they won't listen. The detectives laughed at my tale, told me to get out and not waste their valuable time, while they sat drinking coffee. The clowns. I tried to convince them I could lead them to where he's hiding. I know where he is. And I know who's with him."

"*Who's* hiding?"

She stared directly into the camera. "Who? That dreaded Lenin, of course! The murderous bastard! Won't anyone help? Doesn't anyone care? My visions have told me. I want to tell someone but they won't let me."

Vlad paused the program. "Who in God's name is that wild woman?" asked Boris. "She looks like she's been thrown under a bus."

"She calls herself Madame Zaza the Seer. She claims to be a successful psychic. She says she's had dreams for weeks. Frightening dreams. Telling her Russia is in terrible danger and no one is paying attention, no one wants to listen. She's desperate. Apparently she even tried breaking into Internal Security headquarters, but they tossed her out and gave her a stern reprimand."

"How do you know so much about this scrubwoman?" asked Dimsky. "You have no police or intelligence contacts."

Vlad leaned over the desk, arms akimbo, looking the skeptical colonel in the eye. "There isn't a well positioned media person in all of Moscow that doesn't want my ear. Nadia Ivanova from Channel One's been phoning and texting all morning. Nadia's convinced, and she's nobody's fool. I decided to have one of our news investigator do an objective background check, and also a researcher to dig up anything known about her. I admit she looks outlandish and crazed in the snippet aired last night, but her reputation is solid. She's not a crank. Reportedly she's successfully helped dozens of families in finding missing spouses, children and the like. I've read testimonies."

"You're not seriously suggesting we ask her for assistance?" queried Boris, wondering if Vlad's judgment was clouded by frustration.

"What do we have to lose? I'll go see her by myself. I know where she is. She lives in a crumbling tenement on the ground floor. There's a sign on the door. If she provides a kernel of information it'll be help. Heaven knows we can use every scrap."

"I guess Vlad's right. We have nothing to lose," Boris told Dimsky. "What do we lose?"

Dimsky shook his head in bemusement. "Wouldn't you rather have me send one of my agents to deal with her? They'll get to the truth much faster."

"I doubt threats or a beating will work. Better to go ourselves," Vlad said as he made for the door. Boris grabbed a jacket and followed.

Under pale streetlights a small sign on the narrow street entrance door read simply, *Madame Zaza*. A dog barked from an alley. Boris didn't use the doorknocker. He rapped with his knuckles.

"Who's there?" came a soft, alto voice.

"Internal Security to speak with Madam Zaza. Open the door."

"Come inside."

It was unlocked and he pushed it wide. Boris cautiously entered first, Vlad right behind. Fresh bunches of thyme, basil, and rosemary was bundled and hanging, filling the air with their perfume. They pushed aside a screen of beads. Renaissance music was playing quietly in the background. The lighting glowed softly from several oversized lamps, the room tightly packed with period antique furniture. A large nineteenth century French armoire stood against one wall, a chipped, dark wood Italian chest of drawers against another. Stacks of old newspapers and magazines were piled high atop circular Victorian side tables. Several colorful Moroccan leather boxes sat on the floor near a frayed jewelry box. Lace trimmings adorned a messy desk. An oddly out of place smiling bust of Houdini stood in the corner on a Roman Doric pedestal. Large imitation Rococo armchairs draped with shawls, quilts, and Afghans stood at either side of a once plush expensive sofa, now badly faded. Vlad felt a feeling of melancholic gravity in the middle of it all.

The black-haired woman sitting with her head leaning against an oversized flowery, fluffy pillow absently watched her visitors come in. Behind her hung a tall, narrow neo-classical mirror. A tray with supper sat on her lap, a plate of eggplant, cabbage, radishes and sweet potatoes, smelling of garlic and herbs.

They were surprised to see a white cockatoo perched behind the sofa. It fluttered its wings and screeched an obscenity.

"Hush, my sweet!" said Madam Zaza, waving a hand toward the bird. The cockatoo repeated the obscenity one more time and fell quiet. As Vlad came closer he saw the walls were covered with a variety of old film posters, photographs of international movie stars long since forgotten, along with picturesque magazine cutouts of exotic beaches. She held her fork and harpooned a potato. "Please have the courtesy to close the door behind you. Gently."

He shut it. The musty, dank smell mingled with the fresh herbs and exotic woods. Boris walked to the woman and displayed his identification card. Madam Zaza briefly looked up at his face, then to the photo on the card and back to his face. Vlad showed his own I.D. "You can put that away, I know who you are. I gave up trying to contact you. Your friend Nadia Ivanova did her best, to no avail."

"Nadia passed on your message, though. She told me everything. I appreciate your warning..."

She studied him scrupulously, while tugging at a large rhinestone earring in her left ear, and making the facets sparkle. "Close friends call you Vova, I believe?"

"Yes, they do. But I'm uncertain why it's me you wished to speak with. Aren't you wondering why we're here?"

"I know exactly why you're here, both of you."

"Do you?" said Boris.

"Of course. You're here because you've realized that you need me after all." She took another bite and chuckled under her breath. "And I knew you would be here tonight. That's why I left the door open, so I could eat my supper without having to get up. I still ache from where your bullying gendarmes jostled me."

Getting down to business, Boris said, "We saw you interviewed on television. You claim you know where to find this imposter."

Madam Zaza's smile barely contained her cynicism. She had ravenous, penetrating eyes. Her wide lips were painted bright red; high, projecting cheekbones that were lightly brushed with rouge, She wore a black lace blouse, a black skirt, black stockings and black shoes. Her arms were adorned with bracelets, her fingernails painted the same color as her lips. She was interesting to study, with a mystery of existence about her.

"This man you seek is no imposter, and you already know it," Madam Zaza rasped in reply to Boris' query. "He is as alive today as he was during the October Revolution, and you're aware of that, too."

"How do you know?"

"How do *I* know?" she mimicked. "The same way I know who *you* are. Internal Security doesn't send just anyone to my door to talk. You're an important one, aren't you? I have dealt with your kind before. Clever and boorish, possessing the keen eyes of a cat, but concealing claws like a panther. When deemed necessary capable of cruelty with satisfaction down to the marrow of your bones."

Boris set his jaw, and said nothing.

"As for your younger companion, he's not a policeman at all. I saw him also in my visions. He is helping you, but understands little of these things surrounding him. That's why I pleaded with his friend to warn him."

Vlad said, "I'm grateful for that, Madam Zaza. I was told you believe I'm in danger. You wish to warn me. And I was also told that in your visions you saw the figure of a dead man sucking at the poisoned breast of a strange woman. It was the poisoned milk that brought this man back to life..."

She nodded. "I saw those things, yes. But you did not heed my warning or come when I asked."

"I'm here now."

"Yes—and we must hope it is not too late." She went on eating, unperturbed.

"You sound very sure of yourself, Madam," said Boris.

"You may call me Madam Zaza, if you please. I suppose you wish to know all about me, don't you? You're thinking I'm some drunken old crone looking to squeeze a little money from your coffers. Well let me tell you something, Mr. Internal Security, I have dreams and those dreams tell me things. Sometimes very important things. Unrealistic? Absurd? I know you've already completed your dirty work, checked me out, and learned I'm no charlatan. I went to your police every day begging them. I said I could help find where Lenin was hiding, that visions in my dreams pointed the way. Did they care? Did they take note? I was degraded. They laughed and called me vulgar names, saying fakers masquerading as seers all said the same thing, and I was an indisputable swindler. A liar, a cheat, and a schemer, intent on defrauding the State. They started a smear campaign against me, threatening to transport me to an asylum. Treating me as though I were a criminal. Internal Security, ha! Let the State rot. What do I care? To hell with all of you."

"We are listening now, Madam Zaza," Vlad said quietly, feeling she wanted to talk if only someone would listen. She eyed him with suspicion, as he added, "You have a strange accent, I don't recognize it."

"I speak many languages. Russian was my mother's tongue. She taught it from the time I was a baby."

"But you lived elsewhere for a very long time?"

Putting her dinner plate aside, she said, "You are persistent, so I will tell you. I was born in Lithuania, but my mother was Russian and I was abducted at the age of seven. My full name is Zaza Masha Turetskya. My father profoundly hated the Party and all it stood for, and dared to defy it. They accused him of being an enemy of the State. As an act of spiteful revenge he paid the price— and so did I. They put him on trial. When he was sentenced, KGB operatives kidnapped me and whisked me away to Romania, to a so-called youth camp for those in need of deprogramming. It was several years until I managed to escape, before the collapse of the Soviet Union. I travelled by night, stealing, watchful of the police, and gradually made my way to Sophia, Bulgaria, where I joined up with a band of freedom-loving gypsies, rambling, moving always from place to place. First we journeyed to Hungary, later north to Poland, then to Latvia. I managed to slip back into Lithuania shortly before it became free. When I returned home I learned that my father was released from prison, and died within a year. My mother died too, grief-stricken after months of heartrending sobs. There was nothing for me to salvage. Does that make you happy?" She felt a stab of bereavement.

"No, of course not..."

"Russian police never stop hounding me. They are like crows and rats scuttling in the grass, waiting, watching. They find sadistic pleasure in my pain. The USSR was crumbling. I was in turmoil. Trying to run again I stole a motorcycle. I hurt myself on the road and suffered a serious concussion. I had been a week in hospital, unconscious, they said. Soon after, my paralyzing headaches began; but I know I was fortunate merely to have survived. I thanked my stars. My gypsy lover and I secretly escaped to the West. With forged papers we made our peace and lived in Germany. It was in Berlin that I discovered my abilities. One terrible night, after another of my headaches, I had frightful dreams like never before. My head was still pounding. I woke up sweating, trembling, tears streaming uncontrollably. In my vision I'd seen this bus, this bus filled with young people who appeared to be Chinese, groups visiting Europe on a summer tour. The bus crashed before my eyes. Overturned it lay, and I could see blood, mangled bodies lacerated and disfigured. I heard mournful cries for help I was unable to provide. It haunts me still. That dream tormented me, shook me to my bones. I could not get it out of my mind.

"The very next night I heard that a tourist bus overturned on the Autobahn. It was filled with student visitors, Asians. I was wrong; they were not Chinese students; they were Japanese. And many were killed. That was the first time I had a premonition. I tried to put it out of my mind, but I couldn't. My headaches worsened. Soon it happened again—and again. Premonition after premonition. I lost weight, stopped eating. I prayed and prayed for it to end. It didn't. My dreams became more vivid, and sometimes the people of my dreams spoke. Told me what had happened, or where they were to be found. Some begged for revenge, restless souls without peace. I cried for them.

"Since those days I've had many such dreams. People who know of me and respect me for my work come to me for my skills and tools. They do not treat me like dirt. I've helped many poor souls in distress. I charge no fees for telling what I see. But yes, I do accept donations. A woman has to survive, doesn't she? And our beloved new Russia doesn't always keep her promises, does she? But I get by. I'm not complaining. My gypsy lover is gone, long gone. Good riddance to him, I say. Good riddance to those who came after as well. Valentino and I get along perfectly, don't we sweetie?" The bird made an intelligible sound. "He must like you. He didn't swear. He mistrusts any who might wish me harm. Valentino is assuring me you mean no ill."

"You listen to your bird's advice?" Boris asked without humor. He didn't believe in any ability of divining information beyond the obvious five senses.

She narrowed her glare and met his gaze. "I can tell the difference between right and wrong, good and evil. You are not kind, but neither are you a bad sort. A plainclothesman, a police informer, a scion of the old regime, that's what you are." No reply came. She indicated to Vlad with a long, crooked finger. "I sense I can trust your young friend; he bears no malice."

"Then speak with us, Madam Zaza," Vlad said, coming closer as Boris quietly moved a few steps back. "Everything you've said so far is accurate. You're right. I had you carefully checked before we came to see you. I learned that the police have hounded you many times in many places over many years. You've been harassed, scorned, sometimes forced to flee. But we've come here tonight exactly as you predicted, to ask your assistance. If you truly hated the Party as you say your father did, then you won't want to see it regain power. You won't want to witness the return of Lenin. If you do possess extrasensory perception, please, will you help us?"

The seer studied Vlad's face with a slow and careful scrutiny that was making him uncomfortable. "You wish to learn where Lenin has been holding his secret conclaves," she said at last. She must have been a dazzling young woman, Vlad thought. As fiery and passionate as she was adventurous, with a grandeur and majesty richly infused with humor and sharp insight.

"Yes."

"Because the police have so far bungled the job?"

"Yes."

She indicated for Vlad to sit in one chair and Boris in the other. "I have had the same dream over and over disturbing my sleep for weeks now," she said. "There is a man, a small, sardonic man, and he grins scornfully. He enjoys toying with people, afflicting their lives, I can tell. Admirable but not loved, he is not a nice man. He dresses in a white coat like a physician. He is sly, this one—and smart. He beckons disrespectfully to me in my dream, and desires to reveal something hidden. I follow him, and it grows darker. He has a haughty laugh. His eyes appear large behind thick eyeglasses..."

Vlad and Boris exchanged furtive glances. "Sunavich," Vlad mouthed silently.

Madam Zaza put her hands over her face and rocked back and forth. Her voice remained soft and calm. "The small hateful man has conjured up another from purgatory, he tells me. He gestures. I see someone begin to arise from a... cold table, a table where he's been long sleeping. It appears to be a doctor's office. This sleeper sits up and opens his eyes. He looks around but is frightened, and confused. The small, depraved man basks with pride and soothes him. He supplies a strong drink. When the sleeper finishes it he seems to feel better. Slowly he places his feet on the ground, precariously standing fully, looking directly at me. I view him, and I feel his inner power. I am looking directly at... Vladimir Ilyich Lenin..." She made a little gasp and put her hand to her mouth.

"Do go on," Vlad urged.

She took her time, continuing at last in a throaty voice. "It is the darkest of nights. I hear sounds. Country sounds. A place where horses are herded and sheep raised, where cabbage grows, potatoes, and radishes, too. The sounds of frogs and yipping mongrels teem in the night, endless conversations of nocturnal animals...

"He doesn't bother to lock his door, but he is not a foolish man, this hidden one. He has mastered anguish and loneliness before, long ago, and spends no time fretting over foolish things. He is concerned with power struggles of far away, affairs in the capitals of Russian homelands. He is not defined by how others define him. No. He is different and capable. Many fear him, he knows. The confident small man who awoke him from slumber fears him, too. Russia is a tinderbox, a Sodom and Gomorrah cauldron overdue for destruction, and wherever he goes he shall leave a trail of smoldering debris. He alone carries the match to ignite it..." She paused, feeling waves of cold seeping inside her.

"Down a dirt road stands a tiny village amidst tangled grass and bare ground. The soil is good. Nearby I see a drafty house in disrepair, a wooden skeleton of forgotten history, a sorry place for sorry people. A friendless boarding house, I think, with many small dank rooms. It has a name. I cannot read the name clearly. Vagrants travel there, poor troubled souls with limited money. I hear a crackle of wagon wheels upon gravel. I smell cucumbers. Rabbits and rats burrow in deep grass, waiting for garbage to be tossed. Here he comes and hides, plots and schemes..."

"Lenin is hiding in this place?" said Boris, leaning forward.

The seer nodded. "Behind rusting gates, among the sad, the wretched, longing for a glimmer of hope. No one finds him there, no one disturbs him. Only those visitors who conspire against the privileged does he meet. His friends keep him safe." Madam Zaza rocked again and started to hum an ancient Russian folk song from the North Caucasus.

Nonplussed, Vlad asked, "Aren't there more clues in your dream? No further location to search?"

Her voice was singsong. "At the old boarding house. He goes and comes, he comes and goes."

Boris shot Vlad a glance as if to say, 'the witch is a lunatic'. But Vlad wasn't yet satisfied. "What else, Madam Zaza? Please."

The small man follows him there sometimes. Also there is a woman. Yes, there is a woman, younger than he, fertile and strong. She, too, wields power."

At this point Boris grew intently interested. Was this an allusion to Ilya Evgeny? "If you sincerely wish to help us, then explain anything more you're able. Russia is vast, and there are thousands of boarding houses filled with the poor and indigent. Where is it? *Where?*"

"He will wait until he is ready. But the sun sets in the West and I have seen it go down below the horizon in my dream. The place is to the West. Perhaps near the border, perhaps nearby across. I cannot say."

Vlad jotted a few notes into his phone. "Belarus is west. Lenin had many friends near Minsk..."

"Your friend is quite astute," Madam Zaza said to Boris. "I am not sure you deserve him." She smiled kindly at Vlad. "I also can tell that you are pained by love. Be patient and strong. It will pass, I promise. Better will come." Vlad felt momentarily shaken.

"We do appreciate your help, Madam," said Boris. "And we'll thoroughly check out everything you've said. May I leave you with a donation for your trouble?" He took out his wallet and gazed at her questioningly.

Madam Zaza Masha Turetskya gladly held out her hand.

"I don't give a damn if you have to muster the entire Russian army at dawn," barked the prime minister, convulsing with fury. "They're making bigger fools of us every day. I want this damned grotesque clone stopped! Shoot it. Chop it. Drown it. And then hand me Mikhail Sunavich's head." The prime minister heatedly strode back and forth over the blue-marbled floor, around the edges of the invaluable 17th century Scandinavian carpet. The ceilings were grand in this aristocratic room at the far southern end of the Kremlin. His private offices were spacious jewels that for centuries had belonged to the Czars. Several 19th century Victorian gilded chairs stood at opposite corners. An antique desk holding drawers with distinctive iron pulls was placed in front of two tall, narrow windows. A bronze, crystal beaded chandelier hung from the ceiling. Milonov stood before an eighteenth century curio cabinet, clasping trembling hands behind his back.

"We're conducting an all-inclusive investigation, Mr. Prime Minister," Boris Sokolov told him in his best reassuring tone, avoiding any mention of his clandestine meeting with Madam Zaza.

Unconvinced, Sergei Milonov sulked. "Don't patronize me. Do you have any inkling of how many sighting reports I've seen? Dozens from trusted sources, claiming Lenin is barnstorming across steppe and taiga, assembling ever growing, eager crowds pressing as far away as *Vladivostok*. Vladivostok, the end of the damned world! Why not cross China's border and bestow speeches to the Chinese? That would be a sight! The authorities would twine him in chains and display him in a cage. Then they'd publically have the little shit drawn and quartered." Spittle flew from his mouth.

"I understand fully, Mr. Prime Minister. Some think Lenin's purpose is to provoke the Pacific Fleet in Siberia to mutiny again."

Sergei threw up his hands in disgust, spluttering, "That's what I'm telling you!" he lambasted. "A communiqué on my desk says he's rallied another crowd of degenerates in Irkutsk—at the exact time he's supposedly in Vladivostok. How can someone be in two goddamned places at once? And how can this fabricated Lenin have reached Siberia when reports pinpoint him in Pinsk, extolling drivel to his constituency along the banks of the river like a flaming biblical prophet? Rallies here, rallies there, engulfing us. The blogs are abuzz with this dung. He's become a cult figure, a 21st century Spartacus. It's a travesty, a cyber uprising. Stop them! We're living in the information age of scientific know-how, yet we're spectacularly inadequate to snare a rag-tag, wayfaring *freak*! Is Internal Security totally composed of incapable bumblers?"

"I believe the sighting you referred to happened at Minsk," Boris corrected. "Our best minds are exploiting everything possible to uncover clues where he'll pop up next. Unfortunately he's all too real, having his obstreperous adherents faking sightings to confound us. There's no magic bullet. We're walking a razor's edge."

"I see. He's become a beatified hero on a white horse, miraculously arriving with a mandate to rescue the people."

In the corner, Tinkerbelle the cat meowed and stretched. Boris looked on in consternation while Sergei kneeled and tenderly stroked the feline. Tinkerbelle was brought regularly from home to office; the prime minister loved her so. Sergei Milonov plopped into his chair and stared blankly at the ceiling. "Do you know what I was contemplating just two weeks ago, Boris? Let me enlighten you. I was sitting in this very chair, staring at this very ceiling, conceptualizing how wonderful life will be when I announce my retirement shortly after the Federation's extravaganza. I'd be hailed a State hero amid this roiling world of convoluted Russian politics, honored with awards, endowed with well-deserved gravy envelopes. And then I'd retreat to my modest villa on the Black Sea, eating duck in red bilberry sauce for supper. I'd lie on my ass on the cabana all day, spending nights at the casino and stylish eateries. A proliferation of the world's most enchanting women would cling on my arm, and I'd sit around reflective pools of glamorous mansions and gathering spots, treated like an international mogul. Spend winters at Mallorca and Ibiza on sugar-white beaches nibbling delectable edibles, and attending wine tastings. What do you think of that scenario, Boris?"

"A life tantalizing the senses, envied by every man."

"Precisely." The prime minister leaned forward, elbows on his desk, and shot an angry, red-faced stare at his most artful advisor. "I'll let you in on something. Do you know what's happening to that sublime life I've envisioned? It's being flushed down a toilet in front of my eyes. Poof! My dream seems less likely every passing hour, and the only place for my sorry ass might be a basement desk in Vladivostok. Do you know how dark and awful winters are in Vladivostok, Boris? Give the matter some thought because I'll be bringing you to Siberia. Only you'll be going to Yakutsk for a bit of rehabilitation, 450 kilometers south of the Arctic Circle. You'll spend your days pondering the mysteries and perfidies of life while selling furs and candle wax. And if the situation further deteriorates you'll be shoveling Yakutsk shit in a gulag latrine, maybe hunting sea otter for petty cash. Do you grasp what I'm telling you, Boris?" He pointed an angry finger. "These moronic 'intelligence' reports indicate civil unrest is increasing all over creation even as we talk. He's become a cancer...a malignant cancer we must remove."

"I'm well aware, Sergei, but it's more entangled than you realize. These are posers, lookalikes seeking attention and a little fast money. Drifters, impersonators, con artists. We've questioned many, arrested dozens. Scientists are at work night and day in conjunction with Rabbi Titlebaum to solve this mess. It comes down to old-fashioned, shoe-leather detective work. No one could have predicted how infuriatingly devious and clever Mikhail Sunavich is."

"You're saying this backstabber's duped us? We haven't been able to infiltrate the ranks of this would-be Robin Hood?"

"He's ludicrously intelligent. We're relying on patience and guile to exploit holes within their intelligence network."

"*Someone* will be held accountable in the wake of this counterintelligence collapse. Heads will roll—you know that very well, Sokolov. I want an immediate crackdown against civil disobedience—*now*. Furthermore," he opened the top drawer of his dark wooden desk and withdrew a batch of passports held together by a rubber band. "Before you go, allow me to show you something else of interest. Do you see these? This one is French. The next is British. This other is Canadian, and the final one issued by Australia. And do you know what's fascinating about them?"

"No," Boris replied while the ever-present Tinkerbelle slinked around the corner of the room.

The prime minister beckoned with his finger. "Have a better look. Let's say you have a passport and I have passport. Then we'd have two passports, one for each of us, wouldn't we? But supposing I took your passport and put my own photograph in it. Then I'd have two passports, wouldn't I?"

"I'm not following you."

"Take a peek at these."

Boris took them in hand. "They seem genuine."

"Pay attention to the photographs."

They invited scrutiny, and Boris carefully examined, holding each up to the light, searching for visible embedded watermarks to provide detailed authenticity incorporated into the passports. When he was finished he puffed his cheeks and blew out his breath. "All carry identical photos, the same man with different identities."

"Very good. Do you recognize any?"

"I recognize all."

"Excellent. Please tell me whose smiling photograph adorns them."

"It's the eccentric American assigned by their Department of Agriculture, Floyd Dingus."

"Bingo!" said Sergei Milonov, pushing back his chair with glib confidence. He made a pyramid with his hands. "Do you suppose Floyd Dingus is a Frenchman, a Brit, an American, or perhaps even a Mossad agent?"

"He could be anything, Sergei. If they're forgeries, they're perfect. But passports are easily obtained on black markets. May I ask how you obtained these?"

"You may ask, but I won't answer. Suffice to say this American, Floyd Dingus, freely walks our streets, convincingly playing his role. I've instructed the police not to intervene. We want him convinced we're not on to him. New copies of his passports have already replaced these. *Gospodin* Floyd Dingus will never know the difference."

Boris shifted his gaze from the prime minister to the thick bookshelves lining the far wall. The books were packed tightly for show; Milonov didn't enjoy reading books, which he said were a waste of time, and led to his migraines. "If Dingus is an imposter, what do you think his game is? Do you suspect he's been involved somehow with Codename Chocolate Lenin?"

"I should ask you those questions, spymaster. That's why you and your snitches work for me. Of course I suspect he's a mole, but exactly who he is working for I expect you to learn. Needless to say, Boris, you'll not mention a word of our discussion to anyone—not even your team. I want everyone dealing with Mr. Dingus treating him as though he's just another lame, inept American official. And I mean *everyone*."

"I understand you instruction perfectly, Mr. Prime Minister," Boris replied, trying to second-guess what Milonov was up to. Obviously the prime minister didn't want the president advised of this touchy matter. Under Russia's newest constitution presidential powers weren't balanced by restraint, and mutual mistrust among ranking officials was rampant.

"I hope you do understand," the prime minister said with a touch of menace. "I hope you do."

"Well?" said Alina Vera. "Don't hold back!"

Asher Titlebaum smiled from ear to ear. He stretched his arms and clapped his hands. "I think we have our samples. I received a hastily scrambled text message mere moments ago."

"From Rimsky-Kimsky?" said Vlad.

"Yes. He's slow and exasperatingly punctilious, but a top man." The rabbi looked to Dimsky. "Go on and fill them in, Colonel."

"Our coordinates accessing the telephone conversation were definitive," Dimsky began. "This Lenin is extremely cautious; he uses no email, no mobile phone. But Anya's little chat with Ilya Evgeny has paid off, giving us barely time to pinpoint their current safe house. National Security Police coordinating with crack commandos conducted a daring raid during the early hours before dawn, converging on the refuge. It's a small boarding house sheltered at the forest's edge. Unfortunately, they arrived too late to trap our suspects. But we did locate the room Lenin and Evgeny last occupied. The place is near a small village not far from the kidnapping site in Gorki, about fifty kilometers from the main road to Minsk."

Vlad held his breath. "Madam Zaza was right..."

Dimsky nodded. "Her suggestions were accurate, which the telephone coordinates corroborated. But there were many places to probe before we managed to hone in on this one and plan our assault. How much of a role her psychic abilities played I can't say, but she provided valuable service. We rounded up the boarding house residents for interrogation. Information provided was useless. What a motley bunch, ignorant of enterprise transpiring under their noses. However, our unit persevered and recovered the grand prize." He spoke glowingly of his task force. "We arrested the innkeeper-owner of this leaky dump. Her name is Olga Orlovskya." He whistled. "A real piece of work that one. All indications point to this Orlovskya being in some sort of collusion with Sunavich, Lenin, or both. When we arrested her she was sitting alone in her room eating *kurnik*, festive chicken pie. She jumped up, demanding she be allowed to finish her *kurnik* before being taken into custody, screaming we were 'cruel, inhumane, and degrading,' and infringing upon her civil liberties and constitutional rights. We cuffed her and dragged her away screeching and chewing."

"Nice work," said Vlad. "What do we know about this innkeeper?"

The colonel grimaced. "So far very little. She's coy. A faking consumptive petitioning government benefits. A middle-aged widow who collects a military pension from her deceased husband's lengthy service. I'm glad I wasn't married to her, I can tell you. The poor chap served thirty-five years in uniform until one day he keeled over just like that on the eve of retirement. Very sad. So far, under diligent questioning, the widow refuses to divulge any useful intelligence. She reportedly laughed in the faces of her interlocutors. A staunch apostle of the old ways, for sure, and doubtless she's content playing a small role as a cog in Lenin's clique. She's a stubborn old bat, this Orlovskya, but we'll get everything out of her one way or another. Of further interest, the hotel register shows that a frequent guest was someone calling himself 'Andrei Popov'. He lists his profession as 'harpsichord player'. Handwriting experts examined this Andrei Popov's signature carefully. It has odd flourishes, and virtually identical similarities with the signature of M. Sunavich. After close comparison the experts feel sure it's his handwriting."

"Sunavich!" exclaimed Boris. "Andrei Popov is the alias of Dr. Sunavich!"

"Possibly. I've alerted all police commands, and sent instruction for Popov's arrest on sight."

"Excellent, Colonel! Make certain Inspector Drinkwater of Internal Security is informed. He's been on standby, and he'll know what to do."

"I've already done it." Dimsky continued. "Drinkwater's squad is alerted. As for Lenin, our best intelligence thinks he feels safer across the frontier, not daring to make his way inside Russia until he's secure in popular support and financial backing. Perhaps the Inn's stubborn old bat can provide clues in that area. We'll get on it right away."

"The semen, Colonel!" the frustrated rabbi interrupted. "That's our priority! Did you detect any?"

"Oh. Don't worry, we didn't forget, Rabbi. A careful examination of the room's bed sheets was conducted, and there's no dispute—it contains characteristic evidence of recent post coitus sexual activity. Some sheet stains reportedly were faded. However, our people methodically extrapolated all newer samples for study. Copulation samplings were flown to Omsk in refrigerated containers before our team withdrew."

"The semen is without contamination?"

"Forensic police experts took supervisory responsibility. They swabbed and collected the fresh specimens. That Inn was a virtual brothel, a smelly hovel, infested, badly in need of major repairs. I think the old prune gave approval to local prostitutes to rent out rooms by the hour."

Vlad asked, "How can we be sure it's Lenin's seminal fluid, not someone else's?"

"We don't have conclusive answers yet. The scientific team says preliminary indications show the collected discharge is unmatched. There was quite a bit of ejaculate. A considerable flow emerged. They did an immediate PCR test at a local laboratory."

"What's that?"

"An abbreviation for Polymerase Chain Reaction," explained Alina Vera. "PCR copies DNA efficiently, assuming it's in quality condition." Turning to Asher, she said, "He'd achieved multiple ejaculations?"

"Assuredly so," Asher replied. "His outward appearance may look time-worn, but inside his regenerated body his organs are vigorous and virile, at a prime. He'll be athletic, and fully functioning. Concerning sexual matters he might even be considered virginal."

"That being the case," said the colonel, "after steamy sex I'd speculate he disgorged his flow several times."

"Maybe more," opined Alina Vera with fascination. "My money says she's fucking the old bugger's brains out."

Vlad overlooked the comment. "When can we hope to learn something conclusive?"

"As of now his complete DNA structure is urgently being analyzed, contrasted, and segregated versus tissue previously withdrawn from 'Little Man's' testicles. We're screening Lenin's DNA markers. PCR-based tests are fast and sensitive, but better RFLP testing requires larger amounts of non-degraded DNA. Fortunately, we obtained enough to conduct both. My hope is to add to our arsenal by correlating comparisons to garner incontrovertible profitable evidence within hours."

"Good. And if it's proven his beyond doubt?"

Asher rubbed the crown of his head, fitting his yarmulke in place. "If it's conclusively confirmed, then we'll unearth the method for using his own body fluids against him."

"Since returning to Moscow we're spinning wheels, wasting time like couch potatoes." Alina Vera was rueful and restless. "We should be on the move."

"She's right," said Vlad. "Fighting battles with computers and technology is Dimsky's domain. Our adversaries attack while we squander our time mining more stacks of useless data."

It was true. The shots of their cat-and-mouse game were managed solely at Lenin's whim, while they stumbled to react to his provocations. They'd all drawn the same conclusion.

"I'm unsettled, too," said Boris. "It so happens I have timely job to undertake, except the Kremlin considers me obligated to stay here. So, I want you and Alina Vera to travel to Minsk, interrogate, and evaluate this innkeeper, Olga Orlovskya. You'll be taking my place. She's a clever conniver, not providing a single piece of information. The Belarusians aren't getting anywhere, which doesn't surprise me considering how inept they've been. It's time for a different approach. I trust your instincts, Alina Vera. Your father taught you well. You have the right temperament, and a good nose for smelling out liars. Will you do this for me?"

She readily jumped at the offer. "You know I will."

"Belarus is in economic devastation, suffering from decade after decade of economic stagnation," Boris went on. "Things are bad and getting worse. Radioactive contamination of forestland from the Chernobyl disaster still severely restricts agricultural output. Civil unrest is bubbling barely beneath the surface, and the whole place is ripe for poisonous agitators. The authorities are walking a tightrope, dancing a delicate balancing act to retain control over an unhappy people straining for a whiff of freedom. I need you to find out everything you can elicit from the prisoner. Not merely Lenin's whereabouts, but also information regarding Sunavich. His dirty fingerprints are smeared all over this." He gazed directly at Vlad. "And I don't want Alina Vera out there alone. It's too dangerous. Accompany and assist her in the interrogation. She'll need your help, and I think the two of you make a good team. Can I count on you?"

"I'll do everything I can," Vlad assured. "When can you book tickets?"

"Tickets? I'll charter a plane. That old medusa of an innkeeper is being temporarily held at police headquarters. It's tricky footing until we receive complete cooperation from the Belarus authorities. But they owe us, so it's only a matter of a time until documents are cleared. We're asking she be kept indefinitely incommunicado under their Emergency Terrorism Act. Meanwhile, I'll arrange your flight and expect reports beginning tomorrow."

The chartered night flight was short and uneventful. The Belarus government swiftly approved their undisclosed objective. A chauffeur and car were waiting at the new Minsk National Airport. They were quickly driven along winding, flat roads near forests heavy with pinewood and oak. Spongy, thawed fields with grass sprouting from beneath tangled roots stood forlornly. Here and there an old tractor or combine could be viewed. In less than an hour they approached their destination, a lonely fortification at the unpopulated, outskirts of the capital city. A murky landscape veiled by a bleached, bluish mist.

The prisoner, Olga Orlovskya, had been hurriedly whisked to this marooned location, once housing foremost political prisoners. It was an intimidating concrete and brick edifice reminding Vlad of stories heard during the ominous heights of communist power. A sinister accommodation few ever left—at least while still alive. Its baleful elevated walls and looming sentry towers made him shiver. Alina Vera braced his arm tightly as they walked inside the opened gates of the dreary maximum-security facility.

A century before, Minsk had been a major center for the Bolshevik movement dating to the earliest days of their rise to power. During the First World War, Minsk served as headquarters for the Russian Army's Western Front, then a beehive of military activity. A Worker's Soviet Council was established, and Lenin cherished and venerated. No surprise this locale was considered prime breeding ground for sowing seeds of unrest.

"I'm astonished the Belarusian authorities agreed to all our requests," Alina Vera commented as they entered the foreboding enclosure. A massive steel gate clanged shut behind them.

"They're as distressed by it as we are," said Vlad. "The nation is insolvent. Insurrection will spread here like wildfire, and what better place for this renegade than where he began his first ascent to power? He's shrewdly outfoxed and frustrated everyone, running about, fanning discontent. Anya's attempted kidnapping is just an opener. The authorities here are also desperate to catch him, as impoverished as people are. This place is explosive, just waiting for a match."

"I pity poor Anya. She's such a trusting child. I'm thinking Ilya Evgeny has played the kid for a fool all along, capitalizing on her fame."

"You mean she's a diabolic money-grubbing hustler contriving for an opportunity? Well, I think so, too."

Alina Vera laughed.

They accompanied a prison guard into a sallowly lit holding room. They sat on a bare slatted bench, surrounded by joyless, peeling olive-green plaster walls. The chamber reeked; it was a disheartening, deplorable confinement.

The prisoner was soon escorted inside. She wore a shabby, dirty-patched shawl across her sloping shoulders. Unwashed, uncombed gray hair fell and curled at the nape of her neck. She was a chubby woman, overweight around the middle and thighs, with fleshy arms and large hands. Dark bags were conspicuous beneath cautious eyes, and a double chin that eclipsed her neck. Two long gray hairs grew from that chin, which bothered Alina Vera to no end. The scientist quietly longed for a pair of tweezers, as she visualized plucking out the offending hairs.

As she and Vlad waited on the opposite side of the worn table, the prisoner eased onto the splintered bench with obvious discomfort and indignation. Olga Orlovskya rubbed at her shackle-freed wrists. She squinted, regarding her unexpected visitors with bright, watery eyes glaring with defiance. A fluorescent light above accentuated the shadows across her cabbage-round face. Bottles of mineral water sat on the table and Alina Vera offered one to the woman directly across from her.

"My partner and I have travelled from Moscow to speak with you today. My name is Alina Vera Galina. This is *Pan* Petrovsky." She used the Belarus word for 'Mister'. "I hope you understand the severity of the charges against you, Olga. All we ask from you is cooperation."

"I wouldn't drink that mineral water if I were you. It might be poisoned," Olga said, scowling. She wrapped her tattered shawl tighter to shield a strong draft while scrutinizing the Muscovites.

"I hope you'll take seriously what Alina Vera just said," Vlad told her, ignoring her comment.

"Oh, Moscow's a long way, isn't it? You might as well take your tickets and go home. I've spent plenty of time speaking with the police and said everything I want. Return me to my cell. The stink here is like the smell of sewage on a hot summer day."

"Look, we're not the police," Vlad told her dismissively. "Your guards will take you back after we're finished."

Olga shrugged. "I see. Have it your way." Her lips were large even for her apple-cheeked, buttery face. One of her front teeth was broken, jagged at the corner. "I couldn't care less where you came from, or who you are. It's no matter to me. Last night my guards threatened to beat me—again. Before that they threatened to starve me, even deny permission to use the toilet. Do you think I was frightened? Would you like to hear what I told them?" Her lips curled in a harsh mock smile. She knew she was in a special category of punishment designed for women prisoners who have politically threatened the system. Solitary confinement was only the beginning.

"We can pretty well guess," Alina Vera dryly reprimanded. "Let's not play games, prisoner. We don't need to use threats." She leaned forward, palms on the table. "I think you and I understand each other very well."

"You think someone like you can understand someone like me?" Her thick eyebrows rose with her crooked sneer and vituperation. "I've known your kind all my life. You don't fool me. I'm not ignorant. I went to school. My father sold goods to cushy landowners. I read, write, and count. Maybe I'd have gone away to study, but I was very young and stupid. I fell in love. My father hated the boy, lashed him with his whip, ordering him to never see me again or he'd kill him. So we fled. What could a lowly young man do with no trade? He became a soldier, and a good one at that. My husband served his country, did you know? Is that information in my police folder? The army awarded him medals, gave him citations in cheap frames which he proudly hung on the walls. For thirty-plus years he gave his life for his country, and for what? They emasculated him, and he didn't even know it. He was a sorry fool." She turned her face away with repugnance.

"I read his military file," said Vlad. "He was a good soldier, and a brave one. His commanding officer wrote he served with dignity and pride, and he did the best he could for his family. You didn't starve, did you Olga? You always had shelter above your head. Life's never easy lacking education."

"Oh, I see. Today we're looking down at lowly peasants, are we? What do you know of it? My husband stayed loyal to the State until his dying day. He did exactly what he was told, every time. When he was given an order he snapped to attention and carried it out. He fought in Chechnya and took bullets. Became a prisoner and escaped. And at the end of the road what did he get for all his bravery? Did they feast him on fancy apple cinnamon duck like a rich *Boyar*? No, he got a royal broom up his ass."

Vlad cleared his throat. "Nevertheless, you managed to put away enough money to purchase your little inn."

"Not thanks to your kind," she retorted crossly. "Not that it's any of your business. I learned the hard way to scratch money from lechers; men in expensive suits with fancy educations. They talk sweetly to your face while picking your pockets. I fought for every wretched penny of my money. Was your own ancestor an aristocrat? A spoon-fed duke surrounding himself with serfs licking his boots and wiping his behind?"

"My grandfather was a master craftsman, a carpenter," Vlad replied in a calm, restrained voice. "His own father served in the army during the war. He, too, was decorated after the fighting ended."

Not pacified by the comparison Olga launched into a scolding tirade. "You claim to be a child of the proletariat? If your grandfather was a tradesman you should be ashamed," she castigated. "Why do you do business with his enemies? Your unhappy grandfather must be rolling in his grave, his grandson a lackey for elites bleeding the people." Her burning eyes shot animus toward Alina Vera, flickering with unmistakable contempt. "And why do you work for the likes of *her*? That one has the rot of wealth all over her. Arrogant, a moneyed pretender, she's nothing but a city whore."

Alina Vera leaned coolly across the table, glaring face to face with her antagonist, breath hot against Olga's skin. "I don't give a fuck if you hate me or not," she hissed. "You and your kind nauseate me, too, *Comrade*—but sooner or later you *will* talk."

"If I refuse?" Her voice dripped with vitriol. Their eyes locked tensely.

Her disdain was bluntly reciprocated. "Then you'll fester here. Forever. An unfortunate creature of your own stupidity. Either way your Lenin will soon be a dead man."

Olga leered. She wiped a runny nose with the back of her hand. Vlad handed a few tissues as Alina Vera added, "We'll find Lenin with or without your help."

"You'll never get your wretched hands on him no matter what you do," she scoffed. "The faithful love him too much. He's the greatest leader of all; my own grandparents told me so. When Lenin spoke the proletariat stood mesmerized, clinging to his every word. He brought hope, gave them courage to fight, and made them strong, not like your kind, weaklings who pay to have your dirty work done. You're all nothing but thieves and trash. Your ancestors stole the land, keeping us vassals for a thousand years. The history books say Comrade Lenin returned the land to its rightful heirs. But when I was a child your counter-revolution turned into what you call 'democracy,' stealing it back with pretty words. All lies and empty promises. Worthless slogans uttered by rich, fascist pirates. The people can't eat promises. You sell us out, growing fat off their backs." She lifted her chin and raised her head high. "When the time is right…"

"We already know who's been hiding in that squalid room of yours," Alina Vera flared. "When did you first meet your darling revolutionary, and who accompanied him?"

"The common people accompany him in his heart, because we're not like you. We're not false." She made fists with her sturdy hands. "We are of the earth. We are strong. We cannot be defeated."

"You're refusing to answer is ill-advised. He's using you, but you can't see it. This man is a false prophet. Real misery only began when the Bolsheviks secured power with their profane manifesto, each ensuing leader proving worse than his predecessor, until the nation fell to its knees. Millions suffered in labor camps, millions perished. In the end you'll get nothing but sorrow and heartache from your unstable messianic fanatic."

Olga sat motionless, eyes staring blankly ahead.

"Why not tell us where he's hiding?" Vlad said.

"Go on. Try and catch him if you can. Try it, if you're fool enough. But you can't, can you? That's why you traveled all this way to visit someone like me. You think somehow you'll convince me to help. Even if I did it wouldn't matter. He's too smart. He knows, oh yes, he knows. We common folk are true brothers and sisters. We cradle him to our bosoms and keep him safe. You can't catch Lenin any more than you can catch the wind."

She was a zealot, Vlad saw. A devoted believer, prepared to give her very existence for her cause. The police could beat, starve, and deprive her all they wished, and still she'd treat them with repugnance. No matter what torture they devised, it was useless. She'd only lie or give false information. So he decided to shift tactics. "Did you know that the woman who's sleeping with your Lenin is one of our spies," he said matter-of-factly. "She's been an informer for the police all along."

"You're a liar! She's one of us. She'd die for him."

"I don't need to lie, Olga. Her name is Ilya Evgeny. Does it sound familiar? She's been posing as tennis manager to Anya Andropova for the past several years. I can freely tell you this because while you're in jail you're not a threat. Your hero will be long dead by the time you're released. However, if you're willing to share some information—"

Olga bit her lip; she'd maintained her composure until then, but suddenly something snapped. She peered toward the corridor, sad eyes overflowing with tears. Was it mention of Ilya Evgeny that so disturbed her? Had Lenin's consort caused rifts between them? Deftly sizing up the situation, Vlad quickly realized he'd sown seeds of doubt. Perhaps Olga hadn't fully believed him, but he knew she couldn't be quite sure.

"It wouldn't matter anyway," she said after a moment, sniffling. "He can make love to as many women as he desires. Women everywhere fall at his feet. Besides, soon it won't matter because the true revolution has begun. Can't you see it boiling over, people gathering, whispering? Men, boys, and women prepared for a long fight. Your system is shameless, greedy, stealing the wages of decent citizens. We defeated you before and we'll defeat you again. In time, Lenin also will come to realize who his true friends are, those he can rely on."

"The Belarus police can keep you locked up indefinitely," Alina Vera reminded. "You're being confined under your Emergency Terrorism Act. You won't survive long enough to witness any 'Glorious Revolution'. We could have helped you, Olga, but you insist on refusing."

A grim sort of levity glowed in Olga's watery eyes, and the depth of her hatred disquieted Vlad. She spoke with such passion it jarred him. If Olga Orlovskya proved typical of the new army Lenin raised, then indeed bloodshed would flood the streets. If he hadn't fathomed how deep this enmity burrowed before, he surely did now. Doubtless there were millions of inflamed sympathizers corresponding to Olga among the poor, deprived, and disenfranchised. Ordinary folk held down so long they'd gladly risk life for the chance of overthrowing this reviled established order. He was also acutely aware of how well Mikhail Sunavich had penetrated the minds and hearts of the peasantry, eternal dreamers craving a return to the old ways. They were simple people, pawns of a broader game played out on a vastly broader stage. But things don't always go according to plan, Vlad understood. He wondered if the mad scientist's creation might one day surprise him and turn the tables.

As if reading his thoughts, Olga blurted, "Your eunuchs can't stop us, you'll never stop us. We're an unflinching army hidden in every town, every village. Camouflaged, holding on, biding our time."

"Well, while you're biding time awaiting release from this paradise, at least accept this." Vlad stood and passed her a small box of marshmallow chocolates. Olga stared with bewilderment. "I know quite a bit about you, Olga. More than you think. Don't deny it. These are your favorites, aren't they?"

Her eyes darted back and forth between Vlad and the chocolates. She reached hastily for the box and pulled it tightly to her bosom, trying to hide unexpected surges of emotion.

"I'm hoping we'll have a chance to talk again soon," said Vlad. The interview was over. "I'll try to bring more the next time we visit."

11.

The young boy was timid and nearsighted, squinting constantly, needing glasses. "I'll not harm you, lad," the soft-spoken, dignified man said. The boy took notice of the stranger's suit. City clothes, he realized. City people had money, his father said. They were unproductive, worthless types, usually gangsters who rob the poor. Such people could afford to buy whatever they wanted.

The boy glanced up and down at the stranger's disheveled clothing. His bearing suggested wealth, but on closer examination his suit was ill fitting and frayed, splattered with soil and grime. His leather shoes were pinched and torn. As for the taller, muscular woman, her tailored clothes were unkempt and no less faded and fatigued. She stood on one foot and then the other, her feet raw and blistered. She seemed irritated. The man smiled in a friendly way but she did not.

"I wish your help in guiding us to town," he said to the boy.

The child observed with interest while the man and woman slapped layers of dense dust and chunky mud from their garments. The man's voice was gentle but the woman had unmistakable anger.

"What did you expect?" she said with derision. "Riding all night in that grubby pile of shit? We were hurrying to catch a train, you said. Important people were waiting at the other end, you said. Catch a train, ha! First that sorry nag has fits and gives out. Then the mindless driver gets on his knees and begins wailing beside the swarming flies. Are these the people you say we're depending on? When he bent over beside the dying horse to beg forgiveness I wanted to kick him in his ass, and get back our money.

"We'll walk, you said. The train station is close. Well, the station was broken down and deserted, with a stink worse than a pigsty. Pornographic graffiti scrawled over the walls. And the wind and rain, rain and wind, with no letup." She didn't pause to catch breath while she berated him. "Its already mid morning and I'm feeling weak. I'm hungry, too. My stomach is growling. When was the last time we had a meal, eh? Decent food? We're not fodder to be treated this way. You there, boy, listen well and do as we ask. We'll pay good money for your trouble. Go on! Lead the way quickly to your town!"

The traveler reached inside his pocket and pulled out a small wad of cash. Unscathed by her tirade, he smiled amiably, bending over and handing the boy a few notes. "She's had a hard time of it these past few days, lad. Don't be upset by her crude words. At heart she's a good woman. An exemplary woman, the salt of the earth. Here, lad, take this. Now please lead us the fastest way you know. We've been walking on this bad road for hours." The boy listened and agreed. He greedily took the cash and carefully put it into his own pocket. He walked on without saying a word, his mind occupied by irrelevant matters.

Lenin said to his companion, "It really wasn't the driver's fault that the hapless mare collapsed. You saw the poor fellow trying his best to hurry the animal on. You didn't have to keep yelling and insulting him. Nor spit at him."

Ilya Evgeny stopped cold in her tracks and took off her right shoe. She shook it and a handful of pebbles fell to the ground. Her hair was disarrayed and straw-like. "Look at this. My shoes are ruined, and I have blood blisters on my feet. Now my ankle is swollen, too, and my back hurts like hell. I have sharp pain shooting up and down my legs. I need to sit quietly for a few minutes, OK?"

Lenin looked toward the sun and shaded his eyes. He pulled open his starched collar and loosened his tie. He wished to look his best at all times but it was proving a challenge. The sun was rising higher in a cloudless sky. It was a warm, muggy day, a precursor of the hot dry summers in the hinterland. Yellow dandelions rose amid the grass. Wearily, he picked up the two pieces of worn luggage, carrying one in each hand, and slogged onward behind the country boy.

"There's no time for stopping now, Ilya. You know our agenda. Must I remind you said you were hungry? We'll surely find a friendly little café to serve hot food in the village. They are fine people in these parts. I know them. They'll help us. They won't turn us away." The taste of copious dust was in his mouth; he coughed grit from his lungs, and spat on the side of the road. The slope of open, empty country lay beyond. These backwoods roads of Belarus were worse than the dilapidated roads of Russia. Something needed to be done about it. "How much longer to reach town, boy?" he called. "It's going to get hotter. Walking in hot sun and toting bags is strenuous."

Without looking back the boy responded, "Not far, *Pan*. There's fresh well water on the way, a little ahead. I'll take you there. If you and your wife are thirsty, I'll ask the farmer to let you drink. It's clean and always cool. The farmer is my father's friend."

"Yes, yes, that would be excellent, boy." Lenin trod on at a slowing pace, slightly waddling as he balanced the luggage. His own back was hurting, and he would have paused to rub it but neither hand was free. Ilya's small baggage was far heavier than his own, and he wondered what she might be carrying. Women's garments always puzzled him. "A water well! Wonderful, bring us quickly."

He turned to the demoralized woman. "Now can you understand, Ilya? This lad will take us to the farmer, and the farmer's water will quench our thirst. Do you see how peasants sow their fields and feed the workers? And in turn the workers feed the nation. I'm sure this well water is cold and tasty. Hey, boy! Are we close, eh? Please, Ilya, let's do make haste. We're both exhausted. Perhaps we'll find a clean room at the village. Wouldn't that be nice? You can take a hot bath, luxuriate, and be refreshed for the rest of our journey. There's still a long way to go, a very long way."

"All right. I hear you." Muttering under her breath, she rasped, "You old sod; this isn't a smart way to organize a revolution." So far they'd been unimaginative, slow, generating little real progress. She'd have to whip him into shape and bring him fully into the 21st century.

Lenin began whistling a traditional Russian folksong. He smiled as he observed rolling hills turning lush green and fertile, wildflowers blooming, the countryside imbued with dazzling color and beauty. Birds singing, rivers thawing at last, gently flowing. Bucolic with a sensuous pleasure of frolicsome peasants plowing seed in the lengthy process of nurturing the soil until harvest time. How glorious it all was. Somehow it made the difficult work ahead seem easier.

"I have to take a break and go into the bushes," Ilya announced.

Looking back over his shoulder, Lenin said, "Can't it wait, pretty one? The boy says the farmer's home is near."

"If I don't stop, I'll collapse," she retorted, her nostrils dilating. "Would *that* make you feel better?"

He sighed. There was no use in attempting to mollify her. "Hold up a minute, lad. The lady requires a short pause."

The boy halted in his tracks. Lenin placed the shabby suitcases side by side and sat on one. His elbows rested on his knees, his chin in his hands. His feet were sore. He was sweating profusely as Ilya walked to the side of the dusty road and made her way amidst clumps of thorny bushes. She returned noticeably calmer.

"Are you feeling better, dearest?"

"I am. In fact, I'm feeling much better." Standing with her legs apart she stretched, bending over, arms straight, fingertips to the ground. She was fond of exercise, especially aerobics. Her toned figure was athletic. He noticed her mobile phone was in her hand.

"Oh my God," cried Anya Andropova, "I just received a text message from Ilya."

"Dear girl, read it aloud," said Asher, his heart racing with anticipation.

The tennis player sat at the end of the bed, clearing her throat. Ilya says, "I need the money I asked you for. I'll be able to collect it soon, across the border on my way home." Anya looked up disconsolately. "That's all she wrote. She didn't even ask how I was."

The rabbi thought carefully. Crossing the border must mean they planned on returning to Russia at last. The chess pieces were nearly in place, opening moves prepared. He took a handful of grapes and cashews and ate them slowly one by one, paying no attention to the nagging ache in his lower back.

Alina Vera stood on the sidewalk waiting. She held her umbrella above her head. A leaden sky had opened with a heavy downpour in the morning that had only now abated. Minsk was a city destroyed and rebuilt numerous times, practically turned to rubble after World War II.

During the afternoon they'd strolled market stalls at *Dynamo* stadium. The small, quaint restaurant where they'd eaten dinner displayed a menu in its window that read *pilmeni* and *verenekei*, meat & potato dumplings.

They were a parochial, insular people in Minsk, she thought as they left, pulling her fur collar tightly up to ward off a chill.

Noises in the distance came from the direction of the city center at nearby Independence Square. Vlad followed her outside and stood listening. "It sounds like a demonstration," Alina Vera said with a hint of worry. She clutched her umbrella tighter. "I want to take a closer look."

Prospekt Nezavisimosti, Minsk's main thoroughfare was quiet, motor traffic spare, almost all shops closed. There was a clamor at the end of the street where a nighttime café was doing a good business despite the gloomy weather. Minsk was a quiet, well kept, quaint city, adorned with attractive public gardens and gracious monuments scattered throughout. A police car rushed by in the same direction they were walking.

Vlad reached out and gripped Alina Vera's arm. A crowd was moving in their direction. He drew her deep into the canopied shadows outside an unlit storefront.

The protesters were a tattered and ramshackle group, a collection of working-class young men and women. Several of the leaders marched stiffly, waving flags. Red flags.

"Restore worker's rights!" someone shouted.

"Down with oppression!" they demanded clamorously. They were knowingly flouting a ban on demonstrations, facing severe consequences to address their deep grievances.

Alina Vera tried to contact Boris on her smartphone. "I can't send a text. There's no signal. They've crashed the system, the network's dead."

"Satellite communication's been cut," he said. "They don't want the outside world to see."

"Well, they're going to see it all!" She held up her phone and shot a short video.

"Are you crazy? If they see you—"

"I don't care. These people aren't dangerous."

"More to be pitied, if they're arrested. Put your phone away. Authorities here are draconian; they'll haul every one into District Court, and lock them away—including us."

All the nation's media, television, film, and especially the press were heavily controlled, he knew, and popular opponents of the regime all too often simply disappeared off the face of the earth. He cleaned rain from his lenses and squinted ahead. He estimated there were about a hundred of them, not a worrisome size. Placards called for rights and justice, and an end to brutality. He felt sorry for their plight.

A drumbeat began, a steady cadence growing intense. Alina Vera pointed to another direction. From an opposite direction near the square's fountains another group was rapidly descending from a side street. This new group was brash and provocative, rowdy, and angrier. Vlad held Alina Vera back. The psyche of the population in this authoritarian state was used to living at poverty's edge, and now the long-festering resentment was expressing itself in remarkable declarations of unity. Stifled emotions could no longer be suppressed. Brewing trouble was ready to burst.

Something flew through the air, a shop window shattered. Hundreds of tiny shards of glass erupted. Resounding cheers and catcalls quickly followed. From yet another side street activist students advanced. One held a red banner as they sang a workers' song, lyrics obscured by shouts and slogans from all directions.

A large stone was hurled; it cracked the windshield of a parked car. The car's emergency siren screamed. A small group of students broke off from the main assemblage and started heaving the car over. Others began blocking the main intersection in a human chain. Several passenger cars screeched to a halt. A young woman dressed in blue jeans clambered atop the hood of a parked vehicle. "Long Live the Revolution!" She cried again and again, "Give us Lenin!"

"Revolution!" others shouted, taking up her plea. Soon the cry reverberated, echoing down winding streets and across the wide boulevard. A police siren wailed. Vlad watched while paramilitary sedans screamed to the scene. Police cars with flashing blue lights encircled Independence Square. Ten baton-wielding policemen wearing body armor rushed out, military armored vehicles following closely behind.

One of the armed policemen shouted through a megaphone, "Return immediately to your homes!" He was greeted with jeers.

"Turn around, go home!" The protesting groups rejoiced as they converged beside the square's fountains, pressed closely, shoulder to shoulder. It was an amalgam of workers and students, young and old united in a flashpoint of rage.

"We have the right to protest!"

"We want freedom!"

"Lenin lives!"

In a show of force, dozens of helmeted riot police wearing gas masks clamored from the armored vehicles. Grasping shields, they formed a single line like a Roman phalanx. The beefed-up state security apparatus prepared to undertake a campaign of intimidation and repression to maintain order. The tide of protestors showed no sign of backing down as the police line moved forward. Quite the opposite, while the drum roll rhythmically pounded, the protestors increased in strength and took on the belligerence of a maddened coalition unafraid of any clampdown.

"Disperse now! This is a final warning!"

Their response was punctuated by jubilant defiance. A barrage of rocks and stones showered through the air, bricks aimed at police cars. Riot police lifted shields as a wide swath of rocks slammed over and around them. The commanding officer barked orders to end the lawlessness and the police assault swiftly followed. Tear gas canisters exploded. Screams ensued; the drumming abruptly ceased. In the darkness many fled, scrambling, crouching, but others continued surging forward, bravely taunting the line of police. A handful of protestors unsuccessfully tried to break through the barricade but made little headway. Under orders, riot police started swinging truncheons. Several demonstrators crumbled to the ground. Loud cries arose as more tear gas was fired. Amid escalating hostilities additional sirens shrieked, vehicles delivering fresh reinforcements against the possibility that the uprising might become a true rallying point for transformation. Several armored personnel carriers helped form a cordon. Military checkpoints crisscrossed all sides in a bid to restore order.

Alina Vera and Vlad watched aghast, cringing at sight of truncheons. Although huddled a hundred meters from the crowd they also began feeling the stinging effect of tear gas. "We need to go *now!*" panted Vlad. "They'll shut this thing down by brute force."

"I need more photographs!" she protested. In the distance they heard the chopping blades of a helicopter swiftly approaching.

A gunshot pierced the night. "Live ammunition!" Vlad exclaimed. A menacing armored car rolled into place and blocked another intersection. Buttressed by additional militia pouring in and taking positions, security forces began their own offensive. Tear gas clouds rose high above the streets. Using batons and boot kicks, riot police in shielded helmets pummeled a shouting protester to the ground. More officers fired off salvos of tear gas grenades to disperse the adamant demonstrators.

"Revolution!" sounded another cry. "Long live Lenin!"

Screams continued amid a cacophony of buckling activists retching from the foul gas. Additional military vehicles dashed to the grisly scene. Overhead the helicopter buzzed, circling, searchlight blindingly focused on the fast-disbanding crowd. Its rotors swished and churned crisply. Banners were trampled, the square littered with broken glass, tear gas canisters and debris. Hell was breaking lose in the peaceful city of Minsk. This time Vlad didn't ask; he grabbed Alina Vera's arm and forcibly yanked her away fast and far. Panting, she said, "We need to document what's happening!"

"It's too dangerous," Vlad yelled above the din. She squirmed to break free from his strong grasp. A pea soup of tear gas lingered, the scientist continuing taking pictures until the absolute last moment before clouds obscured everything.

In Minsk, riot police clashed with hundreds of angry youths and workers in the city's central square. Police fired repeated volleys of tear gas to repel rioters hurling firebombs and ripped-up paving stones. A crowd of youths smashed the windows of a nearby luxury hotel. Cafe tables and chairs lay overturned as trash bins burned. Heavy clouds of tear gas lingered for hours, choking chemicals wafting as far away as the parliament House of Government. Hundreds have been arrested and charged with criminal violence, and looting. A curfew has descended on the city, with paramilitary police patrolling the streets, a government official said, speaking on condition of anonymity because they were not authorized to speak publicly about security matters. The chaos triggered a sharp sell-off in global financial markets as investors worried about chain reactions in other countries. Experts conclude that the results of expanding turmoil could be catastrophic...

Boris turned off the television.

"We saw it unfold firsthand," said Vlad. "They're lying. The police provoked it. It didn't have to turn into a melee. At least no one was killed."

"As far as we know," Alina Vera chided despondently. "Those people could still be taken out and shot. Boris, this thing is worse than we realized." Her brow glistened with a sheen of perspiration.

Boris scowled, unnerved as he examined photographs clandestinely taken and posted on the Internet during the protest. Many were dark and blurry, but clear enough to discern major events of the clash and verify his concerns. A myriad of images were filling cyberspace, and bloggers from around the world were writing editorials and articles filled with frosted repudiation and disgust. Along with these emotionally charged missives he deduced a disturbing but unspoken embryonic layer of support for Lenin's call to arms.

At length Boris pushed his chair from his desk. Divorced from the morbidly provoking pictures, he said, "You're right. It's out of hand, and we don't have tools to prevent it happening again. You should have stopped her from taking photos. There are more than enough out there. You both could have been arrested along with the mob."

"I tried to stop her..." Vlad wanted to explain.

Boris pointed toward the door. "I understand. Never mind for now. That American pain in the ass is waiting outside, and I can't hold him up much longer. We'd better get our facts straight and not forget the president's directives. Handle his questions carefully, without divulging a thing."

"I don't trust him, Boris. Why is it so damn important we have to see him?"

"I don't trust him either, any more than thin ice in Gorky Park, but we're committed to stringing him along. Those are our orders. End of story." Boris hadn't yet informed his colleagues of the multiple foreign passports Milonov claimed were found in Floyd's possession, creating another troubling dimension of the enigma. The whole thing gave him bad vibes. He didn't like it. "Let him in, Vova."

Vlad went to the door. "Come in, Floyd. It's nice to see you again." Floyd Dingus smiled his toothy smile.

"Hi there, Vlad." He strode into the room with an easy gait. "It's good seeing you all. Hello Boris, Alina Vera. You're all looking well, but not too chipper, I'd say."

"Oh." Alina Vera examined her fingernails. "What does it mean, this 'chipper'?"

"Oh, just an expression, it means like being happy. Being in a good mood—not like you look now. Your workload got you down?"

"We're swamped, as I'm sure you'll understand. However, because your embassy requested a meeting we made every effort to be available. A token of goodwill in the spirit of Russian-American friendship, naturally. What is it you require? How may we be of service?"

"Well, I'll tell you, may I sit?"

"Certainly." Vlad gestured to a comfortable chair.

Floyd eased down and crossed his legs, allowing his loafers to dangle from his feet. "I love these damn shoes. Absolutely the most comfortable I've ever owned. Handmade. I don't know how they do it. Anybody want to try them on? I picked them up last year in Zimbabwe."

No one knew what to reply so nothing was said. Finally, "Get comfortable," was all Alina Vera could manage.

"So what is your embassy concerned about?" asked Boris.

He leaned in, clasping his hands. "Don't take this the wrong way, but the ambassador is convinced you're giving me the runaround. They sent me to Omsk to inspect the chocolate factory, and your people refused to open the door, stonewalling from day one. So they transported me back to Moscow to check out some other stuff, but it looks like I'm being blindsided wherever I go."

"What are you talking about?"

Floyd scratched the side of his head. "It's itchy. I should have washed my hair this morning when I showered. My scalp's sensitive. Do any of you recommend a particular brand of Russian shampoo?" He sighed. "I hope I don't wind up with a bad case of psoriasis."

"Yes, you should have washed your hair," scolded Alina Vera. "Didn't your mother teach you to wash it every day?"

Floyd paid scant attention. He looked from Boris, to Vlad and back to Boris. "As I was saying, gentlemen, my government is perturbed about these ongoing sightings all over the place. On my way here I saw all kinds of pro Lenin graffiti decorating the city. People are stirred up and turning out in droves, taking to the streets, and mouthing ugly rumors. Pretty dangerous stuff."

"Please don't take any of this commotion seriously," said Vlad. "The closer the Jubilee, the more you'll find fools doing practically anything to get attention and into the press. It's true we've had an upsurge of graffiti in pretty unlikely places, but attention seekers are relentless, you know that, Floyd. Con men flourish with rumors. These things happen all the time in America. Why suppose it's different here? On television I recently saw a man in New York claiming to be Charlie Chaplin. He looked exactly like Chaplin. A double. So what? We all realize he's just a lonely soul seeking notoriety."

"True, Vlad. I saw that Charlie Chaplin doppelganger story myself. That guy was good. He damn sure nearly convinced me he's Chaplin. But that's not what we're talking about here, is it? Some folks around Russia are getting mighty agitated, looks like. My embassy's received so many sighting reports it's ridiculous. Heck, more people are seeing Lenin these days than UFOs, and *everybody* sees UFO's. And these folks aren't garden variety working stiffs. Strange behavior, something's not right."

Boris reached into his pocket and took out an expensive Cuban cigar. He placed it under his nostrils and sniffed. "Cut the kabuki dance. Exactly what is it you want?"

Floyd leaned forward, smile disappearing. "Cut me some slack, okay? I want truth. I want facts." His Midwestern accent vanished.

"We've been telling you the facts all along," Boris answered evenly. "We don't have reason to lie. In any case, whatever happens inside Russian territorial borders is the affair of the Russian government. Please don't take this the wrong way, but frankly it's none of your business."

"Well, when this stuff spills over into other countries that the United States has good relations with, like Ukraine and Belarus, it certainly does affect us."

"Ukraine and Belarus are politically and economically aligned with the New Russian Federation, Floyd. I would have thought you realized that."

"Oh, we certainly do. Nevertheless, this incendiary rhetoric has destabilizing repercussions spilling over and reaching all your neighbors; places like Poland, the Czech Republic, and Lithuania. And those countries, Boris, have become staunch American friends and allies, if you follow my train of thinking."

Boris lit the cigar, clenched his teeth and puffed. Alina Vera lighted a cigarette, exhaling smoke from her nostrils. "Russia no longer bears responsibility for what transpires in those places. The old Soviet Empire disbanded decades ago. You're discussing free, fully independent nations; interfering in their politics and internal affairs is unpalatable. Nor do they interfere in ours. Period."

"That may be, but we're teetering on revolution, and that's a horse of a different color. These political shocks are a pretty hefty matter for everyone, Sport, your leaders and mine. People are polarized. So skip the song and dance. We don't want to see contagion, so we share considerable mutual interest in this business." Floyd's eyes retained no hint of their usual humor.

"Serious business indeed," agreed Boris in a monotone, avoiding a testy exchange. "Are you pessimistic about it spreading to America? That you'll be overrun by wild-eyed, fanatical Bolsheviks forcing reform on you?"

Slowly the toothy smile resumed. Floyd's shoulders relaxed, his disposition resuming its typical laidback joviality. "Naw. Americans idolize money too much to go and have a real revolution. It's too chaotic and messy to go in radical new directions. We're comfortably stuck in our own political malaise. The truth is my government would like to help with your delicate affairs any way possible. You know, curb this restlessness and get back to business."

Alina Vera blew a plume of smoke at his face "You'll help how, shipping over Avian Flu?"

Floyd grinned expansively, waving smoke away. "Not precisely what I envisioned, but I do admire your sharp wit, Dr. Galina. Right now your nation has a credibility problem. And my country realizes the tremendous difficulty you have trying to control these crazy...occurrences. We recognize how much stress Russia is under scrambling to complete all the projects in time for your Anniversary Jubilee. Much needed infrastructure is still in planning stages, new stadiums underway, hotel upgrades to accommodate masses of visitors, plus airport improvements, roads, rail, bus service. Russia is so...big. Loose threads everywhere. The delays could cause a breakdown in public confidence. We're sympathetic to your plight. We'd like to help with some good old American ingenuity."

"I'm confused, Floyd," said Alina Vera. "I thought your occupation was stalking diseased cattle, and in your spare time observing how we make chocolate. Suddenly you're interested in a great deal more."

"Things have drastically changed, haven't they?"

What indeed did Floyd Dingus know and what did he really want? Boris wondered. Who was he really working for? Was he a double agent, a triple agent? Were those fake passports found in his possession actually his, or was Floyd Dingus setup, and no more than he claimed a low-level representative of the United States Department of Agriculture? Boris found himself in a quandary. The forged passports Milonov provided weren't proof of anything, nor was Milonov above contriving subterfuge for his own purposes. It didn't automatically make Dingus guilty of any crime. Yet nor could he be exonerated. Who was really behind the deceit? Who could be trusted? No one.

"What do you expect of us?" Boris said at length.

"Well, for starters, we want to know about this ugly business in Minsk, the demonstration that turned into a riot. That's what it was, and you can't convince me otherwise. It received more notoriety than a US Olympic team. There are web postings and eyewitnesses chattering on a ceaseless stream of news networks, reporting in Arabic to Swahili. All of it documented on video."

"Worldwide media never gets enough of a good story," Vlad observed. "I wish I could acquire that much free press coverage for Russia. We all realize it turned belligerent. But if you're questioning events in Minsk you should be seeking answers from their government, not us."

Floyd looked squarely at the public relations director. "We're on top of it, you can be sure. But what I'm trying to figure out, Vlad, is why you and Alina Vera were down there the other night."

A heavy silence hung in the air. Alina Vera snubbed out her cigarette. These damn Americans had spies falling over themselves, she thought. "Your government is mistaken. They clearly have me confused with someone else, or they're suffering from a bad case of ADD, attention deficit disorder. I've been home in Moscow since leaving Omsk."

She wasn't going to budge.

Floyd shrugged. "Well, I'm sure not going to argue with you about it. Okay, maybe the info my government provided was inaccurate. Maybe those are pictures of some psychotic lookalike. Heck, I don't know. But I sure wish you wouldn't be so defensive. I'm not sheriff of Dodge City. I'm just another working stiff. My country would like to work together with you on this formidable unfolding matter."

"What 'formidable matter' do you mean?" asked Vlad.

"Uh oh. Back to square one. The matter of this flake claiming he's Lenin. Whoever the hell he really is, it looks to Washington like some sicko joke is spiraling out of control. Something's gone haywire. I believe you're aware the President of the United States has held private conversations with your President. It's no secret. We just need to find out how far gone this crazy business is. Look, I've been doing some serious reading since I saw you folks last. I never realized how violent and awful Russia's Revolution was. America is rightly concerned if another might be brewing. Bad, bad business, a real downer.

"America's assumption has been you'd come to your senses and make a deal to forestall catastrophe. Do you people read the newspapers? Financial markets, currency and oil traders across the world are shaking in their boots, not playing chicken to see who blinks first. Your economy is going to go down the toilet, and chances to get out of this bind are dwindling. A lack of stability hurts us all, so you'd better tackle it before it does become insurmountable."

Floyd's astringent rhetoric was not about to make Boris capitulate to scare tactics. He placed his cigar into an ashtray and pounded out burning ashes. "The United States can be one hundred percent assured there won't be any revolution," he insisted. "This perversion fueling discord will be put out of business— by any means necessary. Understood?"

Floyd sighed. "I hope so, 'cause if this mania reels out of control, I can tell you, the consequences won't be pretty."

"You've got to be fucking kidding."

"No, I'm not," Anya huffed to Alina Vera. "Go read the headline for your-self. Right there on the front page of the BBC's homesite."

"Read it to me."

She did. 'New Wave Rock Band Scores Number One on Charts: *Bring on the Revolution*, by pioneering group calling itself, 'Chocolate Lenin'. Not too shabby, huh?"

"Oh Christ," she thought.

"What a weird name," said Anya. "Critics say they're the best band to come along since the Beatles. *'Bring on the Revolution'* has sold almost a mil-lion copies in Europe already. A few weeks ago creepy gorillas abducted me demanding a revolution, and now revolution has turned into a bestselling song. Freaky! Listen to it." Anya began streaming the tune, blasting the speakers. It started with an earsplitting series of electric guitar riffs followed by a wail.

Alina Vera put hands to her ears, moaning. "Keep the volume down, okay? Just read the latest news, and let me know what else they say." She excused her-self, slamming the door, marching into her bedroom.

She speed-dialed her phone and Vlad came on the line. "Don't say a word, I know it already. It's repeating on the crawl of Moscow's *World News Tonight*. Boris has scheduled an emergency meeting. He should be ringing you any mo-ment."

Within the hour the team gathered. Vlad was acutely disturbed by this latest peculiar turn of events, and the collective mood was as disheartening as he'd ever seen. "What is all this populist exhilaration?" Boris decried through gritted teeth, "And how in hell did a bunch of British kids come up with this particular name?"

"Our London agents are investigating," said Dimsky. "As best as we can confirm the band's name was a suggestion given to them."

"Suggested by whom?" asked Vlad.

Dimsky put aside his notes. "We've learned that the father of the band's lead vocalist works for the British Embassy in Moscow. How intriguing is that? He's Sir Alistair Krumm, a high-level deputy. I don't know if any of you are familiar with him but this puppy's known for having close Russian friends—es-pecially among the chess playing community. He's a bit of a chess player himself, in fact. Want more? You've heard of former European chess champion Gregori Nabokov? It appears Sir Alistair Krumm and Nabokov go back a long way to-gether. Nabokov spends a great deal of his time in London and he's pickled in the brine, long suspected of smuggling stolen jewels, and money laundering. He likes living high, and resorts to questionable exploits to ensure affording to do so. We have an extensive dossier, but the police have never proved any of it."

"I think we're onto something," said Boris.

Dimsky agreed. "A tie-in is evident. Get this, Mikhail Sunavich coincidently also happens to be an acquaintance of Gregori Nabokov. We have proof the two met for lunch at least twice this past year. Additionally, on several occasions Sir Alistair Krumm has also has dined alone with Dr. Sunavich. Buddies like the three musketeers. Is this cozy linkage coincidence?" Dimsky sat back, pleased with his investigative work.

"Tantalizing, but what does it prove?" said Alina Vera. "I've also lunched alone with Dr. Sunavich several times."

"It proves a connection," retorted Dimsky, betraying uncharacteristic annoyance. "Some things can be shared and others cannot. Internal Security agents from my division have also suspected Gregori Nabokov of quietly passing information to foreign operatives in addition to fencing jewels and cash."

"Our chess champion Nabokov is a spy?" asked Vlad.

"Former champion. He's been detained but never held or charged. Insufficient evidence, plus slush fund clout he doles out liberally. His friends are influential in the right places, Sir Alistair Krumm, for example. Krumm is favored among British society as well as Moscow brownnosers. We don't know what information Sunavich may have shared, but it's established the two of them occasionally play chess together. Possibly Sunavich gave instructions to Nabokov, and Nabokov passed them on to Alistair Krumm. Or maybe Sunavich gave directives to Krumm. Is it accidental that Krumm's son named the band, 'Chocolate Lenin'? Sir Alistair Krumm fits neatly into our puzzle."

Honeyed sunlight spilled throughout the room. Squinting, Boris walked to the window and pulled down the blinds. "What significance does the band's name 'Chocolate Lenin' have? Could this British deputy have overheard a trivial clever phrase mixing incendiary politics with earsplitting music, and innocently suggested it to his musician son? Not likely. And coincidentally this Krumm has acquaintances with both Nabokov and our Dr. Sunavich?"

Dimsky gritted his teeth. "The song's popularity caught us off guard. We had no way to foresee it, but we're checking everything possible to learn its source."

Vlad said, "Rock and Roll bands frequently devise flamboyant names to distinguish themselves. No need to enumerate."

"I'm not a man who believes in coincidences," said Boris. "A large chunk of my youth was spent living on odd jobs and croissants filched from bars, surviving off my wits. I've been round the block. Does anybody believe it's a fluke that this pop culture hit song is titled, *Bring on the Revolution*? No, this is out and out subversion against the State." He paced to the far end of the room, picking up and randomly thumbing through a book lying on a shelf.

"I'm finally beginning to detect how widely Sunavich has managed to spread his tentacles. The doctor may not have meted out laboratory secrets, but he's gleefully sowing seeds of havoc, and disrupting our efforts to wrack and ruin. He's taunted us with hidden codes at the *Das Kapital Bingo Parlor*, agitated susceptible crowds into a rabid fervor, and now makes fools of us by exposing our secret project through silly song titles and names of rock and roll bands."

"I don't even like rock and roll," grumbled Dimsky.

Boris glanced around for support. "Suggestions how to tackle this?"

"My best advice is not to publically touch it," advised Vlad. "To react to the band's name or song title is the worst thing to do. I suggest we ignore its exploitation, continuing as usual as if nothing's happened. We don't want Sunavich alerted that we're troubled. Let the bastard guess our reaction. Our public face needs to remain upbeat. Russia is prosperous, busily planning and looking forward to the Jubilee. Meanwhile, pull out all stops to track down Gregori Nabokov and grab him, even on trumped-up charges."

"Alright, Petrovsky. We can do that."

Dimsky stirred. "If I knew where he was he'd already be under arrest. Bound, gagged, tortured by a continuous stream of deafening punk rock 24 hours a day. Let's see how he likes it."

Overlooking the colonel's remark, Boris dourly said, "If this isn't bad enough, let me compound our dilemma. I've received a coded text that our trusted top man in Omsk, Rimsky-Kimsky, has been observed in the company of dubious characters with known connections to foreign elements. This is a bad blow for the rabbi."

"Shocking!" deplored Alina Vera. "Rimsky-Kimsky's been passing secrets?"

186

Boris chomped an unlighted cigar. "Word came down from my colleague, Inspector *Bolshoi Utka*, a top special unit security detective. We presume Rimsky-Kimsky has been colluding with a topnotch agent for the Mossad."

"The *Mossad*? The Israelis have become involved?"

Boris didn't respond either yes or no. He looked to the colonel. "Exactly what have you been able to find out regarding Gregori Nabokov?"

"We know he visited St. Petersburg as recently as two days ago. His girlfriend lives there, renting a small flat in a bohemian neighborhood. For some time her name and credentials have appeared on several suspicious lists of possible subversives. Possibly she's acted as a courier."

Alina Vera groaned at the mention of this woman. "May I add something else you might find important? As you know, Anya Andropova and I have become close and she has confided almost everything about her life. One item she recently mentioned I paid scant attention to, and I suppose should have. You see, Anya may be very young but she already circulates among the cream of Moscow society. I can say with certainty she's met Gregori Nabokov at galas and functions, and also been introduced to his girlfriend."

"Your point?"

"My point—and how's this for irony—Nabokov's girlfriend is none other than Ilya Evgeny's sister."

The irony was not lost.

Vlad stood for a long time under the shower's hot water. The steam penetrated flesh like a sauna, and his throbbing shoulder pain eased. He wrapped a towel around his waist, and wiped the foggy mirror as he prepared to shave. He stared at his reflection before applying shaving cream, noticing deepening lines etched along the sides of his mouth, and puffy shadows below his eyes. He didn't like what he saw, and didn't like himself, either.

His entire world had undergone a cruel metamorphosis these past weeks. Barely a month ago he'd stood at the pinnacle of his career, erstwhile director of the largest agency in all of Russian publicity media, secure in his capacity as head of public relations, coordinator for the Anniversary Jubilee. At Kremlin receptions he was positioned alongside ranking cabinet ministers and government undersecretaries. Governors and administrators of Russian Oblasts, mayors, plutocrats, all manner of assorted dignitaries eagerly seeking goodwill and patronage fiercely curried his favor.

And now? He looked despondently in the mirror, his whole life undermined; rescinded temporarily from his post for an unknown duration, Raisa had whisked the girls to Petersburg, and his marriage barely clung by a thread. His daughters, Katya and Aleksandra, had sent several endearing photos and messages to his phone. It was wonderful hearing their voices, and it touched him deeply when they sent a simple text saying they loved him. How pale waking up to all his so-called achievements and acclaim in the world seemed alongside this brief moment. Hoping he might soon see them lifted his spirits, allowing momentary bittersweet refuge from the rabid realities of his hollow new world. Foreign intrigues, espionage, sabotage, not to mention the scientific marvel of all time. Where exactly did he fit into this complex, baffling mosaic? Why was he chosen to be part of this elite team?

Boris was a crafty individual; master spy, former KGB intelligence officer, and fully capable of directing subordinates to unlock solutions for seemingly impossible situations. Then there was Dimsky; key counter-terrorism expert, accomplished military man, archetypal patriot of the highest standing. As for Asher, his reputation spoke for itself.

Next, he thought long and hard about enigmatic Alina Vera Galina. It was undeniable he felt attracted to her, and he'd come to think possibly those same feelings were shared. Beyond that, however, Alina Vera remained a noted scientist in her own right, a perfect assistant for the rabbi.

Together his colleagues comprised an excellent working group, fitting like fine leather gloves. But what role did he play? Apart from a handful of useful suggestions he considered his role superfluous. He obviously couldn't compare himself with the meticulous professionalism of Colonel Dimsky, the cunning and dexterity of Boris Sokolov, and certainly not the scientific genius of Rabbi Titlebaum, or the expertise and savvy of Alina Vera. He made up his mind then and there. He finished shaving, dressed quickly, and texted Boris. Boris agreed to a private meeting and Vlad decided this would be an appropriate time to request permission to resign. What future ramifications on his career this might entail he didn't know; he only knew he felt incompetent and expendable.

Boris savored black tea and listened while Vlad presented his case. When he finished the veteran spy nodded with empathy. "I've suspected for some time how you feel, Vlad. I realize it must be like I threw you into the lion's den. But believe I had good reason for it. You and I have worked closely for some time, although I acknowledge under very different circumstances."

"Then it's all right? I can turn in my resignation at once."

Boris took a cigar from his pocket, toyed with it, deciding not to light it. He looked hard into Vlad's eyes. "You're a creative and capable man; hard working, diligent, never shirking duty, or complaining. I've always held you in highest esteem and value your keen insight."

Feeling damned with faint praise, Vlad leaned forward disconsolately. "It sounds like the kiss of death, Boris. This isn't the time for game playing."

"No, my friend, it's not."

"Then why did you select me? The day we talked in Red Square, why did you divulge things I had no business knowing? I didn't understand it then but I was flattered by your openness. Now I recognize I play no meaningful role in this affair. If the prime minister needed me for arranging press conferences, soothing public opinion, or even handing out misleading propaganda, I could easily do it. I've been whitewashing the State's dirty laundry for a long time. I could lie like a drunken sailor and make it sound as believable as a bishop's truth. But what do I know of subversion or counter intelligence? Nor am I a man of science. I've never even served in the military, let alone become privy to top secret classified military information. And I don't have any of your own expertise in subterfuge."

"You're referring to my former work for the KGB, and Internal Security? I know I'm suspected of being a mole for the prime minister, or a double agent for the president."

Vlad looked away morosely. "I didn't mean it to sound like that. I only meant to say I don't possess your skills."

Boris picked up the blue porcelain teapot and filled both their cups. "Everyone on our team respects you. You're well liked and held in high esteem. I wonder if some may like you a bit too much." Boris didn't explain his cryptic remark although it was obvious whom he referred to. "But that's neither here nor there, nor is it my business. What remains my business is finding ways to reverse the damage Sunavich set loose, the breakdown in public confidence, and the civil unrest this fictitious character is causing. I never dreamed I'd witness State Security so befuddled and stymied. Lurching without direction, tottering on the verge of paralysis. Please believe I do recognize your feelings, my friend. And maybe I'm the one who owes you an apology."

"An apology, why?"

"Because, it's pitiful when honorable men can't trust one another. When suspicion, doubts, and jealousies enter and everything else becomes muddled." Boris indulged in his tea. He spoke quietly, devoid of his usual bravado. "I'm going to share a small secret of my own, Vova. You want to know why I selected you specifically? I suppose now is a proper time to update you. But first allow me ask a question requiring the most honest of answers."

"You can me count on me to speak truthfully, Boris. I've never lied to you about anything. I won't begin now."

"A simple question then, old friend; am I able to trust *you*? Even with my life, should it come to it?"

Vlad was taken aback. "You can. I'd never betray you."

"Thank you. I believe you. You know, your personal dossier is quite extensive. I've seen it. You never realized you had an official dossier, did you? Don't be scared. All enterprising men seeking high positions have one. Yours began long before receiving permission to study in London. Don't worry, it isn't terribly interesting, merely bits and pieces regarding your life, background, family, friends, hobbies, that sort of thing. The State takes interest in everything its citizens do, particularly its smart, ambitious people. I suppose not very much has changed after all." He scowled. "Let me add that I'm fully aware of the gimmicks and tricks you've played over the years to further your career. But I don't blame you. Most committed far worse sins, believe me. You rate very highly. The State considers you reliable and trustworthy, and I fully agree with that assessment. It's a quality more rare than you realize. I admit I selected you for this group because, above all else, I uphold total confidence in those qualities."

"Then I don't see why..."

"It's really a simple explanation." His eyes narrowed. "I brought you into this because I needed to be one hundred percent certain I had at least one person on our team without prior connections to this affair. So I included the single person I knew I could count on to guide a transition. You are that person."

'I'm listening."

"Let me speak briefly about the others. Rabbi Titlebaum worked with Sunavich for years and may have personal scores to settle. Even though his credentials are impeccable this animosity gives me cause for concern. Is he out to get Sunavich more than serving his country out of patriotism?

"Dimsky is a long-time valued colleague and friend, but he was security head at the Alexander Nevsky and therefore feels deep personal responsibility for events gone wrong on his watch, right under his nose. Antipathy can cloud judgment, and I can't permit that. Likewise, Alina Vera worked closely with Sunavich. She rightly feels betrayed, and also might let personal vendettas get in the way of our work. I cannot allow that, either. Though her father and I worked together when he served as a magistrate and I secretly for the police, I mustn't allow my own connections to her interfere.

"As for you, Vova, I knew from the beginning you harbor no vested interest, bear no grudges. Because of this impartiality you're the only one I can rely on for objectivity, doing whatever's necessary despite the consequences. You are literally what your dossier reports declares; reliable and principled." He waited, then, "So I ask you, will you reconsider and remain?"

Vlad sat quietly, unwilling to commit.

"Do you recall the day you and Dr. Galina went for a stroll in the park, and Alina Vera discussed her great uncle who'd lived in the former Red Marshals' Compound?"

"You know about that, Boris? Were you spying? How could you do that? You say you're my friend and I've never given cause to doubt me. You just finished saying how trustworthy I am. Are Alina Vera and I suddenly considered ideological subversives?" He kept his anger in check.

"Of course not. I'm confiding this is only because I want you to realize how valuable you are to me. One of Dimsky's undercover men was instructed to keep a watchful eye, ensuring your safety. It's really Alina Vera, not you, we've had need to stay close to."

"Nevertheless, your agent followed us. You played your old KGB games, recorded and listened to our conversation, didn't you? Does today's Internal Security do things the same old way? Next you'll tell me it was your agents who tried to run us down in the street."

"Absurd!" Boris thumped a fist on his desk. "Why would I hurt the very people I'm counting on? I suspect someone closely connected to Sunavich was behind that incident. And I doubt they intended to hurt either of you, just scare you, keep you off balance."

"Well, they did a first-rate job. And by the way, Alina Vera confided she was nearly run down in Omsk."

"I'm aware of that incident, too. Over the years our pretty scientist has been a choice confidant of Sunavich. Maybe it's his way of ensuring she's too frightened to expose him. But no one will harm her, I give my word."

Was Boris being truthful? Weighing the scales, Vlad decided harming her ran contrary to his vital interests. Reassured, the tension eased. "All right. But I'm perplexed. I'm gratified you possess this faith in me, but I still don't understand my role. If you expect to coerce me into keeping a watchful eye on Alina Vera, or the rabbi, or even Dimsky, you're mistaken. I won't do it. I don't care about any personal cost to me."

"When I said I needed someone dependable, I meant it. An ally with no particular ideology, able to lead in my absence should anything unexpected happen."

"What are you saying?"

"I'm saying we inhabit a dangerous world. If you have faults, Vova, it's that you've remained too passive, reacting with good suggestions but rarely showing initiative to take control. Our team needs that."

"How can I be expected to take over? You're in full control."

"And so I am. But these are menacing times, and we mustn't be incapable of confronting that fact. If something unexpected happened to me, then what? The strike team has to continue its work. The State requires strong leadership beyond reproach. In my opinion, that someone is you."

"You're saying I'd be team leader?"

"I'm saying I can count on no one else. In fact, instructions to that effect have quietly been issued. Are you up for the job, Vova? Now it's my turn to insist that you be straightforward. I need an answer. I've shown my cards. You're smart, talented, and not frightened to stand your ground. I respect that. So do the others. What do you say?"

Vlad offered his hand. Boris took it. "Alright, I'll do my part. You have my word."

"Good. No one needs to be told of this meeting. Just remember your role is indispensable. I mean what I say. During this upcoming phase of work, I wouldn't even trust the prime minister. Milonov isn't what he seems."

"Not trust the prime minister? He organized our team's duties and responsibility, didn't he? If not…who the hell *is* running things?"

Boris sat back and smiled enigmatically. "A good question to be explored another time, my friend. Right now, I'm placing my confidence in you, and I expect the same truth you ask of me. Should anything seem amiss among our team I need you to tell me immediately. And I also need you to put any personal feelings aside. If you discover anything meant to do our country harm, I need to know it."

Vlad regarded him earnestly. "That I promise. I won't serve as your eyes and ears, but I do give my solemn oath I won't betray my country."

12.

Rabbi Titlebaum stood beaming like a proud schoolboy who'd scored well on an exam. "We've got them," he announced. "We've obtained authentic swabs of Lenin's sperm. Parallel results are corroborated by colleagues at Omsk, validated and verified."

"No doubt whatsoever?"

"A perfect match to 'Little Man'."

"Thank heaven," murmured Dimsky, clapping. Vlad shook the rabbi's strong hand, filled with awe, and fascination, as well as alarm at what this crucial accomplishment portended.

"It's true," added Asher. "Lenin's sperm markers were isolated from prior obtained stains. Bed sheets were procured from Olga Orlovskya's lodgings. Security police handled the specimens with utmost professional caution, careful not to contaminate them. They were rushed by helicopter from a local police laboratory to the Alexander Nevsky. Apparently Lenin's gonads are quite active, which of course supplies a plentiful quantity for further examination. Better yet, from within the soiled sheets we've isolated body fluids that can belong to none other than Ilya Evgeny. Hair sample traces swept from her flat confirmed it."

"Finally we proved she *is* fucking the old bugger," said Alina Vera.

"She most certainly is." Boris smiled tenuously. A tall glass of vodka and a good cigar would go well now, he thought.

"Next," Asher intoned, "We need to ratchet up our work, and adapt a way to use his own fluids against him. Think of it like a new strain of flu virus. We'll isolate it, and once we distinguish its attributes we'll develop virulent microbes to enter the bloodstream, launch deadly attacks, and finish the organism off."

"Isolate and kill Lenin?" said Vlad.

"No different than destroying any nasty infection." The rabbi left no room for doubt as to his intentions.

"Not as easy as it sounds," Alina Vera chimed. "Post coitus, mammalian sperm cells can survive within a female reproductive tract five days or more.

However, outside the female body its 'shelf-life' is seriously degraded, sometimes to no more than a few hours. Dead sperm cells are useless to us."

The enthusiasm decreased. "Which means you'll require a fresh, steady supply," speculated Boris. "Colonel, one way or another, your agents have to track every hideout. The clock is running. More sightings and protests are taking a toll."

"News stations and entertainment programs are already poking fun," added Vlad. "Alluding to various Lenin sightings, simultaneously playing sound bites from *Bring on the Revolution* by the 'Chocolate Lenin' band. The song's exposure is hurting our image. Our latest polls report interest in the Jubilee down eleven percent this past week alone. Numbers like that can't continue. It'll ruin us. We'll be defiled, humiliated, made to look like a joke. I've already instructed colleagues in Moscow to put together a new ad campaign I conceived for dealing with this. I want to deflect as much negative press as possible. I think this might work."

"Go on," said Boris.

Vlad paced, speaking calmly. "I've envisioned an entirely new public relations campaign, cutting-edge and clever, kicking out the stale old one. We'll sponsor it across Western Europe as well as the United States and Canada. It'll cost a bundle, but it's worth every ruble. The monies are already preapproved by the Culture Ministry budget." Everyone was well aware how much this effort needed to succeed to salvage the celebrations, he knew. Not to mention how much he needed to salvage his own reputation.

"So here's the plan. Russia will introduce tennis star Anya Andropova as our number one spokesperson. She'll be hailed as the 'New Russian Woman,' our quintessential feminine image, a living cultural icon for the Jubilee. Anya's sexy, photographs beautifully, and is already globally recognized as a rising personality in professional tennis. We'll provide the world with what it's hungering for. Men will fall in love, and women will want to emulate her. We'd never find anyone better suited to personify Russian womanhood. With Anya's natural charisma and looks she can't miss."

"She is a pretty girl," acknowledged Dimsky.

"That she is," Vlad agreed, motioning the angles of TV camera shots. "Utilizing a series of super high definition thirty-second television spots we'll highlight Anya glamorously relaxing in a steamy, hot bath, washing with a bar of soap looking like rich, creamy chocolate. Several spots are already underway.

They have a prolonged focus while Anya sponges delectable light confection over her body, and blows sudsy bubbles at the camera. Off screen, an enticing, sexually arousing voice invites audiences to come visit Anya in Russia during the Jubilee. She'll be waiting for you...

"Our closer will be a close-up of Anya puckering her lips in a kiss. The ads are tasteful, Anya remaining totally wholesome. We'll out-compete rivals for airtime, and blow off detrimental impressions and stubborn misconceptions piling up. I think it's an effective antidote that'll backfire against anyone trying to demean us.

"So far I've viewed only a few daily rushes, but from what I've seen it's a powerhouse. The Minister of Culture is extremely excited. He agrees we've found the proper response to pare losses and turn our image around. I'm convinced that by utilizing chocolate in our ads we'll appear to parody ourselves, and demonstrate we're enjoying the spotlight, even acting as though the furor is some personal joke. I'm betting viewers will soon perceive all these Lenin sightings as part of a staged ad campaign, a publicity stunt. That should diffuse our current dilemma, and at the same time deflate Lenin's media worthiness, while shoring up public support for us." He folded his arms and smiled, pleased with his achievement. "Needless to say, Anya is ecstatic being selected to head up the campaign."

"Brilliant showmanship," exclaimed Boris. "Bloody genius, Petrovsky! Who knew you were such an ardent visionary?"

"We're so proud of you," Alina Vera added with a visible glow.

Eager to explain further, Vlad went on, "We're including an extensive campaign of photographic visuals in magazines and popular cyber sites focusing on fashion. We'll run double page spreads in Europe, but naturally save our biggest guns for North America. We'll also cover emerging markets in South America and Asia. China has already approved expanded TV coverage providing we increase per capita advertising spending. Our side agreed, and it's a done deal. One hand washes the other. We'll blitz local media, tailoring ads specific for the booming Latin market. My intention is to extend the campaign vigorously across the United States, splashing Anya's innocent face and appeal, and launching her new 'lifestyle' line simultaneously in New York and Los Angeles. Time and again Americans prove overly receptive to subliminal erotic marketing, and I am determined to take full advantage of that proclivity. We'll air ads night and day, showcasing our golden beauty's heady invitation. Digital media promotion will compliment our drive."

Alina Vera stirred, animated with a touch of derision. "Now I get it. We're selling a lifestyle of trashy materialism and becoming brilliant entrepreneurs at the same time. Ah, the mysteries and perfidies of life. So that's why Anya refused to divulge anything until you spoke to us first. She said it was going to be a big surprise."

"A humongous surprise. We're naming her exclusive fashion label, 'Attire by Anya'. Catchy, isn't it? Nothing tacky. She'll offer a brand-new, chic line-up of respectable, but slightly provocative fashion; swimwear, skirts, jackets, tee shirts, and tank tops. Maybe accessories too. A treasure trove customized by Moscow's most famous designers. Anya's silkscreened face and figure will adorn smart, casual outerwear, embossed with various inscriptions like, 'Kiss Me With Russian Chocolate!' and 'Let's Boogie-Board the Black Sea Together.'"

"Undoubtedly Anya is receptive to representing this crap?" wondered Boris.

"She's floating on air, totally euphoric in a cloud of giddy happiness. She called it 'awesome', and added she's 'stoked'. The avalanche of publicity will pirouette her into an instant superstar. We'll cyber-galvanize the world with her image. Anya's public persona is going to be enormously enhanced, as will her bank account. In a matter of weeks she'll be all the rage and skyrocket to international fame. The kid's so intoxicated she can barely contain herself. Announcements for our campaign will start selectively airing this weekend. Once Anya's lovely face is flashed onto the small screen she won't merely be a symbol, she'll become *the* symbol of Russian beauty."

"Mother Volga," intoned Dimsky. "I can tell everyone I'm a personal friend of a superstar."

Boris acerbically observed the enterprising brand Vlad was concocting. Without question he was proving his worth as a savvy business operator as well as an excellent propagandist beyond expectation. "You're spearheading a nice little plum for Anya. With all that divine publicity and upfront money, I have a strong suspicion Ilya Evgeny will try to contact her fast, and not miss an opportunity to exert her influence. Doubtlessly she's already calculating how to get her defiled hands on Anya's cash, ostensibly for the rebellion. She won't be able to contain herself. In fact, greed may make her consider dumping Lenin entirely, even selling him out."

Vlad radiated confidence. "Exactly what I'm hoping. Combine moral laxity with avarice, and she'll fall blindly into our hands."

"You certainly have a knack for original concepts!" Alina Vera squealed. "I'd bet Floyd Dingus will love your providing him with one-of-a-kind Hawaiian shirts decorated with Anya's face."

Boris put a hand on Vlad's shoulder. "I feel good about this, Vova. This is a great day for our team. I'm starting to believe we've turned a corner. Because of your effort we have a fighting chance to provide Asher the time he needs to topple Chocolate Lenin once and for all."

Both players concentrated on the elevated chessboard. After a time the first player moved a white pawn one space forward. With a quick countermove, a black pawn was pushed ahead. Then both players resumed their intense study. The younger man tamped a rich American tobacco blend into his pipe bowl. A lithe, well-endowed woman quietly slipped from the kitchen holding a tray. With long, gentle fingers she gracefully served cups of steaming tea. Then, with quiet glamor and appealing movements she set down a small plate of chocolates.

The guest reached for a cup and saucer, sniffing with delight at the heady aroma. It was impossible for him not to take notice of the captivating server. "The resemblance to your lovely sister truly is remarkable, I'm always astounded by it," he commented, no longer examining his white chess pieces. Professional players nearly always prevail against amateurs, he knew, but he was no ordinary amateur.

She smiled at his admiration and flattery. "You should be able to tell the difference by now. In any case I believe my younger sister is the one who resembles me, although I gladly accept your kind compliments." She offered the chocolates. "Take one, please. They're delicious. Manufactured at the Alexander Nevsky, naturally. They cost a pretty penny."

"I know it. And what could be better?" The guest helped himself, letting the chocolate rest on his tongue while it melted. "Russia's finest." There was shimmering humor in his beady eyes as he loudly smacked his lips.

Gregori chuckled, lighting his pipe. "These sisters are so alike in so many ways. Your eyes aren't playing tricks, old friend. You wouldn't think so but at times even I can have trouble telling these lovely siblings apart…"

The guest nodded with polite understanding, eyeing Irina's shapely figure from head to toe as always, admitting to himself that Gregori undeniably had superb taste when it came to women. "Indeed, so lovely. You are a most lucky man. But then, so is your Irina." He smiled warmly. "Sharing life with such a re-spected bon vivant like our Gregori is so much more neat and tidy than traipsing around the Cossack countryside hiding among ill-bred primitives." Both men shared a hearty laugh at the allusion.

"Apparently you misjudge my sister," Irina Evgeny pronounced. "She's never been one to be led by the nose. By all accounts she crossed the border without difficulty. I was surprised hearing how many rustics eagerly assisted her in slipping unseen across the frontier. These people do so adore their heroes, don't they? As if they've been patiently waiting. How much homage he com-mands."

Gregori flexed his heavy brows. "It's still dangerous for Ilya. If she's stopped I hope her papers are well forged. Do you know how she's planning to circumvent this nationwide police dragnet?"

"Forgive me, but I can't discuss that. What I can say is there are numerous sympathizers fanned out across many cities. So much graffiti scrawled the au-thorities can't whitewash the walls fast enough. The Kremlin is convinced Ilya and Lenin remain underground, hidden out by rural folk. But things are moving along faster than anyone expected. The Kremlin's in for a rude surprise."

"They already had one. Sir Alistair Krumm played his part perfectly, to the letter. I was amazed at how easily I managed to dupe him." Gregori winked. "He was so eager for another shot at playing me. During the opening moves I gave a strong defense, but then made a few poor ones to weaken my position. I could see the gleam in his eyes. He had no idea it was intentional. He pounced on my 'mistakes'. All it took was letting him beat me in one single game. After that he was practically eating out of my hand, the crowing bugger. I fed him our story and he felt honestly flattered I was interested in seeing his son succeed in the music business. I fed his narcissistic nature, and convinced him we could help assure that success. Thus a mindless, half-baked rock and roll anthem is going to help take down Russia's government."

Irina glowed at her Gregori's prowess. "Darling, you were magnificent, deluding him totally, boosting his already inflated ego, and giving the credit for the music's inspiration. What a gullible patsy! He was actually grateful to you. When the authorities catch on—if they ever do—the blame will automatically fall on his shoulders. The British will toss the blunderer out of the Foreign Ser-vice. How has he lasted so long? I'm so fortunate to have fallen in love with the smartest man in the world." She bent over and kissed the chess player, lightly pressing a breast against his arm.

"And you, my love, remain more beautiful than your sister in every way. Don't forget you helped write the lyrics. So poetic, yet such a tiger. I predict a grand future for us." Stirred by her sexuality, Gregori blew on his tea to cool it. He placed a lump of brown sugar on his tongue.

Her perfect teeth gleamed with bemusement. She brushed aside loose tendrils of hair. "Do you mean it, Gresha?" she asked winsomely, using a fond diminutive. "When your match is finished let's turn the teacups and read the leaves for our guest. It should be fun to learn what our future holds." She giggled like a schoolgirl.

"We mustn't become complacent," exhorted the guest, also aroused by her womanliness. "Our work's not done, and there's no margin for error."

Irina's dimpled smile radiated from her pleasing mouth. "Don't worry; we're careful. We've worked too long and hard to let anything fail. Enjoy your game, gentlemen. I'll be leaving shortly but will return as quickly as I can." She turned her back to leave. The visitor found himself envious of his fortunate friend who constantly attracted the most beautiful feminine company. In this case, choosing between the two stimulating, curvaceous sisters would be difficult.

"She adores flitting about town, you know," Gregori said, watching the unique sway of her hips. "She has expensive taste, of course, but that goes with the territory. I never demand she give account."

"Is that a hint, Gregori?" asked the guest. He reached inside his jacket pocket and withdrew a thick, plain envelope he subtly slid to the chess master. Gregori Nabokov took it with a single gesture, and placed the fat envelope inside his own pocket without counting the contents.

"You've earned every ruble, old boy. I'm very pleased with your work, and Irina's role, also." The visitor pondered upon the radiant sisters Evgeny; Ilya and Irina, so alike yet so different. Lenin presently had claim to Ilya's affection, but must Irina remain with her Gresha? Perhaps not. Perhaps when this undertaking was done a way might be found for poor Gregori to be apprehended. It would be a shame, but then again, life was not fair. And perhaps, when, in her grief, Irina turned to him he might provide enough solace and monetary diversion to claim the lusty girl.

"Thank you, Doctor," said Gregori, pulling him from his thoughts. "I appreciate your confidence in me, as well as the rapid payments."

The small man grinned expansively. "You are most welcome, old friend. Consider payment only a token of my appreciation for what you and your delightful partner do. But back to our game, do you think *I* might be able to defeat you tonight? That is, without benefit of you letting me win?" He stared at the chessboard; elbows on the table, square chin resting on his hands. A pair of thick eyeglasses sat at the end of his nose.

"We'll see, old fellow, we'll see." Gregori's pipe bowl glowed.

Muted light diffused through narrow lanced windows. Inside, the solid, expansive walls were adorned with multiple embellished frescoes and brushed icons painted in gold leaf. They mystified and delighted the rabbi as he patiently bided his time, peering inside the entrance's wide open doors. Onion-shaped domes towered brightly, gleaming atop the structure. The outer walls of the majestic cathedral were painted in pleasing vertical tones of yellow alternating with white. A slender, raw-boned woman wearing a headscarf slowly climbed the stone steps and paused next to him. "It's very beautiful, isn't it?" she said.

Rabbi Titlebaum nodded. "Quite beautiful and totally harmonious. I've never been inside a church." He admiringly gazed skyward. "It leaves a most powerful impression."

"It's meant to. It appeals to both one's intellect and emotions. Did you know the church itself is symbolic of the universe? The domes above suggest the open heavens, while the cathedral's base represents the earth below upon which mankind dwells."

"I'd never heard that," said the rabbi. "Quite fascinating, I'd like to learn more. Long ago I took several courses in religious studies."

"Perhaps someday we'll have an opportunity to discuss it." Normally she exemplified the epitome of style and sophistication, but today she was a humble woman with little makeup, wearing a simple white blouse and blue skirt. A warm woolen sweater was tied around her shoulders. Her shoes were flat and plain. "I'm pleased you could make our engagement this morning, Rabbi," she said in a precise, pointed manner.

"I'm pleased to be at your service, Madam President."

No one would have recognized Natasha, scion of the Stroganoffs, standing beside the tall cherubic, bearded rabbi. They cut a peculiar pair, he so obviously out of place, she in the role of a prosaic babushka. "Do you have more news for me, Asher?"

A biting chill blew this early hour and he kept his hands clenched deep inside his pockets. "None since we last spoke. Lenin's unprecedented DNA samples are being examined and I'm assured fresh ones are being airlifted to Omsk."

"Very good."

She was serving her second term as President of the New Russian Federation. A smart, determined, cool-headed woman, she'd entered law school by the age of twenty and became a respected State Prosecutor by thirty. Before reaching forty she'd been named First Deputy to the former Interior Minister. Known for her levelheadedness and poise, with an acute, judicious understanding of the shape of Russian history and people, and its deep-rooted longing for sound capable leadership, it wasn't long before senior officials of her political party took notice. By the age of fifty she attained a leadership position, and stunned much of Russia's elite establishment and political pundits by being popularly elected to the highest office in the land. A tireless, rigorous leader, Natasha Stroganoff had skillfully learned to be a politician as an actor studies and learns his way around the stage. The only difference was that in her chosen field, the stakes were far higher. During her time in office some suspected she savored ulterior motives and ambitions, that she relished power too well.

"Have you further instructions, Madam President?"

She shook her head. They sauntered leisurely down steep steps and onto the pavement. The cold wind diminished. A flock of sparrows flew from sight. Morning traffic moved orderly along the street, a mix of buses, cars, and taxis. "Have you been contacted recently by our prime minister?" she asked.

"*Nyet.* Not a peep. He plays his cards very close to his vest, but inwardly I know he's fuming with all his bluster and finger pointing. This has been a rude awakening. As far as I'm aware, Boris Sokolov is one of very few who has his ear, and Boris feeds any information with great caution."

The president appeared decidedly satisfied. "And the rest of your scientific team? Are they adequate?"

"They do their jobs well. Nor can I fault Boris for his choices. Do you believe he had knowledge of this episode concerning Rimsky-Kimsky?"

"I doubt Sokolov knew anything, but I appreciate you being candid. Before we depart, what about our other matter of concern? America's annoying interference by their so-called representative, Floyd Dingus?"

"Frankly, this man has everyone bewildered. No one knows what to make of him. Evidently he plays his part well as a naïve, jovial, good-natured fool. But he hasn't hoodwinked anyone; it's apparent it's a charade. It has to be. Boris and the others wonder how much an actor he is, and above all, what he's really after and whose interests he really represents."

"As I also concluded. Very well, keep a watchful eye on him—and do be careful." She paused, looking at him squarely. "You'll continue keeping me apprised, I trust?"

"My solemn word, Madame President. I promised you long ago, before resigning my position at the Academy, that you could count on me when need arose. I never expected finding ourselves in such peculiar circumstances, but my word is my bond. You needn't be concerned."

Her eyes were graphic and probing. "Thank you, Rabbi. Our country stands on a dangerous precipice, facing a possible renewed civil war. It's necessary to know we still have solid patriotic men like you on our side. Take care of yourself, Rabbi. Good care. Goodbye." She turned and walked down to the end of the street. He watched while she entered a nondescript waiting car and drove off in the direction of the Kremlin.

Asher glanced behind at the imposing church. He stared again at the extravagant domes, speculating how it was possible for religion to give birth to noble and marvelous ideals while simultaneously being the cause of so much hate, strife and destruction. Then bracing against the chill he walked off in the opposite direction.

Vlad sat quietly on his sofa, his mobile phone beside him, battery depleted. He'd placed it there this morning immediately after his conversation with Raisa, and there it remained. How long had it been since she exited his life? How many times had he phoned and texted in recent days, never receiving a reply? How often he'd speculated how his daughters were faring during this upheaval in their young lives. Were they as resilient during this period as he prayed? Did Raisa prevent them calling? This morning's conversation left many questions unanswered. One thing, though, was certain; her mind was made up; she was not coming back. He tried to protest, agree to a face-to-face meeting, but no, she tearfully told him it was pointless. There was too much doubt, too much pain. Why prolong the inevitable? Raisa assured him there'd be no animosity during the divorce. She was agreeable to lenient terms of financial settlement, moreover, she was willing to share custody once he resumed a normal life, and gave assurances that he'd again be the good father he'd once been, the loving parent his daughters had all but forfeited these past two years.

Vlad was surprised how well he'd anticipated this conversation when Raisa finally returned his call. These past weeks were some of the loneliest and arduous of his life, having to act as though everything was fine while his home life was falling apart. He wished it were different. If he hadn't accepted the position as Director of Public Relations his world would never have been so severely influenced. He and Raisa might have made a go of it. But the lure of this job afforded opportunities and connections he could only fantasize, and there was no turning it down. That he'd gained favored status among several key government ministers was proof positive his efforts had handsomely paid off. He believed Raisa understood, indeed shared in the glow of these fulfilled aspirations. Now he realized its toll was greater than she could bear. From the outset of accepting he recognized their life would become trying, but not ruinous. No, he never saw it coming. His psyche was jammed with work like a cluttered hard disc, and he'd been blindsided to the reality. The impact was brutal; he couldn't be wed to this career and Raisa at the same time.

"If you want to dance, you have to pay the piper," he recalled his mother chiding him. Nothing is free, everything and everyone has a price. And now that payment was made in full. What more could he lose? Again he recalled Alina Vera's admonition; remain strong, now more than ever. Did he really care, he wondered, if some lunatic physicist created a monster embroiling Russia in renewed revolution? Was it his business if politicians scurried and trembled at the prospect? He wasn't a politician or a soldier, and he wasn't an espionage agent. When it came right down to it, until a month ago, all he'd been was a family man aspiring to make his mark, like so many others. To hell with Mikhail Sunavich, Boris Sokolov, and most of all this ludicrous Chocolate Lenin.

You're wallowing in self-pity, he told himself. This isn't the time or place. There'll be countless hours ahead for tears, self-examination, ruminations and incriminations. Hold in those emotions until later. Not today, nor tomorrow. He wasn't old; he could look forward to decades of remorse.

The doorbell rang. He stretched and got up leaving his uncharged mobile. "The door's open," he called, pouring a small shot of brandy. Odd, but his shoulder stopped aching. A month ago nothing nagged more than his physical pain; tonight, it was emotional torment gripping his abdomen, and he was powerless to stop it. There was no prescription.

"You look awful, Vova."

He glanced up to see Boris standing at the doorway. "Come in. Want a drink?"

Boris closed the door behind. "Thanks, no. It's time to leave. Have you looked at the clock?"

"Raisa is divorcing me," was all he said.

Boris gazed downward, sadly, almost able to predict word for word what Vlad would say. Something similar had happened many years before in his life with the wife he'd all but blotted from memory. A man can't serve two masters. "I'm so sorry. She's a nice girl. I always liked her."

"I liked her too, Boris." He didn't mean to bare the bitter sarcasm in his voice.

"Bring your overcoat, my friend. We'll talk more on the way."

Vlad nodded, downed his drink, heat rising in his chest. It was all he could do not to break down and cry.

13.

In a sign of international unease, The U.N. Security Council voiced 'grave concern' with deteriorating security concerns deepening in the New Russian Federation, putting aside disagreements that had prevented the 15-nation body from speaking unanimously on the stirring unrest...

Colonel Dimsky sat rigidly at his keyboard, paying scant attention to the radio report. He emailed new instructions to Doctor Yuri Grushin, the newly appointed scientific team leader at Omsk. Shocking news had arrived advising the colonel that current team leader, Rimsky-Kimsky, was to be arrested, charged with passing information to a foreign government. There was little doubt the scientist had clandestinely met with a noncitizen known to be an undercover agent of the crack Mossad. It hadn't yet been determined if or what information Rimsky-Kimsky may have passed to his contact. This was a heavy blow to absorb.

Dimsky had very little information regarding newly appointed Yuri Grushin. However, Rabbi Titlebaum himself had given the go-ahead. Rimsky-Kimsky's loss had struck deeply, the rabbi was forced to act quickly and Dimsky was in no position to question him.

He looked at his watch; the hour was late. A whiff of cigar aroma wafted to his nostrils and the colonel looked up to find Boris and the others finally had arrived.

"Excuse the delay," said Boris. "Our car was stuck in horrible traffic on the ring road. Apparently there are major hindrances occurring at Domodedovo Airport."

"I know. Hundreds of international flights have been postponed or canceled." Dimsky swiveled in his chair, noting Alina Vera agitated and Vlad visibly shaken. "Don't be concerned about me. I've put my time to good use using newly developed digital tools for both spying and destroying. I was scouring cyberspace, searching social networks and blogs, about to download some questionable music into my flashdrive." He showed the flashdrive. "I did download a fresh copy of *Bring on the Revolution* by the Chocolate Lenin Band, if any of you wish to hear it. Subversive, loathsome material for sure, but it's really not a bad tune, even if it is only rock and roll. Good guitar playing, nice riffs and licks."

"Curb you admiration," snapped Boris, tossing his jacket over a chair. "What's the latest regarding this airport mess? Was there an air accident?"

The colonel shook his head. "No. It began earlier at Lvov's newly completed international airport. Initially it was started by a group of whining, disgruntled baggage handlers displeased with their benefits. They showed up for work refusing to load or offload passengers' luggage. The dispute spilled over, and that's when everything came to a standstill. Air traffic had to be rerouted. A subsequent report says there's also an ongoing stoppage at Kiev's terminal, apparently the act of freight handlers. A rally was planned beforehand, a big demonstration along the main highway. They disregarded police orders against blocking airport traffic. We have a sit-in. Large numbers of foreign and domestic carriers have dozens of aircraft idly stacked on the tarmac. It's impossible to unload cargo. Laborers willing to report for work have been prevented by threats and intimidation."

"What cargo are these planes carrying?" Vlad asked. "Explosives, guns? Terrorist bomb-making materials?"

"Not at all. Crates of cheap vodka, mostly. Atrocious knock-off brands, bargain basement dregs and dross we pawn off to others who don't know any better. I'm not sure about anything else. The authorities are making a big to-do. All arrivals are being diverted to still-operating airports. Central air traffic control has directed international flights to land at Petersburg or Moscow, but as other regional airports report stoppages, delays have increased dramatically. It's a cascade of falling dominoes."

"What's the stoppage for?" questioned Alina Vera. "What are the trade unions demanding?"

Dimsky held his breath. Smoke from Boris's cigar was belching like a smoldering volcano. "Alleged abuse over workers' rights," he said, waving offending smoke away. "They claim work shifts are unfairly long, too many hours of toil, too little break time. They say they're busting ass for inadequate pay, and are unwilling to obey supervisors representing anti-worker, bourgeois airlines delivering capitalist cargoes. All respect for authority is tossed out the window."

Boris slumped into his chair, forcing a modicum of inner control during an out-of-control situation. "This is a calamity. Lenin's swill and detritus has gotten to them, everyone spouting the same horseshit." He sat silent, ill humored, his face turning color as he pictured dozens of rotting husks of grounded Aeroflot planes.

"We're awaiting news from Omsk regarding Rimsky-Kimsky's successor," said Alina Vera, as she peered questioningly over the colonel's shoulder. "What are you doing on this music website?"

Dimsky's poise stiffened; he lowered the volume. "For your information, I'm conducting important official work. This is a particularly scandalous site devoted to upcoming British rock and roll bands. I've been carefully scouring for indications of subversive music."

She couldn't contain an artless smirk. "Come off it, Dimsky. Admit it. You're starting to enjoy this stuff."

He ignored her. "Per your Omsk query, I've just emailed an introductory note to Rimsky-Kimsky's replacement regarding protocol. The newly-assigned team leader is Professor Yuri Grushin—"

"*What*? Yuri Grushin is put in charge at Omsk? Are you kidding?"

"Do you know him?" Vlad asked.

She turned around. "Of course I know Yuri. We were at school together. I've been acquainted with him for years, too many years."

"What info can you tell us?" said Boris, looking up.

"Ha. What *can't* I tell you? Yuri's a twenty-four carat conniving prima donna. Barbaric, and ill mannered. You want some enticing dirt? Okay. At school his idea of fun was pinching girls' behinds, then running away giggling. He expressly rides his bicycle the wrong direction against traffic. I once saw him act as though he was going to run down a frightened old lady. He's a mental defective with a brain more callused than his ass."

"I hate bicycle riders, too," consoled Dimsky. "Whenever I'm driving and see one I have the urge to run him over and squash him."

"Yuri's a schoolboy prankster in short pants. He loves juvenile antics like snapping girls' brassieres."

"Can we possibly be discussing the same fellow?" said Boris. "The scientific leader on whose expertise we'll be entrusting?"

"It's the same. Years ago, Yuri enjoyed playing lowly flunky for Mikhail Sunavich. He'd drool for the opportunity to run his errands, buy his lunch, or fold his laundry, whatever. He'd hurry to the shop, pick up a vodka bottle in one hand, and carry a jar of sour pickles in the other."

"He acquired such fondness for sour pickles?" asked Dimsky.

Alina Vera rolled her eyes heavenward. "I don't understand why Asher possibly picked the likes of Yuri Grushin."

"The rabbi must have numerous reasons unexplained to us," Boris said, returning to himself. "Anyway, merely because Grushin behaves like an immature nitwit doesn't mean he isn't a top-rated scientist."

"More an addlebrained clod. A few years back he was a gofer sycophant for the Minister of Science. Maybe he pressured the rabbi. And where is Asher? Why isn't he here?"

"He's still at his lab. He said he'd remain overnight if necessary. I have no specifics, but his hints and tone lead me to believe he's on the right track with his specimens. A fresh semen batch was flown in by military helicopter. Most was delivered to Omsk, but the rabbi specifically requested a small amount diverted here. I think Asher mistrusts everyone since this Rimsky-Kimsky debacle. He said he wants a firsthand look at every new delivery."

Alina Vera nodded. "Asher works best when left alone. I hope he'll soon allow me to assist him at the lab."

Dimsky punched numbers into his smartphone. "Give me up-to-the-minute developments of the airport situation," he instructed an underling. He listened stone-faced, thanked his contact and hung up. "We'd better prepare for a long night." He frowned. "A rally is taking place right now guaranteed to piss Milonov off. The workers are chanting, *'Hey, ho, hey, ho! Milonov must fuckin' go!'*"

Alina Vera tried not to snicker at the profanity.

"Meanwhile," Dimsky dryly said, "the airspace backup is worsening. A domino effect. Moscow military HQ is considering designating a regiment of Army regulars plus freshly drafted recruits to carry out the work if the baggage handlers persist in refusing returning to duty. This could turn nasty very quickly. These hotheads are in no mood to be pushed around, and the military will follow all commands issued, closing roads, suspending air service, shutting transportation. Top staff is closeted, wrangling in around-the-clock strategy sessions, awaiting Kremlin instruction. As of now it's a standoff, but it could turn violent. Lenin's dream is becoming reality, a repetition of what you witnessed in Minsk—or worse."

"My God," Vlad gasped at his disturbing conclusion. "I see what he's up to! He's replicating events of the October Revolution, pitting the military against workers." His eyes widened with awareness. "I think I'm starting to understand his strategy. He's found a way to escalate his crusade to a fevered pitch that's sure to garner international attention, and back us up against the wall. Without firing a single shot he'll be hailed as a courageous dissident, a lone, brave figure standing up to a debased establishment, a shining beacon of hope, while we're pilloried in the press."

"Blah, blah, blah," said Dimsky, exasperated.

"The masses will eat it up and rally. And if our military uses arms to diffuse the protests we'll fall straight into his ambush. Brute force against unarmed workers? We'll see a universal uproar. More unions will walk off the job, more soldiers defect." A simmering volcano was about to erupt spewing lava, Vlad realized. Hopes for rebellion needed friction and divisions to increase turbulence, precursors to sliding into a second civil war. "Colonel, do everything possible to call off these soldiers! Order them to stand down!"

Boris stood. "Blessed holy mother in heaven, Vlad sees it right. Confrontation is what that mucus-for-blood bastard wants! Huge protests cutting across class and ideology, shows of solidarity, defiant parades. I can picture marches broadcast on nightly newscasts. There's no time to lose!"

Dimsky attended his smartphone. Boris took his own mobile and made a frantic call to the prime minister's private number. "Get me Milonov immediately," he growled. "It's urgent—find him!" He stood his ground, legs apart, snorting like an angry bull preparing to stampede. After a brief interlude he snapped his phone shut. "Damn it! The prime minister is incommunicado; he's gone to personally oversee the situation at Domodedovo, escorted by lights and sirens with the Chief of Staff. The army is ordered to declare martial law at Russian airports effective immediately if needed."

Vlad paled. "The military mustn't interfere!"

"They can and they did. Sit down, Vova," Boris ordered. "I need to assess this train wreck with Milonov. Hopefully prevail on him to reevaluate. But Milonov has his own agenda. If I can't convince him, there's no further action we can take. Our hands are tied."

Vlad sat downcast, hating the order of things. He held his head in his hands. "We're serving them their goddamn revolution on a silver platter," he insisted. "If workers are harmed, fresh strikes will paralyze the country from Petersburg to Vladivostok in a tsunami of dissent, impossible to deflate. We'll watch worldwide footage of soldiers beating civilians splashed across TV and cyberspace."

Alina Vera kneeled beside Vlad, seeking to assuage his foreboding. "He knows what he's saying," she emphasized. "He's the only one here showing common sense. Martial law is a harebrained mistake. Why aren't you heeding him? Allegiance among recruits is already divided; this will smother any remaining military morale. You want to see our soldiers defect en masse? I listen to the news reports. All the fear, pain, and hatreds we resolved a century ago will resurface. Why is Milonov pursuing this? Is his reptilian brain that backwards?"

"She has a point," Dimsky darkly acknowledged.

Boris said nothing. The presented scenario was undeniable. The reliability of Governmental response was in question. Lenin couldn't find a better ally to jumpstart a revolution. What in hell was going on?

It was the longest of nights.

The dramatic bond selloff took the yield on 10-year debt to 15 percent across Europe, and 13 percent in the United States. Potentially more troubling is the glaring action by China today when its finance minister declared that Russian financial instability remains untenable, setting off unpredictable effects across already suffering markets. Value of the ruble dropped sharply overnight…

Boris ignored the international business report blaring in the background. After trying in vain for hours to garner support, he sat disheveled and dispirited. Dawn had arrived and his numerous efforts had failed.

"Milonov conjures threats from everywhere," he groused. "He's cocksure rivals are finding cute ways to steal his thunder. He was awake all night, he said, fearful of a widening conspiracy. The Cabinet's agreed to meet with the heads of the largest trade unions to discuss grievances. God knows how that will go with so much animosity existing between them. They loathe one another. The Government is showing a willingness to negotiate, but insists on a compulsory return to work, plus resumption of air traffic. Meanwhile, our bourse is reeling, the stock market is plummeting, and foreign investors are pulling out cash by the billions, and will soon bankrupt the nation. Barring some doubtful quick agreement, the military is preparing for nationwide deployment to prevent a protracted humanitarian crisis. There will be no further stoppages. The prime minister's threat was implicit."

"It defies explanation," said Alina Vera. "Even if the strike's not legitimate, it's dumb to disperse it with brutality and barbarity."

Sunlight splayed across the room accentuating the wall's color. A seemingly endless view of Moscow's ever-burgeoning skyline lay before them. No one paid attention. Alina Vera curled on her settee. The situation remained critical, and they awaited the outcome in subdued silence. The incessant tick-tock of the clock heralded a steady reminder of more precious time being lost.

Boris chewed his cigar and savored another mug of strong coffee. Colonel Dimsky maintained his stoic outlook, laptop in sleep mode, smartphone recharging. His faithful balalaika lay at his feet. He'd been softly playing to help pass the long hours, strumming treasured time-honored tunes, music composed by peoples of the copious forested hinterland.

Vlad ruminated, speculating on what dire events might have transpired overnight at the airports. Circumstances today could mark a defining moment.

Boris's mobile rang loudly. Ill at ease from lack of sleep, he grabbed it with jerky agitation. "Sokolov." Paying rapt attention, he whispered to his colleagues, "they're patching me through to a conference call between the Kremlin and Ukraine big shots." He listened attentively while the Ukraine Minister of Defense conversed with President Stroganoff's trusted Deputy Chief of Staff.

"Are you on the line with us, Boris?" the deputy asked.

"I hear you clearly, sir. And I understand our current predicament perfectly."

Everyone waited with edgy anticipation. Revolutionary rhetoric had reached new heights, spawning international frustration and condemnation. The United States, EU and UN, publically pronounced growing concern, and a menace of unspoken serious repercussions should matters not resolve quickly. Strikes had yet to end, civilian aircraft unable to take off or land inside Russia's borders. Considerably worsening the outlook, a number of Western European airports including Berlin, Paris, and London were voicing worry over their own mounting delays and cancellations. All Europe and beyond would soon be affected.

Asher came quietly into the room. He had also spent a demanding night, and hearing news of this latest crisis left his lab to huddle beside his team. Boris nodded to him, silently concentrating on the telephone conversation. Asher's deep-set eyes were watery, bloodshot with fatigue and concern. From his sagging mien, Alina Vera surmised his own labors hadn't gone as well as hoped. She hustled him off to one side. "Asher, what prompted you to put that sophomoric buffoon, Grushin, in charge?"

Gaunt and weak from long hours of arduous work and solitude, he said, "Between us, there wasn't anyone else I could trust. Grushin may act the clown but he's not white-livered. He'll live up to his responsibilities, and at least he can't do worse damage than the megalomaniac responsible for this mess. It's a gamble we have to take."

Alina Vera listened, too weary to protest.

The conference call abruptly ended. Boris shut his mobile. "All of you need to hear this." He sat at the edge of his desk. "A temporary agreement was reached minutes ago, confrontation is averted for the moment...without guarantees of durability. I think Milonov blinked at the last moment."

Vlad shut his eyes. "I'm thankful for that much."

"Thinking with his brain is hard work for the P.M." said Alina Vera.

"But don't think our trouble is over," Boris quickly added. "The Ukraine and Belarus are both loudly blaming this entire disaster squarely on us, proclaiming ignorance of trade union intent at Lvov or anywhere else. Everything was inspired from here, they insist. They're probably right. Also they're issuing substantial demands for cooperation. It's possible the Americans are pushing them. Our wiretaps noticed an energetic increase of activity at the American Embassy. They're exerting pressure on the president to permit envoy Floyd Dingus total access to our work. Obviously they're dissatisfied with what Dingus accomplished so far. It's causing another diplomatic flap."

He regarded his colleagues with disapproval. "Oh, and one other thing..." he added tiresomely, "Alina Vera, Vlad, I have no knowledge of how the two of you conducted yourselves in Minsk. And I don't know how you questioned this Olga Orlovskya, or if you made any sort of promises. But suddenly I'm told she's agreed to cooperate—oddly, not to cooperate with the Belarus authorities holding her, but with us. Naturally they're upset. Outraged, in fact. Our deputy minister gave me hell. I had to bite my tongue and listen to his foul-mouthed diatribe. Prisoner Olga Orlovskya has admitted possessing important information regarding Lenin's intrigues, and also possible information concerning his whereabouts, and those of his consort, Ilya Evgeny."

Vlad and Alina Vera exchanged puzzled glances. "We did nothing unusual, Boris," Vlad said in innocence. "Nor did we make promises. During the interrogation we role played 'good cop, bad cop' like you see on American crime shows. It's a clever police technique—and it works." He grinned sheepishly. Alina Vera gazed down at her hands.

"I love American crime shows," said Dimsky.

Boris's physique bulked, his voice grew sterner. "Well, whatever the hell you did, you apparently achieved it very well. Your little television ploy worked."

"Oh?"

"Yes. One curious thing the Belarusians mentioned. By any chance did you give this dangerous prisoner, Orlovskya, a gift box of expensive marshmallow chocolates?"

Vlad swallowed hard. "I did. I'd read her dossier on the plane, carefully studying her background. It mentioned she's partial to chocolate marshmallows. It was strictly innocent. Don't worry, though, I paid for it with my own money."

Boris shut weary eyes. "I see. So the two of you grandstanded, playing 'good cop, bad cop,' and afterward, as a meager charity gesture, you provided her with a box of chocolate marshmallows. Her favorite kind, as you noted." He heaved a sigh, unable to decide whether laughing or crying was more appropriate. "All things considered, I don't know whether to call it great skill on your part or plain dumb luck. In any case, it seems the prisoner was strikingly moved by your thoughtful gesture. You touched her deeply, did you realize the effect you had?"

His gaping stare indicated he most certainly had not.

"In that case, you'll be pleased to learn your technique was rewarding, and Olga Orlovskya so influenced by your showered graciousness that she's consented to giving a complete confession. But with one teeny-tiny condition—the only person she'll talk to is Vladimir Petrovsky."

Vlad froze, speechless. Certainly the confession was welcome, but Boris appeared anything but pleased.

"Belarusian secret police worked Orlovskya over for days and nights, using all the tools and expertise at their command, but the pitiable woman didn't budge. She apparently detested Alina Vera, but as for you—well, need I spell it out?"

Alina Vera's mouth opened wide. "Oh Vlad, don't you get it? It's so *obvious*! She's got a crush on you!" Alina Vera folded her arms trying to contain sidesplitting laughter.

"That's not possible—"

"Furthermore," Boris added in mock congratulations, "Belarus authorities feel disgraced and disgusted by this entire episode. So they've not so humorously dumped her on us. After bickering they agreed to permit Orlovskya to be flown to Moscow to continue interrogation. That is, for *you* to personally continue where you left off. No one else is permitted to be present."

"This is priceless," said the scientist, as Dimsky guffawed loudly.

Vlad fumed. "I get the picture. What do you want me to do?"

"*Do?* Buy her another damn box of chocolate marshmallows! Ten boxes! I don't care. Cook a tasty plate of chicken hearts in cream. Go to bed with her, arrange for conjugal prison visits, vow to marry her. But no promises of amnesty—understand? I'm telling you this, you'd better find out every tidbit this atrocious woman has concealed. From the start we've believed her smelly inn played a integral role in hiding Lenin, and maybe harboring other conspirators."

"Sunavich, too," said Alina Vera.

"Sunavich also boarded at that filthy place?" wondered Dimsky.

Boris faced skyward, shaking his head. "Anyone might have boarded at that filthy showpiece. It could well be that Orlovskya's inn—what's its name— is notorious for lowbrow clientele."

"*Peter the Great's Palace.* It's a well-known, frequented establishment in the locality," offered Dimsky. "Part slop-house, part brothel. A decrepit, end-of-the-line dive, and a verminous hideaway for the dregs of humanity. A peculiar name for such a rubbish pile."

"Right. *Peter the Great's Palace,*" parroted Boris. "Feasibly serving as Lenin's provisional headquarters. It serves as a good haven for laying low while contriving his blueprint for anarchy. We've gone through entire lists of telephone records emanating from *Peter the Great's Palace* dating back months. It's amazing how many individuals of fine repute have been secretly paying the cagey succubus considerable sums to maintain a hushed, hellish room there—including an unnamed American congressman! But I digress. More than a handful of logged phone calls have suspiciously originated from there to St. Petersburg. So I ask myself, who in a derelict washbasin like Gorki had reason to call St. Petersburg this past month? Even more fascinating, is that we discovered a number of these calls were made to the home of none other than noted chess champion, Gregori Nabokov."

Alina Vera's sense of evolving deduction heightened; a new piece of the puzzle was emerging. "The great Gregori Nabokov, whom not-so-coincidentally happens to be the boyfriend of Irina Evgeny, the nearly-identical sister of our dangerous friend, Ilya Evgeny."

"Coincidence, indeed!" Boris huffed, turning to Vlad. "Your duty is straightforward, Petrovsky. Olga Orlovskya will arrive sometime later today. Fulfill your undertaking to the best of your ability."

"It's a jungle out there," sighed Dimsky.

Vlad realized he was charged with possibly the most important task of his life. Could this provide the key they badly needed, putting an end to revolutionary fervor as well as Chocolate Lenin?

Olga Orlovskya wore knee-high stockings with elastic bands. Her dress was a few inches shorter, a grey *rubakha*, a plain peasant-style shirt-dress fashioned from coarse linen. The Belarusian authorities delivered her to Moscow dressed in her own clothes, not prison garb.

Boris and Colonel Dimsky summarily escorted her to a small, outlaying lodging house that would arouse no suspicion. It would be better not to treat her as a prisoner, Boris reasoned, opting to deal with her firmly, professionally, but not by using threats or force.

When Vlad entered the room she was sitting in a finely wrought bamboo chair angled at the side of the bed. He stood before her, and she turned off the small television. "It's good to see you again, Olga," he said with a polite smile. "Here, please accept this small gift I brought."

With a hint of schoolgirl joy, Olga reached to accept the box of marshmallow chocolates. "Thank you, sir. I so much enjoyed the last ones you gave me." She glanced down at her new gift with her mouth watering. "Oh! These came from the Alexander Nevsky. The best. You didn't have to spend so much money."

Vlad relaxed comfortably in the chair opposite, crossed his legs, and placed folded hands in his lap. A tiny microphone was carefully hidden under his shirt collar. An unseen microchip earpiece allowed Boris to talk to Vlad if necessary.

"It was my pleasure to buy it for you," he said, immediately noticing that the two elongated hairs growing from Olga's double chin had been removed. Her stringy grey hair was pinned and neatly combed, and she certainly appeared less agitated than during their first encounter at the desolate prison in Minsk. "I hope you were well treated on your flight?"

"How do the police ever treat anyone?" she scoffed. "They're glad to be as rid of me as I am of them. I told you last time how they threatened me and talked down to me as if I were lowborn scum. Well, I'm not. Remember, my father was a tradesman. Had I remained at the Girls' Seminary I might have grown up to be a fine lady, who knows? I had a real wedding in the holy church. What more can I say? I don't apologize for a thing. As to my treatment from the Belarus police, I gave back as good as I got, Mr. Petrovsky."

"I see you know my name."

Olga smiled broadly, unashamed of her lack of dental care. "Oh, yes! I do. Your first name is also Vladimir, isn't it?"

"Yes."

"Just like Lenin."

"No, not at all like that. Olga, do you understand I have questions I need to ask? However, I give my word that in no way would I threaten you or do you harm. I know you told the Belarus police there are certain…matters…you're willing to confess, but only to me, is that correct?"

Olga held a marshmallow chocolate in front of her nose and gazed at it with delectable promise. "I never said anything about a confession. I tried telling you last time; I'm not a stupid woman. I have more education that you know. I told the prosecutors I'd be willing to talk, but only to you. That is, if you had questions for me, I'd give answers to you alone. So please don't patronize me." She put the chocolate in her mouth and made modest savoring sounds as she chewed. After she swallowed, she sucked thumb and forefinger, and smacked her lips. She placed the open box on her lap. The box contained twelve large pieces of marshmallow chocolate, eleven were left, he noted. It appeared she intended to relish every last one.

"Fair enough, Olga. I do have questions, and I trust you'll answer them truthfully."

She nodded, brushing tousled locks of hair away from her forehead. "I always keep my word, sir. Especially to a gentleman." Her eyes made contact with his.

"First, Olga, I'd like you to tell me when and how you first met Mikhail Sunavich, as well as the individual who calls himself Lenin."

She shot a piqued glance. "There's no mistake, he *is* Comrade Lenin."

"Agreed then. Now please, tell me when and how you met both these gentlemen." He reached inside his jacket pocket and handed her a recent photograph of Mikhail Sunavich taken shortly before his disappearance. The snapshot presented the doctor berating a junior colleague. Olga wiped fingers sticky with chocolate on her dress before taking the photo. She tilted her head and pondered.

"Oh yes, it's him. He's the one. Only he didn't use the name 'Sunavich'. He told me his name was Popov, Andrei Popov. He showed up at my inn for the first time, *Peter the Great's Palace*, some months ago. It must have been the middle of winter because I recall the snow was high and it was very cold. I sat with friends playing a card game, *Durak*, 'Fool'. Yes, I remember that. I don't like to lose, and I was winning money that day while waiting..."

"Waiting for who?"

"I pay a local farmer to clear away the snow and ice with his broken-down plow truck, but the lout must have been drunk because he didn't show up until almost dark. His carrying-on could have lost me all my customers, the degenerate."

"Go on."

She squinted inquisitively. "You're not recording me, are you? I won't say another word if I'm being recorded."

"I'm not recording you," Vlad said truthfully, omitting that below in the basement Boris and Dimsky were carefully listening.

Olga picked up another piece of chocolate, licked it, and then placed it between her cheek and gum. This one she didn't chew, she just kept it in place, evaluating his reply. The bulge appeared like a swelling caused by an abscessed tooth.

"These chocolates are delicious. I'm in your debt, and when they finally release me I'd be most happy to have you visit my inn any time you wish. And not just any room for you, no! I keep a special room for very special guests I pamper with private dinners, entertainment and schnapps. Maybe I can find sympathetic company who'll listen to your problems, if you wish." Her intense eyes looked away shyly.

He felt uneasy at her innuendo of seduction. "Thank you, that might be nice sometime. But for now, Olga, let's return to my question. Was it the night of the snowstorm you first met Dr. Sunavich?"

"Andrei Popov," she corrected firmly. "He's the one in your picture, that's certain. His ears and the tip of his nose were cold as icicles that night he showed up. Lips blue, I swear. He politely asked if I had a room available for such an awful night as this. He struck me as a sly one even then. I can tell these things. I asked for his references. I said, 'this is a decent place and we don't allow tramps.'

That was when he told me he was a musician. So I asked him, 'where is your instrument, sir?' He didn't give a direct answer. He muttered about playing the harpsichord, and that he traveled from city to city, giving lessons and concerts to earn his living. Then he asked if I'd ever seen any of his concerts, or if I'd ever seen him before anywhere. I told him, 'No sir, I've never seen you before.' He demanded to know if I was certain. 'Positive,' I replied. That pleased him. I knew what he wanted to hear and I know how to keep customers happy."

Vlad leaned forward, lacing his fingers on his lap. He chewed at his lower lip, trusting their voices were loud and clear to Boris and Colonel Dimsky. Dimsky personally had wired the room earlier.

Olga munched the chocolate marshmallow lingering in her mouth, licking her lips after swallowing. Ten pieces remained in the box. "As I was saying, this Andrei Popov gave me his story and said he wanted a room to let, but he also wanted to know if I was willing to make an arrangement to maintain it exclusively for him.

"I told him I couldn't afford to leave any of my rooms empty. I needed to keep them rented. 'I'm a poor widow and my dear husband was a valiant, patriotic soldier,' I said. I told him the pittance of a pension the government gave since his death wasn't sufficient to feed a dog. He was very respectful and heard me out without interrupting. Mr. Popov assured me he understood my requirements. I could tell by his nice clothes he was a man of some means, although it was hard to believe a harpsichord player could earn a decent living, let alone lot of money. I thought he must come from a wealthy family. He took a gob of cash from his wallet and peeled a number of 1000 ruble notes. 'I can give you this much every month, Madam Innkeeper,' he said. 'Is this enough to satisfy your wellbeing?' I counted it and answered that indeed it would do. That visit he only stayed one night. He was carrying a little suitcase and under his arm was a small computer. I told him that I wished I could learn to use a computer. So many people do these days, even little children. Imagine that. He agreed with me that a computer was a good thing to learn. He said he mostly used his computer to send e-mail letters to his elderly sickly mother. He travelled so much, he added, that his poor mother rarely saw him anymore. She worried that he appeared gaunt and pale and might be ailing. He said he felt guilty about her. She must indeed be a very old woman, I thought to myself, because this Andrei Popov was certainly no spring chicken." She snorted at her humor and chewed another piece of chocolate. Vlad sat serenely, waiting for her to finish while she sucked her fingers and wiped them.

"After that, Mr. Popov would show up from time to time; a bit more frequently when winter winds eased and the roads became passable. I have to say he was good to his word and paid me in cash every time he visited. He never even requested a receipt."

"Then what happened, Olga? Tell me about what went on after the snows and the road became accessible."

"Well," she began as she enjoyed the next piece of chocolate, "Several more rooms rented out, as you know. Around springtime city travelers come my way, wandering from every direction. The world has changed so much, and it's not easy for a widow to make a living."

"Who mostly rents your rooms?"

She shrugged as she thought. "Sometimes I rent to farmers on their way to make a transaction at some faraway market. Sometimes travelling salesmen peddling rubbish to stupid people stop by for a rest. I'm always surprised how foolish people can be. Of course I keep my handful of regulars who enjoy visiting *Peter the Great's Palace* with their gentlemen friends. Short stays for those desiring only a bit of sleep. Hardworking girls, nice girls coming from decent families. No painted streetwalkers allowed. No one will catch congenital syphilis in my establishment, no! I chase that kind straight out. And no drunkards allowed, either. I own a decent little hotel, if you please. I've never permitted cheap women from lowly backgrounds to hang around my inn. I want you to know that. I run a proper establishment for proper folk."

"Never mind these working girls, Olga. That's not important."

She hesitantly took another piece from the box. Eight were left. "It was more than a month ago when Andrei Popov appeared again. On this occasion he seemed very happy, happier than I'd ever seen him. Usually from the moment he arrived until the moment he left he remained in his room. But this time he said he was hungry and apologized for such a late arrival. He asked if my cook could make him something to eat. He said he'd made a long journey for a concert and he needed to make arrangements to have his harpsichord cleaned and repaired. He moaned it was 'so expensive,' harpsichords being so delicate and unappreciated. I offered a plate of steaming cabbage and potatoes with mushrooms and garlic, and slices of black bread. He agreed that would be fine because he was a vegetarian anyway and didn't savor eating red meat. Very bad for your health, he said. Personally I don't care what my guests eat as long as they pay for their supper. But Andrei Popov was never any trouble. So I told him there are chickens loose in my backyard. I buy them cheap from neighbors to keep at the ready for fancy meals or banquets. You can hear those damn chickens clucking day and night. My henhouse has no door.

"Andrei Popov said he felt grieved for the poor chickens. Killing them wasn't right, and he made foolish remarks how workers of the world were very much like those skinny chickens, eaten alive by the rich and powerful. I understood his meaning, I told him, but I never involve myself in politics. A good, proper gentleman's supper would be waiting in the parlor when he was ready. I even offered him one of the friendly girls for company, but he declined, saying he was exhausted and preferred going straight to bed after supper.

"Before leaving the next morning he drank several cups of Turkish coffee. He prefers Turkish coffee. He mentioned that a close friend of his would soon be coming to visit *Peter the Great's Palace*. He wondered if this friend could use his room in his absence. The fellow was also a musician, Popov told me. He asked if this might require a larger deposit. I told him a few hundred extra would do fine. I asked if his friend would want meals or company during visits. He said he didn't know, that his friend would decide. I asked his friend's name and he only told me his Christian name. He said it was Vladimir, an old childhood chum from schooldays. This friend played the piccolo, he said. Occasionally they performed as a duo."

Vlad listened intently. "So, Popov never gave any surname for his old chum?"

She picked out another chocolate marshmallow. Seven remained. "No, he never did. I waited for this long-lost friend, Vladimir, expecting him to arrive any day. He didn't. In fact, it was about ten days before his comrade showed up. This one appeared even stranger than Mr. Popov. After showing him to his room, he kept on his proletarian cap and his scarf, covering much of his face. I wondered if his face was burned or deformed, poor thing. He asked if I knew who he was, and I said I did. 'You're Vladimir, the musician, Andrei Popov's childhood chum, the piccolo player.' He was amused, admitting piccolo music was not rated highly or appreciated these days. He visited and left a couple of times. I didn't pay much attention. But the next time he arrived I recall it was a very warm day, because I was sweating like a dog. I always sweat in the heat. Vladimir the musician showed up without coat or hat. I looked at him, as if suddenly seeing him for the first time. He smiled. He has a nice smile. 'Do you recognize me, Madam?' he asked.

"I gasped and stood frozen, daring not say a word. By all the saints, I swear he was a perfect image of blessed Lenin. I was startled. Was he an actor dressed for a play? Then and there he confided that he knew about my poor husband, my widow's plight, and me. He took my hand in his and soothed me. He swore me to secrecy as a member of the new resistance. He promised to help me and I believed him. He asked if I could keep a secret and I assured him that I could. The police would have to beat it out of me, I said, and he laughed. I offered to share a glass of my finest vodka. He declined, saying he couldn't drink much because drinking clouded the mind and he had much important work to finish, many meetings, and speeches to write and give. Still, I thought maybe he hid a bottle somewhere because he frequently stumbled and sometimes stuttered. Once he tripped down the stairs, and I saw his papers go flying across the floor. He got down on hands and knees to pick them up, cursing. I sensed he must quietly enjoy a little schnapps when alone."

Vlad's eyes grew wide. "Your guest was drunk?"

"I wouldn't call it drunk, only a bit tipsy like after you've enjoyed a schnapps or two at the end of a long day, and it warms you, and makes your belly feel good inside."

"I see," said Vlad, recalling the rabbi's impressions.

In his ear he overheard Boris saying to Dimsky, "It's the rum alcohol coursing through his veins that keeps him this way. It doesn't dilute. Make a note for Asher."

Dimsky replied, "Why do you suppose Sunavich used rum instead of vodka?"

Vlad paid no attention to that conversation. He looked directly at Olga and asked her to continue.

She fixed her gaze at the half-empty box, undecided whether to take more. As if unable to contain herself, her fingers grabbed one and shoved it into her mouth. After she chewed and swallowed, she said, "During all that time, Lenin and I had never even shared as much as a single drink. One night I was standing in the staircase shadows near my own rooms when I noticed him leaving. He noticed me, too, and smiled. I invited him to come inside. 'May I brew you a nice cup of tea?' I asked. He said that would be good. I keep a hot plate in my personal rooms and I brewed a steaming dark Chinese blend. The poor man's brows were furrowed, and I realized there were heavy matters weighing upon it, and I told him so.

"He looked up with surprise. 'There is, in fact, a great deal upon my mind, and how observant you are to take notice.' I explained how owning my inn over the years brought me into contact with many different types of people, and that a woman learns her guest's wants without asking. He needed someone to talk to, a friend, I said. I believed he was lonely, poor thing. He answered that I was a very wise woman." Olga smiled with pride, blushing slightly, remembering and cherishing the nice compliment.

"You liked this fellow Vladimir very much, didn't you? I mean in a romantic way."

She shied, aware her feelings were revealed. "He's a well-bred, attractive man and I'm a poor widow, aren't I? My dear husband ascended to heaven more than three years ago. I loved him very much, but a woman grows lonely, and winters are so long and cold. In the dead of night the morning seems far away, doesn't it?"

"I know what you mean."

"Do you, *Pan* Petrovsky? Are your nights long also? I realize it's none of my business. But on the night I was speaking of, Lenin took me into his confidence. Me, a peasant woman, a nobody, unworthy, yet he trusted me." She glowed at the memory. "I had already pledged secrecy, and now I'd pledge full loyalty. He said that great things were coming, that he had friends taking up the cause to carry the word across Russia and beyond. And he asked if I were willing to become a simple soldier in his grand army, a partner in his worthy cause. I would be proclaimed a hero of the struggle. Right then and there I gave my word. I would stand beside him always. He gave no details, but said his agents were biding time for the uprising to begin."

She presented such a harmless, gullible poise, Vlad thought, as though she was uninitiated in the seamier sides of life. Lenin had struck a chord profoundly into her essence. Gone was the hard, bitter edge she maintained; in its place he caught a glimpse of the young starry-eyed girl Olga once had been, fleeing from home to be with the boy she loved. "So you believed the things he told you?"

"Of course! We're discussing Vladimir Ilyich Lenin, the greatest hero in history. I told you I gave my solemn oath. I would serve without hesitation, a soldier in his army. My life was his to command. He smiled at me that day, and said my words pleased him very much." A shadow crossed her face.

224

Vlad fidgeted. Some thought flashed through her mind, troubling her. "What happened next?"

"That night he thanked me. We drank tea with lemon and sugar. I offered him jam. We talked and laughed. It grew late. I would have permitted him to share my bed, but such an important man; a great thinker, his thoughts were elsewhere, far away. It wasn't my companionship he sought. The best I could offer was my support. I trusted him and I knew he trusted me."

"Something must have broken that trust, Olga. What made you decide to tell me all this? You didn't have to divulge this. You could have kept your pledge and your secrets. Why did you change your mind?"

She ate two pieces of chocolate, one after the other, chewing quickly, without savoring them, he noticed. A long moment of silence passed before she resumed, speaking with wandering, listless eyes. "It was because of that shameless woman." Pain marred her face, etched with great anger and buried hurt. "It was because of that heartless, soulless bitch who stole him away. That false deceiver without decency or conscience."

Vlad sat stiffly, raptly paying attention. He'd touched the sore wound, he realized, striking raw, intense emotion. He also knew that to win Olga's confidence she needed to be treated with gentle compassion. He reached over, lightly placing a sympathetic hand to her shoulder. "In today's world it's hard to find sympathy. Life is cruel. But you can confide in me, Olga. I'll cherish your trust, not spurn it. Please accept my word on it."

She sniffed, distracted, large tears spilling from sad eyes. She glanced around, searching for tissues. Vlad handed a box. Olga's shoulders slumped with dejection. "Every morning, after my prayers, I made a point to listen for the latest news about blessed Mother Russia. I was thrilled, so impatient for his return. There were so many protests and marches; the workers had been awakened, as if Russia's people had finally stirred from deep slumber. It was wonderful to hear. My commander, my *friend*, spoke the truth. My heart pounded with joy. I couldn't wait for his return, until he walked triumphantly through the doors of *Peter the Great's Palace*. Oh, I yearned to look upon his kind and gentle face. I would throw my arms around him, hug and kiss him, squeeze him with my happiness.

"I could hardly sleep. You understand, don't you? I paced inside my room, nervous with the prospect, but fearful the authorities might hunt him down. I would die if they caught him! I'd throw myself into the river. I knew he would always be safe while he remained with me. But when would he finally return? I smoked cigarettes all day. They cost me a pretty penny, too. I paid no attention when guests complained about lack of heat, or odors in their rooms. I told them the furnace was broken and I didn't have money to fix it. I told them to go to hell, to find somewhere else to stay if they didn't like the smell. I didn't care about their worthless lives. *He* was all that mattered, you see. Lenin, *my* Lenin!

"Days passed, then a week. I waited some more. I was frightened. But at last the fateful moment arrived. The front door swung open. At last he had come back! His tea was prepared and waiting. Sugar and honey, too…but then I saw that he wasn't alone—he was with *her*! A single glance told me what kind of a woman she was. She clung to his arm while they laughed and giggled. I stood there, watching him fondle her breasts, and seeing her kiss him and whisper into his ear. She bubbled and blathered like a child. And, to my shock, Lenin wrapped his strong arms tightly around her, and carried her up the stairs to his room! *My* stairs in *my* hotel! He slobbered all over that tramp, *Pan* Petrovsky. How dare he sleep with her in my home? Lay with her inside the very chamber I'd rented to poor, sweet Andrei Popov! How ashamed Popov would be if he could bear witness.

"Everything changed. I attempted to speak alone with him but I was ignored, unheeded when I called his name. This happened in my own home! Why was I being punished this way? What had I done wrong? That night I could not eat my supper. I threw the samovar to the ground. Tea with sugar, indeed! I crept up the stairs and huddled in darkness, listening from the next room. The worn mattress squeaked and squeaked. The headboard pounded against the wall. Boom, boom! Boom, boom! They bounced like jackrabbits, writhing and thumping. It was disgraceful. I tell you it was a scandal, and degrading to my establishment!" Olga paused, blew her nose, and took another chocolate. Only a few remained. Perhaps he should have brought two boxes, Vlad thought.

"I heard the tart cry out, 'Oh, my love!' and 'Oh, my sweet!' I could imagine her arms wrapped around him, taking him to her, using him." Olga sneered. 'Oh my love,' indeed! Yammering and jabbering, she was manipulating him, couldn't he see? Was he so blinded by this…low streetwalking trickster? What a buffoon he proved to be, to be fooled so easily. What had happened to our magnificent leader, to our glorious revolution? She was ruining him. Brazenly spending him and draining him! It was so obvious. He moaned and fell asleep. I heard him snore. I'm very well acquainted with loose women like that, and I know what they're after, money and power. This fast-talking strumpet wasn't interested in Lenin's cause or revolution. She wasn't a devoted socialist, you could tell.

"I cried bitterly, Vladimir Ilyich what have you done? Where is the noble man of dignity? Our refined gentleman, commander of the revolution? Where is he? In bed with a woman! A whore who cares nothing for our cause, the people's cause. He'd betrayed it. He'd forsaken those who'd given him their trust and money, risked their lives and offered honest love. Our Motherland would continue being looted by those he swore to crush." Olga broke down and sobbed loudly. Her anguish and grief flooded to the surface in a torrent. "Oh Lenin!" she wept.

Vlad sought to comfort her, but then thought better of it. He sat patiently, troubled by hapless Olga's woeful tale. Ilya Evgeny had indeed won Lenin's heart. From Olga's description it was clear Lenin wanted and lusted after this woman. So he had an Achilles Heel after all, Vlad thought. If Ilya did control him, he'd stumble one day, making a fatal mistake. The wily rabbi was correct, and Vlad now realized the brilliance of his hypothesis. Lenin would spend himself, sucked dry, diminished in essence and abilities. And from this lethal combination would come his downfall.

"Please excuse my tears, sir," Olga sniffed, wiping wet cheeks, embarrassed and sorry for her rash outburst. She blew her nose again and held the tissues tightly. "I knew then nothing could come but grief—at least as long as this evil woman was allowed to ruin him. Early the next morning they left together, arm in arm, laughing like children, two fools, Lenin the greater."

"They were lovers," whispered Vlad.

No more tears fell from her eyes; they glowered with scorn and resentment, her pupils' fiery coals. "I would have my compensation, I decided. Yes. I vowed right then and there I would kill this woman! Rob her of life, just as she'd robbed the Revolution. It was the only way, you see. Never in my years had I committed or even imagined such an act, but never in my years had there been so much reason for it. Lenin had given hope again. With him, we'd regain our rightful places; our lives would have meaning. But not while this bloodsucker sucked breath into her perfect body. Without Comrade Lenin to lead us there'd be no uprising, no tossing out the thieving scum controlling our lives. There'd be only emptiness, and the dream of so many millions would extinguish like a candle's flame. But if someone had to pay the price so the dream might live, it would be Ilya Evgeny. I knew what to do, all right. I plotted my revenge. I sharpened a small kitchen knife and kept it constantly in my apron, at the ready. By the name of our Holy Mother Church I'd obey my vow to all Russia's people. I'd pounce with teeth like a lioness, and with Ilya's drenched blood pooled at my feet Lenin would be restored back to his senses, shaken awake from slumber. He'd realize why I committed this act, proving myself, and my worth for the cause. *Our* cause." She hung her head, slouched, swallowed several times, and finally found strength to reach for another piece of chocolate. Only one remained.

"But I never had my chance," she continued with crestfallen, tragic pathos. "Mere days later, in the dead of night, punk-infested secret police stormed *Peter the Great's Palace.* They ran up the stairs and broke into the rooms like cockroaches. Poor working girls screamed, running naked into the corridors. I jumped to my feet in my bedclothes, without even a chance to dress in my robe before horrible men in leather jackets grabbed me, placed my hands behind my back and handcuffed me. They even refused to let me finish my supper. 'Olga Orlovskya, under the State Terrorism Act you are placed under arrest! Come with us immediately. If you resist you will be shot!'" Her head bobbed up and down.

"I had no choice. I gave up. I'd failed. In my heart of hearts, I knew Lenin didn't really love such a woman as this filth, Ilya Evgeny. I understood that in his way he'd used her, too. I'm not old and stupid. Women know exactly how men think. And I knew my sharp little knife could have changed the world."

Here her story came to a conclusion. She held the last piece of chocolate in her palm and squeezed. When she opened her hand her palm and fingers were smeared with melted chocolate and marshmallow mixed to fudge. She made no attempt to lick it. She took the used tissues and wiped her hand. Instead of being cleaned, the soiled tissues smeared her even more.

"Now I hope you understand, *Pan* Petrovsky. The greatest man in Russian history had become my friend, my ally and confidant. Of all those he might have chosen for his confidence, he'd picked me. I gave him my allegiance and would have died for the cause, gladly, died for him. But how did he repay me? He threw everything away for a painted Russian whore." She closed her eyes and said no more, unmoving, as if buried with her own cocoon.

"You have my full sympathy, Madam Olga. I believe every word, and I know at heart you're a good woman. It's not within my power to release you or promise you freedom. Nevertheless, what I do promise is that when you come to trial I'll be a witness on your behalf. I'll do everything I can to set you free to return to your beloved *Peter the Great's Palace,* where you may resume your good life and care for your many guests."

Vlad lifted himself up. He glanced down at the lonely, crestfallen woman curled in her seat, seeming so frail. He wished he had another box of chocolates to give. Quietly he left the room. Olga Orlovskya remained motionless.

14.

Boris shut his phone, panting, "They've trapped the criminal, Andrei Popov, near the church at Dubrovitsy, the great estate outside Moscow near Podolsk. Let's go, Petrovsky. You won't want to miss finally meeting with our elusive harpsichordist, better known as Mikhail Sunavich."

A clever if surprising site to hide in, Vlad knew. Lenin himself reportedly lived in Podolsk for a short while during his younger years. Today, a museum in his honor stood there. Perhaps there were still sympathizers. Vlad felt his heart race as he put on his seat belt. Boris gunned the engine of his blue Lada Samara. Moscow was a city of perpetual traffic jams, hazy road rules, and questionable lanes, but Boris wasn't deterred. "We're not going far," he said, as they detoured around traffic on the main highway from Moscow south to the Crimea. "Popov has just finished giving a harpsichord recital. Hardly anyone was in attendance so there was no need for crowd control. Our people were waiting until he walked offstage. Then they jumped him and knocked him to the floor. He was surprised, all right. And best of all, this Andrei Popov, harpsichord player, had a woman with him. An accomplice. I'm praying we've caught Ilya Evgeny, too. They're in the custody of a top security agent who's waiting for us."

"Did anyone even know Sunavich played the harpsichord?" wondered Vlad. It was a rhetorical question.

The drive to Dubrovitsy took longer than it should. Another anti-government, spontaneous demonstration was in progress nearby, bystanders lining the streets, many cheering the demonstrators on and booing nearby police. Two gray-haired women were dancing topless in an open window. Neither man talked as Boris made his way through the commotion.

Soon they arrived. The quaint area was famous for its estate and church. There were graceful, numerous statues everywhere. The church's ancient architecture of carved stone was spellbinding with its remarkable white tower, surmounted by a great gold tiara and cross, a landmark over the serene Pakhra River. In place of the usual cupola of most Russian churches it had a tall crown of gold. Empress Catherine the Great had purchased the estate as a present for a court favorite, but the unlucky owner wound up spending half his life under house arrest. It was in this setting that Popov and his cohort glumly sat hand-cuffed.

A huge man in his late forties with strikingly Eastern Siberian features greeted Boris as he got out of the car. They shook hands firmly and kissed one another on both cheeks. Vlad realized they were close friends and colleagues at Internal Security.

"Petrovsky, permit me to introduce you to one of our best men in Mother Russia. Agent Drinkwater, please meet Director Vladimir Petrovsky, Public Relations man extraordinaire, in charge of the Kremlin's 25th Anniversary Jubilee."

"A pleasure, Director Petrovsky." A massive hand gripped his. The smile was full, the eyes joyful and sparkling.

"Good meeting you, Inspector Drinkwater. I've heard Boris speak of you. An unusual name. Are you Inuit?"

The Internal Security man expressed friendliness. "Partly. My father originally came to Russia from Alaska. He ran away from home as a youth, traveling to Siberia for adventure, and to work in the oil fields, thinking he'd find riches. Instead he met my mother in Ostrov Ratmanova, where she was finishing school. She was an indigenous Chcuchi woman. They fell in love the day they met—or so everyone says. My father remained in Ratmanova, and soon they married. I'm the eldest of eleven, so that must tell you something." The Inspector laughed, and continued.

"Pop found himself a career policeman instead of an oilman, and only recently retired from his job. My mother's brother also worked for Internal Security, placed in a fraud unit, which is how I first met Boris Sokolov, when he headed a national squad policing mineral mining extortion. So I guess police work runs in my blood."

"It must, Inspector," Vlad said cordially.

"You can call me, Big Duck."

"All right. May I ask how you acquired your name?"

"Everyone asks!" he bellowed in humor. "While my mother was pregnant she unexpectedly went into labor away from home near the lake. She fell in pain, unable to get home. The loud quacking of nearby ducks alerted fishing villagers that my mother was about to deliver her first child. They ran to help. Mama gave birth to me right then and there, and so I was born on the edge of a pond. I was a very large baby among the nearby ducks, so the fishermen suggested naming me, *Bolshoi Utka,* Big Duck. What do you think of that! All my life my friends call me, 'Big Duck'." His smile deepened.

Boris, a head shorter than the affable policeman, clapped him on the back. "All right then, Big Duck. Show us your prisoners."

Bolshoi Utka led the way. His voice echoed as they went inside the building. "This man, Popov, denies everything. But intelligence reports indicated he would be deceptive and elusive. A sly bird. As for the woman, she calls herself, 'Princess Valeria'. She says she's a circus acrobat down on her luck. Too old for that, I'd say. But see for yourselves. They're being held in the next room on the left." He gestured.

Boris entered first, then Vlad, lastly the wily Internal Security Inspector.

A skinny, soft-complexioned man sat forlornly on the bench. His eyes were expressive and bloodshot. Dried tearstains formed lines down a long, thin, despondent face. Boris exchanged a quick glance with Vlad. Big Duck Drinkwater stood quietly, hands behind his back, his persona very different than when Vlad was introduced minutes before. "This man's identity papers appear in order. Nor did he try to avoid any of my questions." He spoke in a resonant, authoritarian voice. "We're checking for authentication." Big Duck shot an ominous look the prisoner's way, and the man in custody on the bench trembled.

On the stage behind, several of Big Duck's security men were carefully disassembling a harpsichord. "They're checking for hidden explosives," the broad-shouldered Inspector explained. "Terrorists will go to any lengths…"

"I keep telling you, I'm no terrorist! That's my musical instrument. My livelihood. Be careful! It's an expensive antique, the only thing I own of any value."

"Shut up!" one of the policemen said gruffly. He sneered, and pretended to kick the harpsichord with his boot. Mortified, the prisoner looked on. "Keep blabbering and we'll chop the damn thing up for winter firewood."

Boris walked closer to the suspect. "You say you're Andrei Popov, the harpsichord player?"

"Yes, yes. I am. You have my ID card. All my papers are in order. Why have you arrested me? Why am I in handcuffs? I'm no criminal. I promised my landlady I would get her the remaining rent money she says I owe. I only asked for a few more days. I try hard to make a living, but in these times people don't have respect for beautiful music. They listen on the Internet for free. Rap,

Hip-Hop, Screaming Punk that hurts your ears. Kids download all they want illegally, and then sell cheap CDs on the streets. It isn't my fault. The economy is so bad I lost my janitor's job, too. But I gave the old landlady my word she'd get her rent money in full. I swear under oath. I always keep my word. Never once did I cheat her." He choked up with emotion. "She didn't have to call the police on me."

"Is your landlady called Olga Orlovskya?" demanded Big Duck in his deepest, coercing voice. His powerful tone alone often elicited confessions out of criminals.

The prisoner leaned forward, veins bulging from his throat. "I told you, Inspector! I never heard of anyone named Olga Orlovskya! Or anyone called Sunavich, for that matter! Who are these people? Why don't you believe me? Please, don't take me to prison. I haven't done anything wrong. I had permission for my concert today. A recital on the Art of the Fugue. You saw my permit. This is a travesty of justice!"

Big Duck snickered with mockery. "And I suppose you've never heard the tune, *Bring on the Revolution?*"

"*Bring a…Revolution?* Are you crazy? No, *never!* I have no idea what you're talking about."

"And we are supposed to believe you?"

"He's telling the truth, you bullies! Let him go."

Boris and Vlad turned to see a rawboned, underweight woman with bleached blond hair sitting with her back straight against the opposite wall. She also was handcuffed. Vlad felt his heart sink. The scrawny, gangling lady wearing black nylon stockings did not fit the description of muscular, seductive Ilya Evgeny in the least.

Big Duck said evenly, "She's his accomplice. A keen one, all right. They make a good pair. Her papers are being authenticated, too. If we find out she's lied…" His implied threat went unfinished. Andrei Popov hung his chin on his chest, shackled and friendless.

"You say your name is…?" Boris asked the woman.

"Princess Valeria," she replied proudly, tossing back her head of thinning hair. "And my companion is *the* Andrei Popov, the virtuoso concertmaster. A composer, as well as musician. He's spent a whole life bringing fine music to the masses, not that they deserve him. You men aren't good enough to lick dirty snow off his boots in winter. I assist whenever he holds a concert. He's a fine man, an outstanding human being. We agreed to band together to try and earn a little extra money whenever we could…"

"Never mind him for now. Who are *you*?"

Her eyes grew spirited and disdainful. "Who am *I*? Ha! I am an *artiste*, for your information. An aerial dancer, a star performer, formerly with the Moscow Bolshoi Circus, ever since childhood. My parents were circus people, too. I was once a debutante, performing for kings and presidents at courts across Europe. I dined in fashionable restaurants with intriguing people of good position who say little but eat like gluttons. If you want to know, I've travelled throughout Mother Russia for as long as I can remember. I've played the top theatres for thousands of people in every city. Spectators gasped at my prowess. Haven't you heard of the breathtaking Valeria, Princess of the High Wire, sir? Take off your hats. My name was legendary, acclaimed on posters from the Baltic to the Pacific." She snorted. "Now look at me; do you see how cruel life can be? Asphyxiating. But I refuse to bow low to anyone. To make my pittance I sell cigarettes and American bubble gum in a kiosk from dawn till evening. Only for a genius of Andrei's caliber do I pass the hat to sweaty, hairy-chested souls on city stink corners. What do you think of that?" She remained audacious and truculent in her squalor and shackles.

Boris squinted, looking her over with insatiable curiosity. Her appearance was a shambles, a raw-spoken wreck, but her speech, vocabulary, and comportment evinced a totally different pedigree, in fact the antitype of coarse, brutish Russian peasantry. Something deep within lost cognizance stirred. He recalled a faint, all-but forgotten memory. Yes, it had been at a circus, a very long time before, a free, charitable performance conferred by the Socialist Workers' Party for Labor and Collective Families. Everyone within the great tent sat on folding chairs, packed in like sardines, hot and sweaty, eagerly awaiting the main act while a handful of juggling clowns and wrestling midgets performed burlesque antics inside the single ring. High above hung the trapeze. A snare drum announced the arrival of the star performer, more famous than even the Flying Manzini Brothers who had earlier impressed the enthusiastic crowd. Everyone quieted. The Princess took off her golden robe with a flourish, and handed it to an assistant. Athletic and attractive, she wore a risqué bathing costume, and slowly climbed up to the top. She was as voluptuously beautiful as she was daring, he recalled. No wonder so many young men reputedly fell madly in love.

Then she took hold of the pedestal bar, building up her swing from a still position, using the momentum to execute her tricks, at times seemingly hovering mid-air. With dynamic movements requiring fastidious timing, the swinging trapeze rocked from one end of the tent to the other, while the lovely trapeze artist swung back and forth in sprightly rhythm, gracefully twirling, balancing on one foot then the other, finally letting go of the ropes as she bowed before the gasping pleasured amazement of the adoring crowd. She was fearless and phenomenal, dazzling as a fairy princess, as alluring as any American film star. When she was finished with her daring act the entire assembly jumped to their feet, clapping, hollering, and whistling for the lovely lady. She bowed again and again to the roar of applauds, throwing kisses, laughing and tossing her head back, precisely the way the woman in front of him just did. The crowd was pleading for more, and she did a single encore, a death-defying balancing twirl without a safety net. The circus crowd and even fellow performers went wild in delirium, intoxicated by her courage and dexterity. He had never quite forgotten. Perhaps he too had been a bit intoxicated, infatuated with the beauty and pageant of this daredevil. Her name was Princess Valeria.

"She's telling you the truth," cried Andrei Popov, the harpsichord player. "Please don't harm her. She's too old to work now, and her eyesight is weak, although admitting it to you would shatter her pride. I hire her to help me out. Whether playing concerts or street recitals, Princess Valeria holds out the hat for donations. She's polite and thanks anyone who spares a kopek or two in appreciation. We make a good team, her and me. Please, don't make her pay for my misfortune; she's done nothing wrong. She doesn't steal or beg, and she doesn't owe my landlady any money. Arrest me, if you must, but please set her free."

"No one need feel pity for me," Princess Valeria snapped, skittish yet full on with disrespectful effrontery. "I remained a good, loyal Party member. Always! I did whatever was asked—gladly, a true patriot, but still I'm waiting to receive the pensioner's checks I was promised. Where is the money owed to me? Who's stolen it?" She stared at Big Duck without a trace of fear. "You're a policeman. Go and do your job! Arrest the government thieves who've taken my money!"

Boris looked at the Inspector, and back to the woman.

"The State gave their word she'd receive a regular monthly pension," explained Andrei Popov. "She barely has money to buy food. No one cares anymore that once she ruled the high wire, that she was the envy and emulation of every young schoolgirl, and the secret love of every schoolboy. They forgot the excitement of the band playing, the drum banging with anticipation, the thumping hearts as she flew gloriously like a golden bird across the sky." He lowered his gaze. "Now she's feeble and becoming a bit senile, I fear. I check in on her, bring hot tea to her room. Yes, she's gloomy and sarcastic, but it's been hard for her in recent years. Everyone turns a cold shoulder. She has no family left. She's all by herself. I try to give her a bit of my own money whenever I've earned something, but these days it's not easy. People have become tone deaf. No one loves good music anymore, nobody cares..."

Vlad touched Boris lightly on the elbow. It was plain this venturesome man was not Dr. Sunavich, and the trapeze artiste with the shredded legacy certainly wasn't the woman plotting a prelude to Lenin's return, Ilya Evgeny.

The pleading in Vlad's eyes touched Boris. "Uncuff them," he gruffly told a waiting policeman at Big Duck Drinkwater's side. "These are not our suspects."

Andrei Papov's wet eyes glanced thankfully at Boris.

Big Duck snapped his fingers at his underling. "You heard him. Release them both—now." Inspector Drinkwater saluted smartly. "We'll speak soon regarding that other matter," he said. The Inspector nodded.

No one noticed Boris slip a folded hundred new ruble note to the thankful harpsichordist as they left.

The Communist Manifesto, by Karl Marx and Frederick Engels, read the title. Floyd Dingus relaxed in his bubble bath, sank low and held the book before his face. He glanced at the cover photos of both Karl Marx and Frederick Engels and eagerly began to read the first section titled, *Bourgeois and Proletarians*. It began, "*The history of all hitherto existing society is the history of class struggles...*" Floyd yawned. It was going to be a long night. Outside the tub his mobile rested within reach. It rang before he finished the first paragraph of the first page.

Floyd leaned over and picked up the phone. "Hello."

"Good evening, Floyd. This is Boris Sokolov. I hope I'm not inconveniencing you at a bad hour."

"Hey Sport, how the heck are you? Listen, hold on a sec. I've got soap in my eyes." He stretched his boyish neck, reached for a washcloth, wiped his face and tossed the cloth aside. He glanced at his bottle of bubble bath, squinting and tearing as he read the label, 'No tears, no burning,' and wondering why his eyes were burning and tearing anyway. He picked up the phone again. "Okay, I'm back. Hey, it's been a while. Not that I'm complaining, but I've been getting strong vibes that you and your friends are avoiding me."

"Avoiding you? Not at all. You know what working for the government is like. They demand thirty-hour days and eight day weeks."

Floyd chuckled. "I hear that loud and clear, Sport. Sounds just like home. Especially with all these so-called 'disturbances' going on. What's up? Is this call business or pleasure?" Floyd tossed his book toward the bathroom door, holding the phone to his ear with one hand, rubbing soap bubbles over his stomach with the other.

"A bit of both. I wonder if you could answer a few questions for me."

"I'll do my best. Shoot."

"Thank you. Your ambassador tells me that in America you belonged to a chess club. From what I understand, you're a pretty good player yourself. You've even entered a few professional competitions."

Floyd scrubbed his chest. "That's really nice of the ambassador to say. Back in the day I did enter a couple of minor competitions. My dad taught me to play when I was a kid, back in Waterloo, Iowa. My old man was a darn good player himself. You know how that goes, Boris. Don't tell me you're challenging me to a match?"

"That's not what I had in mind. It's rather complicated. There's a particular chess master we understand you've met on several occasions."

Floyd listened. "Well, I've come across a few of those boys over the years. Americans, Canadians, well known competitors in the chess world. I've also met a fair number of Russian players. Several live in the US, but most are still right here in Russia. I hope to enter a tournament again someday. I've gotta hand it to you, these Russians sure are tough competitors. The cream of the crop."

"Our government will be glad to know you hold our virtuosos in such high regard. Among these Russians you're familiar with, there's one in particular I'd like to ask about. His name is Gregori Nabokov, three-time Russian champion, a winner in a number of international tournaments, including America, of course."

Floyd burst out laughing. His soap slid to the bottom of the tub as he raised himself up. "Nabokov? Sure, I know that name. Who doesn't know Gregori? He's a pretty flamboyant guy, and a real lady-killer. But during a match he's fiercely competitive. Make the slightest noise while he's playing and you'll get a cold stare that'll kill you on the spot."

"When was the last time you spoke with him?"

Floyd puffed his cheeks and scratched his sandy hair. "He was entered in a pretty serious competition in New York a year or two ago. I saw him afterwards. We had a few drinks and laughs, chatted about the old days. I'm no kid, but Gregori goes back way before my time. I can't think of anything we share in common except maybe a love for hot chocolate. I take mine with lots of whipped cream and sugar; he doesn't."

Boris hesitated. "I don't know how to say this, Floyd; I'm certain it seems odd, but I need to ask you to give me and my team a little assistance. Please don't misunderstand, we don't wish to interfere with your own work."

"You're asking *me* to lend you a hand?" He sat up straight, reached for a towel and climbed out of the small tub. Water splashed and dripped, forming a pool at his feet. He leisurely dried himself.

"I hope my request hasn't upset you, Floyd."

"Heck no, Boris. Au contraire. The prospect has me pretty jacked up. I'd be more than pleased to provide whatever assistance I can. I mean it. Don't get me wrong, but since I've been getting the runaround I really haven't had all that much to do. My ambassador's been hollering a lot lately, but damn, it isn't my fault your boys keep obstructing me from doing my job. Don't be insulted. Nothing personal, but that's the way it is."

Boris looked at his phone with a hint of confusion. "No, I don't take it personally. Thank you for your willingness; it's most generous. Tomorrow morning come by my office. You recall where it's located?"

"I sure do. Last week a very pretty Russian escort gave me a grand tour of the Kremlin. She slipped me her phone number afterwards." He grinned. "The Kremlin's a stunning place, magnificent, filled with so much history about Grand Dukes and Czarist palaces. Say, even your boy Lenin lived there. Your agency is part of the government office complex, right? I never realized you were such a big shot."

Boris took the compliment lightly. "I'm hardly what you'd call a big shot, Floyd. What time suits you? Shall we say around ten?"

"Tell you what, Boris, you provide a samovar of that finely ground Turkish coffee and I'll make it my business to show up early."

"A deal. I'll have a driver waiting at your hotel."

"Sure, that'd be swell."

"Your Turkish coffee is ready. Prepared exclusively for you with pistachio grains."

Floyd entered the office with a spirited gait. Boris and his team were waiting. The first one to greet him was Asher. "It's good to see you, Mr. Dingus. I've heard many nice things about you. Let me add that I dearly love both America and the American people."

"Why, *Spasibo*, thank you, Rabbi. It's certainly nice to meet up with you, too. You're a quite talked-about man in these parts."

The American sat down and cordially reached for the demitasse Alina Vera provided. It was steaming hot and he held the saucer carefully.

Vlad sat next to Colonel Dimsky on the divan along the far wall. Boris remaining on his feet. Despite smiles and greetings the mood in the room was tense and businesslike.

"The samovar is full," Alina Vera told him. "Hand me your cup whenever you're ready. I'll be happy to provide, what do you Americans call it, refills?"

"Refills, right. If I'm late I apologize. It's a zoo outside. Unshaved, witless protestors at the Occupy Gorky Park camp are being evicted, and traffic is snarled. Police lines had the streets blocked because of a rush-hour flash mob, and it looks like some dissidents calling themselves Occupy Squads are chaining themselves around trees and benches. There was a lot of shouting, cops, hoots and hollering, everyone mad at everyone. I heard chain saws, too. Meanwhile, some smaller group was parading outside our embassy, waving condoms blown up like balloons. The bigger group carried signs proclaiming the refrain, 'Lesbians for Lenin'."

Chewing an unlit cigar, Boris did a slow burn, a bad taste in his mouth. Vlad sat mute, eyeglasses in hand, peering at the lenses. Colonel Dimsky was stiffly uncomfortable, his beloved balalaika close by.

"You do know some of Lenin's appearances have gone viral?" added Floyd. "They're all over the Internet. Google it. Lenin at the river, Lenin at a factory, Lenin calling on mothers to boycott the upcoming Jubilee...Rock bands are doing covers of this 'Revolution' song online. It's been dubbed with voiceovers in dozens of languages. Some of it is real funny stuff. *Bring on the Revolution* in Chinese sounds damn clever. It's spreading like an epidemic. There's this hysterical one called 'Bozo Lenin.' In fact—"

"*We know all about it!*" snapped Boris.

Since gaining notoriety, Internet videos were spawning increasingly numerous rallies across the country. The most brazen demonstrations were trying to appropriate public spaces and plazas in the name of liberty. Speakers poured out their souls at Moscow's *Triumfalnaya* Square, aggressive activists emboldened by progressively sympathetic news reports reaching the West. In this unstable environment anything could happen.

"Better change the subject," Vlad advised tactfully.

"OK." Floyd sipped his coffee. "This is real good. Thick, piping hot. I haven't tasted such a robust brew since I was sent to Istanbul, and don't ask how long ago that was." He winked at Alina Vera. "Say, you haven't drugged my coffee, have you, Dr. Galina?" No one was amused at his lame attempt at humor. He shrugged it off.

Alina Vera handed him a small plate of exquisitely wrapped chocolates. "This is special confection straight from the Alexander Nevsky. I made it my business to order samples especially for you."

He accepted one and ate it slowly. His face alighted with gustatory pleasure. "That's one helluva delectable piece of chocolate." He closed his eyes and chewed expressively. "Oh my." When he was done, he said, "Listen, despite everything else, it's nice to see you all again. And before it slips my mind, let me compliment your driver, Boris. He was prompt, polite, opened the door when I got in and opened the door when I got out. He only cursed when we got slowed to a crawl because of the demonstration, and I couldn't blame him for that. I don't know his pay grade, but I'd like to put in a good word, suggest you give him a raise."

"I'll make a note," said Dimsky.

"I see. My driver's one of your security men, huh?"

"We all work together," said Vlad. "We're a team."

Floyd finished his second cup and with a wave of his hand rejected an offer of a third. Alina Vera seated herself beside Vlad, crossing her legs, and pulling her tailored skirt below her knees.

"So here I am, Boris, just as you asked. What can I do for you?"

The streetwise counterspy scanned the room with narrowed eyes, abruptly turning to Dimsky. "You've had this office swept for detectors again?"

"It's clean. You can speak freely."

Boris nodded, voice firm, unhesitating. "Floyd, I want us to talk openly, man to man." He rested against the edge of his desk, looking evenly at his visitor. It was an overcast gray Moscow morning, chilly breezes blowing. Noise from the vast city outside was dampened. It was a pivotal moment in their relationship with the perplexing American. "Sometimes in life we all have to take risks, bite the bullet and put our trust in someone. In our business, that's not easy, is it?"

"Not easy at all, Boris."

"I'm glad we agree. So please understand I need to ask an important question, and I need to know you won't take it in the wrong spirit."

"Can't say how I'll take it until I know the question."

Usually the epitome of caution in delicate matters but steeled for a combative reply, Boris asked plainly, "Floyd, are you a spy? Do you work for the CIA?" There was no trace of hostility. He spoke frankly, expecting an equally frank reply.

Rattled and stung, Floyd said, "I serve my country the same way you serve yours. I consider myself a patriot. As to your question, let me shatter any illusions. No, I'm not a spy."

"Not for America—or anyone else?"

"You have my word."

Vlad observed carefully, scrutinizing the American's body language for indications of guile or deception amid these interwoven crosscurrents. Satisfied Floyd's reactions were genuine, he said, "I'm willing to take the chance."

"I concur," Alina Vera cautiously agreed. "I don't see any reason for suspicion."

"Not exactly true," corrected Dimsky.

"Oh?"

"The colonel's statement is legitimate, Floyd," said Boris. "When you've been burned by soup, you blow on your yogurt. This isn't a good day for diplomatic niceties so please permit me to be blunt. We've obtained a number of foreign passports said to be sequestered in your hotel room, all bearing your photograph."

Floyd Dingus stirred uneasily. "Are you kidding me, or what?" For the first time the affable American appeared genuinely flustered and angry. "You take me for a total doofus? Go on. Question me. Knock yourself out."

"Unfortunately, this information is confirmed. I personally saw the evidence. There were five foreign passports. A serious criminal offense under our Emergency Terrorism Act, as it is illegal in every country. What do you say? You're a diplomatic guest in Russia. Why would an official from the U.S. Department of Agriculture wish to assume numerous foreign nationalities?" Their eyes locked in an unbroken cold stare.

"It's a blatant lie—unless someone's got reason for planting forged documents to implicate me. Either way, they're not mine. I have diplomatic immunity; I don't need to fabricate anything."

Boris waited, not yet satisfied. "A very high level official brought them to my attention."

"In America an accused man is advised of the identity of his accuser. And a man is presumed innocent until proven otherwise. We've had a pretty good judicial system for a long time. You want to incriminate me, Boris? My diplomatic immunity's out the window, and I need a lawyer? Is this why you really wanted me here today?" The barrage of questions came fast and incensed.

"Of course not. I didn't mean to sound harsh but I need to be certain. We can't afford ungainly mistakes. Frankly, I believe you. I wouldn't be surprised to learn these were forgeries intentionally planted to cast suspicion. Forgive me for being brusque; these have been thorny weeks. Under the circumstances I hope you'll understand." A despondent expression crossed Boris's features. Being at loggerheads with someone whose favor you hoped to curry was not smart. He fondled his cigar, unable to decide whether to light it or not. He chose to leave it in an ashtray.

Floyd Dingus looked on soberly, undeterred. "Seeing we're being frank, let me provide a little unadulterated honesty of my own. Since I was posted to Moscow you've done anything and everything to prevent me from carrying out my assignment in a timely manner. I feel like a pariah, bounced around like a punchy boxer. That includes you Vlad, Alina Vera, and above all, you, Boris. Shenanigans and stonewalling only makes my superiors and me all the more suspicious. This isn't about divulging nuclear secrets. I was sent on an honest mission and instead I've been rebuffed and impeded every step of the way. Your credibility is nil."

Dimsky grumbled. "Our government is not accustomed to permitting foreign representatives access to our inner apparatus—"

Boris curtly cut him off. "Floyd is correct. He didn't know the nature of our work made access impossible to permit."

Floyd smiled without his typical humor. "Suddenly that's all changed? For some remarkable reason you want my assistance?"

"I'm afraid that's right." He folded his arms. "Better drink another cup of strong coffee. I have a long, complicated story to unwind."

"I'm listening..."

"You know my team, and I'm proud to tell you I trust everyone in this room with my life. I've been acquainted with Vlad since he graduated from university and received his first post at State Television. I've known Alina Vera since she was a child. Her father was a close friend and confidant, and I'm something of a godfather." He turned to Dimsky. "I've had the privilege of working with the colonel over many years, and he and I share total confidence in one another. As for our esteemed rabbi, his credentials are impeccable. Although I haven't known him long, I've come to rely on him completely."

Floyd poured fresh coffee. "Okay. So how do I fit in? I'm a total outsider. You have no reason whatsoever to lay bets on me. To you, every American is a cause for suspicion, a CIA operative, a rogue agent on who-knows-who's payroll. And you want to hear something? I can't say I blame you for the cynicism. Washington's a hotbed of mistrust and neurosis, too. In that respect Moscow's no different."

"Exactly what I've been thinking," Vlad said in accord.

Floyd took off his baseball cap. "Look, I was sent by the USA because of some really ludicrous rumors. As I learn better every day, they're not rumors. From what I've seen and read all hell is breaking loose around here, and I don't understand it. Day by day increasing bedlam; protests, disorder, strikes, and confrontations demanding the rights and aspirations of the Russian people, all supposedly caused by a dead man whose embalmed corpse lies on display less than a mile from here. This 'non-existent' insurrection is followed by a hushed flurry of government crackdowns against a rebellion you say isn't happening. You claim some flimflam pretender is bewitching people and perpetrating a hoax. But video and eyewitnesses prove there's someone a lot like Lenin paving the way, and our own voiceprint studies show the voices to be identical. What gives? If I were Russian maybe I'd get a handle on it. But I'm not, I'm an American."

"Precisely, Mr. Dingus," said Asher. "The very fact you are American makes us believe we might place our trust in you."

"He's right," admitted Vlad. The idiosyncratic American didn't appear anywhere as stumbling or naïve today as he usually did. "Floyd, there are serious events happening within the New Federation only a handful of people in the world are aware of."

"Like your 'secret' Lenin Project?"

"Exactly like our Lenin Project," said Boris, conceding its existence without skipping a beat. "The nation will suffer extensive harm if its sensitive nature is mishandled, and there will be formidable ramifications for the world. Colonel, please spell out a few facts for Mr. Dingus."

Dimsky nodded reluctantly. The military man was candidly hesitant to divulge internal secrets. "We're putting our reliance in your integrity, Floyd. I hope it proves justified." He took a deep breath before speaking. "The prime minister of our country, Sergei Milonov, is notorious for his ambition, flaunting his ascendancy to power, and intimidating any willing to confront him. Some might say he's cold-blooded, that he professes loyalty neither to the State nor the government he serves. In short, a man who'd stop at nothing to satisfy his appetites."

Floyd sat listening, searching all their faces. Apart from the colonel's transparent contempt for Prime Minister Milonov, each was unreadable and impossible to evaluate.

"And so," Dimsky went on, "we recognize that Milonov retains a covert agenda, raising the specter of a troubling split within our Duma's already fractious atmosphere. Based on gathered intelligence, we've concluded he's using political upheaval as an excuse for preparing a mendacious plan to seize governmental control while the rebel forces are making substantive progress..."

Floyd's mouth hung open.

"We foresee a coup d'état, plotted while Russia diligently works to contain Lenin's damage. Milonov reasons that under the current situation, absence of the rule of law gives him opportunity for dictatorial fiat. Initially, he was undeniably outraged and frightened by popular calls for rebellion. However, he soon concluded that as fear gripped the land he could use it to his advantage. So while publically demanding swift action, he secretly was pleased with the increasingly chaotic situation. Behind the scenes he's worked tirelessly and illegally to interfere with preparations for the Anniversary Jubilee. Normally that alone would justify removal from office, and indictments. However, it hasn't been possible while we're struggling to contain this fevered uprising. Our current position is too dire. But we do have other means for deterring his plans—incontrovertible proof leading to prosecution on charges of sedition."

"Holy shit," Floyd murmured. He leaned back, stupefied. He was well familiar with numerous felonious intrigues engulfing the globe, but nothing rivaling this level. "You have proof of this?"

"We do," said Boris. "But at the moment we find ourselves in the unenviable position of urgently needing to deal with this Lenin first, even while gathering evidence on Milonov." He looked again to Dimsky. "Go on, Colonel. You might as well reveal everything. What do our pockmarks and blemishes matter now? If we're caught, one side or the other is going to kill us anyway."

Dimsky placed his balalaika on his lap and plucked a single string. It resounded loudly. "Our prime minister and his wife have a cat. This cat they dearly love, treating it as though it were their child, and a rotten, spoiled child at that. The pet is indulged with many gifts, especially at holiday time. This past Christmas, Boris asked me to give the cat a little present of our own. During an official meeting at the prime minister's residence, I excused myself to use the restroom where I employed a special tincture to anesthetize the creature, a harmless concoction. Next, I carefully made certain the cat's toys were amply filled with long-lasting potent catnip cooked up to keep her feeling happy. While pretending to pet Tinkerbelle, I meticulously injected a small microchip into the cat's neck. This microchip records all Milonov's private conversations to wireless computers set up at a secret location. You may listen to these recordings, if you wish. Graft, embezzlement, and monetary crimes are the least of the offenses. He's concocted a murky meshing of public and private interests rarely seen. We've overheard him discuss the most incredible contrivances, from rounding up and imprisoning political foes, to contemplating kidnapping. He's prepared to use his despised security for an aggressive campaign to snuff out discord any way required—from torture to assassination. Mother Volga!" He plucked a decidedly sour note.

Floyd remained dumbstruck.

Boris continued. "Bit by bit we've eavesdropped and recorded—illegally—exactly what Milonov has premeditated against the State. We've determined his stratagem. His contingent of security agents is composed of well-paid, loyal underlings, totally treacherous characters. The magnitude of revelations shook me so badly that for a long time I found myself mistrusting everyone, including Vlad and Alina Vera.

"Milonov's clique would happily barter their mothers for the right price," interjected Dimsky. "And he's dispersed plenty of cash to purchase allegiance. That leaves only us remaining to block his way, the last fortress of loyalty to the New Federation. However we have our own pressing dilemma; the implanted microchip creates severe problems. As our information was gathered illegally it can't be used as evidence in court, diminishing prospects of a trial. Therefore, it's crucial that the microchip be removed, and it can never be disclosed that his precious cat functioned as our tracking device." He smiled deviously.

"Go on, Sport. You've got my full attention. What's your proposal?"

Boris said, "The nature of your employment takes you across America, supervising cattle, sheep, poultry, and so forth. With your veterinary skills you undertake personal inspections whenever deemed necessary, and your government counts on you to assure livestock are healthy, factories are cleansed of unhealthy bacteria, and other detrimental organisms. Am I correct?"

"Yes. I attended veterinary school straight from college, that's why the Ag Department hired me. If necessary I order questionable foodstuffs removed from the market. I work with all manner of animals, not only cattle. Heck, I even diagnose cats and dogs."

It began to rain, a soft patter lashing against the windows. "Perfect qualifications. Your skills are ideal for our requirements. Perhaps I've no right to ask, but there's no one else to trust. Will you work with us, help us?"

"You're placing your trust in me, and not your own people? Me, the potential spy in your midst?" The toothy smile reappeared. "Yikes. Interesting. That's sure a gamble on your part, isn't it? You know, until now I thought just Democrats and Republicans mistrusted each other."

Mincing no words Vlad said, "Being an American we recognize you harbor no secret allegiances to Milonov or...*anyone* else. You're our best hope, maybe our only hope."

Boris acknowledged with sincerity. "It's true. We need your skills—urgently."

"What skills?"

"You'd be able to make an incision and cleanly remove the cat's hidden microchip without scars or traces, with as little fuss as possible."

"*Surgery?*"

"Don't worry; Colonel Dimsky will provide all the medical instruments you require. You do have the expertise for a fast surgical procedure like this?"

"You mean a fast *illegal* surgery," muttered Floyd. "If they catch me I'll be shipped to some forsaken Siberian prison."

"Without doubt," Dimsky drily agreed. "There'll likely be a big show trial for an American spy. A national televised spectacle broadcast in Super High Def. How much we do love catching spies. In America you'd call it a three-ring circus. Of course you'll probably receive a life sentence. And naturally if they decide to torture you, we don't need Siberia anymore. We've built a quite interesting secret facility quite near to Chernobyl."

Floyd gulped, spilling coffee. "Are you all right?" asked Alina Vera.

"Sure, why wouldn't I be? Just because I feel like I'm being sucked into a bottomless black hole. You don't ask much, do you, Sport?"

"We'll do everything humanly possible to protect you," Boris assured. "We recognize the risks you're undertaking."

He made no reply.

Asher entered the conversation, regarding Floyd with thoughtfully crafted advice. "A famous rabbi once said, 'The whole world is a very narrow bridge, and the most important thing is not to be afraid.' It shall take a very special individual to pull this off, bravery above any call of duty. We haven't made this request lightly. Only your own inner conviction can overcome your doubts, fears, and vacillation. The challenge is to allow the knowledge within of your abilities to shine through. Let that be your guide for your decision."

"Please listen to him," Alina Vera added with sincerity.

Floyd gazed downward, wavering. "You people sure ask a lot of a guy. And I thought my fraternity initiation of running onto the playing field mooning the marching band at a game during halftime was risky." He drew a deep lungful of air, weighing the request one way, then the other, shuddering at the consequences of failure. "I must be as nuts as the rest of you, but my conscience is telling me it's the right thing to do."

"Then listen to your conscience," prodded Asher. "It's man's greatest source of wisdom."

He puffed his cheeks, exhaled. "Okay. Count me in."

A huge sigh of relief resonated across the room. Alina Vera got up and planted a fat, wet kiss on Floyd's pudgy face.

Dimsky showed his earnest gratitude with a powerful handshake. "We'll do everything in our power to clear the way for you. Tonight there's an unofficial meeting at the prime minister's private offices. I'll be attending, and so will Boris and Vlad. You'll be wearing a Russian Army uniform, accompanying me and another soldier as my personal adjunct. No one will question you, I'll see to that. You'll wait quietly down the hallway for the meeting to end. At some point either Boris or Vlad will casually play with the cat. Boris often does, so it won't arouse suspicion. The cat will run out the door Boris will open, freed as if by an accident. We'll shout for help. You'll be in a position to catch the animal down the hallway. You'll have scant moments to use a quick-acting drug to momentarily put the animal out while we divert Milonov's attention. You'll use a surgical scalpel to remove the microchip, and clean off traces of blood. Then you'll innocently bring the cat back, as if you'd just caught it. At best you'll have two or three minutes."

"If they catch me, I'm fucked."

"If they catch you we're all fucked," Alina Vera corrected.

Floyd whistled. "Wouldn't it be easier to report these treasonous activities directly to the president? Let her deal with it. She dislikes him, anyway."

Boris picked up his cigar, turned his back to the American and stared ponderously out the window. Down below a picket line of young protesters were merrily singing the chorus of *Bring on the Revolution,* despite the rain. Watching police kept them from spilling into the square. He grimaced and closed the blind. "If only we could report it to our president—but there are other considerations at play. Unfortunately, Russia often returns to her historical Byzantine ways, a swampy morass laden with landmines. You see, my American friend, I'm afraid we have more explaining to do."

"What more can there be?"

"Let me tell you. Unfortunately, perfidy doesn't end with Milonov. Our president, Natasha Stroganoff, maintains quite a treasonous agenda of her own. From her point of view, shall we say, the more anguish our country suffers the stronger her position.

"Our president is not known to be of a democratic nature. In fact, she's quite the autocrat, opposing constitutional and legislative reform, personally desiring nothing better than witnessing bloody violence taking place in the streets to further her ambition. Thus, Lenin's uprising plays directly into her hands. If anarchists gain free rein to run amok, burning and ransacking, the temperature of the land will turn to national outrage, and a hue and cry for political stability under any circumstance. Our nation will reel.

"The repercussions of such an occurrence encourage the perfect climate for denying civil liberties and imposing martial law. Effectively she'll take total control of the country. With Lenin running free she'll call for emergency national unity along with some meaningless window-dressing cabinet reshuffling, doubtlessly followed by a stringent military crackdown. She'd like a collapse of authority as her way of justifying a crackdown and discrediting her enemies. At which point we think she'll summarily shut our parliament, the State Duma, by invoking the Emergency Terrorism Act. With despotic powers available she could also shut our court system as well. Judges opposing her will be arrested together with opposition parliamentarians, leaving her free to persecute anyone posing a threat. If you believe Milonov to be cold-blooded, Natasha is ironfisted and relentless."

Discerning Floyd's confusion, Alina Vera spoke up. "Hundreds of years ago, Imperial Russia aspired to becoming the world's 'third Rome', a huge empire extending all the way from Europe to Siberia. The Stroganoff family would gladly pick up that mantle and reignite those fantastic dreams of dominion. If given the chance, our president would return to the days of Catherine the Great, overthrowing all vestiges of duly elected democratic government, and sealing her grip with a single pen stroke. Rigged elections will follow with impunity, and stuffed ballot boxes will provide any 'proof' needed to demonstrate that Russia's people stand steadfast with her. The Stroganoffs are dangerous, and never to be underestimated."

"Rigged elections, stuffed ballot boxes? Is this a return to communist rule?" said Floyd.

"Quite the opposite," said a glum Colonel Dimsky. "She despises the communist regime. You must understand that our president belongs to a very historic, aristocratic family. Following the October Revolution when the Bolsheviks and Red Guards seized power, the Stroganoffs largely managed to flee to Paris, essentially remaining intact. She's not a Red by any means. Many of her family members returned over the years and quietly integrated into society. Nevertheless, animosity toward the revolution has always simmered. Just as Lenin's uprising can be helpful to the prime minister, so it's also expedient for her. We've strong reason to suspect all the Stroganoffs harbor monarchist ambitions."

"Monarchist? Kings and queens?"

"Our Colonel is informing you," Vlad said, "that this president would, without hesitation, readily return Russia to a monarchy. Natasha is a truculent, invective woman, and if anyone could pull it off she'd be the one. She believes she has the bona fides to proclaim succession, and would gladly proclaim herself Natasha the First, Czarina, Empress of all Russia. Once anointed, she'd restore the imperial St. Petersburg Winter Palace to its former opulence and splendor, a Czarist symbol, demonstrating Imperial Russia's magnificence and power."

"Czarina? Empress of Imperial Russia?" Floyd's face turned a shade of grey. "Is there more coffee? I need a stronger cup."

Alina Vera poured. "We realize how implausible it sounds. Vlad and I only learned of these dire circumstances these past days." Her face was sepulchral and unflinching, expressing her seriousness.

"It's one thing suspecting Milonov's deceitful ambitions," said the rabbi. "I've known him much of my life and have been wary for some time. But when the president personally implored my help after Dr. Sunavich fled, she swore me to absolute secrecy. Her political rhetoric was brazen enough to hint at a grab for power should Lenin's call to arms gain popular momentum. Of course she claimed it was for the good of the nation, and that since she was elected to serve the people's interests she'd take whatever actions required, no matter how totalitarian. I think deep down Natasha believes she has a divine calling."

Floyd stared blankly, feeling like he was punched in the solar plexus with a one-two combination. "Let's see if I have this straight; your prime minister is conspiring to take over as a dictator, while at the same time your president is conniving to anoint herself Czarina and restore the monarchy. Meanwhile, amidst these Kremlin intrigues, an unhinged and unglued new version of Vladimir Ilyich Lenin is preaching massive revolution of the proletariat."

"That's a succinct appraisal," agreed Alina Vera.

Floyd added with despair, "And suddenly lots of people are heeding him because they're alienated and disillusioned by fathomless corruption from top to bottom. Pardon me for being tactless, but it sounds like Russia is in one helluva mess." He downed the dregs of the coffee. "Gee Boris, you were right. This story is too incredible not to be believed."

Boris nodded. "Anyone would think us demented, but every word is true. Turmoil's been simmering below the surface for a long time. Now it's going to explode. Let me elucidate."

He lighted a cigar, sucked in smoke and blew it high toward the ceiling, framing his thoughts long and hard before speaking. "As some surmise, I've acted as a covert agent for years answering to our prime minister. However, no one suspected during this same time I was a double agent on the president's behalf. Both believed they were using me, but in truth my first loyalty has always been to the State. There are still many good people in Russia not about to let our freedoms be stolen. Secretly, I've been instructed by the head of Internal Security to take hold of this entire affair. See it through, and follow wherever it takes us—even should that path lead to the doorstep of the highest prevailing political incumbents. Until recently my entire life has been one of subterfuge and undercover activity, however now it's taken new meaning and urgency."

He set his jaw and looked inflexibly at his colleagues. "I am no longer that mercenary. I've watched great leaders rise and fall, witnessed the Soviet Union crumble and experienced the birthing pains of a shifting political landscape that became a democratically independent Russia, which faltered. Now, these years later, our New Russian Federation has taken shape. I'm not often proud of my past. If you'd confronted me during my youth you'd have found little more than a thug. I admit to committing acts in the name of the State and patriotism you'd consider despicable. Looking back I feel ashamed. Yet what's done is done and I can't alter the past. Some time ago I came to the realization that my sole fidelity is to the people—not unscrupulous, ambitious leaders." He blew perfect smoke rings. Alina Vera lit a cigarette of her own.

"You might regard this speech as pangs of guilt," Boris added in an introspective monotone, "or merely an aging man's sentimental prattle. But today I clearly understand my duty. If I don't do everything in my ability to preserve our country's emancipation, I can never redeem myself. My entire existence will be reduced to total failure. I'm disgusted watching a brain trust of megalomaniacs ruin our beautiful land. I desire Russia to be rid of her outmoded past, to prosper, and boast her rightful place among nations. Maybe a younger man does need to replace me. All I know is that I cannot stand by while this disaster unfolds. With the rabbi's assistance and Colonel Dimsky's abilities, we've learned the bitter truth regarding both the prime minister and our president." He flicked ashes.

"It's depressing to concede that I doubted you as well, my fellow team members. But matters progressed to such a fragile degree that a brooding darkness made me feel no one was trustworthy. I'm glad to say I was misguided and wrong on all accounts. Not long ago I shared these perceptions with Vlad. I put faith in him because I knew he harbored no vested interest or ambitions in this affair. He held no vendetta. Vlad helped me realize how insane this fear was; that I was privileged to work alongside such a wonderful group. I am forever grateful for that. The rabbi has proved himself a man of impeccable character and highest moral standing. Our president badly miscalculated when she presumed he would succumb to her whim or kowtow to a role of debasing himself by abetting her dirty work. On the contrary, Asher brought his dilemma directly to me, exposing his own vulnerability by gambling I wasn't a counteragent who'd incriminate him. In other words, Asher also risked his life. Putting our heads together he and I concluded the best course of action was for him to continue pretending to pursue his role as an informer."

"So Boris is a reluctant hero after all," said Alina Vera, feeling a depth of pride she didn't know existed. "I also have an admission to make. I had serious qualms regarding him from the start. I didn't trust him, didn't want anything to do with him or his team. I'm joyful to discover I misconstrued his motives, and that I was wrong. There's no one better suited to do the right thing. And I know whatever is decided here stands to alter Russia's future for countless generations." She sniffed. "I'm proud to play my part."

Totally out of character, Boris lowered his head with palpable humility. He unsuccessfully tried to hide a tear delineated at the corner of his eye. Colonel Dimsky put a brotherly hand to his shoulder.

When Boris regained composure, he said, "Now, I must sadly make an announcement. A man we've all trusted and relied upon, Rimsky-Kimsky, this morning was taken into custody, and has been placed under arrest." There were gasps. "The charges against him are severe: Espionage and sedition. He's accused of being a sleeper agent for Israel's secret service, the Mossad. Vlad has ensured that sensational bulletins of this arrest are leaked to all major news organizations." Boris waited while the shock sank in.

"However," he quickly went on, "I'm pleased to disclose that this is a political ruse. He hasn't been an Israeli spy at all. At my personal behest the Mossad agreed to play along, feigning to have enlisted him as their agent."

"Then he's innocent?" asked Alina Vera.

"Not exactly. Although he played the part of bootlicking flunky to Sergei Milonov, Rimsky-Kimsky has for some time had the dubious distinction of secretly being in the employ of the president's clique, contracted for one singular purpose—assuring the Lenin Project would fail, even as he pretended to save it. Time after time he threw wrenches into the Omsk team's work. It became incumbent upon Colonel Dimsky and me to make certain his arrest was expeditious and promptly blamed elsewhere. Working in tandem, a Mossad operative allowed himself to be clandestinely photographed meeting with Rimsky-Kimsky at a public café. This sleight-of-hand permitted us to take him immediately into custody. *Bolshoi Utka*, Big Duck Drinkwater, and his men picked him up leaving the rendezvous. Rimsky-Kimsky was mortified. And our president can't object without tipping her hand. Obviously it's imperative she never suspect we knew he was her illicit informer. Rimsky-Kimsky's been detained in strictest isolation. Big Duck personally interrogated him and now he's beside himself, vomiting names and facts, terrified he'll be shot. *Bolshoi Utka* can be very intimidating, I promise. Rimsky-Kimsky has signed a full confession, one that includes incriminating much of the entire Stroganoff family."

"Wow," said Floyd.

"Accordingly, with unnerving fears of insurgency increasing," Dimsky went on, "Russia's citizenry wouldn't question unpopular controls the president may have seized—including declaration of martial law. The nation's fragile political fabric risks being reduced to tatters, divided between Bolsheviks, anarchists, democrats, libertarians, socialists, and monarchists; each surreptitiously encouraged by nefarious, rich, international moguls. A tottering Russia would swiftly be brought to her knees. With a shoddy veneer of respectability, Natasha can claim plausible rationale for her unilateral presidential takeover. Tantamount to handing her power on a golden platter."

Boris clenched his teeth with consternation. "I'm determined to see that won't happen—ever. An alarmed populace clamors for stability and protection, rightly insisting on what you Americans like to call 'law and order'. Our president would seem heroic by summoning the Army, paving the way for a new order. Tanks in the street would assure democracy in Russia thrown back a century."

Floyd apprehensively leaned forward. "This has more twists and turns than a Sherlock Holmes tale."

"It does place us in a pickle," agreed Dimsky.

Floyd twiddled his thumbs. "You've given me lots to think over. No doubt your prime minister deserves what he gets, and I'd sure like to help out. But one thing troubles me. When you phoned last night you were discussing your chess master, Gregori Nabokov..."

Boris coughed loudly, putting out his cigar. He pounded his chest with a fist. "I've got to quit smoking," he said with a croak. "What a terrible habit. Alina Vera, why are you still smoking those vile American cigarettes?"

"I've been trying to quit for months. Maybe we should join Smokers Anonymous?"

Floyd lifted his hand. "Excuse me folks, but you're avoiding my question. How does Nabokov fit into this?"

"I was going to get to that next." Boris appeared embarrassed. "You see, we have another little favor to ask."

"Risking my life in a Russian prison isn't enough?"

Run-of-the-mill espionage and power hungry politicians were mundane fare compared to their immediate crisis, Boris knew. However, explaining to Floyd how a crazed Dr. Sunavich had twisted his vaunted project by inculcating a living, life force into the chocolate-blooded Lenin would tax the limits of credibility.

"I didn't hoodwink you, Floyd. As a matter of fact, Gregori Nabokov was indeed the purpose for my call. We've been shadowing this reckless chess master until he slipped out of sight. Due to Colonel Dimsky's diligence and special agent Inspector Big Duck Drinkwater's perseverance we've finally located his whereabouts. It was a shocking discovery learning Nabokov betrayed his country by playing an integral role instigating this revolutionary mob. Moreover, we discovered his girlfriend is the sister of none other than Lenin's consort, Ilya Evgeny. She's been on the run for weeks. Lenin's smart and elusive, here one day, gone the next. We're trying to track them down in an expansive, exasperating manhunt, so far without success. Lenin and Evgeny are becoming folk heroes in the neglected countryside; hailed as defenders of the common man, living legends, with followers willing to hide and protect them."

"Lenin's a folk hero like Jesse James?"

"More like Bonnie and Clyde," growled Dimsky.

Vlad said, "He's been engraved into the popular consciousness, winning their hearts and minds. He's always retained an uncanny understanding of the proletariat, and he's an expert at fear mongering, citing injustices, projecting dire consequences, harbingers, and omens."

Floyd scratched his head. "You just lobbed a double whammy explaining how both your president and prime minister are each scheming to overthrow legitimate government so they can return to totalitarianism or monarchy. How is this Lenin character any different? Am I missing something here?"

Boris had regrettably reached similar conclusions on his own; conclusions that did not bode well under analysis. Dodging a direct answer, he said, "Our paramount concern is capping this embryonic insurrection. Once it's ended the reasoning our treasonous politicians would use for seizing power will be removed. We'll capture this Nabokov soon enough. For now I ask your indulgence; each of these monsters will be decapitated at the appropriate time."

"They're all equally slimy," said Alina Vera with scorn. "But Boris is right. Battling the insurrection is our priority. Above any consideration Chocolate Lenin must be stopped."

Floyd's eyebrows rose. "*Chocolate Lenin?*" he parroted. "What the hell is Chocolate Lenin?"

She gasped, quickly putting a hand to her mouth. The cat was out of the bag. Vlad took off his glasses, inclined his head and pinched his fingers at the bridge of his nose. He shut his eyes, sighing at her accidental, regrettable slip of the tongue.

"Oy," muttered Rabbi Titlebaum.

"Well Colonel," pronounced Boris, muted vexation marring his fretful features, "aren't you going to whine, 'Mother Volga'?" He turned to the baffled American, tormented by this inopportune indiscretion. "Floyd, *Tovarich*, instead of coffee how would you like a nice shot of overpriced vodka?"

15.

"*In Washington, D.C., today, it was categorically denied by the American Secretary of State that the United States government has embarked upon a highly-secret project in an effort to replicate and restore to life their beloved sixteenth President, Abraham Lincoln. Lincoln, of course, was assassinated in 1865 after the conclusion of the Civil War in the United States. Furthermore—*"

"What possibly can come next?" Sergei Milonov's scabrous feature grew crimson as he shut the replay of Canadian news broadcast. His spasmodic tic worsened in a face pinched heavy with fatigue. "Mass marches across Red Square? Moscow district troops demonstrating with presidential cavalrymen?" He sank despondently deeper into his chair. His cat, always nearby, didn't attempt to sooth but swiped a paw his way instead. "Shoo Tinkerbelle, Papa's busy." The spoiled cat meowed with a huff and scurried away, tail held high.

Everyone avoided engaging one another; instead they cast fretful gazes downward, blinking, shuffling irrelevant papers to shy from searing criticism. "We shouldn't allow ourselves to become carried away, Mr. Prime Minister," voiced the husky Deputy Minister for Internal Affairs, a long-standing, well-experienced bureaucrat who'd seen prime ministers come and go.

"I heartily agree with my colleague," said the Minister of Commerce, a fleshy faced, pimply man sprouting a thick moustache in the manner of Stalin. "Who could take such ridiculous reports seriously?"

Muscles around Sergei Milonov's lips tightly contracted, a sure sign he was dissatisfied and straining to hold back a lapse in self-control.

"We can never underestimate the influence of the media," said Vlad, finding the fortitude to speak. His heart pounded fiercely inside his chest, his palms were sweaty. Did anyone notice his edginess, he wondered. Would his nervousness give him away? Boris sat directly at the right of the prime minister. Colonel Dimsky sat opposite, his hands folded on the table. Dimsky remained typically quiescent, and Boris portrayed his usual earnest countenance, prepared for the night's business.

"What's your view of this news report, Petrovsky? Can Washington be taken seriously on this? You're our expert media man. Tell us." The prime minister looked him squarely in the eye.

Vlad cleared a lump in his throat, answering with measured words and mature calmness. "Sir, in my capacity as senior advisor I suggest your office issue no statement. And unless pointedly asked at your scheduled press conference tomorrow, say nothing. That's my opinion, although I'm certain some in attendance here would disagree."

"Go on."

"In my view, if you are asked you should welcome this American effort profusely. Assure attending journalists that, to the best of your knowledge, such a fantastic development appears all but impossible. However if accurate, and America's talented scientists have indeed reconstructed someone of Abraham Lincoln's unmatched stature, rather than expressing angst, I recommend you vigorously applaud such brilliance and abilities."

"You do? What else?"

Vlad thought fast, adding. "I'd pleasantly say, 'As a matter of fact, President Abraham Lincoln has always been a personal hero of mine.' Continue, pointing out how you personally idolized Lincoln's most noble ideals. You've read numerous books of his humble beginnings and life over ensuing years, and how he demonstrates for everyone that a man lacking formal education can attain the highest, most prestigious and powerful office in the world. Tell them President Lincoln is a man after your own heart, an underdog who mustered great courage against enormous odds to stand for his beliefs. That it would be an honor if one day you should be privileged to meet his incarnation.' That's pretty much how I'd handle it."

A gradual smile appeared, the prime minister exhibiting unfeigned interest at Vladimir's suggestion. "You wouldn't be trying to massage my ego, Director Petrovsky?" General laughter ensued.

"No, sir. I just want you to realize that this barrage of foreign reports can be manipulated to our advantage every bit as easily as those who use them to our disadvantage."

Elbows on the table, Sergei wagged his head, putting his chin in his hands, saying, "I like you, Petrovsky. But you knew that, considering I'm the one who appointed you." The laughter grew louder with recognition that the prime minister was pleased.

Boris used this brief pause by casually standing and stretching. The time to act was ripe, Dimsky saw. Diverting Milonov's attention, the colonel said, "Director Petrovsky's advice has valid points. I believe such glowing comments serves to enhance your overall leadership image." As Dimsky continued, Boris lackadaisically ambled across the room, effortlessly kneeling to pet the playful cat. Dimsky, the picture of efficiency, went on with his critique. "The more I consider it, the more I appreciate the point of view of our public relations director."

"Really? Then you're also an admirer of this Abraham Lincoln, Colonel?"

Boris quietly interrupted the exchange. "Mr. Prime Minister, while we debate America's quirkiness reaching new heights, would it be all right to have fresh tea and coffee brought?"

"As you like." Milonov proved eager to return to the banter.

As Dimsky continued, Boris informally opened the conference door widely, seeking the guard on duty. He snapped his fingers in the air. "We need you, soldier," he called. Unnoticed, he gave the cat a swift push with the tip of his shoe. Tinkerbelle meowed and scrambled out the door. "You there," Boris barked to Dimsky's attentive adjunct. "Fetch the prime minister's cat and be quick about it!"

Looking sideways, the prime minister said, "Don't let her stray! If she's lost, me nor my wife will sleep a wink."

Vlad caught Sergei Milonov's attention again. "Frankly sir, I see a wide-ranging press conference as an unexpected opportunity. You'll get good coverage on primetime news. With a few well-placed allurements, I might be able to have the broadcast include that your own childhood and Lincoln's shared numerous flattering parallels; two smart boys born into poverty, overcoming limitless obstacles but still rising to the top. A short documentary recounting your own life could be put together, also."

Milonov listened with increasing enthusiasm. "Yes," he said, "Yes. I can see it."

Scant seconds later, Boris was standing at the doorway cradling the cat. He lovingly nuzzled her and gently placed her back on the floor. "I'm pleased to report that Lady Tinkerbelle is rescued safe and sound, Mr. Prime Minister." The cat scooted under the conference table. Boris stood with his arms open wide taking a bow like a theater impresario. The mood in the room had decidedly lightened into one of joviality.

Vlad added to it by standing and giving a round of applause. Then he said, "I trust you didn't forget the coffee. I'd be grateful for a cup."

"Best we resume our important business," growled Dimsky with fraudulent irritability. "The question needing resolution is how seriously to take this American endeavor to recreate a living Abraham Lincoln."

Russia's U. S. ambassador currently recalled home for debriefing, spoke up. "I doubt concern is founded. I'm familiar with how these Americans operate. They love to brag. Possibly a major university or institution is seeking larger endowments, and by flaunting this fantastical tale of resurrecting Lincoln they plan on gaining public attention and major funding. Grandstanding, showing they do things bigger and better is an old American tradition. Don't forget the lessons of Sputnik, how stunned Americans were when Russia auspiciously placed the first satellite into orbit. How quickly they vowed to send a man to land on the moon. They achieved their intention with incredible fanfare, gloated over their success, and increasingly lost interest. Look at their space program now. It's in tatters, a shadow of itself. No, I don't believe them to be on the verge of furnishing the world with a new Abraham Lincoln." More laughter followed.

"You believe this report's merely propaganda? Seeking notoriety to reclaim the scientific spotlight?" Milonov cracked his knuckles. "And it avoids misrepresenting difficult truths regarding their real abilities."

The ambassador leaned forward with dutiful candor. "Doubtlessly the United States has obtained a smattering of information regarding our Alexander Nevsky project. They may even possess minimal understanding of our dilemma. The Pentagon definitely is exhibiting concern, as well as their Secretary of Defense. But I believe this president to be a pragmatic man. He'll not hastily jump to conclusions. He'll require definitive proof."

"I've met their new president on several occasions," Sergei Milonov boasted. "I agree. He's a colorful and charming personality, but a pragmatist. Nevertheless, I'd wager the White House finds sitting back and constraining to be exacting. If I were the American president I'd already have directed the scientific community to move full steam ahead, discerning whether creating a reincarnated Lincoln is plausible. If our scientists obtained a breakthrough, why couldn't they succeed in duplicating it, too? The Americans couldn't bear the notion of their scientists being inferior."

The coffee arrived and was subtly given. Boris resumed his seat and sipped, a sugar cube melting on his tongue. "What's your opinion on this Lincoln rebirth, Sokolov?" Sergei demanded.

As was his way, Boris took his time before replying. He inched forward on his chair. "If I were advising this American president, I'd recommend losing no time in catching up. I'd designate an immediate secretly funded project, much like their Manhattan Project, which we know produced the first atomic bomb. Today, some believe that America has fallen badly behind, capable only of producing rock and roll music and superior cinematic special effects. However, I do not share this pessimistic view. I believe their president and Congress will allocate enormous sums and move expeditiously with their own version of the Lenin Project, perhaps dubbing it, the 'Lincoln Project'."

"You think they're capable of restoring Abraham Lincoln back to life?" asked an incredulous Minister of Commerce.

"I do. If we achieved it, why shouldn't they?" said Milonov.

"In point of fact," noted Vlad, "it's debatable to claim we've achieved anything. A single demented scientist formulated it entirely by himself. If Dr. Sunavich hadn't gone rogue we wouldn't be here."

"Quite so," agreed the prime minister. "You carry a good head on your shoulders, Petrovsky, with a fine future to look forward to. I predict it." He pushed back in his chair, drank from his porcelain cup. "I've decided to take your advice at my press conference. I'll praise and hail the Americans as super achievers. Reiterate I consider them the premier economic and scientific power of the world. These Americans adore being adulated like little children, don't they?" He glanced to his fingernails; he sorely needed a manicure before appearing before television cameras. "Gentlemen, I believe we've gone as far possible for tonight. Are there any other matters to discuss before adjourning?"

No one spoke. Vlad peered at Boris, glad to see the vigilant, double-dealing counterspy pleased with himself. The meeting was adjourned.

"My mother would leave the cooking pot simmering on the stove all day long. You'd smell potatoes, carrots, and a variety of spices bubbling, blended with the overwhelming odor of boiled cabbage."

"Poor Dimsky," lamented Alina Vera, "Is that what your mother gave for supper in Siberia?"

The colonel chewed on a toothpick, picking balalaika strings. "She was a woman of angelic modesty, and it was a filling, healthy meal for hungry children of moderate means. She governed our home with clever economy. The only thing missing was garlic; we could never get enough. All my siblings love garlic. It was a contest to tell which smell was stronger, the garlic or the cabbage." He continued playing.

"That's a pretty tune," said Vlad, lying flat on the couch, hands resting on his stomach, a medicinal heat patch adhered to his left shoulder. It was late and they were tired.

"It's a Central Asian peasant tune my grandfather taught to me. He owed his education and job to the Party, and in that absurd time they encouraged you to sing revolutionary songs. So with unalloyed patriotism he'd croon odes to the Motherland with friends—until extremists accused him of disloyalty and my family fled to Western Siberia. When I was little, my father would drive up to the Mongolian frontier on business. I treasured the jaunts, such adventures for a boy. I watched the magnificent horsemanship of the Mongolian traders and tribesmen. Not even a sandstorm stopped such enduring, robust horses riding wild across the Steppes. It was astounding to witness these saber-wielding horsemen galloping, leaping hurdles through great rings of fire. It's amazing. I'd visualize the vast armies of Genghis Khan passing once under this very night sky, conquering the world. Bold, brave soldiers, and without doubt the world's finest horsemen."

"They take my breath away," agreed Alina Vera, having seen such spectacles herself. "What was your father's trade during your years in Siberia?"

Dimsky's eyes twinkled with memories. "He was considered an honorable, independent businessman. He regularly traded back and forth along the frontier with Mongolian tribesmen. They were savvy barterers, but good to their word. And they had confidence in my father, too. He never lied or cheated them, and always paid up front in hard cash. It was a long, good relationship."

Vlad laughed. "Your dad was a smuggler, Colonel."

Dimsky shrugged, unabashed. "During difficult times contraband dealing was considered an honest trade." He continued playing.

"And exactly what did your father trade?" Alina Vera pressed.

"Yaks. He did a brisk business. Have you ever tasted yak milk? When I was a lad my mother made a tasty treat; home-baked black bread with yak butter and jam." He smacked his lips in recollection. "I can still almost taste it. At other times she gave us black bread with *salo*, a traditional dish made from salt-cured pig fat."

"Sounds wonderful." Alina Vera muttered.

"It was. My father sold yaks to local farmers in our area. Nothing regarding a yak is wasted. You drink its milk, cook its meat, and burn dung for fuel. It was a happy time. As a matter of fact—"

"I hear an engine." Alina Vera sat up straight. They listened as a car pulled into the driveway.

"At last," said Vlad. The front door opened. A blast of cold air accompanied Boris and the rabbi. Boris disclosed no sentiment but it was plain the rabbi brimmed with satisfaction.

Boris rubbed cold hands together. "Well, isn't this is a cozy little scene? I hope you've spent a nice evening visiting my home. And you, dear Alina Vera, look the perfect part of a content housewife."

She turned her head and frowned. "We've sat around all night to hear that?" she fussed. "At home I could at least read tea leaves with Anya."

The rabbi took off his coat and hat, and settled into a recliner. He leaned back with his feet propped. Atop his head his yarmulke sloped askew. Dimsky put down his balalaika. Vlad looked on eagerly. "So?" Vlad asked.

"Wait while I clean up," Boris said to Asher. "Not a word spoken, all right?" Boris sauntered off toward the bathroom.

Alina Vera went to the kitchen and poured green tea. Boris returned to the parlor as she finished serving. "I believe we're onto something," he announced. "Rabbi, would you mind sharing your news?"

Asher straightened in his chair. He rubbed reddened eyes and stifled a wide yawn. In the last several days he'd hardly left his laboratory, ate very little, slept less. Light-headed and muddled, he cleared the webbing eclipsing his mind. "The motility of the latest batch of specimen sperm was superior. From it I extrapolated faint elemental traces of rum tinctured with chocolate, thus isolating the basic formulaic ingredients Sunavich perfected. I contacted Yuri Grushin's team for their conclusions regarding life force subatomic molecular structure. After exhaustive effort I saw their trials concurred with mine with 99.7 percent certainty, an incontrovertible conclusion."

"You seem pleased."

"I am."

The news lifted their spirits; but before becoming euphoric, he cautioned, "Don't get too excited. The evidence is preliminary. Assuming my hypothesis proves correct we've made a significant breakthrough. We've shown Lenin has earthly limitations after all. Understanding his unique molecular composition opens the door. Now we find a pathway for deconstruction, molecule by molecule."

Alina Vera placed her teacup on its saucer. "You've formulated a plan, haven't you? I feel it. I sense it. Please, allow me to assist you. I want to work, to contribute anything of value. What do you say?"

"Wish granted, Dr. Galina. I can't manage alone, I admit. I'll need you just like the old days at the Institute. We'll begin early tomorrow. Report to my lab prepared for the hardest work of your life."

She squealed with delight. This was everything she'd dreamed. Not only working beside the rabbi, but also thrown into the cauldron, becoming a part of am exciting scientific search begging to make history.

"Would either of you like to share what's up?" asked Vlad.

Asher glanced toward Boris, who cautiously nodded assent; it was pointless in trying to keep the news under wraps.

"This solution I've advanced can't accurately be called a weapon," Asher disclosed. "Nevertheless, once revealed it will prove to be something human eyes have never before witnessed. As we know too well, our antagonist is more resourceful and resilient than we ever imagined, and our own efforts feeble at best. We've been trying to catch a rabbit on the run, dashing through a warren. Given those circumstances we might as well give up and sell vegetables in a market. That elusive rabbit will not be caught without exploring unprecedented avenues."

"What 'unprecedented avenues' have you found?" Dimsky asked.

"Our challenge is to render Sunavich's genetic compound ineffectual. I frequently asked myself if it was even possible. Tonight I declare that it is— by introducing a deterrent able to break down and completely decompose our chocolate friend's anatomy and microcosmic foundation."

Vlad looked sidelong at Alina Vera. "In plain words, Asher's saying he's found a way to destroy Lenin," she said.

"Destroy him without catching him?"

Asher frowned. "I dislike the term 'destroy'. Let me posit it another way. Our vaunted secret police have failed miserably, our army insufficiently trained for this, and our network of underworld informers unmotivated, ineffectual, or double-crossing. Even Internal Security is stymied. We've stumbled and bumbled in an endless runaround, unable to locate let alone eradicate the world's foremost revolutionary. Meanwhile, the uprising's popular following continues unabated. It was crucial we find ways to take the initiative, and now we can." Asher made a pyramid with his hands, placing laced fingers to his lips. "As we're unable to stop, catch, or render Lenin helpless, I concluded only one alternative." After a pause he spoke with determination. "Simply put, my solution is to melt him."

"*Melt* Lenin?" mimicked Dimsky, eyes popping wide. "Mother Volga!"

Alina Vera appeared disquieted.

"Does such a thing pose a moral dilemma?" the rabbi asked rhetorically. "I think not. I've pondered long and hard, deliberating, scouring numerous books and texts for guidance. Evaporation is our neutralizer, not a weapon of destruction, but is the sole technique for eliminating him without requiring knowledge of his whereabouts. Let's review our facts and findings:

"His anatomy was bestowed with human needs, his copious sperm attesting very well in that regard. Unknowingly, Ilya Evgeny has well amplified that point. Through their extraordinary neutrons, electrons, protons, positrons, and neutrinos, his semen provides a roadmap. This knowledge works to our advantage…But in the final analysis my theory can't be proven in a test lab. We must employ it. Only then can we properly assess the neutralizer's abilities. Because Lenin moves freely with impunity we're unable to target him. The only option is to expand our horizons from one end of the Motherland to the other, and beyond."

"We're going to blow up the Motherland?" a puzzled Dimsky asked.

"You know me better than that, Colonel. However, we need to prepare for a worst-case scenario. Broadening our scope is exigent. With Lenin removed from the equation the insurrection's momentum will subside. The balloon will lose its air. Without the head of the snake it will limply fizzle out."

Vlad swallowed hard. "Destroying the world in order to save it? Haven't I heard that sort of talk before?"

The rabbi wasn't amused. "On the contrary. Our plan will assure the world's safety. Remember, the operative word is *melt*."

"Your intent is to melt the Earth?" queried Dimsky.

Asher rolled his eyes in consternation. "No, Colonel! You're entirely missing the point!" He waited. "Let me caution that my formula isn't completed—and even when finalized there's a possibility it won't work. The direct and indirect effects can't be precisely predicted. Failure to neutralize brings us right back to square one. Thus, My conclusion is straightforward: Fight fire with fire. Therefore, the only conceivable method of stopping Lenin cold is by development of the most unimaginable weapon in mankind's history. I'm beyond rudimentary genetic equations for its debasing formula, and aiming for total anomalous formulated deconstruction."

"Deconstruction?" Alina Vera held breath. "You're planning what I think?"

"I am, Dr. Galina. This is an outstanding high point. Locating Vladimir Ilyich is irrelevant—yet destroyed he most certainly *shall* be. Our magnetic arrow shoots directly for the heart. We're going unleash unimaginable quantum force, counterattacking with a single, universal strike. With this matrix we're going to melt Chocolate Lenin."

16.

Floyd's jaw hung low. "You're asking me to do more dirty work? Heck, I just finished putting my life on the line, Boris. What now? I'm not a member of your team."

"We could appoint you as an associate member," offered Vlad lightheartedly. "Launder your Russian military uniform, keep it safe just in case."

There was a round of exultant laughter at the table. Asher tossed seedless grapes, and cashews into his mouth, brushing away palls of lingering cigarette smoke. Tonight the scientist rabbi was clearly indulging himself. "Enjoy your deserved hero status, Mr. Dingus. You may not fully appreciate it, but you've helped save Mother Russia from irrefutable tyranny."

The sky was darkening, and a large, butterscotch half-moon loomed above. They sat relaxing in a popular smoky café called, *Crime and Punishment*, near *Strastnoi Bul'var*, a hilly district offering exemplary panoramic city views. An extensive multitude of basement cafés dotted Moscow's outer boulevards, a locale where aspiring artists, writers, and intelligentsia gathered. The brightly hued walls were decorated in a palette of pastels, French Impressionist prints randomly hung. The team's mood was upbeat and gratified; lazing, trading barbs and compliments on a job well done. Pungent aromas of espresso, cappuccino, and Turkish coffee permeated the bistro's smoky air. Every table was occupied, a mixture of after-theatre couples, models escorted by wealthy businessmen, and tourists among locals fighting for limited space. Unknown to most, a spattering of low-level criminal bosses were on hand. Colonel Dimsky kept a quiet eye on one table in particular set diagonally from their own. Russian alternative rock music blared from scattered overhead speakers.

"Time for a smoke," said Boris, wiping apple *vareniki* cake crumbs off his shirt. He took several fresh Cuban cigars from a humidor and offered them. Floyd Dingus, doting on the last morsels of his own cake, accepted gladly as did Alina Vera. Boris struck a match, lighting the cigars one by one.

"You did a wonderful job, Floyd," said Alina Vera, puffing. "You impressed me with such adept expertise at removing the cat's microchip. I never dreamed you were a daring risk taker. And by the way, you looked really sharp in your

Russian Army uniform. Most handsome!" She was in an exceptionally good and talkative mood after spending a worried, anxiety-filled day.

"He did look rather distinguished," admitted Dimsky. "I made certain his shirt, jacket, and trousers were perfectly tailored to explicit specification. I don't have faith in military outfitters. They have no sense of style. Nevertheless, if Floyd had been caught, likely they'd have taken him out back and shot him on the spot."

"Maybe, but he'd still have looked spiffy lying in a pool of his own blood." Alina Vera winked.

"They'd shoot you first, Colonel, if they knew what we were up to," aggrandized Vlad.

Floyd grimaced at the thought of a Russian firing squad. He sucked in smoke and exhaled a series of perfect rings. Everyone watched them sail through the air, applauding as they slowly vanished. "Well, I admit being plenty scared at first, but then I took to it like a duck to water. I've never done anything remotely like this before. Back in the day I sure would've enjoyed signing up with the CIA, and becoming an espionage agent like my brother. But that wasn't the job I was offered." His shoulders slumped. "Don't think it's fun working around smelly cattle. Some Ag Department folks enjoy being out in the field with their boots squishing in cow dung, but not me. Hooking up with you people sure gives a new perspective. Say Boris, do you do this espionage stuff regularly?"

Boris shook his head. "The good old days are gone, my friend, and my KGB years long behind. However, tonight did make me feel nostalgic, I admit, because for me the question remains, what next? I refuse to spend the rest of my life sinking into senility. I ponder the future." He puffed deeply on his cigar.

"You're becoming quite philosophical in your dotage, Comrade Sokolov," said Alina Vera, tapping ashes, undeniably irritating him with the salutation 'Comrade'.

"Decrepitude is a state of mind, my dear."

"Oh? Then why don't you explain to Floyd what you've lined up for his next assignment? You can tell how eager he is." Gloating, she puffed her cheeks in an attempt to blow her own smoke ring, failing miserably, and muttering, "Shit."

Dimsky slapped her gently on the back. "It takes lots of practice." He turned his attention to Floyd, speaking more seriously. "At the small table over there, do you see the man and woman sharing a quiet conversation?"

"You mean the guy with the short, graying beard, wearing a Greek fisherman's cap?"

"That's the one. Don't stare. Staring isn't polite."

Floyd squinted. "Something's sure familiar about him but I don't know what. I've never seen his wife, either."

"That's not his wife," said Boris. "Take another peek but don't be overt. A good spy is always inconspicuous. Good. This time, try and picture the fellow without his beard."

Floyd allowed his saucer to fall to the floor; he pushed back his chair, kneeled down to attain an unobstructed view. The couple sat leaning in, elbows on the table, lost in an intense, animated conversation. Floyd observed carefully, and then resumed his place. "That guy looks like Gregori Nabokov." He gritted his teeth. "Yeah, it *is* Gregori. So that's the reason you brought me here. I thought we came to celebrate."

"We are celebrating," Alina Vera assured with a sparkle. "I assume Nabokov's showing up is merely a coincidence."

"Some coincidence. Talk about mine-infested waters. You set me up."

"Floyd's on to us," admitted Boris, demitasse in one hand, cigar in the other. "I suspected Nabokov would be here. His girlfriend frequents this establishment. We've also learned that she and her sister, Ilya Evgeny, maintain contacts with powerful underworld figures who come here, too."

"Like the mafia?" said Floyd

"Call it a homegrown version," corrected the rabbi, grapes in hand. "These are powerful, ruthless men, venturing into everything from stock manipulation to human trafficking. Likely Evgeny's connections may help fund their enterprise. But we're onto them, and trying to track that money."

"Holy moly."

"This establishment is a habituated hangout for shady types," Boris disclosed. "Tonight's a perfect time to see if you still recognized our chess master, and apparently you do. That's a good thing."

Peals of laughter abounded across the cafe. Two generously bosomed women in low-cut black dresses and black stockings arose and sauntered out the front door, followed behind by two burly blond men in tailored suits. Floyd's eyes drifted towards the women. "Better check out some other girls," said Alina Vera. "Those two are high priced, how do Americans say, 'hookers'?"

"Never mind that," grunted Boris, seeing Floyd's disappointment. He placed a hand on Floyd's arm. "You told me you wanted to be an undercover agent. Alright, I have a special job for you with a mountaintop perch."

"That important? It seems to me everyone around here gains something out of this messy business. I don't mean to be a party pooper, but what's in it for me?"

"Your reward is helping to save Russia from grave risk, and perhaps America too," Dimsky said.

"Gregori Nabokov is in league with your prime minister?"

"Not exactly," Vlad said. "He's secretly working with a wanted, extremely dangerous woman. A woman who, in her own way, is as power hungry as Milonov ever was."

"Oh, I get it. Sure. You're talking about Ilya Evgeny. Don't tell me. That's her sister shacking up with Gregori?"

"As a matter of fact, yes. The two are essentially identical in more ways than one. We believe both are conspirators with Nabokov," explained Boris. "Internal Security has concluded Ilya Evgeny was sent to Moscow to collect a large sum slated for funding the revolution."

Floyd was about to reply but stopped cold in his tracks at the mention of revolution. "This whole affair, this *Chocolate Lenin* business, you've been very vague. I need to know more if you expect my help. I want to be filled in on the whole shebang."

Vlad placed his arm around the American in a gesture of camaraderie. "I think Boris explained as much as permitted. It's a tangled mess, and only now are pieces of the puzzle falling into place. This inflamed Lenin character is not only promoting overthrowing our elected government, but personally vows to restore the worst days in our history. We can't allow that, Floyd. Russia has suffered too much."

"I'm getting a good idea of what you mean. Remember me looking for a copy of *The Communist Manifesto*? Well, I found one. I've been reading up. Let me tell you, those boys Marx and Engels were pretty tough stallions."

"Yes they were. So you know about the gulags, the tortures, and disappearances?"

"I know enough."

Vlad sighed. "If Lenin assumes power that scenario could return. As an American, I expect you wouldn't like to resume the Cold War?"

"No I wouldn't." He stared into his empty coffee cup. "I get your point. Hey, Alina Vera, how about reading the grinds for me? Should I accept Boris's offer?"

She took his cup and held it in her hand, turning it slowly and gazing. "I see a bird in flight, Floyd Dingus, a large bird with a very powerful beak. Yes. It appears to be an eagle." She looked up at the American. "This eagle, this is the symbol of the United States, is it not? I thought so. I can see in your cup, Floyd, that *you* are that eagle soaring..."

"Hot damn! No one's ever buttered me up as good as you. Quite a snow job, but I gotta hand it to you, you're the best." He roared.

"Why thank you." Smiling mischievously, she returned his cup.

"Waiter," Boris called, snapping his fingers, "another round over here."

"All right, let's suppose I let you bamboozle me and agree to your little assignment, it's because I want to, understand? Not because you talked me into it."

"Understood," replied Vlad. "Your excellent work won't be in vain."

"Uh oh. Don't look now," said Alina Vera, "but Nabokov and his companion are leaving. He's just paid his bill."

"The cheap bastard didn't even leave a tip," grumbled Dimsky.

Floyd turned sideways so the chess master couldn't see or recognize him. The couple walked briskly out into the pleasant night air. Nabokov hailed a taxi, and within moments they were whisked away.

"We have eyes and ears routinely watching Nabokov," Boris said. "An expert team directed by Inspector Big Duck Drinkwater, one of our finest. Your task, Floyd, should be a snap. Tomorrow at noon you'll 'accidently' run into Nabokov on the street. You'll recognize him and start up a cheerful conversation, chatting about chess, common friends, and so on. At all costs divert his attention. He'll try giving you the brush off, but don't let him. Slow him down, grab his sleeve, and don't let him out of your sight. A money drop is going to be made directly to Nabokov by Lenin's consort, Ilya Evgeny. She'll be delivering it by hand; so all the cash will be sitting in a briefcase. He's got skillful connections for laundering it outside the country.

"Meanwhile, our man *Bolshoi Utka*, Big Duck, will await Evgeny at her end of the drop. Her protégée, tennis star Anya Andropova, has already fed Ilya the bait. Drinkwater and his police will nab her. Once she's safely in custody we'll surround Nabokov and arrest him, too. You'll act surprised, confused, like you

271

know nothing. Pretend to aid your friend. No one will ever find any link to your involvement."

Floyd whistled. "It's crazy learning a respected master of Gregori's standing would get involved in such muck. Are you sure there's no mistake?"

"No mistake. He's in it up to his neck, together with his girlfriend." A new round of coffee was brought by the sweaty, busy waiter.

"We'd better be leaving soon, too," said Vlad. "Tomorrow's going to be another long, demanding day. We need to ready bright and early."

"I hate getting up early," muttered Dimsky.

Alina Vera looked askance. "I doubt any of us are looking forward to losing sleep, but Anya and I are both greatly looking forward for our chance to finally confront Ilya Evgeny eye to eye."

"You perverted, damned liar!" A tennis shoe sailed across the room and hit the wall with a dull thud. Anya Andropova clutched the matching shoe and made ready to throw it with the grace and strength of a tennis serve. Alina Vera quickly grabbed her arm.

"You phony, worthless fishwife! I gave you my trust, I believed you!" Anya wailed.

"Anya, I swear I did you no harm."

The tennis star glowered with alienation, her face turning darker than her eye shadow. Blond hair splayed wildly as she threw her head back and spit. "You deceived me from the very start, you shrew!" Warm tears streamed. Alina Vera steered her to a seat, and remained beside the girl.

Vlad and Dimsky stood levelheaded and erect at the door, eyes downcast. "I learned the *real* truth, you streetwalker!" Anya blurted, her intonation dripping acid. Before Alina Vera could prevent it, the second tennis shoe flew across the room. Ilya ducked.

"You're responsible for my kidnapping! You purposely made me take that lousy trip with you! You knew those primitives were waiting. You knew they'd hold me for ransom, and you pretended to be a victim, too. What would have happened if the police didn't intervene, huh? What would have happened if those gargoyles managed to drag me to their filthy hideout? Would I be beaten, raped? Was your repulsive lover planning to seduce me, too?"

"Anushka, where did you hear such horrible things?" Ilya protested, tears flowing from her steely eyes towards the corners of her mouth. Under arrest, aware the chances of being found not guilty in a Russian court of law were virtually nil, the muscular coach decided to plead her best case. "Where did you hear these second- and third-hand fabrications? He's not my lover. I didn't know a thing. I've been an innocent dupe, too. These zealots needed me to be a scapegoat. I never agreed to anything. I was forced to phone you and demand money. I had no choice, and I never intended to actually show up for that money drop. My plan was to escape beforehand." Her demeanor portrayed an abused victim incredulous at being cast into a villainous guise.

"This one acts a good role," muttered Dimsky to Vlad. Vlad nodded, gazing straight at Ilya. So this was the infamous woman responsible for so much anguish during their formidable manhunt, the secret consort who not only aided Lenin in dodging the police, but also ambitiously plotted her own rise to power alongside him. Ilya Evgeny noticed Vlad's stare, and glared back defiantly.

Anya Andropova wiped her mouth with the back of her arm and spit again. "You make me sick! I believed in you. It wasn't my career you cared about; it was advancing your own fortunes. OMG, you used me from the very start, you pious bitch!" She lunged so fast Alina Vera didn't have time to blink. Anya pounced atop the shocked woman and the two of them fell to floor, rolling, grappling and hitting. Fists flew. Dimsky ably snatched the well-toned, robust Anya off her antagonist, and yanked her back to her chair. Vlad assisted in lifting Ilya Evgeny to her feet. She was off balance, unsteady, her lower lip swollen and bleeding, a trail of blood trickling from one nostril. A bluish welt formed beneath her puffy left eye. He handed her a few tissues. She took them as she struggled to regain composure.

"You landed a few good ones," Dimsky said quietly and gratifyingly to the panting, sweaty tennis player. "Especially when you kneed her in the groin." Anya's blouse was mauled, exposing cleavage, and she bent low, placing her hands on her knees, catching breath. "I'm not done with you, I'll rip your gullet!" she hissed venomously. Ilya shuddered.

"I'm entitled to a lawyer," Ilya implored, impelled to run away but with nowhere to go. She wiped the blood. "I know my rights. I demand judicial process."

"We maintain complete discretion as to your 'rights'," the colonel informed her with disdain. "We can hold you incommunicado indefinitely under the State Emergency Terrorism Act," "In fact, we can make it so you no longer exist."

"But I'm not a terrorist—"

Anya sprang; this time Alina Vera caught her in time and shoved her back down. Her choleric expression assured Ilya to expect more assaults any moment.

"Give me a smoke," Ilya said, holding out a shaky hand. Alina Vera took out her pack of American cigarettes, lighted one and handed it to the bruised manager. She took a drag, saying, "I won't fall for all your tricks, gimmicks and traps."

"Listen, Ilya," said Vlad, "we've learned much more than you credit us for. And not just about you. We've discovered the conspiracy between your sister, Irina, and her gentleman friend. Don't try and protest. Gregori Nabokov is in custody even as we speak."

Vlad knew everything had gone precisely as planned. A barely disguised Ilya had shown up promptly, waving to the waiting Anya Andropova while the tennis star stood meekly on the corner clutching a small bag filled with cash. Anya had raised every ruble, converting them into dollars to convince her manager she was keeping her promise.

"Doubtless, your Gregori will spew his guts telling everything we need to know," said Dimsky with authority. "How you passed the money to him, stuffing it into his empty briefcase. All are treasonous acts—for you, him, and for your sister. If you sincerely wish to save your neck, Ilya Evgeny, you'll answer every question posed to you." He looked toward Alina Vera.

The scientist stood to her full height and coolly strolled to the quivering, prickly tennis manager. As the daughter of a police magistrate she'd gained a potent understanding of interrogation techniques. She would now be the closer for this case. As a child she'd often sat on her father's lap as he lovingly told stories of vile criminals he'd condemned. She adored listening, wishing she, too, could become a judge. This was her first real chance to put what she'd learned and dreamed of into practice.

She lit a cigarette of her own and inhaled deeply. The sun was beginning to set, a rosy tint from a small window spilling through the room. "You can make this easy for yourself, or choose to make it a special category of punishment," she stated bluntly. "It's up to you. Personally, I don't care. I've had it up to here with your kind. So Ilya Evgeny, while you still have favorable circumstance, our fundamental question is, where is Vladimir Ilyich Lenin concealed? Where is Dr. Mikhail Sunavich?"

Ilya's fingertips brushed against her painful, rising welt. She leaned hard against the wall. She had no idea where she'd been brought, only that it wasn't a typical police station. All signs pointed to being in the custody of the abhorred secret police, a wretched, dehumanizing place of punitive confinement behind reinforced steel doors. A place where one might easily disappear, found dumped ignominiously in a swamp, or along some faraway rutted road. "Who is Mikhail Sunavich?" she stammered. "I don't know anybody by that name."

"Lying whore!" screamed Anya Andropova, unbridled, straining like a racehorse. She desired nothing more than delivering one last solid punch to render her former manager unconscious. Alina Vera looked sternly at Anya, quieting her with an angry motion.

"You've never heard of Dr. Mikhail Sunavich, you say?"

"No. I've never heard that name."

"But you do admit having spent numerous nights and private moments with Lenin at *Peter the Great's Palace*? Amorous nights."

"If you mean that pigsty owned by that creepy witch, I willingly admit it. What of it? I'm a free woman, and Russia is now a free country. *Private moments!* I can sleep wherever I choose." She threw her head back insolently.

"You admit the room was the fleabag belonging to Lenin?"

Ilya folded her arms, cigarette between her index and forefinger, thin smoke drifting toward the ceiling. "I have no idea who it belonged to. I had no choice; he forced me, understand? His obnoxious hands always groping, bad breath suffocating me. It was humiliating. Did you think I *liked* it?" She spat with scorn, as if her own sexuality and unapologetic tumescence played no part. "Anyway, his cronies were lurking nearby. I had nowhere to run, nowhere to hide."

Alina Vera comprehended this woman was determined to remain resistant to the bitter end. A wild beast in a cage, and if there was any chance of shattering her will that time was now, squeezing until she went squish. She leaned in close and hard, tilting her head and her stance, the way Humphrey Bogart did in so many crime movies she loved watching, growling her words huskily.

"I see. Your narrative is revealing. You were merely a fleshy bauble for his sadism, you say. Very well. This private room you intimately shared, how many times did you visit *Peter the Great's Palace* either with or without him? Think hard what you reply, Ilya Evgeny. Your answers will go far in determining your fate."

Alina Vera's fabricated life or death threat shook Ilya to the bone. She was being forced to divulge a full description of her chronology with the harbinger of the Revolution. Uniformed, severe Colonel Dimsky stood nearby, eagerly waiting for her to be caught in deception; trapped between the hammer and the anvil.

"I'm not sure," she stammered. "We always traveled late at night. It was safer, he said. We were on the run, sleeping in farmhouses, sometimes in fields or stinking barnyards with nowhere to bathe. Vladimir Ilyich has many friends in the countryside. But yes, I do admit visiting that smelly rat hole, what's it called, *Peter the Great's Palace*? Ha! A palace you say? More like a sewer. Did you think we sat drinking fruit punch on the verandah? It's an affront to all civilized people. A reeking cesspool, nauseating and offensive. The walls are paper-thin; you can hear prostitutes plying their trade above, below, and from every which way. Beds banging against the walls all night long, women and men moaning. It was disgusting."

"Who did Lenin tell you the room belonged to?"

Alina Vera tried to penetrate through her brash, hardened features. Ilya shrugged expressionlessly. "He said it belonged to a friend, a bosom buddy from student days was paying for it. It meant nothing to me. What did I care about his friend, anyway? And why are you wasting time asking these questions? Is this an official interrogation? Are you the secret police? Obviously I'm already condemned without even benefit of a trial."

"I ask the questions," seethed Alina Vera. "You answer them. Revolution is treason; you do understand the penalty for treason is death, don't you? You've put yourself in serious trouble, but if you're cooperative, some benevolent magistrate may decide not to cast you off to a Siberian gulag, a place where you'll grow old very, very, fast, I promise. Your lavish good looks will vanish in months, and in two years you'll be a hag, wishing you had been executed. If you dream of ever seeing the outside of prison walls again you'll find it very much in your interest to assist us. Think it over, but quickly. Be sensible. As I said, your hold your fate in your own hands. Believe me, my friends are not as nice as I am." She glanced sideways toward Dimsky, whose posture overflowed with unequivocal menace. An army pistol was plainly holstered at his side.

Alina Vera stalked close round Ilya, broiling and twitching, blowing cigarette smoke her way but not looking directly point-blank, a tried and true melodramatic method. "This dear 'bosom buddy' Lenin spoke of, his old school chum, was his name Andrei Popov, the harpsichord player?"

"Popov sounds correct. I believe that was the name, yes. But I was never told anything about his playing the harpsichord."

"Did you ever personally meet this Andrei Popov, either with Lenin or alone?"

Ilya swallowed with difficulty. It was clear the prisoner felt deep distress at her unenviable situation. She took her time answering, carefully weighing her options; how she might best downplay her part to convince she was merely an inconsequential, if not innocent player, in the unfolding conspiracy. She could sense the lacerating glare of Anya Andropova's disapproving eyes riveted upon her. At this moment the blossoming tennis star, icon of the Jubilee, would gladly trade all for another chance to render one final substantial blow.

"I may have met this man Popov, yes. Vladimir Ilyich held many meetings during those weeks. Workers and delegates traveled from all over. I wasn't privileged to hear all the conversations but I did occasionally overhear a few discussions on strategies. They debated demonstrations, inciting revolts, and burning farms and estates belonging to oligarchs and rich landowners. They reviewed how many soldiers had given promises, risking court-martial to flee and fight under the Red banner. Lenin became obsessed. He lives and breathes his revolt. He dispatches his closest allies to cities and towns. They serve as his eyes and ears, he says, a network of spies and couriers. He rubs his hands and chortles after fruitful meetings, blabbering to himself on what comes next. Often he gets hungry. He's not a fussy eater, but he does have his likings. He especially enjoys eating chocolates, and sardines out of a can."

"A bad diet," said Dimsky.

"He's insane I tell you. He sits up at night writing and rewriting speeches given more than a hundred years ago. He practices giving them in front of me, but often forgets his place. His mind gets foggy. Sometimes he blames me, saying I distract him, or that it's my fault pages are missing. Other times he sheds tears. He goes from mood to mood. I often saw him strolling at daybreak wearing night-clothes, licking dew from tree leaves, dirt caking his bare feet. He can turn visionary, melancholic, tormented and inspired within minutes. He raves about some dead French poet he admired, Gerard de Nerval, and how Nerval liked walking his pet lobster, Thibault, on a ribbon through the Palais-Royal gardens in Paris…"

"*Gross!*" exclaimed Anya.

"Please believe me, I played no part in his ragtag insurrection. I swear it. I was kept strictly for his pleasure. His nighttime playmate."

"I bet you were real good at that," sniped Anya.

Ilya looked to her inquisitor. "You must believe it! These men were armed and dangerous. One odious crony kept a pistol constantly pointed at my head when I telephoned Anya. I was directed to solicit monies from everyone. Lenin was crazed with finding funds. It was expensive, he kept insisting. There was no refusing. He even made me solicit the Salvation Army, saying they had good underground affiliations, including recruits and followers ready to join him. In fact, he says they've quietly become as powerful as the Freemasons, a nefarious influence on behalf of the current elitist regime. Does that sound like a man with a sane mind?"

"I'm a Freemason," muttered an offended Dimsky.

"All right, enough of that. What I want to know where you first met Andrei Popov, the harpsichord player."

Ilya banged the back of her head against the wall. "I've already told you it could have been anywhere!" she insisted. "We were constantly on the move, with shadowy, grim men sometimes accompanying us. There was this one particular man, a devious little fellow who wore thick eyeglasses. Cool as a cucumber, that one. Cold blooded. He frequently came to talk to Lenin, denigrating politicians, and I believe he also played a role goading gullible folk at rallies. The little man with thick eyeglasses seems to hold some queer sway or authority in a narcissistic way, instructing him to do this or that. He alone knew what was best. He said Vladimir Ilyich was too bumbling, repudiating his superiority, and so on. For a time Vladimir Ilyich listened, but soon he refused to be degraded and humiliated this way, he said. They argued, sparring loudly. The perverse little man went into furious fits, insulting Vladimir Ilyich, behaving like the revolution was his accomplishment, saying he was being flouted and rewarded with ingratitude.

"Vladimir Ilyich was understandably concerned and upset. The little man with thick glasses was no longer his friend, he confided, and he pined for halcyon days. I saw true sadness in his eyes. That little bully had been something of a father figure to him. Oddly, during that time I felt compassion for poor Lenin. I cradled him while he wept. In time he began to grow stronger, more sure of himself, taking the breakup well. After that, he made every decision personally. I understood what he wanted."

"Go on."

"You have to realize that his attention span is very short. He has peculiar tendencies. He often rambles during speeches, at times stumbling, especially on multisyllable words. If you didn't know better you'd think he'd been having a few drinks. But he hadn't. So strange. He likes frequent little naps. Sometimes when he wakes he doesn't recognize where he is, and I have to calm him. Once he was positive he was in Bishkek, Kyrgyzstan. *Bishkek*! We argued about it. Finally I pretended he was right about our whereabouts, just to keep him placid. Yet other times he says his naps invigorate him, and then he pontificates for hours on end, shunning meals or drink. He can drive anyone to insanity with his constant diatribes and winded historical speeches. Especially when he cobbles together mixed passages from tripe like, *The Ideology of Marx*, *The Communist Manifesto*, crap like that. His favorite speech from the first Revolution was, '*How to Put an End to the Oppression by Landlords and Capitalists*'. Sometimes he'd go on blathering until it hurt my ears and I wanted to scream, *Fuck the Collective*!"

She shook her head sorrowfully. "But on other days he'd weep like a child. He'd bawl with dampened spirits, and beg me to console him. Tears ran down his cheeks. He'd confide he only did what he did because he had no choice. The rich, as in the old regime, were abusing decent folk, taking advantage, stealing the nation's oil and mineral wealth for personal profit. The downtrodden counted on him. Before their falling out, the little man with thick eyeglasses—"

"Will you please stop repeating 'the little man with thick eyeglasses'!" huffed Dimsky.

Ilya quickly apologized. "I meant to say, his friend egged him on continuously, especially at first. He said that was why he'd brought him back. I didn't know what he meant by that, but he presented Vladimir Ilyich with lots of cash, and he suggested places for suitable hideouts or recruiting eager allies. I guess that friend must be the one you keep referring to as the 'Andrei Popov' you need to find."

"We didn't say anything about 'needing' to find Andrei Popov,'" Alina Vera said, looking squarely at Ilya with narrowed eyes. "First you tell us you aren't sure who Andrei Popov is, who the man with the thick eyeglasses is; then maybe they are one and the same, you say. But then you tell us you're not sure where you met Andrei Popov, but add that the little man with thick eyeglasses personally directed Lenin's actions. Quite a few contradictions, Ilya Evgeny.

"What we wish to learn," Alina Vera went on calmly, fully enjoying her new role, "is if you know Dr. Mikhail Sunavich, and where he is. His whereabouts are important, and your help will go well for you with the judge."

"Wow." Anya Andropova sat with her chin on her fist, mesmerized as her manager's confession unfolded.

Ilya Evgeny stood immobile. Mascara smeared beneath her eyes. A vein pulsed in her neck. She blew her nose. "Popov, Sunavich, what does it matter what he was called? He's the man you're after, isn't he?" Her lower lip trembled. "This is crazy...No way to run a country..."

"Tell us about your sister, Irina, Alina Vera demanded, switching deftly to a multi-pronged attack. "What was her role in this little drama?"

"If you hope to save your skin and help your sibling, you'd better tell the truth now," added Dimsky.

Ilya sighed. She wiped her moist eyes, face drained of color. "It was her boyfriend's doing, that louse Gregori Nabokov. He's the one that drew Irina into this conspiracy. So suave, so charming, and such a damn rogue. He's the one who convinced me to follow suit."

"When did this happen? How long has Irina been helping him?"

"Months ago he convinced her, I'm not sure precisely when. But there was one particular man Irina told me often came to visit Gregori. He liked her, Irina said, he flirted, and she had the feeling that he'd happily screw Gregori behind his back if she showed mutual interest."

Vlad looked at Alina Vera. The scientist knew they were onto something. "Your sister was fond of him, too?"

"Oh no. She thought him...disgusting. Petty, always leering, a lecherous snot. But he's rich, and she did like that. She laughingly refers to him as her 'little hunchback of Notre Dame'. She'd plainly tease him, perhaps linger a moment too long, stand too close, and whet his appetite. You know..."

"Why lead him on if she didn't like him?"

"I told you, because he's wealthy. He paid well and on time for services. Once, while Gregori was bone weary and fell asleep during a chess game, the dirty little fellow made suggestions that she belongs in a place like Paris, London, or New York. He hinted that he might bring her there, buy her jewelry, expensive clothes, after things settled down. Irina is a born sucker for that. But she knew his game. He wanted to steal her from right under Nabokov's nose, I think. Not that I would give a damn, either way. I know what a venomous cheater and liar her *Gresha* is."

"This person of interest, he came to visit frequently?"

"Whenever he could. Clandestinely. Sneaking in and out at night, my sister confided. Puffed up in his coat, scarf, and hat he'd hop around like a frog. He loves chess, too, you see. They'd play for hours, sometimes one game lasting throughout the night. Can you imagine?"

"Was this 'little hunchback of Notre Dame' the same little man with the thick eyeglasses you referred to?" Alina Vera pressed.

"I never gave it any thought." She shrugged. "The frog could have been your Andrei Popov or Mikhail Sunavich for all I know. I just counted the cash Lenin received."

The tennis star stood. "Really? How much did they pay you for my capture?" Anya asked, recognizing the full extent of Ilya's duplicity, a gnawing knot eating away at her gut. The realization of her genuine motives made Anya sick.

"Answer the question," Dimsky snapped, in no mood for any machinations. "Don't dig yourself deeper into a hole you can't climb out of."

Ilya looked down, her shoulders drooping. Her face was spotting purple from Anya's punches, and a floodtide of misery creased her features. "Me?" she said woefully. "I gained nothing. Promises, only promises; I never received single ruble. They convinced me I'd be a wealthy woman when the work was completed. The plan was to buy a villa in Switzerland. Somewhere beautiful in the Alps, near a lake so they could waterski. Popov mentioned an intention to maybe open up a karaoke club with Gregori as his front man. Keeping customers happy, plying them with expensive booze while they sing silly songs. Then he'd dump Gregori when the time was right. Doesn't sound much like Socialism, does it?" She exulted. "Popov receives monies through a numbered Swiss bank account, I learned. Believe me, he's not the old, stodgy sod you might think. He has an itch, and his appetite won't be consummated until he can frolic alone with Irina."

"He'd throw Nabokov under the bus?"

"Without hesitation. The chess master's role would be finished. Popov freely spends these bankrolled funds, bribing pencil pushers, gaining the trust of honchos here in Moscow and other places, and instigating protracted turmoil he believes will eventually wear down the State. There is no shortage of libertines willing to sell their mothers."

Vlad and Alina Vera exchanged worried glances. It was troubling to digest the momentousness of what Ilya divulged. How high up in government circles might the treachery climb? Alina Vera drew her face close to Ilya's, hot breath causing Ilya to flinch. She imitated the way she'd seen it in detective films. "Let me be clear, it appears your role isn't innocuous at all. You admit being well acquainted with Popov after all. We've caught you awash in your web of lies. And Irina is in this game as deeply as you. Don't try denying it. There's nothing I'd enjoy more than watching you dragged from this room straight to prison, the kind of special, reserved accommodation few know exist."

Ilya felt herself at the bottom of a great abyss, enumerating the pitfalls awaiting her inquisitor's will.

"Back to basics. You freely admit to conspicuously leading Anya Andropova into a trap, orchestrating this getaway under the guise of sharing a brief holiday. And when time came to return to Moscow for her tournament, you made sure to be near the village of Gorki the moment Lenin's goons lay in wait. You knew full well Anya would never reach Moscow to play her match. You knew their intention was to kidnap her."

Ilya shook her head vehemently, relating in a low voice, "it wasn't supposed to end that way. I was devoted to Anya, and only learned the truth afterwards. It was Gregori's idea, his doing. He's the one who insisted I convince Anya to take this little trip, travelling to the countryside near my ancestral birthplace. I keep telling you, that slimeball Gregori Nabokov is not what he appears."

"How do you mean?" All eyes focused intently on Ilya.

"My sister did a little snooping of her own a while back. She accidently found information that startled her. Receipts. Peculiar notes, and scribbled instructions. Gregori Nabokov, she confided, has for many years been secretly on the payroll of a multinational conglomerate, collecting assorted classified information on their behalf. The information he provides they then use to bribe and blackmail, worming their way into the highest officialdom of the Kremlin. A ranking British Embassy deputy is also involved, I believe. I never learned his name."

"Which international corporation is responsible for these crimes?" Alina Vera demanded.

Ilya shut her eyes, fearful of repercussions even greater than she faced now. "They're powerful, these people. Ruthless in searching out those prepared to complement or enhance their efforts. And they'll run roughshod over anyone or anything in their way…"

"Tell us the name!"

"It's…the famous company known for theme parks across the world— Mouse Universe."

"*What?*" Cranking out her glut of information, Ilya now provided a shocking disclosure, unprecedented, as it was unbelievable.

"It's true, I tell you!" She wiped a mixture of tears and blood clotting over her puffy cheek. "These slippery people played Gregori like a fiddle. He's arrogant, filled with himself, and susceptible to all sorts of flattery. Inflated by an overblown ego, his ear is always to the ground looking for opportunities. Many view him as a smug playboy, a bon vivant living a lusty life, but that's largely a façade. His prominence and stature in the chess world affords him virtually unlimited access to conspicuous people in high places. These trained theme park operatives were eager to learn as much as possible regarding Russia's arrangements for its 25th Anniversary Jubilee, but for some reason they were especially interested in gathering knowledge concerning recent activities taking place at the Alexander Nevsky Chocolate Factory."

"Oh? Why would that interest them?" Alina Vera felt her heart skip a beat. The plot was growing more sinister and frightening.

"I don't know the answer, but they're unscrupulous. Apparently, Gregori was instructed to periodically pass them summarized documents, dossiers, and schematics he no doubt received from Andrei Popov, your harpsichord player. I believe they were highly interested in stealing some classified secrets concerning chocolate making."

"Chocolate making?" Alina Vera tried to act disinterested. "And Popov served as primary agent on their behalf? Are you certain of this, Ilya Evgeny?"

"I believe so. Gregori confided that this multinational corporation intends to utilize a highly guarded secret formula for their own special purpose, which they hid from me. I did overhear that each Mouse Universe theme park contains a secret labyrinth of tunnels beneath their compounds. An intertwined network of air-conditioned bunkers, stocked with supplies stretching for miles, chambers with computer servers, laboratories for scientific studies…"

"Absurd," goaded Dimsky, "Americans are quite adept at processing excellent chocolate. I eat it myself. What secrets could they steal from the Alexander Nevsky?"

"Try industrial espionage," said Vlad. "If Andrei Popov, aka Dr. Sunavich, transmitted secrets to Mouse Universe, it means he's been in collusion with them for a long time. Perhaps even from the very start." The implication was obvious; the famed conglomerate was planning its own duplication process for perfecting a life force based on Sunavich's formula, unleashing perfect replications upon the world. The web of intrigue was growing by leaps and bounds.

Alina Vera was about to probe the prisoner further when Colonel Dimsky's smartphone rang. The colonel moved off to the side and hastily put the phone to his ear. "*Da*, go on. What? *Nyet*, we didn't know." He listened for a few long moments, saying, "I'll inform our team immediately." He put the phone down, opened the door and signaled the security men outside. "Return this woman to her holding cell. She's to be kept in strictest isolation, understood? No contact until I say so." Head hung low, tightly containing her anger and hostility, security men took Ilya rigidly by her elbows and escorted her away. The colonel's face was ashen.

"What's wrong?" asked Vlad.

Dimsky shut the door and looked up toward the ceiling shaking his head. "Riot police have been called out tonight in Paris to quell street disturbances. A curfew has descended on Stockholm. All of Europe is strained to the breaking point. We're facing worldwide furor. There's going to be an emergency meeting of the United Nations Security Council. The insurrection is spreading."

"*Mother Volga*," Vlad mimicked softly.

17.

Diplomats in New York have claimed that the Security Council's image has been seriously tarnished due to its inaction over escalating calls for revolution inside the New Russian Federation…diplomats slammed the United Nations Security Council over its ineffective handling of the turmoil…The Council faces deep divisions among members prior to the meeting, and is the 15-nation body's first substantive action on Russia's months-old uprising.

Outside the famed United Nations diverse flags of the world's nations fluttered in multicolored splendor. It was a beautiful spring day in New York. The waters of the East River gleamed reflective sunlight so bright it hurt the eyes. Tourist buses en route to U.N. headquarters found themselves barred by police blockades and turned away down crowded side streets. The entire area surrounding the U.N. was cordoned off. Police helicopters circled. There were two demonstrations, the larger held directly across the street, well contained by police barricades keeping antagonistic protesters distanced from one another. A small group within this crowd repeatedly chanted in unison, "Long Live Lenin! Bring on the Revolution!"

Down the avenue a smaller group marched behind separate barricades in solemn procession. They held up anti-revolution banners decrying the 'Lenin Rebellion' as it was now universally dubbed. Stern members of the NYPD SWAT teams backed up by Federal Marshals, made certain the strained atmosphere remained under control. Clandestine FBI men took photographs and covert video. Passersby, businessmen, tourists, and office workers stopped and looked on with wonder. Once again, the disputes of Europe had reached the shores of the United States.

Within the austere halls of the hallowed United Nations, indeed within the honorable chamber of the Security Council itself, matters were taking a decidedly different turn. This special emergency meeting was hastily requested by Uruguay and Togo, nations deeply concerned about the crisis. On this morning the chamber was crammed; dozens of members of the press sat in attendance, representing countries of every continent. Live television was covering the extraordinary meeting. The cozy visitor's gallery was tightly squeezed with curi-

ous onlookers and invited guests, as well as many wishing to express support both for and against the mushrooming Lenin Rebellion.

The current presiding President of the Security Council, a wispy, dapper man from Nepal ordered the assembly into session. He markedly warned that no outbursts from the visitor's gallery would be tolerated under any circumstance during the discussion of a new draft resolution. Nor would any out-of-order discourse from representatives of member states be permitted. All Council rules were to be strictly obeyed. Everyone hushed as the first member was called to speak.

The British Ambassador, a former university lecturer best known for his thesis on jungle warfare during the 19th Century, coughed into his handkerchief as he brought his ruddy-complexioned face closer to the microphone. Several days earlier he had circulated a draft resolution including an embargo and sanctions against various officials. "Mr. President, as we have sadly witnessed, events emanating from within the New Russian Federation have begun taking an increasingly dangerous toll across Europe. We are viewing a bellicose debacle of immense proportion unfold. It appears that due to an inability to prevent extensive widespread anarchy, the government of the New Russian Federation has thereby permitted the situation to deteriorate. Thus, Mr. President, it behooves us today to canvas support for an alternative to put an end to this ridiculous nonsense. Therefore it is our obligation to request swift action be taken forthwith by the Security Council before events spin totally beyond control."

The Russian Deputy Ambassador grunted with displeasure at this direct slight, quickly stating, "Sir, my government strongly protests the British Ambassador's blatant attempt at interference in the internal affairs of my country. In no way shall the New Russian Federation agree to or tolerate—"

The president of the Security Council curtly cut him off with a bang of his gavel, putting his thumb on the scales in favor of the UK. "You will please wait your turn, Mr. Ambassador. I urge you not to interrupt again. There will be ample opportunity to respond in accordance with the Council's bylaws." There was a long flurry of murmuring among the many aides of different countries represented as these remarks were translated into numerous languages.

"Thank you, Mr. President," the British Ambassador went on self-righteously. "For some months now all of Europe, indeed, the whole world, has stood by and watched in silence as broad numbers of the Russian people have demonstrated their grievances in ever-growing numbers. Larger and larger demonstrations have in some cases turned violent, increasing in multitude and acrimony. His Majesty's Government calls upon the Security Council to exert its authority and immediately convene and appoint a fact-finding commission. We suggest this body fly to Moscow, where they shall confer with official government representatives, and also with independent members of the opposition. This will determine what will be required during this current hostile atmosphere. Of course we additionally request that the New Russian Federation fully respect the commission's independence and findings, whatever they may be, and wherever they may determine the fault lies. Also, we propose that this commission serve as an intermediary between the various warring parties to seek a fair and equitable solution to this dilemma. In the meantime, we urge that a United Nations policing force be directed at once to play a peacemaking role between the antagonists. The UK, as always, will be most willing to do its part to make sure a lasting peace will prevail."

The Deputy Russian Ambassador spluttered in disbelief. "What arrogance, Mr. President! Never shall my government permit foreign troops on its soil to interfere in our own political matters—"

"We only wish to assist in a helpful way, as we always do," responded the UK's Ambassador.

The French Ambassador picked up his hand and was recognized. "*Merci*, Mr. President. Surely the Russian Ambassador will admit that the situation in his country regarding this new 'Lenin Rebellion' has now spread far beyond Russia's own frontiers, and has systematically begun to infect neighboring nations. Mr. President, I name Belarus and Ukraine to be the first victims of this cross-border turbulence. *Oui*. Indeed we consider the situation perilous and deteriorating, becoming a dire threat to all. I must report that in cities and towns across France, in Paris, Lyon, Marseilles, there are ongoing demonstrations in sympathy with the spreading 'Lenin Rebellion' occurring almost on a daily basis. The French people also wish to play a major role in seeking a just peace agreement between pro-Lenin forces and Russia's government."

"I repeat," scolded the dismayed Russian, with the air of a maligned schoolboy, "my government alone is responsible for its internal affairs." He held up a dossier. "As a matter of fact, it's come to my government's attention that some inside the UK itself have willfully agitated the situation in my country. The music known as," and here he asked a colleague for an accurate English translation, "'*Bring on the Revolution*', has done great harm across Russia. It has provoked young people everywhere, and caused an upheaval in nearly every community. As proof of my accusation, Mr. President, I need only offer the name of the performers that have written and recorded this offensive tune; the 'Chocolate Lenin Band', invoking the name of the revolt's leader with accompanying music demanding revolution. We find this blatant arrogance on the part of the British radio and music television industry, permitted by their government. They earn huge royalties on the backs of these hooligan musicians, and insist on relentlessly playing this offensive music clandestinely over our airwaves, and the Internet. It subverts the susceptible, deepens the problem, and despite my government's plea to the UK to both censure and block this music, they promote its incessant air time." He pulled out another small folder and said, "I have here documentation, Mr. President, positive proof that a member of the United Kingdom's Ambassadorial staff to Moscow has been personally linked to subversive elements inside my country. This dossier shows beyond doubt that the Deputy British Ambassador himself bears responsibility in selecting the Chocolate Lenin band's name; a purposeful act of outrageous sabotage against the State. It saddens me to report that the subject in question cannot be arrested and placed on trial in my country because of his current diplomatic status. Be assured, however, that Sir Alistair Krumm was ordered to depart Russia immediately and returned to the UK. And I demand that once returned home Alistair Krumm be arrested as a co-conspirator in the Lenin rebellion. We retain signed confessions by several of his accomplices. The charges are straightforward, aiding and abetting violence and subversive overthrow of our elected government."

The din in the hall grew louder than before at the open affront of accusing one UN member state of subverting the integrity of another. Nonplussed, the Russian representative continued. "We've been able to track the source of these thousands of Internet videos, and almost every single website emanates from the UK. Many of them also pointedly personally insult Russia's Jubilee representative, Anya Andropova, with disparaging remarks as to her character and physical attributes. We consider this disrespect as an assault on all Russian womanhood, and we demand a public apology."

More murmurs erupted at the allegations.

"The UK is a land of freedoms, sir, unlike some. How dare you accuse a member of the British Government's ambassadorial delegation of such insidious acts? Ridiculous! For shame! Do you seriously expect anyone to believe that the mere name of a band and a song title are responsible for causing political unrest in your country? Come, come, my dear fellow, use some common sense. And in addition I remind you—"

"Common sense?" The Deputy Russian delegate's face darkened and his lower lip trembled with rising infuriation. He appeared virtually on the verge of apoplexy at the aspersion. "You are a nation free to subvert others with your long history of insidious economic colonialism! I accuse the UK also of inciting rancor and rivalry among the great powers so they will conflict with one another as they've successively done throughout modern history. Moscow demands London cease and desist its interfering behavior at once!" The scorn mounted, the air magnetically charged. Taunts and hisses abounded. Someone amid the visitor's gallery hurled an object through the air. Several ambassadors and deputies ducked as an egg splattered directly in front of the British Ambassador. His face and eyeglasses were showered with dripping yolk and egg white. Some watched in outraged shock while others put hands to their mouths to muffle laughter.

"Outrageous, Mr. President!"

Signs appeared, demanding rights for oppressed people everywhere, an end to societies divided by rich and poor, and an outburst of chants.

Then came the dreaded rebellious call to arms. *"Bring on the Revolution!"*

At that battle cry, a torrent of fresh invectives arose among the fifteen permanent and elected Security Council members. Angered envoys shook fists and hurled derision and slanderous mockery at one another. Many sought to settle old scores, long festering. Shoving matches and traded accusations ensued; it was conduct most unbecoming.

More eggs were summarily thrown, followed by a shower of shoes, belittling and insulting to all.

This caused conditions to degenerate into near pandemonium as numerous deputies and representatives of various nations broke into disdainful hoots and catcalls. Protestors mingling amid the press corps leapt to their feet and loudly shouted slogans and demands. Cameramen representing major worldwide networks were knocked over in the rush as agitators jumped from the visitor stands and towards the delegates.

"Long live the glorious revolution!"

"Anya Andropova is a slut!"

"Israel, out of the West Bank!"

More shoes rained down. The lights of the Security Council flickered, went on and off. Fearful cries ensued.

United Nations' police intervened swiftly, grappling with the heckling protestors and flinging them away impetuously, one by one. Badly outnumbered, they did their best amidst an unexpected torrent of verbal abuse and hostility. Cheers and ridicule echoed in unison across the prodigious and dignified chamber.

"Revolution forever! Down with warmongers!"

Who was on which side became ticklish to determine. The vainglorious and flatulent enshrined halls of the lauded United Nations quivered.

The American Ambassador rapidly conferred with a bevy of numbed aides. The din grew so boisterous it became all but impossible to hear instruction. The President of the Security Council banged his gavel again and again, entreating for composure. After a time a semblance of order was restored, the first egg thrower identified and roughly removed. The shoeless woman shrieked vulgar epithets without a letup while overtaxed guards dragged her away.

"The government of the New Russian Federation is urged to act at once to quell these demonstrations," the American Ambassador, Hetway Dingus, spoke into her microphone. "While my government does not agree with our French and British colleagues on an immediate need for a UN-sponsored commission or police action, we do request that the New Russian Federation remedy their internal situation—"

There was a loud splat. First came one banana, then a second, then a dozen oranges one by one, followed by carrots, heads of lettuce. Then banana bunches were flung from the spectator gallery. One knocked over the speaker's microphone. As if in a final indignation, a large milkshake rained over the council like an umbrella; spraying over suits, ties, shoes, baldheads and toupees alike, helter-skelter with no compassion for whomever it struck. An assortment of deputies and aides bobbed and dived, slithering and colliding as they completely fled the chamber in a careless effort to retreat from the ruckus.

The British Ambassador picked himself up from the floor, futilely wiping his smeared eyeglasses. "Things are quite out of hand," he observed. "I need a cup of tea."

***

"Our president was disbelievingly watching every minute of the commotion in New York," Boris said cheerlessly. "She was most displeased at the Security Council's repeated attacks directed at our country."

Vlad closed his laptop and contemplated his distressed colleague. The Jubilee would be a premier casualty among this unbelievable string of ominous events. "The latest headlines are atrocious," he said. "Worse, the European Union has issued severe back channel warnings demanding this rebellion be squashed and order restored. If not, they intend to announce a total boycott of the 25th Anniversary festivities en masse."

Dimsky's jaw drooped; he stopped mid-note on his balalaika. "Everyone blames us for their problems," he lamented.

Boris put a hand to his forehead. "Do you know how many billions have been spent on this worthless Jubilee? Treasure tossed down the drain. From the start it's been riddled with obstacles, coming apart at the seams, squandering enough money to buy a small country outright and anoint me king. We'll all be ruined. Milonov warned my next job would be in Siberia. I'm telling you now, if we don't act swiftly you'll be accompanying me."

"There were more European demonstrations today." Vlad dourly enumerated, "Copenhagen, Oslo, Athens. Thousands of students marching, demanding entitlements, and chanting the chorus of *Bring On the Revolution...*"

"Chairman Mao must be convulsing with laughter in his grave. Doubtless our president considers this derangement a pretext for her cabinet of cronies declaring emergency law," Boris said, heaving a resigned sigh. "I feel it in my bones. She's chomping at the bit. With a single edict she'll create a fait accompli to Sergei Milonov's ambitions. Our secret recordings of his contrivances are enough to keep him in indefinite purgatory, thrown into the worst Siberian hellhole imaginable. About him I couldn't care less, but I fear within weeks she'll also find cause to seize the Duma, and disband all political parties. Once she's got away with that, Stroganoff will shut down the judiciary. We'll have total governmental takeover conducted by her personal internal security forces. She'll have consummated power beyond her wildest ambitions. Russia will have undergone a bloodless coup d'etat, and the monarchy will reign."

"That's the end of *my* career," uttered Dimsky. He plucked notes from *Long Live the Revolution* with the enthusiasm of a convicted man awaiting the gallows. "And so much for Anya Andropova becoming Russia's national icon. Poor child. She'll be thrown out on her ear, lucky if she's allowed to peddle tennis shoes."

"No one will remain unscathed. It's the demise of all our careers," corrected a melancholy Vlad.

"Well, it was good while it lasted," ruminated Boris.

"Perhaps we're not quite done for," came a familiar voice.

They turned toward the open doorway. Alina Vera stood motionless beneath the doorframe. "I'm back from the lab—finally." She was fatigued, pallid and drawn, puffy dark bags under her eyes. She'd spent a virtual non-stop seventy-two hours working to exhaustion.

Slowly she walked to a cushioned seat, kicked off her shoes, collapsed and curled up. "The rabbi will be back soon," she said, her voice hoarse and husky. "He's been holding a last-minute video conference with Yuri Grushin. Omsk's team has carefully replicated Asher's latest formula. No one's positive; it still needs scrutinizing, but the matching DNA compound sequence is complete. I think Asher's on the verge of a molecular antidote."

Colonel Dimsky brought tea. "Molecule antidote," he repeated, "will the thing work?"

"Only the rabbi can answer that."

Boris grabbed his mobile and left the room.

Several hours went by. Alina Vera had fallen asleep, her first decent sleep in days. Vlad sat near her, lost in thought, hoping that if nothing else there'd be one more opportunity to spend time with his daughters before all hell broke loose. More than ever, the stupendous efforts of the past few years appeared wasted, creative ideas and energies pointless. The ladder of success had brought him to a woeful collapse at the hands of misfits and carnivorous pilferers, the sorriest of human specimens. The usual way of advancing a career in Moscow wasn't by impressing prospective employers, but by your connections. Russian society wasn't much interested in hard-working, smart young minds. Leaders amounted to a hodgepodge of bureaucrats feigning to regulate and supervise the country's welfare while in reality they were embroiled in personal ambition and ensuring well-lined pockets. A world comprised of stock market manipulators, blackmailers, unethical businessmen, and nefarious multinational corporations, all unleashed. One big hoax, a circus devoted to keeping the nation pacified while merrily screwing sober and steady working people. Hadn't Alina Vera warned him, told him he was naïve, to be careful, to realize he'd been dragged into something far over his head. Was it this bad everywhere? Not every government could be so self-serving, underhanded and unscrupulous, could they?

Time seemed never ending until Rabbi Asher Titlebaum finally arrived.

Dimsky and Boris hunched at the small table in Alina Vera's kitchen, playing stud poker. Several cigar butts sat smoldering in an oversized ashtray. Boris chomped on one. The doorbell rang, Dimsky jumped nervously from his seat. "At last," an awakened Alina Vera breathed with relief. Asher's broad frame blocked the entrance.

The weathered rabbi came into the flat. "I'm bone tired," he said. "And there's so little time..."

"Come and rest. You're exhausted." said Vlad.

Asher hadn't arrived alone. Inexplicably, Floyd Dingus stood meekly behind him. "You look surprised at seeing me here."

"Most surprised," muttered the colonel.

"It's all right, Colonel," said the rabbi, waving the wary military man off. "I requested Floyd attend." He placed his large hand in his pocket as he sat. The package his fingers sought lay crumpled and empty; there were no more grapes. Silent moments lingered heavily. Finally he mustered energy. "As Alina Vera has probably already explained, I've developed the solution, albeit a dangerous one. I dare not speak of it yet. Suffice to say, what I've accomplished may prove a twin-edged sword, and that reality weighs heavily on my conscience. I knew I couldn't share accountability for its potential, and I alone bear totality of its implications."

Hushed anticipation clung in the air. Boris put aside his cigar, sitting beside Vlad. "Importing someone new into our project at this late date is troubling, to say the least. You haven't explained your reasoning, Rabbi. I'm certainly disappointed."

Asher's eyes met Boris's evenly. Both realized that the trust painstakingly established between them stood to be irrevocably broken. "I only ask you to hear me out, Boris Sokolov. You need to understand the significance of this weapon. Its geopolitical ramifications are so immense that no single nation can be permitted a monopoly on its existence. Nor could I live with myself if I believed it might be put to use more than once."

"We don't even know what the hell you developed."

Asher remained resolute. "I will fully inform everyone now. Because of its awesome, terrible capacity, I need to ensure that the formula will be promptly destroyed after its singular use. You are all friends, and I've grown most fond of each of you. But there are times when a man must be guided by his conscience. Therefore, I recognized the necessity of looking beyond our team for assurances my wishes aren't defied. I admit acting without authorization, Boris Sokolov. Alina Vera played no part, nor anyone at Omsk, or anywhere else. Only I bear responsibility. If there is punishment to be meted out, I accept it. After much soul-searching I decided on a course of action, to contact our mutual friend, Floyd Dingus. I requested he accompany me for this meeting. I hope you'll understand and affirm my actions after I relate my reasoning."

"In that case, you might as well sit down," Vlad said to Floyd. "It appears you've become a full team member whether we like it or not." Floyd hesitated, glancing at Boris; the spymaster displayed no emotion. "You have a lot of explaining to do, Rabbi. It seems we have little choice. Go ahead, Floyd, make yourself comfortable."

Asher sighed with fatigue, wearisome of having to again explain, something he thought to be done with after resigning from the Academy. His throat was parched. Alina Vera brought him a glass of mineral water. He thanked her, leaned his head back and consumed almost all.

"Will you share your findings?" asked Vlad.

"I'm willing to share everything—but first you need to hear certain terms I've set. To alleviate my ethical and moral burden, and ensure total destruction of my formula after its use, I've enlisted Floyd's valuable help. The plan is simple enough; America's Undersecretary of State will shortly be notified and requested to come directly to Moscow. This official will be charged with a grave responsibility. It will be his obligation, in conjunction with Russian and international monitors, to ensure every scintilla of my formula and anti-molecular design are deleted forever. A courageous act of undisputed unilateral disarmament, with all trace of my work forever nullified. Meticulously erasing evidence of its terrible compound, the weapon's total destruction to be verified to everyone's satisfaction."

"Why are you entrusting this to an American?" demanded Dimsky. "Our own people can capably handle it."

"Because too many among our own people can't be trusted. The weapon's high-risk value to the unscrupulous is unlimited." The rabbi turned to Floyd. "Please explain our agreement," he said.

294

Floyd leaned forward, hands clasped. "I've given the rabbi my full assurance to comply. The most honest man in this whole world I'm acquainted with is America's Undersecretary of State. His word is his bond, his reputation flawless. I personally vouch for his total integrity, and I'd be willing to stake my life on it."

"What makes you so sure?" said an unconvinced Boris.

"Because this man is my twin brother, Elmer."

"He's *what?*" Jolted, Alina Vera sat up straight. She cleared cobwebs from her brain. "Your *brother* is the American Undersecretary of State? You said your brother is an active CIA operative."

"Oh. Sure, I said that. But then I was discussing my younger brother, Dexter. Don't worry about him. He knows how to take of himself. He's gone undercover, sent on special assignment somewhere in the Middle East. Frankly, I wouldn't put much trust in Dexter, either. He's crafty, I admit. But if you're discussing old Elmer, well, that's another story. He's beyond reproach. Elmer will do whatever the rabbi requires without reservation or hesitation. He's famously known for his integrity. You can read a neat biography about him on Wikipedia."

Boris grimaced like a man stricken with an unknown ailment. An American government official was being brought into their confidence, and formally requested to personally take custody of the most guarded, secretive formula ever developed.

"And the rest of your requirements?" asked Vlad, more eager to hear than troubled. He fully understood the awkward position in which Boris was placed, but he also knew Asher would never have proceeded without solid reasoning. His formula must be a terrible weapon indeed.

"As we know too well," the rabbi went on, "Lenin could be hiding anywhere; inside Russia, Europe, or far beyond. Since Ilya Evgeny's arrest I came to understand why our manhunt has strategically widened, making me all the more convinced we need to proceed with extreme caution."

Vlad said with a frown, "No doubt. Interpol's alerted, and there's a global dragnet underway. A huge reward has been placed on his head."

"Two hundred million New Rubles," said Boris. "Paid to any mercenary, government, or criminal enterprise that finds him or provides information leading to his capture. No questions asked. Paid in cash, dead or alive."

Dimsky whistled. "More money than the State Lottery."

Asher said haltingly, "Then we understand each other?"

Boris reluctantly nodded. "We do. But I caution you: if turning over scientific secrets to the Americans backfires any way whatsoever, believe me, you'll never see your beloved Esther again."

"I have befittingly considered all ramifications," Asher retorted with typical understatement.

Tension rose and Floyd tried to diffuse it. "Say, we're all still friends, aren't we? On the same team? Rabbi, can you explain how you finally concluded your formula?"

He took his time replying. "A few weeks back I had my initial flash. After finishing yet another dreary analysis of collected sperm, I had a stray thought, a glimmer of a hypothesis. It happened while listening to music. Utilizing sub-microscopic samples, with plenty of ejaculate samples on hand for study, I ran a series of alternate computer tests to discover what form of superbug could most rapidly break down particular DNA compounds." He shut his itchy inflamed eyes, searching pockets for his eye drops.

"My first task was to assault Lenin's immune system, outsmarting friendly microbes that out-compete invaders. I needed an ultra-resistant nemesis to overwhelm his body, a surgical innovation of blazing speed overpowering every defense. To a physicist the world is simple. There are universal laws governing any complicated phenomenon. To take down a house you smash it with wrecking ball. For me, I needed that wrecking ball to crumble his DNA…

"DNA is composed of four building blocks containing information for assembling every organism, from a blade of grass to a human being. Genes are segments of this DNA, located on chromosomes, containing specific instructions that make each one different. Every cell contains thousands of proteins to regulate function, accumulating like bricks, forming into columns, and giving the cells shape. Think of proteins like parts of a car engine, each handling specific tasks. Collectively this makes the entire system run efficiently. Human bodies are built like that, each cell playing its unique role."

Alina Vera couldn't hide her enthusiasm, eager for Vlad and everyone to hear. "Explain how falling asleep gave you the clues." She looked sideways, beaming.

Asher smiled inwardly. Like Boris, he'd noticed the increasing closeness between the attractive scientist and the cooperative public relations expert. For some time he was well aware of their growing mutual interest. Over the years he had seen Alina Vera change from an eager, vivacious young woman to a more mature one spiritlessly accepting her role in life with wistful cynicism, disappointed by lost opportunities. It made him sad to watch, and helpless to do anything. He also knew of Vlad's difficulties and sorrow, and felt unexpectedly heartened to see that these two different souls had out of the blue met and bonded. It pleased him to observe their budding relationship unfold, and prayed it would continue to flourish.

"I'll do my best to fill everyone in." The rabbi spoke without pride, but rather, as a man who'd made a frightening discovery and discussed it with great caution. "After a while my eyes were so tired I napped on the small sofa in my office. I felt a chill, realizing the temperature had been set artificially low to be certain the adjoining laboratory maintained its cool climate. I slightly adjusted the thermostat, snoozing for an hour. When I awoke and resumed work I noticed one untouched genetic sample had mutated, severely deteriorating. I examined it with curiosity. Something within the environment was susceptible; the slight alteration in room temperature chipped away its cellular structure, diminishing it, shrinking it surprisingly fast. I retested my finding, raising the thermostat half a degree, Celsius. It became obvious the sperm strain was vulnerable, heat responsible for modifying the subatomic organism's structure. Something clicked. I ran rigorous tests using computer models of protein structure and function. I found increasing heat modified entire molecular systems in odd ways, releasing a contamination absorbed into our prototype's bloodstream, injuring blood vessels throughout the body. Were these the effects of my desired superbug?" He smiled. The question was rhetorical.

"Blood supply chains can be impossibly muddled to untangle. If we'd been dealing with common tomatoes, cucumbers or lettuce, I might have fathomed it more quickly. But rum infused with a chocolate molecular base structure? Well, you see my point. Still, there was but one conclusion to draw; heat allowed my formula to expiate contamination into Lenin's otherwise healthy cells. A severe destruction."

"You've discovered Sunavich's blueprint, haven't you?" said Vlad.

"I believe I have." His tone left no doubt, and no one spoke.

"The machinery within the nucleus of a cell reads its genes, and produces peerless molecular messages. The end result, I discovered, was that the sperm's chocolate molecular cellular structure collapsed, dispersing, disintegrating, and dematerializing before my eyes."

Morale was quickly rising. Vlad heaved a sigh of relief.

"But I realized the necessity to employ another compound to further accelerate the process," the rabbi continued. "A spiraling biological agent to cause widespread disease to its host, to destroy the organism at super-accelerated speeds, instantaneously annihilating it, not a slow corruption. How, though, to override an entire immune system response? What pathogens could I create? I speculated employing carefully screened cultured samples. It posed a severe test. And then I hit upon it: Molecular mimicry. To bypass the immune defense system fortifying the body I duplicated and reduplicated until I found a way to ransack safeguarding molecules and substitute them with catastrophic ones. Once secured, my molecules would take command and fill the gap, beginning rapid, unstoppable annihilation. Still, I faced a crisis."

"What crisis?" Dimsky said. "The quicker it's dispatched, the better."

Alina Vera sighed. "Colonel, the rabbi's not concerned for Lenin, but for his discovery's deadly potential. A possibility of contagion by molecular mimicry is great, and its unknown consequences even greater if our work isn't rigidly controlled. It could run rabidly."

"Collateral damage," said Vlad knowingly.

"Precisely. Picture a densely populated swarming anthill," said the rabbi. "We wish to identify and destroy a single poisonous entity among millions of healthy ants. How to exterminate our target, without this lethal weapon potentially annihilating everything else? We mustn't risk harming innocent life. As scientists we're obligated to protect not merely human life but all living organisms. Disease control agencies would condemn us outright if they had an inkling of what we're up to."

"Chocolate molecular mimicry's usability remains mysterious until activated," Alina Vera added dolefully. "I shudder to imagine repercussions if we fail. But we're working under a severe time constraint. Fear of causing epidemics or new disease is a concern—and rightly so."

Boris rolled his cigar round and round between his fingers. "I hate to interrupt with mundane matters, but do you have any idea of the intense international pressure we're under? Warned, threatened with sanctions, denied promised funding. Bankers have tightened every screw. From Wall Street to Hong Kong jittery stock exchanges are plummeting, and speculators are having a field day. Even Russia's considerable oil reserves won't be enough to bail us out. They say this panic is due to our failure in dealing with this political upheaval. Until there's stability the World Bank will keep frothing, scapegoating, and making grotesque accusations. They want to humiliate and emasculate us."

"The ruble's value is sinking fast. Soon it'll be as worthless as stale bread," offered Vlad. "Creditors are demanding cash payments, rejecting government-backed bonds. Our credit rating was drastically lowered to barely above junk status, and our own major corporations are turning against us. Soon financial institutions will face insolvency. This frenzy's gone viral. The greater the calamity, the greater the hazard we're on the precipice of collapse. Ruined. We've hit rock bottom."

Dimsky said with a pinched face, "Squeezed by the balls."

Boris groaned and slapped his forehead. "It's a herd mentality. We're drowning. This is a tidal wave, and we're at the point of no return. The rabbi's right. The president has reason enough already to declare martial law. Do you see the insanity? I recognize the barbed implications of this super weapon, and the necessity for supreme caution. But our clock's winding down."

"We're clobbered," Vlad concurred, personified by his long face. "Bashed by a mélange of a rabble-rousing soap-box orator created by a psychotic scientist, abetted by a traitorous chess master, and a paranoid tennis coach." He laughed bitterly. "Our president is salivating to be crowned Czarina, our vainglorious prime minister is slobbering over dreams of dictatorial power. Not to mention huge angry crowds marching to a battle-cry rock 'n roll song!"

Vexed, Alina Vera said, "Add to this shit pile, repugnant public servants falling over to align with thieving multinational corporations. What's not to understand? The world's lined up against us. If we botch this chance Russia will be done for." Glumly she summated, "And so will we."

"Don't forget the sleazebag rapscallions from Mouse Universe," reminded Dimsky.

"You're sure caught between a rock and a hard place," Floyd said sympathetically, understanding now how horribly awry matters had turned. "If your weapon is successfully fired, Rabbi, what happens?"

"My good man, it's obvious. Lenin will *melt*! Reduced to atoms. The crisis will subside, and life shall at last return to normal."

"So you *are* ready to use it," said Boris, in strikingly stark language, remaining dubious of foreign involvement.

"We have no choice. All remaining to accomplish, as Alina Vera knows, was recalibrating traditional parameters for devising an historical gateway for our nimble delivery system to pinpoint and demolish its target. We achieved it a few days ago. Surreptitious and sneaky, but quite effective. I was listening to music because it helps me concentrate, especially when my back is bothering me. Mostly I enjoy classical music, however, while running rudimentary tests I found myself listening to balalaika melodies, which I've become addicted to. You're quite talented, Colonel. I'd venture to speculate that when you retire you could be a gifted musician. So you see, in a roundabout way it was Dimsky who furnished the original spark." His tired eyes glimmered. "Alina Vera and I downloaded several discs of popular, vintage balalaika folk tunes, like our colonel entertains us with. On a thought, I used a powerful music program to integrate harmonic vibrations of the instrument's strings.

"Matter vibrates at different speeds, you see, and if high and powerful enough, vibrations begin turning molecules into atoms, atoms to particles, and particles to sheer energy. Developing a simple computer music program I configured a random test concurrently combining multiple frequencies of musical expression. I based my program on various forms of the balalaika. First I vibrated the pitch of a prima balalaika. Faster and faster, scrutinizing vibration until it oscillated abnormally beyond the pitch of human hearing, but not beyond canine hearing. Next I utilized the simulated strings of the sekunda balalaika, following the same rigid regimen, mapping subatomic connections. Again I increased vibration and tonal speeds beyond natural frequencies." He sketched out his preliminary code on a notepad Alina Vera provided, drawing rapid calculations.

Dimsky beamed at the idea of his beloved instrument being responsible for such an important role.

Asher's face brightened. "The amplitude of vibration is directly proportional to the amplitude of its force. Thus by doubling the force, the vibration increases commensurably. For additional harmonies I included a bass balalaika's composition, followed by an alto motional timbre, and then a contrabass. My research created a version using average values with octaves sounding homogeneously. Every eighth note was held for an identical time, each quarter note twice the length of an eighth note.

"Thus, the springs I'd loaded were ready to let loose. I held my breath and my ears. I mixed and turned up the pace. The acceleration unleashed was inconceivable; it left both Alina Vera and me overcome. We were thunderstruck, realizing it towered far beyond any known musical program's abilities. Next,

I simplified and fine-tuned, painstakingly calculating the system's thrashing mass. The whole system would vibrate when set in motion by an initial disturbance—and I assure you my aforementioned computerized balalaika strings created quite an initial disturbance! My ears still hurt and haven't stopped ringing.

"Alina Vera first noticed the fevered pitch had unexpected effects on chocolate molecules within Lenin's singular cellular structure. I made accommodation for accelerated putrefaction. We were almost there, excited but frightened. For good measure I removed tonal equivalents from a rare piccolo balalaika. When I ran the test the resonance of these delayed waves flew off the measurement scale. With additional adjustments, I set the pulsing beat higher, splitting its fragmentations.

"I gave my earplugs to Alina Vera, and put cotton in my ears. Hesitantly I pressed the button. The ensuing surge was shocking and painful. Molecule mimicry had not only worked, it worked with a vengeance! I lost my balance, and we both were knocked to the ground by its initial burst. I ached so badly I feared I wouldn't be able to stand. Alina Vera leant a hand, and painfully gaining back our senses we managed to stagger from the lab, disoriented, realizing such incredible efficacy endangered our very lives."

"Poor Asher's eyebrows were standing on end from magnetic field effects," said Alina Vera.

Asher nodded. "It's true. After a time we regained our composure. We forged ahead from my annexed lab, patching programs into our computers, reworking finalized calculations by hand on a chalkboard. I was concerned with immunity defense mechanisms within Lenin's sperm cells, mechanisms that specifically recognize and disable intracellular pathogens. When I remixed continuous rhythms at immeasurable speed, integrating them into my supra heated-protein molecule mimicry structure, the results were virtually instantaneous and astounding.

"Its bloodstream's chocolate-infused molecules deteriorated at super-acceleration, hammering, crushing colliding cell structures. Distending their physical and chemical properties, such as boiling and melting points to the limit, whether soluble in water or acid. In short, a domino effect spread across the entire subatomic architecture of our sperm sample in nanoseconds. With barely further effort the existing repertoire of the cells instantaneously decomposed, imploded before our disbelieving eyes. The evolutionarily, innate immune system and its antibodies were helpless against our pathogen-derived mimicry attack. Helpless! With so much dramatic elation, I hardly noticed my trembling hands and my middle ear dizziness. I was woozy and groggy, feeling as though my eyes were popping from their sockets. We were dazed, engulfed by what we'd done. What terrible energy force had we unleashed?

"Again, after regaining composure, I held my breath while Alina Vera ran further test models, fielding a huge diversity of immune recognition molecules, adjusting for variation. To my delight, each and every test subsumed identical effects. Piccolo string tone sustained a last necessary touch required for subatomic acceleration. There was no doubt; the theoretical model was perfect. With Alina Vera working diligently at my side, we'd finally discovered the weapon capable of stopping Dr. Sunavich's creation. Needless to say, without having enjoyed Dimsky's balalaika, this super-heated accelerator might never have reached fruition." He paused, as elated as he was weary.

A small, satisfied smile crossed the colonel's face. "The executioner has lifted his axe," he intoned.

Boris stood to his feet, applauding loudly. "Rabbi, you're a bloody genius!"

"Kudos to you, too, Colonel," said Vlad. Dimsky looked down with bashful discomfort.

"It's damned magnificent!" raved Alina Vera. "We've perfected our weapon, developed its neutralizer and antidote together." Realization dawned that ending the threat of revolution was no longer a mere dream.

"Yes, we've developed our neutralizer," resumed the rabbi. "However, it's imperative we remain cognizant of the ancillary consequences our weapon is capable of inflicting. As to potential side effects induced by chaotic particle colliding we can only speculate. But the endgame is in sight; time itself has become our greatest foe. Our modus operandi is enabled, and we have but one single opportunity to use it. Only a small window remains available."

"What method delivers the super-heated accelerator?" asked Vlad. "Striking without inflicting tremendous collateral damage? Have you devised a super refined laser beam?"

"Not a laser at all. I prefer to think of it as an accomplishment on a scale formerly unimaginable. A challenging breakthrough, nearly beyond mortal capabilities, meticulously engineered with Alina Vera's invaluable, insightful assistance. Allow me to unveil it for you. Today we are unleashing the era of the Molecular Chocolate Bomb."

18.

After youths ripped up paving stones and set trash bins on fire, police fired tear gas at those hurling rocks near the State Duma in an effort to quell anger. It was a dramatic, confusing day unleashed by threats of a general strike as Russia's parliament debated increasing unrest and menace of rebellious confrontations. Some residents have built makeshift barricades of everything from streetlights to cinderblocks and old tires. Traffic is snarled throughout the capital...

"If we actually manage to survive this thing what are your plans?" asked Vlad.

"Assuming we're not dragged from bed at midnight, arrested and shot, I'm resigning my position from the Academy retroactively. I'm fed up. I've had enough, more than enough."

He eyed her with interest. "Disillusionment is widespread. I've been thinking like you. I finally had my long overdue conversation with Raisa today. She plans to go ahead with the divorce, and to my surprise I didn't try to sway her. She's agreed to let me visit my girls as frequently as I want without legal haggling. She also says she'd like our relationship to remain cordial. That's good. Less emotional trauma is better for everyone. These past few months have changed my outlook dramatically. You warned me, but I suppose I didn't understand until now. You were right all along, but my ego wouldn't allow me to see it. This glorified directorship job became altogether contrary than what I thought I signed up for. Now I realize it nearly destroyed my life."

"So you're quitting your esteemed post, Mr. Director of Public Relations?" She sat swinging her leg like a little girl.

"I'm fed up sucking up to buffoons like Moscow's playboy mayor, and his host of subservient flunkies. I couldn't care less what repackaging finally happens with the Jubilee. I was a dreamy-eyed idealist, believing I had something to offer. I would invigorate the State's stale, outmoded media apparatus. But hindsight is useless, and now my opportunities for PR work will be reduced to writing fortune cookie proverbs."

"You *did* have something to offer—but you got caught up in the worst of everything; the new ruling class behaving no different than the progeny of the old. It's a pity you ever got dragged into this mess. What will you do next?"

He smiled as if remembering something warm and comforting. "I've been waiting for the right moment to tell you. I've asked Rabbi Titlebaum to consider accepting me as a pupil. You've heard him discuss the realms of the Zohar?"

"I have; he adores alluding to it. I've been reading up myself on explanations of the *Tree of Life*, depicting a map of Creation...They say it's the process by which the Universe came into being." she recited. "Kabbalah, mystical secrets of the Jewish Torah, clarifying the origins and structure of the universe. Ultimate wisdom, studied since medieval times, yet contemporary scholars constantly find new symbolic influences. It's remarkable, with a thousand years of influence, commentaries, and interpretations from great worldly thinkers. Vova, I think it's a delightful idea and opportunity. I hope Asher agrees, because I know you'll soak up every moment. I envy you."

He smiled and took hold of her hand. "The rabbi is a gifted man. If his teaching abilities are a fraction of his scientific skills, I'll be learning from one of the finest minds in the world." He beamed with the idea, unable to conceal his excitement. "But how about you, Dr. Galina? If you quit the Academy, then what...? You adore science, it's your life."

Alina Vera gracefully walked across the parlor of her flat. She pushed the silken curtains aside and peered from the window. Streetlights of Moscow glittered. It was a warm humid night, couples strolling crowded boulevards. Traffic typically snarled, snaking along the city's expanding ring road. Everything seemed unnaturally normal. Of Moscow's fifteen million citizens did any have an inkling of the drama about to unfold, she wondered? Should the full-blown power of the Chocolate Bomb malfunction there would be no second chance. She wasn't concerned for her own wellbeing; she was beyond that. Rather, she felt burdened for the millions who might innocently suffer because science had played its eternal, irresponsible game of attempting to play God. Because a lunatic in a laboratory trivialized the potentially disastrous consequences of his feckless actions, and by so doing unleashed a chain reaction no one could have ever imagined. Failure was not an option; the Chocolate Bomb was ready, qualified, equipped and set. Win or lose nothing would ever be the same. If it didn't work, Russia would soon return to its warring, feudal past, governed by absolute monarchs or worse, a dictatorship reminiscent of Stalinist terrors.

If the bomb failed and in the end Lenin's revolution succeeded, the likes of Ilya Evgeny at one end of the spectrum and Olga Orlovskya at the other might be redeemed after all. Released from shackles, they'd be universally hailed as revolutionary heroes, perhaps even sharing the limelight alongside Lenin himself.

Alina Vera's personal belief was the president would convincingly prevail in her power struggle against Sergei Milonov with a series of quick, bold strokes. One way or another Milonov was finished, no matter how hard he tried to squirm out of it, and that was a good thing. On the other side of the ledger, within weeks the nation might be crowning a new Czarina on the Russian throne. The radical Stroganoffs would wield iron-fisted power, recast, and bit by bit subjugate the nation. Russia would regress, relinquish its newly found freedoms and be thrown back a century or more. Alina Vera groaned with disgust; she loathed politics and politicians more than ever.

Rebounding from morbid thoughts, she said, "Do you know what I'm thinking, Vova? I'm going to get a dog, a poodle. I've always liked poodles. They're a smart breed and you don't have to worry about allergies."

"I like that. I love dogs, too."

She smiled inwardly; she knew he'd feel that way.

"I was never allowed to have one," he said. "My parents were very strict. A dog wasn't permitted."

"That's a shame. I had a German Shepherd when I was little. I named him Trotsky." She smiled her charming smile. "Trotsky and I would wander the forest during summer, and I'd take him ice skating during winter. It was such fun watching him slide on ice while I glided. My parents had a dacha. I don't know if I told you about it."

"I remember you saying he was a policeman."

"A police magistrate," she corrected. "I'm flattered you recall."

"I remember everything you've ever told me. I have a confession to make; I badly misjudged you when we first met. I thought you were cold and calculating. Maybe even a bit ruthless."

"Oh?" She lit one of her American cigarettes, making herself comfortable in a plush chair. "Well, if this is confession time, I admit misjudging you, too. For the life of me I couldn't fathom why Boris wanted a public relations man for the team. But I suppose I'm also guilty of underestimating Boris Sokolov. It didn't seem you had any business getting involved. For a while I was sure you

305

were a cover for Internal Security's Secret Police, possibly even a mole working for Milonov's enforcement henchmen."

Vlad grimaced at the nauseating thought. "I never liked Milonov, and now I've come to despise him. I'm grateful Boris and Dimsky had foresight in having Tinkerbelle bug his office." He tried repressing laughter.

Alina Vera giggled girlishly, also breaking into a bout of unrestrained gratification. Their laughter grew louder, and soon neither could contain themselves. "God bless our colonel," said Vlad, wiping his eyes. "He's a good man."

"Quite a character, our Dimsky. I could tell you more Dimsky stories than you could handle." She added, "He's a man on the move, and also my uncle."

"Dimsky is your uncle?"

She shrugged as she looked at him. "Remember the day we strolled in the park and I told you about my very elderly uncle who'd lived in the Red Marshall's residence, upholding his legacy? Well, Dimsky is his sister's grandson. Technically he's a cousin I guess, but because of the large age difference I've always thought of him as an uncle."

Vlad took off his glasses and pinched the bridge of his nose. There was no end to the surprises unearthed.

"Well, I was being fully honest when I told you my family was influential," she admonished. "I hope you won't hold it against me."

"Of course not, but it's nothing compared to my own modest upbringing, the son of two ordinary school teachers. No spies in the family, no intrigues, no ranking army deserters. Nothing dramatic at all. But I do have one wish; that you and I had met a long time ago."

She snubbed out her cigarette. Their eyes locked. "I wish that also, Vova. I wish it with all my heart. We'd both have saved ourselves a lot of grief." She sat quietly, lost in thought, and for a time they didn't talk.

"I'd better get going," he said at length. "I received a text from my girls, and I promised to telephone Katya and Aleksandra this evening before they go to bed."

"Stay just a minute longer. There are still troubling things I can't get out of my mind. To be honest, I've come to rely on you, Vladimir Petrovsky. Me, of all people! Remember, I'm the one who told you never to trust anyone."

"I remember that very well." He smiled impishly.

"It looks like I didn't heed my own advice. It's still hard for me to admit, but I've come to trust you completely. You're instincts proved better than mine.

Those purported 'accidents', I can't put them aside, or explain them away. They grate at me like low-grade fever. Who do you think really tried to run me down in Omsk? And the day when we left the park? Was it Milonov's people? Nabokov could easily have been paid to do the dirty work...Possibly Sunavich himself?"

Vlad mulled it over carefully. It had been troubling him greatly. "We may never know for certain, but I'd wager it was on Rimsky-Kimsky's instruction, or some other collaborator connected to the original scientific team. By the way, I've heard rumors that Rimsky-Kimsky's been singing like a bird to his jailers. Maybe Big Duck's security men tortured it out of him, because an odd assortment of people have rashly been arrested in recent days, queued up while cramming onto flights, trying to flee the country. This time even bribes didn't work. There's a major purge underfoot to cleanse the system..."

"Thank heaven for waterboarding."

"As best as I can put the pieces together, President Stroganoff was determined to have us fail, no matter at what cost. As a researcher working first closely with Sunavich, then also with the rabbi, your interaction made you a key component, a crucial one. Your tie-in stretches all the way from the Academy to the Alexander Nevsky. Scaring you provided an easy way to dislodge any perceived threat, while sending a warning to the whole scientific community. Meanwhile, Rimsky-Kimsky served a perfect contingency by monitoring all our handiwork for the president's eye. With his unknown assistance she always knew exactly how far we'd come every step of the way."

Alina Vera listened and nodded. Vlad untangled it well; his interpretation made sense. Who better than a scientific colleague to betray them yet again? "And what about Sunavich? He's still on the loose and dangerous."

"Oh, that little man with thick eyeglasses is out of luck," Vlad said derisively. "You can put money on it. Irina Evgeny's 'little hunchback of Notre Dame' had his day; the anarchy he introduced is finished. And I believe even had his Lenin creation taken power, Sunavich would be shunted aside by some desperado Stalin-like dictator waiting in the wings. Our mad doctor would find himself a palace stooge, too dangerous to be allowed freedom, let alone given a laboratory. They'll lock him away. But even if he managed to elude whoever came out on top, he'd still be hunted down like a dog for the rest of his life. Let's just pray the Chocolate Bomb does its job."

"It will," she said quietly.

"You have that much faith?"

"I do, Vova."

He stood beside her at the window, placing his arm around her shoulders. "Whatever happens, Verochka, you haven't seen the last of me. I'll be at your side. We're still a team."

"And you haven't seen the last of me, either." They regarded each other with longing eyes. She moved closer, embracing him, raising her face and kissing him on the lips. Her fingertips gently stroked the side of his face. "When you feel ready, Vova," she whispered. "When you've made your peace with your daughters and your own heart, wherever I am I vow you'll find me waiting."

19.

The first forewarning of meltdown began in Paris.

Along the prestigious Champs-Elysees where rents run as high as more than a million Euros annually, the band of twenty-something young caterers pranced, strutted and danced among the luxurious shops on their way to the banquet hall. It was exciting to be playing an important part in such an expensive and grandiose wedding reception. Two of the young men clenched silver trays above their heads. Upon each tray stood a large white chocolate mousse especially prepared for serving immediately after the reception's sumptuous dinner. Behind them three more catering assistants carried buckets with chilled bottles of the finest champagne. Onlookers watched with bemusement and joy at the enjoyment the young men seemed to take in their work. What a wonderful wedding it was to be. The blond young man with the silver tray stumbled along the sidewalk. "Be careful Pierre!" one of the friends admonished. "Have you any idea how much this chocolate mousse is worth? Half the art in the Louvre!" They all laughed.

No one noticed the faintest hum of vibrations satiating the air. A svelte, well-tailored woman of a certain age wearing black high heels and an oversized black hat was walking her dog near the Café des Beaux Arts. She felt the sudden tug of the leash. Her white bull terrier began barking loudly.

"Hush, Maxim! Don't scare the nice young men!"

"You have a beautiful bitch, madam," one of apprentices said, "How old is she?"

The dog pulled to break free, snarling and snapping. The young man recoiled in surprise and bewilderment shared by the dog's owner.

"Maxim, what's come over you, *cher*? Be sweet to the nice young man. He just wants to be your friend. Remember Uncle Alain and all the nice lunches he fed you? My new friend Uncle Bruno has a new tasty one for you today." Maxim paid no heed; he snarled again, beginning to foam at the sides of mouth. "Stop it now!"

"Your animal's behavior is most peculiar, madam," snorted the second apprentice, snubbing the blushing woman and her vain attempts at apology.

She stamped her foot and wagged a finger. "Now look what you made me do, Maxim! I broke a heel, you little..." The woman could only stand there shaking her head. Never had her dog reacted in such a manner. Meanwhile, Maxim continued barking. With a leap he broke free and fled across the busy street, dodging pedestrians and people alike.

"Maxim, come back before you get killed!"

Simultaneously overhead a flock of birds scurried in unison across the sky. One of the catering youths felt a biting shiver of cold air. "The wind's picking up, I'm chilly. Let's hurry."

Amid honking horns Maxim ran zigzag while his owner remained motionless.

No one noticed that the full-bodied red raspberries atop the white chocolate mousse had begun to alter in color. A faint trace of dew hung in the air, barely detected that evening. The mousse shimmered in dimming light. Its carefully blended recipe of egg yolks, whipped cream, gelatin, quality white chocolate, confectioner's sugar and liqueur of cognac began to melt, at first soggy, then running down in streams onto the tray and forming pools. It wasn't until the thick liquid drizzled over the fingers of the younger of the tray carriers that they became alarmed. "What's the matter with this mousse? It's dripping all over me." One by one drops splattered on his expensive polished shoes.

"What did you do, Maurice?"

"What the hell's the matter with you?" he shot back. "I didn't do anything. Look at Pierre's tray."

"Mine is melting, too," cried Pierre, aghast.

The ruined, sinking mousse arrived through the back corridor of the opulent, aristocratic banquet hall filled with lavish displays of conspicuous consumption. Meanwhile, several hundred genteel guests gathered across the Italian-marbled floor. They were Parisian haute bourgeoisie; the gentlemen wore notched and classic tuxedos, while, dripping with diamonds and pearls, the ladies attired in low silken dresses and artfully draped bustier gowns with long flowing skirts. Two by two they passed through the cream-colored marble doorways of the unsurpassed ambience of the great lyceum. The haughty, tony mother of the glowing bride, a woman with the expensive curator look of a Mayfair matron, stood proudly in her dress of white satin, the bodice, cut low and square, embroidered with small musical instruments and scales. Bon vivant family members walked alongside in flowing silks and tulle, fabrics whipped into flattering, slender-waist silhouettes covered with shimmering sequins. They gathered like buzzing bees, heaping compliments, awed by the resplendent bash, preening and posing for photographs certain to be leaked to the press.

After delicious rich and creamy *pate de foie gras* and *cuisses de grenouilles*, and warmed goats cheese with sweetbread and roasted figs, the social shakers and celebrities were treated to dessert. Surrounded by carts of apple tarts, boozy strawberry soup, meringue with a custard sauce, and custard topped with caramel, an extra large four-tier chocolate fountain was placed in the center of an adjoining elaborately catered salon. The tiers of the fountain rose grandly over a heated basin at the fountain's bottom. The chocolate was melted in the basin then pulled up through the augur and continually flowed over the tiers. Enthralled guests gathered around the fountain, dishes of ice cream and cake in hand, expecting to dip confection into the deliciously warm, melted chocolate. Crystal wineglasses filled with champagne clinked musically amidst gaiety and resounding laughter. Ladies showed off bedazzling jewelry with debonair flourishes.

To everyone's dismay, chocolate began to pour from spouts, bubbling, dripping off the fountain's bowl. A pernicious gurgling noise ensued, a retching intonation, sinister and sickly. Dumbfounded guests shuddered.

With a grievous burst the fountain spewed, showering a fusillade of chocolate liquid containing vegetable fat, splattering hither and yon. The fashionable guests, luminaries from the world of music, literature, and the arts, jerked backward. The fountain rumbled, quivered, and shook.

"Claude, what's happening?" a distinguished, well-heeled book publisher from Montparnasse reproached the stunned host, his mandarin-collar tuxedo shirt sprayed with mottled, proliferating stains.

An invited impish fashion designer of Marais stared dumbstruck by the spectacle. A naughty Italian film ingénue stood rooted, licking fingers while her soccer-hero husband wiped his stippled face with the back of his hand. "I told you not to pick your nose in public!" she hissed, hooped earrings flopping.

Oozing machinery at the fountain's base whirred, clanking and gumming up as pulpy chocolate climbed faster up through the augur. Dulcet chocolate surged through skewers, shooting into the air, exploding like water balloons. Splotches of fluidic, brown substance swatted anxious faces, ruined hairdos, exquisite dresses, and monogrammed gentleman's attire alike. Unbridled, it sprayed, spitting minuscule chocolate pellets bursting like hand grenades.

Across the gleaming floor it cascaded, forming sticky coagulating pools. Some guests slipped, others toppled, yet others careening and dancing to maintain balance. Afflicting the slender and beer-bellied alike, those that were able fled, nuptials be damned, howling gross profanities in a less than refined manner.

The bouffant-haired photographer had his pricy unpaid-for 60-megapixel 40 x 54 mm sensor camera knocked out of his hands. A snorting baron, trying to avoid tripping in his platform shoes, made an unparalleled dash to take his leave. The enchanting occasion now gave way to a rebirth of speed sprinting worthy of an Olympic tryout.

Likewise, the hired crooners and comedians on the small stage observed in trepidation the decaying cinematic free for all. Musicians made a radical change in musical direction, hastily throwing instruments back into their cases, trolling for direction to the exits. The party became a premier showcase for human ability to flee danger at accelerated speeds.

Mists of deviant, thin fog rolled in waves. Along Paris' charming *arrondissements* the first of the crashing chocolate smashed through the decorated windows of a Saint-Germain confectionary. Buckets of sodden mass gurgled and poured over walls, onto pavements and into gutters. Taxis, motorcars, and lorries hit their brakes and skidded, tires sloshing amid slippery sludge. It quickly spread to Neuilly, Boulogne, Saint Cloud, Versailles, and all Paris suburbs.

"Mother Volga!" exclaimed Dimsky, eyes bulging, watching a live broadcast on the widescreen television. "Super High Def. is so graphic!"

Asher covered his forehead with his hand. The television showcased a pristine village in the Alps inundated by a broad stream of flowing viscous chocolate. It resembled lava from a volcano infringing steadily down toward the Village Square. The British-accented televised voiceover spoke with typical understatement.

"Such scenes as these are being reported in an ever-growing list of cities and towns over the world. London, Oslo, Madrid. Several chocolate factories in Switzerland have reported severe equipment breakdowns as a gelatinous coconut cream-melted-sludge pile has jammed gears and rollers. Entire operations have been temporarily shut. Unusual atmospheric pressure changes are being documented, noteworthy clouds of fogs and mists reducing visibility. Complaints of unaccountable, so-called 'vibrations' are now reported within the substratosphere by weather observatories ranging from the Sahara to Antarctica. Intermittent mobile telephone outages are accumulating, cell towers in all probability affected by these uncustomary 'vibrations'. Many city sewers are backing up with residue. Many residents of Oslo inexplicably report a smell of rotting meats and moldy bread. Similar odors are reported in Toronto and Seattle.

"The President of the United States is expected shortly to be making a statement from the White House regarding this dire situation. Remain tuned for his remarks carried live on our network..."

Alina Vera fervently bit her cigarette's filter. Vlad clutched his coffee mug with both hands, watching with astonishment. Vast swathes of terrain on every continent were experiencing varying degrees of meltdowns.

Floyd Dingus puffed his Cuban cigar. He was wearing a sweatshirt that read on the back, 'I LOVE ALASKA', and printed on the front, 'I CAN SEE RUSSIA FROM MY HOUSE'. He sat tensely listening to the broadcast.

"...Outside of Tulsa, Oklahoma Turnpike operations officials said two hundred or more cars were disabled on the toll road when an unknown sticky goo akin to pothole sealant covered their tires and wheels. Several state police and turnpike maintenance vehicles had to be towed themselves after getting stuck in the tar-like substance, according to the Turnpike operations center. Lieutenant Willie Johnson, official police spokesperson, said, 'It seems like no one knows what it is, or what to do. It's crazy, man. It's this incredible blob of... some kind of paste, blocking lanes in both directions. We have no idea where it came from yet. It's piled on my own tires thick as mud. This sticky mess is hindering travel plans for thousands...'"

"The world's sure in a dither trying to figure this one out," he said, fondling his Chicago Cubs baseball cap. "Back home I bet they're going apeshit. I'd better telephone my mom as soon as a cleared line becomes available."

"How sweet to make sure your mother is all right," said Alina Vera.

"Oh, it's not that. Mom's a tough old bird who can take care of herself. Actually, she's the mayor of a small city in America. Didn't I mention that? They love her there, they surely do. Cleopatra Dingus, mayor of Waterloo, Iowa. She's serving her third term."

Boris chomped on his cigar. "Is chocolate popular in your hometown, Floyd?"

A toothy smile appeared. "We're a nation of addicted chocolate worshippers, Boris. All Americans have a sweet tooth—and cavities galore to prove it. Dentists have it made in America."

The news anchor appeared with a breaking update. "Unconfirmed information from our stringer in Wellington, New Zealand, now reports a tidal surge along the capital's stretch of beautiful beaches. But this particular surge is reportedly composed of sea-watered chocolate...it's being referred to as a chocolate tsunami..."

Asher dismissed the notion with derision. "Ridiculous. What's the matter with these people? Water can't turn itself into chocolate! Absurd. Possibly a chocolate warehouse in the vicinity collapsed with ingredients falling into the sea. Or tons of melted chocolate could conceivably have seeped off a ship into the ocean, then headed to shore with a stiff current, providing these false impressions." He huffed, chewing grapes and cashews. "*Chocolate tsunami* indeed!"

He got up and went to Alina Vera's refrigerator. "I think it's time we check on our little experiment," he said. Sitting in the middle of a large porcelain plate was a chocolate-coated energy bar. He held the plate in both hands and carried it carefully to the parlor table. He placed it down gently, motioning for everybody to take a look.

"My God," said Vlad. The energy bar's paper wrapping was all but swallowed by a leaching mass of gurgling, blistering chocolate.

"Amazing," observed Alina Vera, in her professional tone. "It seems to be taking on a life of its own."

"I saw a movie about a killer blob that looked just like that," said Dimsky. "It's more than melting, isn't that right?"

Asher deliberated, nodding with strict seriousness. "Energy bar ingredients are tightly bonded, especially packed with brown rice syrup adhering to its barley malt component. It's a subtle process. I'd have expected the progression to be slower, considering how cold we kept it in the refrigerator. However, I notice its fractionated palm kernels act as a decisive corrosive factor. This conclusively proves no ordinary wall or structure can plug seeping effects caused by the Chocolate Bomb."

"It sounds like a mess," said Vlad.

"It is a mess," said Alina Vera. "Palm kernel oil is a vegetable equivalent of wax, defying the most concentrated digestive enzymes that speed through your bowels. It makes you burp a lot. And you'll be very thankful once it's fully expelled from your body. In short, this stuff tears your insides apart."

Colonel Dimsky felt a knot squeeze his stomach. "Then even Little Man, locked safely away in his vault, has melted?"

"Without doubt, good Colonel. Little Man is completely dissolved. Wasted, broken down into clumpy wet crumbs and heavy jelled liquid. Altered by now into little more than a small puddle with the consistency of a chocolate milkshake."

Alina Vera wiped wet eyes with a tissue. "Poor Little Man. None of this was his fault. It's sad how the innocent are made to suffer with the guilty."

"We can mourn poor Little Man later," a grumpy Boris said. "Right now we need to get back to business."

"You must admit," observed Vlad, "no one ever expected anything like this—deluge. We assumed the bomb's radius to target only Lenin's proximity."

Anya Andropova, wearing fashionable, especially worn-out jeans, sat on the floor with her legs wrapped around a bowl of buttered popcorn. She painted her nails, attentively engrossed in the incredible unfolding events. "Check it out! Were things supposed to explode this way? Chocolate's smearing the world like shriveled, dripping molasses. Sick!"

The rabbi peered at the screen, rattled. This represented an unexpected and unwelcome conundrum. "I clearly warned of collateral damage," he reminded in a chafed voice. "We had few opportunities for small scale tests within our rigid time constraints. Boris insisted we utilize the bomb immediately—and he was right; the world was grappling with rapidly escalating jeopardy. But I admit not foreseeing the weapon's extensive scope. The onus remains on me. When the laser focused skyward and I released the Chocolate Bomb into the atmosphere I didn't anticipate sunspots causing such dramatic velocity of upper atmospheric winds and turbulence. The combined absorption spectra of gases have apparently ferried the bomb's infrared molecules farther and wider than predominant calculations."

"Meaning it can't be contained?" said Vlad.

"Due to the wide-ranging sunspot turbulence, it's a fair guess our Chocolate Bomb is unexpectedly inundating the entire world," Alina Vera added morosely. "Every continent. I feel supremely terrible for all the children's birthday parties. Their chocolate and ice cream cake turning into pasty, saturated pools of inhibiting glop."

"As thick as jam," Asher agreed gloomily. "I hope they won't be traumatized for life."

"Not to mention millions of outraged parents having to clean up the shambles," added Dimsky. "It's a good time to invest in heavy duty cleaning companies. Stockbrokers will make out like bandits."

"They always do," sighed Vlad.

Alina Vera went into her kitchen where a huge pot of cabbage soup sat bubbling on the stove. The *bliny*, traditional pancakes served with honey or sour cream, were ready for preparation, hearty Russian comfort food. The pungent essence of cabbage wafted through the air.

Colonel Dimsky reached to his coat pocket and took out a chocolate bar he'd preserved for his own experiment. Its paper wrapper was soggy to the point of disintegration. At a touch, a blob of sticky melted chocolate covered his fingers, and he withdrew a hand coated with jellied raspberry stains. The creamy chocolate had dripped in blotches, smearing the coat's pocket and lining. "My best coat is totally ruined," he complained, wiping recalcitrant viscous chocolate away, most adhering stubbornly in place.

"You should've worn gloves," Alina Vera called as she stirred the soup and watched Dimsky's face distort with disgust. "There's a bar of antisepticised brown soap in the bathroom. Use it—and scrub well. Chocolate is tenacious. It'll smear everything if you're not careful."

"Is this crap going to happen to everyone?"

"Everyone within close proximity of chocolate, good Colonel," conjectured the rabbi.

"Do you think the bomb's dynamic effect is powerful enough to pass through solid wall, like stone or concrete?" Vlad asked.

"If it works as intended, it will inundate Earth's atmosphere, permeating everything composed of chocolate in an unseen, ferocious storm. A blizzard of anti-chocolate molecules radiating electromagnetic waves, invisible to all except acutely sensitive optical instruments, microscopes, spectrometers and other advanced detectors. Even your friend Olga Orlovskya, sitting lonely in a damp prison cell, will definitely encounter efficacious effects from the latest box of sweets you sent." He thought upon it, feeling a distinct shudder. "I pray you didn't ship her peanut brittle chocolates. That would indeed be bad, Vlad. Very bad."

"Vova, you've been sending that horrid innkeeper more boxes of chocolate?" asked a wide-eyed Alina Vera, wiping wet hands on her apron, and standing in her kitchen doorway. "I didn't know about that."

Vlad stuttered with embarrassment. "I guess I was feeling sorry, locked up in solitude and friendless as she is. I thought it might make her feel better while awaiting trial. I was told it wouldn't be long until the authorities decide what crimes she'll be charged with."

"Because of her cooperation in the hotel room they'll most likely reduce her sentence," predicted Dimsky. "At this moment, however, she's probably bathing in inky goo and not considering you much of a friend. That old hen is a shrewd one. Be on guard. She'll whisk you off your feet before Alina Vera can blink. What did happen between you two in that hotel room, anyway?" He chuckled under his breath.

"Oh, go play your balalaika," flared Alina Vera.

"Wait! There's a breaking story on the news."

"The imposing British luxury cruise ship, HMS Queen Mary III, is reporting having lost two of her massive twin diesel engines due to unidentified gross clogging of their internal combustion systems. It's said to occur during the ship's gala Captain's Masquerade Party. We were informed that the normally rapid expansion of combustion gases driving the engines' piston downward was blocked by an 'oil-like, heavy substance' dragging on the gear train. The twin engines' stable idling speed was disrupted by this unknown substance and over-speeded, resulting in apparent destruction. The opulent vessel travels with some four thousand passengers plus a crew of approximately eighteen hundred. Currently the colossal ship is said to be limping under her own power towards the island of Bermuda, three hundred nautical miles northwest. The ship is also experiencing sporadic power outages. Food is spoiling. Passengers are reportedly in good health but quite upset. We will, of course, continue to keep you updated on this Atlantic Ocean crisis."

Colonel Dimsky sat engrossed, scanning multiple English-language news sites on his laptop. "An article states that a small number of Saudi oilfields are encountering congested clogging difficulties due to some 'dark, muddy sediment smelling like chocolate ingrained with bourbon truffles.' He made a face, shaking his head. "Can't those pinheads tell it *is* chocolate?"

"Probably some slovenly, overweight oil workers kept extra large chocolate bars sticking out of their back pockets to munch as snacks," said Asher, peering over Dimsky's shoulder, rubbing at his lower back which was beginning to bother him again. "Likely the chocolate fell out, accidentally spilling into the rig's inner components, impeding the mechanism's abilities. Hopefully it didn't include peanut butter filling. Normally, this might cause minimal damage, but under such atrocious circumstances…" He let his words trail off. Peanut butter mixed with chocolate was the worst offender of all.

Boris visualized a nightmare of huge greased pistons, crown blocks, and drill lines all shackled by peanut butter's ultra-sticky substance. Every oil well in the world might suffer blockage and breakdown. Entire oilfields could be taken out of commission, jettisoned maybe for good. Stock market oil futures would catapult to astronomical levels, renewed fears of worldwide oil shortages overshadowing political stability and causing panic. "Drill pipes could jam a mile deep," he muttered. "You couldn't stop it with a bazooka. This is a fucking disaster."

"Don't fantasize. Details of these forecasts are extremely confounding. Any comprehensive effects of our Chocolate Bomb aren't yet properly under-stood, never mind borne out. It will be weeks before any reasonable assessment can be drawn. Moreover, we'll be studying repercussions and consequences on atmospheric alteration for years. It appears we've created a whole new field of scientific study! I dubbed it, Effects of Combustible Confectionary Molecules Upon Earth's Atmosphere. Universities will hold symposiums and offer class-room investigation. Lecturers will trot out to make the circuit and gain new fame to revive their dead careers. Tenured professors will vie at each other's throats for grant monies!"

"Back-stabbing among academics is already an art," noted Alina Vera.

Dimsky said, "I had a professor at the Academy who wore clogs instead of military boots."

"How does your bomb work? Vlad groused.

"My presumption is that affected molecules increased standard diameters exponentially until exploding," Asher continued. "Assuming this, I'd posit that one single extra-large chocolate bar could gum up an entire oilrig and all affili-ated paraphernalia. More extensive damage will occur if the chocolate includes, for example, a caramel ingredient. Imagine truckloads of dense caramel seep-ing down your street. That'd make anyone shudder. So yes, I'd say the story is believable."

Dimsky said, "This French report accuses the CIA as likely culprits."

"What do these French know? The CIA will defer to the Israelis," Alina Vera added caustically.

"In any case, the prime minister's office will have to answer all allegations," commented Boris. He blew uneven smoke rings in agitation. "They'll have a hell of a time trying to pin it on someone else." In the background, television footage showed carriages of a derailed freight train, its cars overturned at skewed angles. The engineer had escaped injury by breaking a window and jumping onto the chocolate-layered tracks.

The world was as upside down as the railroad cars, Vlad thought.

Dimsky sat nonplussed. "Lawsuits will fly. Ambulance chasing lawyers are probably already lining up clients in anticipation. Anyway, I shouldn't think any of it matters regarding Milonov, not with the intelligence we've gathered. Once the scandal is publically exposed he'll be forced to resign. President Stroganoff will make him her scapegoat, and rudely ship him off to his new appointment in Siberia."

"Good riddance to that dipshit," growled Alina Vera. "Our country deserves better."

Anya wiped popcorn butter from her fingers onto her designer jeans. "What will this mean for Ilya?"

"She'll probably get a life sentence," said Boris. "However, because she's agreed to provide evidence against Gregori Nabokov to the prosecutor, they might show leniency and have her time reduced. The same goes for her sister, who's also blubbering whatever she knows to the police. I guess they weren't mere pawns after all." He chuckled. "I'm acquainted with the State Prosecutor, a friend for many years. If I read Ilya Evgeny correctly, she's already plotting to work on him with her feminine wiles."

"What about that Sunavich guy?" persisted Anya. "That spaz creeps me out. The nasty old bugger, aka Andrei Popov, harpsichord player, started this whole mess, didn't he? Aren't we going to nab him, too?"

Boris guzzled a bottle of American beer Alina Vera provided. "For now he remains on the loose. But his identity theft scheme backfired badly. Inspector Big Duck Drinkwater is leading the case at home. Interpol has fanned out across Europe. The International Court of Justice has also indicted him, and international arrest warrants have been issued. Our internal MVD police are searching, and the Americans are hunting him with drones. My personal guess is eventually the Israelis will apprehend him in disguise somewhere, unless Big Duck finds him first. But even should he successfully elude them all his reign of terror is finished. He'll spend the rest of his life hiding in caves and hovels, on the run, stalked like an animal, unable to show his face. And he'll never again possess the ability to threaten mankind. He's shot his wad. Mikhail Sunavich is finished; the charlatan Andrei Popov, harpsichord player, has given his final concert." Boris lifted his bottle in a mock toast and guzzled his beer.

"Which reminds me," said Asher, "I received a text from Yuri Grushin in Omsk. He and his team finally reconstructed the secret code hidden among the bingo cards at the *Das Kapital Bingo Parlor.* All remaining cards can now be safely destroyed."

"A bit late, wouldn't you say, Asher?" said Alina Vera. "Now Yuri can get back to his usual pastimes."

"I think city bicycles should be outlawed," grumbled Dimsky. "They're always on the sidewalk getting in my way."

Anya looked up excitedly. "Hey everybody! It says the Americans have sent a series of scientific balloons into the atmosphere to spy on the laser's residue, hoping to dissect its formula."

"Yeah? Lots of luck with that," snickered Floyd. "We're just showing off."

In Quebec City crews placed sandbags around the governor's mansion as the St. Lawrence, connecting the Great Lakes with the Atlantic Ocean, a river wide even on a normal day, spilled over its banks, covered with a veneer of slogging dark chocolate debris tantamount to a flood. About 40 miles northeast, the local police chief advised residents to prepare for possible evacuation due to chocolate sludge moving downriver, suggesting they take clothing, food and prescription medicine. He also asked city businesses to close their doors by noon...

"Oy," said Asher. "Its reached Canada."

More reports of clogged roadways, bridges, and tunnels ensued in quick succession. Then the words 'Breaking News' suddenly flashed across the television screen. The somber face of the American president came to the podium.

"Good evening fellow citizens of the world. By now, almost everyone has become aware of today's monumental events. The world is in a moment of transition. I wish to assure everyone that humanity is completely safe from harm. What we have experienced is something unknown in the annals of mankind. As is evident to many, the world is currently undergoing a chocolate meltdown. A worldwide meltdown. In every nation across our beautiful earth this event will be remembered as remarkable and historical. For reasons of security, details behind these incredible occurrences cannot be revealed at this time, but again, I assure everyone that they are free from danger, and life will resume normally within a few short days. In the meantime, as many of you already know, the source of the chocolate meltdown being endured began in Russia. Even as I am speaking, my Undersecretary of State, the honorable Elmer Dingus, has been dispatched to the Kremlin on a mission to oversee the process of destroying forever the formula responsible for the meltdown. This is as agreed between the New Russian Federation's President and myself. Under international law, we will ensure total compliance. I personally take President Stroganoff at her word that neither her nation nor any other will ever under any circumstances possess the code to employ future chocolate destruction. The unveiling and one-time use of this terrible weapon of mass destruction was undeniably critical. As a devoted chocolate lover myself, it grieves me to recognize the untold tears and sadness that will ensue. Nevertheless, the undertaking of this mission was imperative. The alternative was unspeakable. Permit me to assure that had a better solution been available to prevent use of its awesome capability the New Russian Federation would have readily done so. Unfortunately, immediate usage became not only necessary but also urgent. Thus, the day of its utilization will forever be memorialized as The Great Chocolate Meltdown, to be respectfully commemorated annually.

"Lastly, I especially applaud the scientists and other members of Russia's unnamed Security Strike Team for its swift, heroic, and decisive efforts in extinguishing a significant threat to world peace. Without the talent and abilities of this exclusively selected group, Russia, indeed all of humanity, might today be facing far graver challenges."

He looked into the camera. "Thank you, and God bless you all."

The president walked stiffly from the pressroom, waving and smiling, but unwilling to answer the endless barrage of questions shouted from the crowd of world media representatives.

"I suppose the president was referring to us," Alina Vera said with a smirk. "We've become Heroes of The Great Chocolate Meltdown."

"Old Elmer somehow always winds up getting the glory," Floyd lamented. "But at least this time we get some credit, too."

"I always wanted to be a hero," Dimsky said thoughtfully.

Boris clapped him on the back. "And now you surely are, good Colonel, now you surely are."

20.

The world will be completely annihilated, according to a country preacher in Colorado, a self-proclaimed prophet with a following of thousands. With a moralistic and pu-ritanical tone, he claims that the Chocolate Meltdown has been prophesied for millennia via an ad hoc mix of biblical texts only now coming to light due to his diligent research. Following the Meltdown he says we will soon experience intense earthquakes and volcanic eruptions that will torment and erode planet Earth for months before its final destruction. We'll witness social chaos, mass famine, and bottomless depths of depravity. 'Invisible judgment' is upon us, he proclaims. Appearing before the Gate of Heaven drenched in chocolate will not be well received. Mayan and Hindu calendar influences also have con-verged proving the validity of his claim, leaving only the righteous to be blessed, while the rest of humankind will disintegrate into galactic dust...

A carpet of wildflowers grew in abundance. It was a beautiful day in *Ermi-tazhnyi Sad*, Moscow's Hermitage Garden Park. Couples, families, joggers, bik-ers, dog-walkers mingled peacefully, ambling along tree-lined, winding paths leading to adjacent theatres, monuments, and the famed *Novaya Opera*. Tourists snapped photos amid a plethora of colorful varieties of leafy foliage and flowery shrubs tall in warm sunlight. Shivering winds dissolved, winter passed. Chil-dren pranced around cascading fountains under the watchful eyes of mothers and grandmothers.

"I'm feeling disillusioned with everything." Alina Vera commented as they strolled. "I look around at the collection of misfits, revolutionaries, and imbe-ciles who dearly paid for participating in Lenin's rebellion. The sheer stupidity of it astounds me. For the next hundred years we'll be bombarded, serenaded, and swallowed up by an outpouring of books, films, plays, theses, television talking heads, and computer games based on the Chocolate Bomb..."

"All getting a taste for new angles to make money."

She thought more and added, "Maybe there'll be a timely soap opera themed around a band of brave heroes fighting to save the Earth. Of course they'll have to include a love interest. I wonder which actors will portray us, Vova?"

Vlad clutched her hand tighter at her using his affectionate name. "Beautiful young American actors, no doubt. I hope they get some of the facts straight. These ongoing arrests, show trials, charges, and counter charges, are a useless waste. Tilting at windmills after the fact. The whole world lost in this debacle." He looked into her eyes. "Except maybe for us."

She smiled ardently. "Boris indicated Stroganoff is preparing to address the nation with an official announcement. He says behind the scenes she's huddling with lawyers and advisors for ways to squirm out of trouble."

Vlad eased himself onto a bench, feeling warm pleasure surrounded by the plush, undulating park, sniffing scented flowers. They mingled with an odor of dampness from the morning's showers. "I heard much the same. Her position's been compromised—irrevocably. Internal Security's made preemptive arrests among her loyal deputies. They've gone belly up, busy denouncing anyone and everyone, proclaiming innocence, ignorance, and declaring they'll be vindicated in court." He could not hold back a laugh. "This is monumental. Natasha is confused by the convulsive political shifts underway. There are so many sit-ins you can barely walk in the street. Parliamentarians composed of all Duma parties are loudly demanding her resignation, as are major news organizations and newspaper editorials, saying she's dishonored the nation in a shocking and disgraceful way. People are blaming failure to stop the confrontation directly on her shoulders. That she could have taken decisive action to safeguard the nation, but was too self-absorbed by her own agenda, and stood fiddling while Rome burned, as it were. Others said taking swifter action might have averted need for the Chocolate Bomb's detonation. We know the truth, of course. She staked her future on this gambit, and lost badly. The uprising brought hundreds of thousands into the streets, paving the way for her downfall, many of them former supporters now whooping with delight."

He was amazed at the cold ferocity the human species was capable of. Slaughter before lunch, tea in the afternoon. "The Stroganoffs won't ever realize the dream of restoring the monarchy. Plans for declaring Natasha as Czarina are scrubbed forever."

"I hope she slinks out of town before some unruly mob shoves her down a trap door."

Alina Vera seated herself beside Vlad. She glanced at her cigarette, dropped it, snubbing it with the toe of her boot. "I've finally decided to give up smoking, quit cold turkey. Enough poisoning my lungs. From now on, I'll just enjoy the occasional Cuban cigar Boris provides." She peered up at two small sparrows side by side on a nearby branch. The scene made her smile. "Do you have any idea what Natasha's going to say at her press conference?"

"No. Her ship's sinking faster than the Titanic, and she's got no lifeboat. Polls put her popularity at zero, neck and neck with Milonov. Backchannel sources say leaders of her Peoples' Democracy Party are outraged and searching to name a new leader, someone with clean hands—if such a person exists. Unconditional resignation is a bedrock demand. Constitutional amendments will guarantee a peaceful transfer of power. All her plans backfired, and if she values salvaging herself she'll retire quietly to her Black Sea dacha. But never count out the Stroganoff family. I learned that much from Boris. If we're not watchful someone of her ilk will be hatching new plots soon enough." He reached inside his jacket pocket and took out two cellophane-wrapped Cuban cigars. "Boris sent me a box. Want one?"

"I'd love one." She took the cigars, retrieved her silver cigarette lighter, placed both between her teeth and sucked until they were lit. She handed one to Vlad. They sat puffing like delinquent children. Ripples of hazy smoke dissolved amid bright sunlight. Passersby stared with peculiarity at the forty-something couple resting on a park bench attempting to blow smoke rings, loudly coughing with every inhale. Clearing his throat, Vlad stretched his arms wide. "It's so nice not to be living with constant anxiety. For the last two years I've been under such drastic pressure I didn't even recognize the toll it was taking."

"I can relate to that," Alina Vera agreed. She amused herself with her cigar, twirling it between her fingers, sniffing like a hound at the ballooning smoke. "Dimsky mentioned that one of his staff officers works with a dog rescue group. He's going to find that poodle I've been wanting."

Vlad successfully blew a perfect ring. He beamed at his handiwork. "I'm happy to hear that. I can't wait to meet your new puppy."

"I prefer a female dog, but it won't matter much. I've already decided on an appropriate name, male or female. A name is important. It gives the animal a sense of identity and pride. So, I've decided to call the poodle 'Lenin'. What do you think?" Mischief glinted in her eyes.

Vlad roared, and almost choked. Alina Vera passed him a bottle of water from her bag. "Lenin?" He made a mock frown after he drank. "You know something? I like it. It's fitting. I recall your childhood dog was named Trotsky, so I'd say it's a perfect match. Another rebel in the family."

"That won't be much of a stretch, I promise. By the way, my family's already heard stories about you, Vova. I'm looking forward to your meeting them."

The thought made Vlad happy. "I'm looking forward, too. I've also really taken a liking to Dimsky, you know. I didn't trust him at first. He seems so stiff and awkward, and so *military*. Every time he looked my way I thought I was going to be arrested. I'd never have imagined that you and he were actually related by blood."

"We are it's true. He's something of a long, lost relative, though. After the Soviet Union's upheaval some distant family members fled to remote locations. During this political turmoil Dimsky's grandfather settled near the Mongolian border, but don't ask me why. You do realize it was Boris that finally brought us all back together?"

"No, I didn't." A group of children skipped beside the path, tossing a rugby ball back and forth, laughing, oblivious to the cigar-smoking couple. Vlad said, "Boris said he'd been a good friend of your father. Is that true?"

"Quite true. My father said that as children they became an inseparable duo. Practically like brothers, even though they were forever wrangling. My father went on to study at university while Boris, well you know. He chose a different path."

Vlad looked at her full on. "Your dad grew up in Moscow slums the same way Boris did?"

She shrugged. "Sure. They joined the Party as youths, remaining loyal members until the old regime crumbled. Boris ingratiated himself with preeminent people during Yeltsin's government and became indispensible. He'd always find suitable ways to maintain important connections, no matter who came to power. My father preserved their friendship even though they soon became political antagonists. Blood is thicker than water, I guess."

"Boris Sokolov is a blood relative?" Vlad was taken aback.

"You didn't know that, either? His mother and my grandfather were cousins."

Vlad's eyes flared with more surprise. He shook his head in fascination. This certainly helped account for many unconventional things, he realized. "You know, I was determined to resign from the team. One day I pleaded with Boris to allow me to quit, right then and there. He talked me out of it, persuading me that I was the only one he could trust. He said I was an outsider without an agenda. I didn't understand what he meant at the time. But I never imagined he was hinting that much of the team was composed of blood relations."

Alina Vera was unabashedly bemused. "Boris always had a flair for the dramatic. But I admit he had a point. This assignment gave us all reasons for mistrust—even among ourselves. You know what they say regarding family. They're at each other's throats, especially when it comes to an inheritance. My sleazy corporate lawyer brother still hasn't forgiven me for successfully buying out his portion of my flat. You should have heard the screaming matches, threats flying back and forth. Well, that's all in the past. I adore my flat and I wouldn't sell it for anything. Fortunately, the lease on my place in Omsk is up. I don't have to go back there, ever."

Once more she attempted blowing smoke rings the way Floyd Dingus had taught. Nearby, a small girl with braided blond hair watched the misshapen smoke circles with intense curiosity. "So, Mr. Public Relations Man, that's my tale. What about you?"

"Me? These past few nights I've slept like a baby. It's nice to be able to rest for the first time in months. I didn't even bother going to see the Minister of Culture when I handed my resignation. I sent the clown an email directly to his private account. Rude, huh? And while I was at it, I critiqued our work together, and told him exactly what I thought. I must have been feeling pretty brave that morning because I also informed my undercutting, backstabbing, insubordinate staff what I think of them, too. Believe me I'll never receive a single government job offer again. I'm a free agent for life."

"You're kidding, Vova. What about the Jubilee? All those grand festivities and carnivals you'd thrown your life's work into?"

He looked into her eyes. "Who cares? After what we've been through, I surely don't. But don't be concerned. All the sensational hype amounted to nothing. The whole thing's turned into a total dud. Everybody knows it. Money sucked down a sinkhole to pay off boosters and trustees. I heard talk of an embarrassing postponement even before Sergei's abrupt resignation. Competitive advertising operators are jockeying for position, clawing atop themselves, ready to maim and mutilate for a chance to replace me. Whoever's finally selected won't stay happy for long. The whole department is in utter disarray, and has been for months. A nearsighted bunch of ass-kissing losers. The only one I'm grateful for is Nadia Ivanova for hooking us up with Madam Zaza. At least she helped put us on the right track. I sent the seer a big bunch of white carnations…not chocolates. I even invited Madam Zaza to join our celebration today, but she declined. She's still suspicious of Boris. But she did promise if I ever need her again she'll be there."

The scientist smiled at his wickedly snarky attitude.

"It's no secret that many of the illustrious planned projects remain unfinished," he added. "Stalled, or so tentative there's no possible way of ever catching up. I had to constantly cover up for how bad things were, making up buttery excuses. Lucky for me my lung capacity was well developed. Since my departure, bureaucratic encumbrances have deteriorated completion efforts. Bigger bribes, endless kickbacks. A bloodletting feast. Nothing changes. Now I can see that the whole project was doomed to failure from inception. Countless billions disappeared—except for the graft lining pockets from top to bottom. It's a shame it turned out this way. I'd guess Mouse Universe people had a heavy hand insuring its undoing."

"Why? What do they have to gain?"

He frowned. "Much more than you think. Our Anniversary plans would have caused great competition and disruption. They were deeply worried. Upstaging the Jubilee means all that lucrative foreign vacation money gets spent on their theme parks, resorts and hotels, not ours. We'd have become serious competition. It doesn't take much graft to pay off our apparatchiks, so any outlay is worth billions to them over the long run. And if Dr. Sunavich has indeed been on their payroll, it means they knew all along about Codename Chocolate Lenin. Of course they'd salivate to get their grubby hands on the formula, but now they won't dare risking exposure. With what we learned about their secret underground facilities, think what wonders they might have conceived by bringing replicated famous historical figures back to life. Imagine replication real princesses and adventurers from every era posing for photographs with millions of squealing little girls. It would be a goldmine for them. So these scheming entrepreneurs cleverly paid off people like Gregori Nabokov and his ilk to ensure the Jubilee would go down the tubes…"

"Shocking."

"Several arrests have taken place, and investigations are ongoing. The consensus is more indictments are expected. A Special Prosecutor is being named to head the inquest, but it takes time for legal machinery to budge." Vlad crossed his legs and tried to count leaves on a branch.

"I doubt Mouse Universe itself will ever face any charges, let alone be convicted," he added. "This affair will be forgiven and forgotten. At best a few low-level officials will be hoisted as sacrificial lambs to calm the public's heated rhetoric, while their corporation continues corrupting and trafficking as long as greed remains a prime human sin. Legally, their hands are clean. And because of our ruination the value of their stock has skyrocketed. Maybe they're the true winners in all this after all."

"The inhumanity of it makes me want to puke."

"Listen to this: I've also been told that as a face-saving measure a *new* 30th Anniversary project announcement is in the works. Of course it's not my problem anymore. The nation will survive and so will I. I've managed to save a bit of money. Most of it I forwarded to Raisa toward my daughters' care. It should last a while."

"What about you, Vova?" Her round eyes were filled with concern.

"No more expensive Italian-tailored suits, but I'll get by. When you come right down to it, I don't need very much. And I'll finally be able to get some good therapy for my shoulder. Oh, and by the way, last week I spoke with a savvy moneyed Moscow real estate investor I know. He says my neighborhood is hot, and I should take advantage. So, I signed a contract and my flat's already on the market. Some filthy rich foreigner will scoop it up. I still owe a lot, but there'll be a small profit left over. University degrees aren't much good when you're blackballed by the State…but I can still teach. The need for fluent English is strong, and there'll always be a post somewhere." He placed his cigar under his shoe and crushed it. "Anyway, I'm not the only one who's been hurt during this business. I count my own fall from grace lucky compared to how many lives are ruined. Poor Anya Andropova's been crying her heart out since being informed she's no longer dubbed Russian Icon Girl."

"Don't feel sorry for our little elegiac tennis star. She'll make out fine. Primped and pawed, I know she was antsy to start as spokeswoman for the New Russia, and all that. She'd aquired a whole new wardrobe to parade in. Too bad, because top fashion designers were begging her to show off their latest ensembles. Didn't your TV makeup artists enhance her sexy aura? Glamor magazines were chasing her to pose, libidinous moguls hungry to date her. She was distraught and raving when she learned she was out of a job."

Vlad muttered a few well-chosen vulgarities regarding advertising trickery. "But her line of clothes, *'Attire by Anya'* is still humming. If nothing else she can get back in shape and play tennis."

Alina Vera snickered. "Your cynicism sounds pretty out of character, Mr. Sensitive Nice Guy."

"I suppose. Maybe I'm evolving in the aftermath."

"Maybe we're all evolving in the aftermath." She nuzzled closer.

In the distance they heard the floating jingle of a wagon selling *morozhenoe*, ice cream, passing nearby. A large number of park visitors hurried eagerly toward the gay music. "Want some?" Vlad asked.

"Thanks, no. I'm content with my cigar." She sat lost in thought, putting to bed unresolved tensions that had lingered for too long. Absently, she said, "Vova, do you think chocolate ice cream will be available again soon?"

"I haven't heard any negative reports. No unexpected molecule explosions or exposure risks lately. Not a pop. But you should know these answers. You're the scientist."

She smiled, slowly shaking her head in reflection. "Looking back, the whole thing is like a dream. I'd wager my last ruble Asher never had a clue the meltdown would prove so pervasive, unexpected sunspots or not. I know he prefers claiming otherwise, but it's bravado. He's thankful and relieved it didn't escalate further out of control."

"Who could've conceived such a thing?" Vlad quoted a sentence from a newspaper article he carried in his jacket pocket. *'The Great Chocolate Meltdown rendered our world supine in a nanosecond as tides of liquefied goop rendered streets and roads impassable, choked major pipelines, and wreaked havoc on infrastructure...'*

"The aftermath is grotesque and comical at the same time. Hardly a family in the world hasn't been affected in some way. Frankly, we could have made a killing in the stock market, investing in companies producing strong chemical detergents and the like. Dimsky saw it coming."

Intending a bad pun, Alina Vera said, "I guess we could have cleaned up."

Vlad grinned. "Fancy the thousands of tons of ruined fabric and clothing, not to mention damaged machinery. Yesterday an editorial in the *Moscow Financial Journal* predicted it will take half a century for already-pending lawsuits to work their way through the court system. Thousands are filed, and that's just the tip of the iceberg."

Alina Vera flicked gray ash from her cigar, a softened tranquility about her. "Homo sapiens. What a monstrosity we are. They made our escapade sound like thermonuclear war. Thankfully we're not held accountable. As agents for the State we're protected, exempted from lawsuits. Anyone seeking reimbursement will have a long, long struggle taking on the Russian government."

He beamed at the lofty idea of hauling the government to court. "Lots of luck with that. They don't have a ray of hope. They'll do better in the International Court. I only pray my flat sells quickly so I'll have enough extra pocket money to tide me over." He looked at his watch. The breeze blew harder, and he pondered whimsically, "If we could fly toward the sun on a chocolate atom we'd probably reach California by dusk. Have you ever visited America?"

"I did, several years ago at a scientific symposium in New York. Actually, both Rabbi Titlebaum and Dr. Sunavich were in attendance. It was lots of fun. I had a chance to tour the city and experience American food." She quipped, "I'd never eaten a taco, or had a slurpee before."

"A taco's not American, it's Mexican," he corrected.

"Whatever. It was tasty. Which reminds me, what's holding everyone up? I'm getting hungry. The purpose of being here is a picnic, isn't it?" Just as she spoke, Floyd Dingus came sauntering down the path, carrying a large woven basket on one arm, cradling a small grocery bag in the other.

"Hey there Vlad, Alina Vera, where's everybody hiding?" He peered at the landscaped fauna as a group of rollerbladers waved as they passed.

"We were wondering ourselves, Floyd. Have a seat, there's plenty of room on the bench."

"Something smells good, 'Sport'. What do you have there?" Alina Vera asked.

The famous toothy smile appeared. Floyd diligently opened his basket. "I brought us buckets of spicy, crispy fried chicken. American Southern-style, deep-fried in lard, lots of grease, preservatives, salt, and fat. You know, just one of the ways we love it back home, grilled, baked, barbeque, roasted. I tried buying a couple of loaves of that tangy, delicious Russian black bread and some pastries at the bakery, but they were sold out." He opened up the basket, lowered his head and sniffed. "There's lots of chicken, though, more than enough for everybody. Help yourselves." The aroma wafted invitingly. Alina Vera took a skinless breast. Vlad took a leg. Floyd provided paper plates, and handed out plenty of napkins.

"Where are the knives and forks?"

"It tastes better eating with your fingers. C'mon guys, sink your teeth into it."

Unused to this odd custom Vlad and Alina Vera shrugged and nibbled. "Mm, it really is scrumptious. A feast worthy of a gargantuan appetite. Where'd you buy it?"

"I cooked it up myself. I used my mother's closely guarded secret recipe my sister gave me. Better than anything you find in a deli, huh?"

"Crunchy good. Compliments to your mother."

"Thank you. I'll pass it on. You know, my sister Hetway Dingus is Deputy American Ambassador at the United Nations, always running around, attending parties with dignitaries and hotshots. People think Hetway's a foxy career woman, but I'll tell you, she's quite a cook and spice expert."

"How is your mom, Cleopatra Dingus?" asked Alina Vera, poking her way to find another warm, spicy piece.

"Just fine, thanks for asking. I talked to her yesterday. She says they've just about scrubbed the last chocolate remnants off the nearby Interstate. I had no idea how much chocolate Waterloo people hoarded. What a town full of junkies. The newspapers wrote about tons of sticky stuff choking the streets during the Meltdown. I shouldn't laugh, but imagine strip mall confection stores with their windows blown out and melted chocolate oozing all over the place. Frantic mothers screaming, little kids crying. Vehicles spinning in circles, mired in chocolate mud. If any works its way into those engines, drive trains and drive shafts, look out, that's all she wrote."

"Wipe that grin off your face," Alina Vera admonished.

Floyd couldn't help himself. "Stalled vehicles zigzagging across intersections, pickups sliding over milkshake-dense gooey pools. No one will ever forget The Great Chocolate Meltdown. A day for the history books. Oh well, enough swapping stories. Come and gobble up some more. I brought as much as I could carry."

"I'll try a bit of that." They looked up to find Colonel Dimsky standing tall and proud dressed in a new civilian blue suit. On his chest was pinned his awarded Hero's Medal of Honor, a commemoration bestowed unanimously by the full State Duma in honor of dutiful service in tracking down the disparaged chocolate terrorist Vladimir Ilyich Lenin.

"Classy! Don't you look the stylish gentleman!" exclaimed Alina Vera, nibbling, wiping her mouth.

Floyd reached deep into his basket and handed the colonel the largest chicken breast of all. "This one's for you. A Hero of the State deserves the best." They shifted on the long bench to make additional room. Dimsky placed his balalaika case at his feet and sat hunched at the edge, chomping, devouring, and licking his fingers. "This is wonderful, Floyd."

For the while there was scant chatter while the four of them sat munching.

"I hope you saved leftovers for us."

Vlad turned toward the voice. Nearby Boris and Asher stood grinning, clearly having shared a glass of schnapps or two before coming to the park.

"Get off that cold bench," Boris called. "I found a nice spot on the grass. We spread blankets next to the trees, and I brought good Russian comfort food as well as bottles of the finest vodkas."

"Pursuant to the art of living and eating well, I provided fresh baskets of fruit," said Asher. "Apples, pears, peaches, fresh strawberries and of course, seedless grapes, compliments of Esther's overnight special delivery imported shipment."

They settled across the rumpled blankets in happy camaraderie. Boris passed around *irka*, a briny and sharp caviar, served on small slices of dark, crusty bread. Next they enjoyed Russian kebab, known as *shashlyk*, a piquant skewered combination of meat and vegetables, brought cold to the picnic.

The sun dipped, evening was approaching, and the first stars were shining. The temperature cooled. Alina Vera put on her jacket and Vlad wrapped his sweater around his shoulders. Floyd Dingus wore his 'I Love Alaska' sweatshirt. They continued talking, eating, joking, passing around small paper cups of vodka. The colonel took out his balalaika and played a jolly folk tune.

"I'd like to propose a toast," Floyd said, standing up, wiping his mouth and smacking his lips. "I think we've got a great deal to celebrate."

"A toast it is," seconded Boris.

"Who are we toasting?" asked Alina Vera.

"Well, first I propose we toast Vova," said Floyd. "I hear our rabbi's accepted him as a pupil at his Yeshiva." All eyes turned to Vlad, comfortably sprawled on his elbows.

"It's true," he said quietly. "Rabbi Titlebaum consented to accept me as his student. I'll be working for him part of the time and doing intense study. I want to learn as much about Kabbalah and the Zohar as I can, while I can."

"A most worthy endeavor," agreed Dimsky. "To friend Vova and his studies!" They all gave a rousing cheer.

"We also owe a toast to Alina Vera," said Asher in all seriousness. "Without her help I might not have completed work on the Chocolate Bomb as swiftly as we did. In addition, she took me into her confidence recently, confiding the long-rumored belief that she really does wish to become a wife and mother. Now our next assignment is to find someone for her to fall in love with. Remember, Einstein said, 'Gravitation is not responsible for people falling in love'."

Her face turned beet red and she sheepishly looked away. Vlad lowered his gaze. It was an open and shut case, everybody knew. Rippling effects of romance had been unfurling for a while. The public relations man and the molecular biologist were doubtlessly in love.

Another exhilarating cheer ensued.

"And I believe we owe you a toast, too, Boris Sokolov," Floyd quickly added. "You were prominently instrumental in keeping your government free and democratic, standing boldly and firmly against tyrants of all stripes, and preventing the crisis from being used as an excuse for political upheaval. Not to mention guiding your team to a successful conclusion."

More cheers followed.

"And just one more thing," Floyd said. "I've gathered information from my own spy sources that Boris and the lady friend he never discusses, his beloved Turkish belly dancer, are planning to elope and start a fresh life in New York."

Boris's jaw dropped. "Where did you obtain such information?"

Astonished, Vlad searched for words. "Is that true?"

The cagey espionage operative hemmed and hawed, refusing to give a direct response. "If you recall, Vova, a while ago I mentioned I'm getting too old for this business. That maybe it was time to retire, allow a more qualified, younger man to take over at Internal Security."

"...Take over at Internal Security?" Dimsky imitated. "Mother Volga! All this time...it's been...*you*? You're the 'phantom', the anonymous Chief of Security? No one had a clue. Your disappearances were always so artful, your sleuthing so hush-hush and well-timed." He struggled to put it all together. "You played your role with such expertise you even fooled me. So it wasn't the military brass echelon that assigned me to Omsk and the damnable Lenin Project—*you* ordered it yourself!"

"He's the consummate spy," Asher said matter-of-factly. "His exploits could fill novels."

Unfazed, Boris said, "I'm not the so-called 'phantom'! I brought you together to Omsk because I wanted to see my relatives." Everyone booed at the lame excuse. "All right. Mea culpa. I swore an oath to do my duty to the State, that's all. I collect a paycheck the same as any one else. Why would you think such a thing?"

"Oh yes, he's the elusive 'phantom', Colonel!" Floyd said, pointing a finger. "We Americans have him caught red-handed! Signed, sealed, and delivered. I even happen to know that Boris personally has recommended *Bolshoi Utka*, Inspector Big Duck Drinkwater, be named his successor at Internal Security. He'll continue keeping things in shape."

"No better man in the Motherland for the job," chimed Dimsky. Ambushed and waylaid, Boris stammered and stuttered.

"Comrade Boris isn't denying anything because he can't!" cried Alina Vera. She put her face close to his, and sniffed like a bloodhound. "What do you say, *Tovarich*? Eh?" No reply came. She smiled an icy, police investigator smile. "You're right, Dimsky. He's guilty. Why didn't I see it, too?"

"Now we have a triple surprise," said a chortling Rabbi Titlebaum. "Steely Boris Sokolov, the Commissioner of Internal Security. After so many years of active subterfuge he's actually decided to draw his pension! And that belly dancer he doesn't discuss will soon be giving him orders. It's about time he gets a well-deserved taste of his own medicine. How did you come across this top secret information, Floyd?"

"You think my embassy doesn't have its own slate of Russian spies on the payroll? Nobody can keep real secrets anymore, Boris. Not in our information age. You of all people should know that." Floyd grinned, happy with his surprise, and again held his cup high. "To Boris!"

"To Boris Sokolov," hailed the rabbi, giving the salute. "Remember always," he quoted, 'Days are scrolls: write on them what you want remembered'."

On that poignant note began an animated, triple toast, the rabbi willingly refilling the vodka cups.

"Enough about me," said Boris, exultant for an opportunity to change the subject. "We have another toast we surely can't forget. Paying tribute and respect to the most formidable adversary I've ever encountered: Vladimir Ilyich Lenin."

Dimsky looked into his empty vodka cup. "And where do you suppose Lenin is now?" he wondered. "What fate did he suffer during the Great Chocolate Meltdown?"

Alina Vera looked to Vlad, and Vlad looked to Boris. Boris looked to Floyd. Floyd turned to Dimsky and the colonel gazed at the rabbi. Asher lifted his gaze skyward. The first evening stars were twinkling, a hazy half moon hung low. "His depleted life force is akin to the dazzling glow of a setting sun in its final glory. A faded force never having achieved its cherished goals. By now Vladimir Ilyich has evaporated completely. Reduced to a pool of chocolate cocoa, granules washed by rain, wind, and nature. Any residue has lifted high into the atmosphere, condensation caused by the warmth of the sun." He stood to his full height and clutched his cup tightly. "Historians and pundits will evaluate and sort out mankind's reflections on this time. Our battle is done. Fare thee well, Vladimir Ilyich. Fare thee well."

There was a long silence, broken when Vlad said, "In an odd way I'm going to miss the old boy. He taught us a lot. He brought attention to the corruption and political abyss ruining our nation, and now we'll finally have true reform. Word has spread to similar regimes across the globe. We see dissatisfaction turning into political action happening everywhere. For that much we owe him a debt of gratitude."

"Very true. We can credit his call to arms as being responsible for upheaval in government," noted Boris, lighting a cigar. "His uncanny understanding of what the common people wanted, even through revolution, provided us opportunities to catch our deceitful big fish at the top. No more Sergei Milonov to worry about. It's cold at the Arctic where's he's been demoted. And would-be Czarina Natasha can't scurry out the door fast enough. There's going to be an independent interim president replacing her. And if the police don't provide good protection I'd wager she'd be hanged by angry street mobs. A caretaker government will assume control until upcoming elections. So yes, in a back-handed way, we do owe him much."

"He's also responsible for bringing us together," added Alina Vera. "Without him I'd never meet Vova."

It was true. Without the startling exploits of their arch foe, their strike team would never have been formed. It was a diffident moment for reflection. In unexpected ways Lenin had shaken up and altered the nation. A bloodless revolution had taken place.

Boris smiled fully. "Did any of you know we have a very special candidate standing for office in the upcoming elections? Someone who's dear to us all."

No one knew what to make of this, silently regarding one another with varying degrees of surprise. Floyd Dingus bit into an apple and shrugged.

"Don't dither, Colonel, and don't be bashful. It's time to spill the beans." Boris insisted at last.

Dimsky abruptly stopped strumming. "All right. As usual, Boris is correct. A group of independent parliamentarians came to visit me shortly after the political crisis erupted. They've had conclaves with politicians, academics, lawyers, and journalists to evaluate the ongoing situation. It's agreed we can no longer afford a debauched patrimonial system of political dysfunctionality. Too long our politicians have peddled cushy government jobs, projects, and favors in return for payoffs, while opposition parties face increasingly higher obstacles to winning seats in parliament. Behind closed doors the leaders of several main parties offered me a leadership role to implement our Duma with a new, nonpartisan, progressive face. Some in the press are hailing me as a national hero, a savior of sorts during this quagmire we've endured. I know it requires a radical cultural revolution to revise things, but—Mother Volga—some say I'm the one credited for salvaging our entire democratic way of life!"

"You're starting to sound like a politician already," Alina Vera noted.

"I know you've been roundly hailed for restoring law and order," acclaimed Boris. "Of course all those flattering newspaper and television articles and interviews Vlad planted helped make your name a household word." He winked theatrically.

Dimsky listened and agreed. "You planted enough stories to have *me* willingly crowned Czar. Mother Volga, every word Vlad explained about the power of the media is true! I'm bombarded with endless fan mail, including several hundred importune offers of marriage!"

"Choose an unrepressed, wealthy widow," suggested Floyd.

"I only wed for love, not the instincts of a primitive man," the colonel replied.

"That's true," confirmed Alina Vera. "Ask any of his six ex wives. Seven will undoubtedly be the lucky charm."

"I don't like to tattle, but our colonel's quietly been dating Madam Zaza, you know," said Vlad.

"What?" Boris crossed his arms and tapped his foot in consternation, holding back a disparaging remark.

Dimsky acted like he was not embarrassed, and without skipping beat, continued. "Duma bigwigs are convinced I'll eclipse any candidate standing against me in fair elections. I had incongruous feelings, but when I recently saw graffiti with my name scrawled on walls, my intuition told me they're right. So I had little choice but to give the matter serious consideration. I discussed it thoroughly with Boris, and after his strenuous coercion decided to accept the honor of nomination. By the conclusion of this parliamentary session, after a transitional administration, I'll be publically announcing my candidacy to become the next President of the New Russian Federation."

"Madam Zaza guarantees you're a shoo-in," added Vlad. "She says you're destined to become a great historical figure."

Mouths hung open. "Meanwhile," Dimsky continued with ersatz distaste, "I've resigned my military commission. I'll spend this upcoming year relaxing, composing music on my balalaika, and playing with Sergei's abandoned cat, Tinkerbelle." He scrutinized his taken aback friends. "When Milonov fled Moscow the cat was discarded. Some animal lovers they proved to be! I felt it my solemn duty to step up and adopt the poor creature after all her loyal service. Sergei and his wife have been permanently ousted and exiled from the capital. And I'll make sure they never return."

"Relegated to the scrapheap of history," said Alina Vera.

The rabbi wasn't particularly surprised at the ex-colonel's news. He blithely passed around boxes of freshly baked cinnamon rolls, and sweet apples. His back was feeling better than it had for weeks and his mood was buoyant.

"Indeed the mystical texts of the Zohar are infallible," he intoned. "The mysteries of our world will never be fathomed by we mere mortals. The Talmud teaches: *We do not see things as they are. We see things as we are.*" Then he grinned, peering up at Vlad. "Which reminds me, I'll be giving our Vova an intense year of arduous study plus lots of homework. And I'm a stickler for detail. He'll have to buckle down. A single year's duration is all he has because next year Colonel

338

Dimsky will need the finest public relations man available to take charge of his presidential campaign. If Vlad accepts the post, that is."

Surprised and speechless, Vlad listened without appearing to understand; Alina Vera spoke up for him. "Oh, he'll gladly accept the colonel's generous offer. Hey, a job's a job, right? It's not what I'd refer to as 'honest work', but it's an opportunity he can't refuse, and he'll need to earn a sufficient living if he expects to ever support a future wife." She shot Vlad a wishful look from the corner of her eye. The former director stumbled for the right words. Giving up, he pulled her close and kissed her.

Dimsky and Floyd Dingus whistled while the rabbi and Boris applauded loudly. "That settles that," said Boris, pouring the final contents of the last bottle of vodka. "To President Dimsky's new press spokesman!"

"Hear, hear!" cooed Floyd Dingus genially. "Oh, and by the way, Vlad, I noticed in the newspaper that your apartment is for sale."

"Yes, that's right. How did you know?"

"Well, I've been checking the real estate sections of the local newspapers pretty closely for a while. It sounds like your flat is a pretty good deal when you exchange dollars for depreciated rubles."

Alina Vera looked at him. "Wait a minute. Those classified ads are printed in Russian. You can read Russian, Floyd?"

"Heck, yes. I can read pretty fluently now, write and speak some, too. Remember when you found that pretty tour guide to show me around the Kremlin and keep me busy? Well, she's been giving me exclusive private Russian lessons on the side." He winked with his toothy smile. "You only have yourselves to blame. While you gave me the runaround I had loads of free time on my hands. Anastasia and me have become real good friends. Anyway, the Department of Agriculture advised me to always be nice to my Russian hosts. In the name of diplomacy, that is."

Boris scratched his head. Would wonders never cease, he thought, blowing smoke rings upward toward the sky. By any account Floyd would be hanging around Moscow for a long time.

"Anyway," Floyd went on, "about your place for sale. It seems my oldest brother, Phineas, is discussing finding a place in Europe. He's in Europe so frequently he feels it's better to own than paying so many expensive hotel bills. I've been telling him Moscow is an up and coming town. A good bet to put your money on. I think Phineas agrees."

"Did you just say Phineas Dingus is your brother?" asked a curious Alina Vera. "By any chance, would he happen to be *the* Phineas Dingus, renowned classical musician and composer?"

"*Da.* He's the one. You've heard his name?"

"Of course I have! Every serious music lover has. But I had no idea he was related to you. I guess I never put two and two together." Vlad placed a greasy, chicken-stained hand to her shoulder. "So who's this latest Dingus sibling?" A nearby large dog on a leash loudly sniffed at the zesty aroma.

"It so happens Phineas Dingus is one of the most notable harpists in the world, in a class totally by himself, a coterie of critics says. He's had sold-out concerts from Beijing to San Francisco to St. Petersburg. In addition, he's written sonatas, concertos, and symphonies. I saw him once in concert a long time ago and purchased an autographed CD. His 'Symphony Number 72, The Hopscotch,' is considered a modern masterpiece. Orchestras everywhere play it to sold-out, standing-room only audiences."

"Well, how about that!" said Floyd, impressed by her knowledge of contemporary serious music. "Phineas will be so pleased to hear your opinion. From now on you'll get as many autographed CDs as you can handle. I told him lots about you all, and that I've been giving you some help in classified matters. Phineas confided that coincidently he's been writing a new festive concerto dedicated to a forgotten Russian musicologist colleague he hasn't seen for decades. An outstanding harpsichord player, the genuine Andrei Popov. He told me that Popov is the best, an unsung virtuoso of period-instruments, with an effortless style beautifully pure and rich, never showy. He's also expert in Bach's keyboard repertoire, and church cantatas. Now get this, he wants Popov to play and record the debut performance here in Moscow. The big payoff is his recording company will release a boxed set of Popov originals, including full scores and notes. It'll raise Popov's standing to international fame for sure. He spoke with Phineas yesterday, and now my brother's really eager to finish and begin rehearsals. Can you believe it?"

Vlad beamed at the news. Boris smiled. The real Andrei Popov deserved a break after what he'd been through, and Princess Valeria would no longer need to hold out the hat.

"Better sell your place fast, Vova, while the market's hot," opined Dimsky. "Get a fat deposit from Phineas Dingus quickly. And to think, all this is happening because of Lenin and that deluded schizoid Sunavich, may he rot. Without them we wouldn't be here celebrating today."

"Or become such good friends," Vlad observed sympathetically. "I think we owe old Vladimir Ilyich a more generous toast than we anticipated."

"He's right," chimed Alina Vera. "If anyone *is* deserving, it's certainly departed Chocolate Lenin."

They held paper cups filled to the brim toward the darkening sky. Innumerable stars were sparkling. They cried with joy and camaraderie, "To Chocolate Lenin, may his melted soul peacefully rest, his chocolate atoms forever abound across clear blue skies."

A placid stillness overtook them until Dimsky finally said, "Our task is finished. The Strike Team is disbanded. When the opera's over you walk off the stage."

And once more they drank deeply, laughing and laughing at their ordeal, their surroundings, and themselves.

Slightly tipsy, Vlad inhaled with vigor. "You know, this is one fine day. And it is a good life. And maybe, just maybe, this old world of ours is a good place to be, after all." No one disagreed, each invigorated with the joy of living.

"Let's not forget Ilya Evgeny," reminded Boris, his ruddy cheeks flushed. "I forget to tell you, she's going to have a baby."